ALEXANDER HALL

THE WOVEN FIGURE

ALEXANDER HALL

WOVEN
THE

FIGURE

Mereo Books

1A The Wool Market Dyer Street Cirencester Gloucestershire GL7 2PR
An imprint of Memoirs Publishing www.mereobooks.com

THE WOVEN FIGURE: 978-1-86151-897-2

First published in Great Britain in 2018
by Mereo Books, an imprint of Memoirs Publishing

The address for Memoirs Publishing Group Limited can be
found at www.memoirspublishing.com

The Memoirs Publishing Group Ltd Reg. No. 7834348

Typeset in 9/12pt Bembo
by Wiltshire Associates Publisher Services Ltd.
Printed and bound in Great Britain by Biddles Books

But I cannot deny my past to which my self is wed
The woven figure cannot undo its thread.

(Louis MacNeice, *Valediction*)

1

The auctioneer's voice was one that commanded attention, one that swept up to the highest vowels and plunged down to the deepest consonants, giving it an incantatory quality. Earlier it had coasted through the numbers like a bobsleigh gradually gathering speed on the run, but now that the kill was in sight for one of the primal beasts in the room it lingered almost playfully over the ultimate figure. The hands moved asymmetrically in a routine piece of choreography, the gavel describing efficient little arcs of anticipation before its descent.

'Are we all done then?' The voice, almost querulous in its intensity, sent out its final appeal. 'For one-hundred-and-sixty-three thousand pounds, for the third and last time...'

He had been through these situations countless times before, the moment when all his expectations either came crashing to the ground or soared aloft on a surge of euphoria, when the knot in his stomach would either twist and turn before hardening irreconcilably or unclasp itself and dissolve contentedly against his spreading waistline. He still had a split second to move his right hand or nod conspiratorially in the direction of the auctioneer. It was all a game, wasn't it? By outbidding everybody else in the room you notched up another victory, you came out on top, you landed yet another success. Not rocket science at all.

And then it was too late. The thud upon the auctioneer's table felt like a guillotine blade cutting home, the words 'Sold to the gentleman on the left' like the passing of a great Solomonic judgement. He had hesitated and lost. He hated the feeling of circling in on the prize, of engaging in the ritual of pushing the numbers up, sometimes far beyond what was initially his set limit or indeed what was justifiable in market terms, and then seeing a more powerful and risk-hardened player elbow him aside and walk off with the trophy. Defeat gnawed at his self-esteem, failure corroded his confidence. He loathed the realisation that he had been trumped, even when there were doubts about the price that had been paid. But he would be back. He would try again, and he knew there would be victories to come.

He heaved himself away from the pillar on which he had been leaning and brushed a few specks of masonry scurf from his sleeve. He straightened the knot of his boldly-striped tie and pushed the stubborn fold of midriff flesh below his smart leather belt. He was ready to move on.

Suddenly he felt a hand on his shoulder. 'Hi, Laurence. Haven't seen you for a while. How are things?'

He turned to confront the face of his interlocutor. Around them people were squeezing out of the tight rows and pushing past towards the double doors of the auction room, still clutching their catalogues and clipboards, impatient to be revived by alcohol or nicotine or the rush of cooler air on their faces, held captive for too long in the simmering warmth of a poorly-ventilated space. The air suddenly crackled with the cries of recognition, the clearing of throats and the nervous cackling of familiar voices.

'Well, if it isn't my old mate Steve,' replied Laurence. 'You don't normally come to these auctions, do you? Did Patrick send you?'

'That last property you were bidding for, the Rosemont Avenue terrace, that was actually where my gran lived before she had to go into a nursing home, so I had something of a personal interest. Patrick didn't have anything to do with it, I just wanted to see how much it went for. I could see you in front of me putting in those bids, but you weren't within hailing distance. And signalling in your direction would in any case have given the auctioneer the wrong idea. Are you disappointed to have missed out?'

Laurence raised an eyebrow and corralled a few straying locks of hair into place. 'Not really, Steve.' Putting a brave face on things was part of the game. 'What with the uncertainties in the market at the moment, it would have been something of a risk, I grant you that. I think if anything it went for more than it should have done, but I'd still have been happy to add it to my portfolio.'

'Ever the optimist, eh? What do you make of the Lehman Brothers business? That's knocked quite a lot of people for six, me included.'

The makings of a smile creased Laurence's face. In days gone by, when they had been sitting opposite each other in Patrick Costley-White's estate agency, the younger Steve in his restless wiry frame would often look across at Laurence and crave his opinion on a mutual client or the true worth of a particular property, his forehead furrowing in alarm at hints of the unexpected.

'Steve, my friend, everybody's getting worked up about something that will eventually blow over. A crisis is by definition short-lived. Never forget that the media thrive on this kind of thing. They have to build it up into mega-proportions. Don't expect them to give you realistic assessments.'

'But this is different, Laurence. This is not just a correction in the market, it's a full-blown financial crisis. We're all going to suffer. Surely you can see that.'

'I agree the outlook would appear to be bleak. At the moment, yes. It's the banks that are having to take it on the chin. But you mark my words, the property business will continue to flourish. It always has done.'

Steve Beech met the reassuring gaze from Laurence's deep brown eyes. Where did he draw his inexhaustible optimism from? Or was it just the fact that Laurence was his senior by fifteen years? Perhaps that accounted for the differences in attitude, the fact that he had seen endless previous fluctuations and could talk authoritatively about the negative equity of the nineties and then the steady recovery that followed. Perhaps that was why Laurence was prepared to quit his job working for Patrick and launch himself as a property developer and landlord when Steve spent every moment of each morning worrying about the next house he was going to sell and whether he would even be in the same workplace a few years from now. He shook his head at Laurence's response but said nothing.

'Where've you left your car?' Laurence wanted to know, as they passed through the entrance hall, with its high arching windows and flaking yellowing plasterwork, echoes of an earlier chapel existence. His short stout legs had a habit of kicking out to the sides, as if to distribute the heavier load above more securely. At times his head and shoulders appeared to be out of the perpendicular, leaning forward in a thrusting motion as if wanting to be ahead of the rest of the frame.

'It's still at the office. I decided to walk here, it's not that far after all.'

'Well, if you've got a car, you might as well use it, that's what I always say. Care for a lift back?'

The late September sun was still wrapping itself around the rows of Victorian buildings on the high street, the air carrying a welcome note of freshness from the sea a mere mile away. Steve's walk to the auction room had taken him away from the constant ring of office phones, the hum of the computers and the splutter of the printers disgorging property particulars, and he was glad to be in Laurence's company again. At the same time he was just a little envious that the man at his side, in his mid-forties with a wife and two lovely kids and a splendid home on the edge of town, all supported by his own flourishing business, always seemed to be going somewhere, his mind focused on the next project, whereas he fretted his way through HIPs and EPCs, market appraisals and the breakdown of chains, couldn't see past his next bank statement and, in his personal life, was fated to drift in and out of relationships.

'OK, thanks, where are you parked?'

Laurence led the way into one of the side-streets that hung from the main thoroughfare like the stays on a whalebone corset. In the far distance a tug signalled its presence in the outer reaches of the harbour. The gulls above strimmed the air with their scissor-like wings, wheeling and then scattering.

There was an expensive-sounding swish-swoosh as Laurence activated the unlocking device on his car. 'Hop in,' he said.

Steve looked approvingly at the spread of dials and switches behind the padded steering-wheel and the wood trim, and settled into the plushness of the leather seat. 'Here, this still smells new. Is it?'

'I thought you knew. I always trade my model in after the first year to chime in with the new number plates. Absolute reliability is what matters to me. And you can't beat German engineering.'

'Well, you say that. A client who's just come back from the US was telling me the other day that over there they call them BM-Trouble-Yous.'

'Oh, why's that then?'

'So many things going wrong and needing product recalls.'

'Well, that's just sour grapes, isn't it? If the Yanks could come up with a first-class product in the first place, we'd all be buying their cars instead of helping to boost the German economy.'

It was no use trying to foot-fault Laurence. He recalled overhearing a client reeling off a list of objections to a property Laurence had been keen to sell. Each reference to yet another snag or drawback was countered with a firm but reasoned rebuttal: the deficiencies were entirely cosmetic, the defects could easily be remedied and the downsides of the neighbourhood were being unnecessarily exaggerated. Above all, it was value for money. He wondered how many of Laurence's sales successes in the past had been down to sheer persistence, a war of attrition in which any potential buyer's fortress of certainty was gradually chipped away and then ground into dust, or simply the undeniable air of bonhomie he exuded, the warmth in his voice and eyes, the sense of being entirely comfortable in his own skin. Laurence was a good friend; he'd never stab you in the back or at least, if he did so, he would surely have the decency to warn you of his intentions well in advance.

Steve decided to change the subject. 'How's Rosie?'

'Fine, just fine. She's busy helping two guys set up a new restaurant on the Portchester side of town. She's been at it since last month. Keeps talking about it.'

'Has she given up selling flowers then? I thought you said she'd invested in the business.'

'No, no. She still works in the shop part-time – you try keeping her away from that – but now she's advising on décor and that sort of thing for this new place.'

'Branching out like you, I guess. You always said it pays to have more than one string to your bow.'

'I don't think she's trying to do that. Don't quite know how she got into it either. She might have told me, but I can't say I remember. I'll have to ask her once the subject comes round again. It's something musical though, I mean there's a musical connection to the place.'

The BMW purred along, the reserves of power underneath the bonnet which Laurence loved to unlock ready to be released with the merest touch of his foot on the accelerator pedal. How very different from the first car he had ever possessed, a clapped-out Austin Allegro he had acquired immediately after passing his test at the first attempt, soon after his seventeenth birthday, a minor personal triumph he attributed to the years spent helping the father of a classmate during the holidays in return for unofficial driving lessons on the family farm deep in the Hampshire countryside. It had been followed by a succession of scarcely roadworthy vehicles that his mother had pointedly refused to travel in, citing her safety concerns, while he scraped his way through his building engineering course and RICS exams until his first job as a technical surveyor in a Southampton architects' office, after which had come a succession of second-hand Audis before he had taken delivery of his very first brand-new BMW.

By now Laurence had taken a left turn off the high street and was heading towards the Costley-White agency on the coastal side of town, where it was strategically wedged between coffee bars, a pharmacy and a fitness studio. Ahead of him was a small green hatchback that was beginning to weave erratically across the surface of the carriageway.

'See that, Steve, the driver ahead? Looks like a woman inside. That's a crazy way to drive. It's a bit early in the day to be three sheets to the wind, isn't it?'

'There's never a wrong time to be blotto, if that's what you're into.'

In the days after the incident Laurence was to play the sequence that followed over and over in his mind, his finger unable to engage with the fast-forward button, reliving each millisecond of what was unfolding, frame by frame. He saw the vehicle ahead suddenly pick up speed and then lurch sharply, veering across the street to the right and narrowly avoiding an oncoming delivery van, before taking to the air and plunging down a slip road that led to an underground car park. It was as if a wounded bird was flapping its injured wings before dropping to the ground below, as if Icarus was making his first attempts to fly in a mechanical contraption.

He pulled over immediately. 'Christ! Something's wrong with the car or the driver or both. Come on Steve, we'd better see if we can help."

There was a small plume of steam rising from underneath the crumpled bonnet, the left-hand side of the hatchback having taken the full force of the impact against the render of a side-wall. Laurence raced round to the driver's side and tugged at the door. The woman was slumped over the wheel, her open mouth slightly twisted, and he gently eased her shoulders back into the seat. There was an agonised murmuring, a gasp as she took in some air and a look of disbelief at what she surveyed. 'I – I – where am I? What happened?'

Laurence bent closer. He could smell no alcohol on her breath. The woman was probably in her late forties, short and dumpy, with long straggly hair and large owl-like spectacles, and she was wearing a dark, shapeless sweater.

'You just came off the road,' he said. 'I was immediately behind you and noticed you were wandering about a bit. You were lucky you didn't hit another vehicle. It could have been a lot worse. Do you remember anything?'

The woman was obviously struggling to make sense of the situation. 'No. No, I've no idea what I was doing. It's all a complete blank, I'm afraid.' She began to shiver.

Laurence took out his mobile and dialled 999. 'I'll stay with you until they come. You might just be shaken up, or it could be more serious. There's always the danger of concussion. Thank God for seat-belts!' he added with a smile.

Steve was at his side, having secured Laurence's BMW. 'Is there anything I can do? Perhaps I can signal to the ambulance as soon as I see it coming.'

By now a small crowd of rubbernecks was gathering. Laurence and Steve waited patiently for some ten minutes, surrounded by a hubbub of excited voices, before an ambulance arrived, followed a short time later by a police patrol car. They watched as the woman was put onto a stretcher and disappeared from sight, together with the paramedics. The police officer thumbed his way through a notebook with a routine air and jotted down the two men's personal details before reviewing with them what they had witnessed.

'Could you come into the station and sign an official statement?' he said. 'We'll get it typed up as soon as we can.'

Steve decided to walk the remaining distance to his office, leaving Laurence to head off home. Glancing at the Rolex on his wrist he realised he was a good half-hour behind the time he'd given Rosie that morning. Quite recently, one of the girls in the newsagent's where he bought his lottery tickets had asked him, 'Is that a real one or one of them fakes you can get in Turkey?' He had been more than a tad aggrieved at the assumption that somebody who was as smartly turned out as he was would be the kind of person to buy a cheap imitation on a package holiday.

He wondered why it was that so many of the people he had dealings with managed without some kind of timepiece on their wrist. He remembered the first watch with a plastic strap his mother had given him, well before he was into long trousers. 'So now there's no excuse for being late,' she had said. Admittedly, mobile phones were taking over this function, the human body's fifth limb, but he still liked to feel the comforting clasp of his Rolex, the spread of keys in his trouser pocket and the thin gold chain round his neck. Metals that yielded to no other material. It was the accident which had set him back; that was the reason he was technically late. Never mind, he thought, it could have been a whole load worse. The poor woman might have ended up with really serious injuries. She might have killed herself. She might have moved into the path of an oncoming vehicle and he might not have been able to brake in time. All of them could have been part of a massive pile-up. Just when he was getting used to all the extra features in his shiny new car.

2

It was the early evening rush-hour and the main coastal roads were choked with local commuters and goods vehicles in transit. There was no point huffing and puffing about any delays in getting home. Laurence knew that would never speed his passage, but there were thousands who failed to get the message. Every day he heard the hooting and the honking, saw the shaking of fists and lip-read the cursing going on around him. He quickly texted Rosie that he was caught in the usual traffic madhouse and waited for the flow to pick up again. She hated it when he arrived home long after he said he would, especially when the whole family was forced to wait for their evening meal. Even after all this time she still had problems accepting the fact that frequently something else intervened, some unpredictable event upset the apple cart, sending all her washing off the line in an instant.

When he had first started driving, he had tried bellowing at the windscreen if he was caught in a jam, but he soon realised that the emotional force he was actively stoking up inside him was having no effect on the rate at which traffic was moving. It was his inability to control what others were or weren't doing which had given him a sense of impotence, a feeling that he was at the mercy of something completely beyond his reach. Over time he learned to accept that in some areas there was nothing, absolutely nothing, he could do to rectify a situation. That was the way things were: things just happened, unexpectedly and without warning, like the episode with the green hatchback that afternoon. But such incidents also made him equally determined to exercise control whenever his reach could be extended, whenever he was in charge of the flow.

Nor was he entirely happy if vital pieces of the jigsaw evaded his grasp. Where had the woman been going? Why had she come off the road? Contrary to his first impressions, alcohol hadn't been involved. What was the name she had mumbled at him? It had sounded like Miriam. She had squeezed his hand just before the paramedics arrived. There was no wedding ring or any other obvious jewellery, for that matter. Nothing to suggest that she cared deeply about her appearance, not even a line of lipstick. She didn't seem to fit into any standard category either. But then he'd seen all types come through the doors of Patrick's agency and later the small premises in the higher part of town from which he ran his company. Everybody needed a place to call their own, and facilitating the perfect match between individual client and available property was a recurring challenge: it was after all one of humankind's primary needs, and the beauty of it was that the need could be endlessly replicated and manipulated. A bigger house, a better area, more features, a smarter exterior, an investment with increased potential. Children were born or in-laws needed taking in, and then extra bedrooms and a bigger footprint became essential. After the kids had flown the nest and retirement edged ever closer, downsizing beckoned. The escalator was moving all the time, either up or down, nothing ever came to a complete full-stop.

The small estate on the edge of town where the Stewart family had been living for the past five years lacked in individuality what it offered in ostentation. It had screamed at Laurence when he first saw details of the project in a bright glossy brochure – executive homes for the aspirational classes, a face that represented style to the outside world, an address with a touch of class, extra inside space to display and demonstrate, flexibility instead of functionality. Buying off-plan and with the benefit of an additional discount which he had charmed his way into getting meant it was an opportunity that was simply too good to miss. Rosie had raised objections initially, annoyed at the haste Laurence had applied to the deal and the extra distance she would now have to cover in order to get to her job at Florabellum. Laurence had responded to her protestations by softening the blow with the gift of a smart-looking runabout which she could call her own. Finding the right pill-sweetener had been an art in itself, and he had worked hard to soften opposition and repel reluctance. But Rosie had only just got everything in their Victorian semi on the Gosport road the way she wanted it to be, from the hand-made linen-weave curtains in the living-room to the patterned tiles in the entrance hall that she had in some cases replaced and then scrubbed and polished to perfection.

'But I'm really happy here. Why do we have to move?' she had wanted to know. Laurence had been adamant that market conditions were right, that a spanking modern property was less prone to maintenance issues and that they'd be in the right catchment area for better schools for Kieron and Estelle. Laurence was prepared for the upheaval; she wasn't. He saw the forthcoming summer sun; she foresaw the grey skies of winter. Her silent resentment at not being properly consulted in such matters was mitigated by the new kitchen gadgets and improved domestic technology that came her way at Christmas and coincided with her birthday in early February. If there was one thing Laurence clearly wasn't, it was mean. 'It's better to be looking at, rather than for,' he had repeatedly said during the first year in their new home, to which she frequently thought, 'Who said I'd been looking for anything different?' even if she couldn't bring herself to say so aloud.

Once again Rosie had left her hatchback standing in the driveway instead of putting it into the double garage. He left his BMW parked in the street outside the detached house with its generously pitched roof and the aluminium window-frames that gleamed in the light of the sodium street lamps. The property, like all the others in the estate, was still too young to have Virginia creeper covering the exterior or the clouds of wisteria that had clambered up the walls of their previous home; it still needed to sit and mature like grape juice lying in vats before it could have any claim to character.

He paused in the lights of the porch, admiring the profusion of carmine in the late-flowering clematis Rosie had planted in a half-barrel tub, and let himself in. 'I'm home,' he called and walked into the kitchen at the end of the long hallway. She was standing at the sink with her back to him, her glossy brown hair resting on her shoulders, an apron wrapped around her floral-print skirt. He wanted to kiss the nape of her neck and wrap his arms around her waist, as he had so often done in the past, but she forestalled his intended approach by turning around immediately to face him, her generous hips gently swaying. 'It's all ready. It's been ready for some time. The kids have had theirs. Do you want to eat now?'

He noted the slight edge in her voice. Even after seventeen years of marriage he was finding it difficult to read her recent moods. He wanted her always to be the way she had been when he had first glimpsed the new girl in the flower-shop down the road from where he was then living, a bubbling vivacious presence in a cotton smock decorated with large ethnic motifs, her large aquamarine eyes beaming at him, her fingernails picked out in primary colours, her cheeks heightened by a rosy bloom. 'What can I help you with?' she had said with more than a hint of a northern accent, the warmth flowing from her voice like chocolate oozing from a fondant. 'It's...' and he had paused before continuing, surprised at his own sudden loss of words. He recovered to say, 'My mother's celebrating her sixtieth birthday next week. I want her to have a nice surprise, so it has to be something out of the ordinary.' And the two of them had connected with the utter inevitability of a bolt pressing home against the backplate.

When he had called round after work to see his mother on her special day, the bouquet had been placed in a large stoneware jug on the dining-room table. She had been ecstatic at the myriad colours of the blooms and the richness of the foliage. 'Where did you find these little delights, Laurence? It's the middle of November, after all.'

'That's all Rosie's doing.'

'Rosie? Who's Rosie?'

And in the weeks that followed, her name came up again and again during her son's weekly visits. She couldn't conceal her annoyance at no longer being the undivided centre of his attention. 'Rosie, Rosie, Rosie. That's all I hear now. Laurence, why do you keep on talking about Rosie?'

'Mum, I think I'm in love with her.'

'You think? But Laurence, she's only a shop girl. You can do better than that, surely!'

He had swallowed hard at hearing his mother dismiss his choice without having even met her, lacerated by her assumption that Rosie wasn't good enough for him. And then they'd had their first big row since Laurence had departed the family home. 'How can you say such a thing? You've been scrubbing for other people for most of your life!'

'Laurence, how dare you! If I hadn't gone out to find work after your father's death, you wouldn't be where you are today. And never forget, I may have started off cleaning other people's houses, but I've been running my own business for years now. And I've given employment to others. And I've contributed to the local economy. And all through hard work. What have I always told you? It's work alone that gets you from where you are to where you want to be. Laurence, you need to want things!'

At that he had remained silent, conscious of the sacrifices his mother had made in the past, as she never stopped reminding him. But he had already committed his heart, and now his own happiness had to come first. They stayed out of touch for several weeks, mother and son each bristling with wounded pride, until the light covering deposited by a February snow melted away and an invitation was extended to both Laurence and Rosie to take Sunday tea in the house nestling in the rolling Hampshire countryside high above the spread of nautical domains that stretched along the coast.

For several weeks after the initial encounter, his mother quite deliberately tried to stall the engine that he was already revving up.

'Laurence, you're not even twenty-seven. You don't need to commit to anybody just yet. Think of your career!' When she heard that Rosie was a year older than he was, she looked askance at him. 'Really? It's always better for the man to be older. Never forget your father was ten years older than me.' When she realised he and Rosie were pressing ahead with wedding plans, she sought out areas of objection that might appeal to the practical side of his nature. 'You don't need to get married. Lots of people just live together now. Think of the expense! You could put all that money towards a sensible investment. Build something else up before you settle down.' To which he merely said, 'It won't be a big affair. Rosie and I don't want too much fuss.' But his mother never gave up without a struggle. 'Where are you going to live? That little flat of yours isn't right for a married couple. And what will you do if you decide to start a family?' He noted the "if" rather than a "when". 'You do realise that if you go ahead, you won't have time for all your friends. What are they going to say?' To which he in turn said absolutely nothing.

Rosie was pushing the last remnants of a pasta bake around the plate, having listened abstractedly to Laurence's summary of his day.

'I think you should have a word with Kieron,' she said. 'Haven't you noticed the way he's become so withdrawn? This has been going on for a good two weeks now. I just don't seem able to get through to him.'

'Rosie, love, he's fifteen. All teenagers are like that. It's puberty. Mood swings and all that.'

'But Estelle's only two years behind and she's no different to what she's always been.'

'Why do you keep getting worked up about things that will pass? It's just the same with the media, constantly focused on the financial world. There've always been problems in the road ahead, but things get sorted in the end. Kieron'll pick himself up in next to no time, you'll see.'

'And how do you think that's going to happen if we never talk about things together? He's our son. Doesn't he deserve our attention?'

'Rosie, I do what I do for all of us. I have to keep the wheels turning and I'm happy to do that. You're home far more than I am. You talk to him. That's what women are good at. I bring home the bacon. You dish it up.'

There was no point in pursuing the matter. It was the same with her mother-in-law. 'I'm Laurence's mother. He calls me "mum", so that's the name reserved for him. You can call me "mother",' Roberta had told her a few days before the wedding. It was a foretaste of what was to come: lines were set in the sand, territory staked out and made safe against rebel encroachment. Responsibilities were allocated and needed to be adhered to. That was the way Roberta saw the world and that was the way her son expected family life to run. Like mother, like son. Which was why she was already looking forward to her next visit to the Callas restaurant and seeing Lee and Matthew again.

3

The Callas had not yet opened to the public. 'Who'd be stupid enough to start up a new restaurant in the current climate, and with a name like that?' was Lee's comment, uttered with more than a little forced irony, one August afternoon when he walked into Florabellum, while the fierce sun seared its way through the heavy exterior blinds outside the shop.

'What brings you here anyway?' Rosie wanted to know.

Lee, a willowy figure with large and earnest watery eyes, allowed himself a faint smile. 'You've been recommended to us as one of the best flower shops around. We're looking for a regular supplier for all the table decorations.'

And so, a few days later, she found herself standing outside the fading façade of a former ironmongery, the whitewashed windows hiding all signs of its previous identity. Once past the rickety entrance door she blinked repeatedly as her eyes adjusted to the gloom of an interior space littered with mops and other cleaning utensils. In her nostrils she felt the sharpness that came from carbolic and soda crystals fighting the years of neglect. Lee steered her gently towards a compact figure with a neatly-trimmed beard, his sleeves rolled up for further assaults on the layers of grime.

'May I introduce my business partner – and also my civil partner,' Lee said. 'This is Matthew.'

'Matthew? Not Matt?'

'No, Matthew. I hate shortenings.'

'Just like my husband. He's called Laurence, but he refuses to answer to Larry.'

'If we're being particular, is that Laurence with a "u" or with a "w"?'

Rosie grinned. 'I could tell you the whole story, how his mother named him after the matinee idol Laurence Harvey, but I won't bore you with all the details. Tell me more about this place and how you think I can help you.'

They quickly moved into the details of how the project had got off the ground when Lee lost his job, after the music magazine he was working for suddenly folded, and he agreed to take up Matthew's suggestion of starting a new life away from London.

'So Matthew's going to do all the catering?' Rosie asked.

'Not completely on his own, of course. We'll probably manage with one or two additional staff until we get established, and then who knows? To begin with, we're planning only to be open in the evenings and for Sunday lunch.'

'And you're hoping to make a go of it?'

'Nobody, as far as we can see, has anything like our big idea,' Lee said.

'And how did you hit on that?'

Matthew put down the pail he was holding. 'Lee's an opera buff. He used to be out at Covent Garden several times a week while I was working as a senior sous chef. We're going to have piped music with one opera after another in which Maria Callas was the star.'

'Was she somebody really famous? I don't know much about opera at all.'

'You bet! Just possibly the greatest female opera singer in the last century. According to my other half, of all time!'

'And the walls will be covered with huge black-and-white photographs of the lady herself,' Lee added.

Rosie looked unconvinced. 'But why start up something like that down here? Why not in London?'

Lee sighed. 'Have you seen the property prices in the capital? Far too expensive. And there are plenty of music-lovers down on the south coast. Plus being down here gives the foodies in London a reason for taking a trip out of town.'

'But do you honestly think people are going to come and listen to background music when all they want is good food and good company?'

'I know it sounds risky,' Matthew said. 'But it's our unique selling point. And if the food's exceptional, that's going to draw people in. The music's secondary, of course, even if Lee doesn't like me to say so. We're both determined to make it work, and if you can help us that would be fantastic.'

They discussed aspects of the refurbishment that was still in progress, the décor that would be most appropriate and why the table linen and other furnishings needed to tie in with that, why textures and materials mattered, why certain kinds of lighting were more effective than others, especially given the limited natural light, and whether Rosie could commit to creating floral arrangements for the twelve tables and reception area on a regular basis.

'Well, I'm not the sole proprietor of Florabellum,' she said. 'I'm a junior partner in the business, but I only work there part-time. I have a husband and two teenagers to worry about.'

'But you could oversee things and guarantee that everything's delivered on time?' Lee queried.

'Oh yes, doing something slightly different from my usual routine would be fun. When exactly are you planning to open?'

'Probably by the middle of November. We'd like to get some of the pre-Christmas business and even run specials over the holiday period. It's all full steam ahead at the moment. I've still got a lot of things to consider, like advertising and the recruitment of additional staff.'

'Fine, Lee. I've got your mobile number now, so we'll keep in touch.'

As she drove home, Rosie mused on how some people suddenly took an unexpected leap of faith and committed to an idea that could as easily go wrong as it might come right in the end. It wasn't that such individuals refused to acknowledge obstacles in the road ahead; they found ways of side-stepping or wriggling round smaller objects in their path and tussled with or heaved against anything that was large and seemingly insurmountable. She thought of Laurence and how he set about pursuing whichever objective was next. He always had one lined up. It wasn't enough to deploy a few counter-arguments whenever he pulled in a direction she had reservations about. Her emotional side needed to come into play: sometimes she raised her voice dramatically, but that was a weapon that had to be used sparingly and only at critical moments. When her passions were engaged her accent broadened noticeably, adding colour to her bursts of rapid and plain speaking. Sometimes her opposition would express itself in sudden silence, with all her sensory systems apparently in shutdown, locked into a calculated freeze-frame, so that he was made to pause and look at her quizzically, instead of continuing on his current flight of fancy. Occasionally she would wait for his intake of breath and then quickly change the subject, returning to whatever had been on his mind much later in bed, when she would surreptitiously extend one hand, and then another, waiting for the shudder of his body as she homed in on the places where he was utterly defenceless. 'To come back to what you were saying earlier,' she would whisper huskily in his ear, knowing that his attention would now be on other things.

As she pulled up at the next set of traffic lights she peered into the rear mirror and examined her face. What had one of her customers said the other day? 'Age is only a number on a scale.'

Nevertheless she couldn't escape the fact that she was rapidly running through most of the numbers on that scale, far faster than she had ever thought possible. As each number was flagged up, her body provided confirmation in counterpoint. The crow's feet that became more pronounced whenever her face broke into a smile, the lines on her brow that yielded only to a judicious application of concealer, the jaw-line that was no longer able to withstand the repeated entreaties of gravity and the streaks of grey that added a faint metallic glitter to her glossy hair. Here she was, heading towards fifty with an increasing awareness of the importance of security and stability, quite unlike Laurence, who was still happy to take a risk on almost anything. She hadn't really wanted to make the move away from the city centre and the place they had called home for a good ten years. She had allowed Laurence to fill her mind with a vision of modern living on the fringes of the coastal urban sprawl within striking distance of the open countryside, and make her think that the transition would be entirely smooth and trouble-free. Nor would it have made much difference had she not given her reluctant blessing when four years ago he had thrown in the towel with Patrick Costley-White and become Laurence Stewart Management almost overnight. Laurence would have pressed on regardless. That was an increasing source of bother: as he aged, he seemed to listen less to her concerns and more to his own inner voice.

At one point, while he had been in the middle of buying run-down properties for conversion into flats, she had felt she had to call into question his ability to keep the family ship on an even keel. 'But Laurence,' she protested, 'we've already got quite a big mortgage with the new house. Why take on new commitments? Is that really wise?'

'Oh, don't worry about the finance. The banks are happy to lend. The buy-to-let market's taken off, so we'll have a guaranteed income from the new properties. And I intend to go into developing in a big way. I've got the skills and the contacts. Then there's always property management. Looking after other people's investments and drawing a nice big commission from the owners. You can see how things are still expanding. It'll all be fine. Just trust me.'

It wasn't that she didn't have a passable business brain herself and couldn't see the attractions of Laurence's growing business empire. After her parents had both died unexpectedly, within months of each other, she and her two much older sisters had come into a bit of money, so when the offer of a business partnership in Florabellum had come her way she had seized the opportunity. But she couldn't really understand Laurence's obsession with growth all the time. What was wrong with consolidation? Why did you always need to have more to show than twelve months previously?

She had followed the increasing media coverage of what they had called a developing financial crisis, but tended to switch off mentally whenever matters became too technical. Why did she need to know about sub-prime mortgages? What were derivatives anyway? All these details were hardly going to impact on her own life. And was bailing out the big banks and effectively nationalising them such a rash thing to do, as some pundits were suggesting? After all, the downsides of the privatisation craze that had swept the country in the eighties, while she was still struggling to decide if she was cut out to be an interior designer, like her eldest sister Lucie, or whether she should commit completely to the floristry business, were now all too apparent.

The cars behind her were suddenly hooting in impatience. She had become too absorbed in her own thoughts. There was Kieron to worry about and now Estelle had confided in her that her periods were proving particularly painful. And with the opening of the Callas coming up in a few weeks, there was still a lot to consider. She would have to make some pretty accurate costings. She headed home.

4

'Laurence, it's Steve. Have you seen the local paper?'

Laurence pulled himself away from the sheaf of property particulars in front of him and gripped the receiver a little more keenly.

'No, haven't had time, mate. Been too busy with other matters. Is that why you're calling?'

'That accident in Pride Street.'

'What, is it in the monthly rag?'

'There's not much. You know the usual stuff, lucky escape and all that. But there's a picture of her and that's the first thing I noticed. It's the same woman all right. Anyway, the police wouldn't give her our details – data confidentiality, apparently – and she's appealing for us to come forward so she can thank us properly.'

'That's a nice thought, but there wasn't a lot that we did. Except hold her hands metaphorically until the ambulance and police arrived.'

'It's pretty clear what she wants though. Shall I give the paper a call and make the first approach?'

Laurence hesitated. He'd been happy to assist on the day, but he didn't really have the time for additional socialising. At least, not now. There was an important auction coming up. He'd managed to secure the property management for a new block close to Portsdown Hill, his mother's seventy-eighth birthday was just a few weeks off and Rosie was nagging him again about Kieron. On the other hand, a quick coffee somewhere wasn't going to eat too much out of a precious working day.

'Okay, go ahead and keep me in the loop.'

He returned to the property particulars. The location was Warsash. Not far from the sea. Not far from where he had spent the first few years of his life, now little more than a blur in the past. Not far from the double-fronted Georgian villa he vaguely remembered from the snapshots in a family album, tucked away in one of the sturdy cardboard boxes his mother kept in the cupboard underneath the stairs. The squat but semi-derelict Wesleyan chapel in front of him presented like a prize fighter in the ring. 'Who'll take me on? I pack a bigger punch than you might think.' He thought back to the last time he'd been inside a place of religion. Eventually the memory resurfaced. It was his mother-in-law's funeral almost a decade ago now. They had all gone up to Huddersfield to sit in the hard pews of a grey stone church, listening to the wizened figure of an elderly priest recounting details from the family history. The human being for whom the grains of sand in the hour-glass seemed to run, just as they had in her husband's case, at a much faster pace than for most other mortals, the woman who had been the life and soul of the local community, the wife who had worked tirelessly at Trevor's side to ensure the family business continued to flourish, and yes, the warm-hearted mother from whom his own wife had undoubtedly inherited her effervescence, the mother-in-law who had enveloped him with her broad smile and open arms on their very first meeting, so very different from his own mother's cool reticence and wariness towards strangers. They had all been there on that icy December day: the three Wingfield sisters, Lucie, Dulcie and Rosie, with their husbands and children and all the other members of the extended family. People he only occasionally saw, since the whole clan was scattered across the different ridings, wrapped up in their own provincial lives. Yorkshire seemed an entire world away.

'So you're the only one?' Rosie had asked, when they started going out together.

'Yes, there's just little me. We're a very small family. My dad died not long after I was born, in fact I didn't know him at all. One of his brothers died young and the other one emigrated to Australia after the war. And my mother had just one sister, my lovely Auntie Joyce. She died when I was about ten, I think.'

They had talked animatedly about their childhoods, the one driven forward in an automatically reloading belief in self-autonomy and the other bathed and nurtured in a network of familial relationships. 'You have to be able to stand on your own two feet,' his mother had said. 'Friends are important, but you have to believe in yourself. Always remember that you can only take out what you first put in.'

He looked again at the chapel. Religion seemed like a closed book to him. What did he really know about the mysteries of the universe? He was far too fixed on rolling out and fencing in the immediate territory of his own existence. Was that so wrong? You got up in the morning, you went through a mental check-list of things you wanted to do, you saw your kids at the breakfast table (if you were lucky), you kissed your wife goodbye, you climbed into your swanky limousine with the personalised number-plates, you headed off into your own little empire where nobody could boss you around or tell you stuff you already knew, and at the end of the day you returned home believing you had made the lives of Rosie and Kieron and Estelle just that little bit better. Wasn't this what life was all about?

He remembered coming home from primary school and then, with either his face pressed to the front window or his eyes glued to afternoon television, waiting for his mother to return from her programme of cleaning jobs, proudly notching up new additions to her rota of clients like the rows of glass ornaments that grew surreptitiously in the confines of the display cabinet in the front room. Every day a little more, forever onwards and upwards.

It was a remarkably good guide price for such a large building, obviously a reflection of the slippage in values he had already noticed in the market. Perhaps the bubble had been pricked, but only slightly, surely? Downward market corrections would be followed by a period of continued buoyancy. That was the natural rhythm. The way things had always been. There was nothing more solid than bricks-and-mortar or a piece of land to call your own. What was the point of staring at a bank account and counting the number of zeros, or ringing up your broker to shift stocks around, or having the key to a locker in a bank vault containing those oblong bits of heavy shiny metal that the rest of the world worshipped? Why else did people say that something was as safe as houses?

The stained glass was an especially fine feature of the building, according to the blurb. Laurence peered more closely. It wouldn't all be intact, for sure, but there were craftsmen around who could restore what needed to be restored. How many ever got the chance to live in a building like that? If people stopped believing in God, there were many other things they could believe in. And God's buildings could still be put to good use. An idea was already forming in his mind as he reached for his phone to contact the agent.

5

Laurence hated November. It wasn't just the mess of leaves on pavements and in the gutters waiting with unerring patience for a few falls of rain and the heavy trudge of feet before spreading itself like a coating of thick cheesy gratin as far as the eye could see. It wasn't just the colours that drained away from gardens and people's complexions, giving everything and everyone a pasty appearance. It wasn't just the fact that property was the last thing people focused on as the prospect of family feasts loomed large on the horizon. Food and drink knocked bricks and mortar for six as the countdown towards Christmas picked up speed. It wasn't just the fact that the clocks had gone back and the afternoons felt as though a shroud was being pulled over the rest of the day. It wasn't just the fact that you could look up into a leaden sky and search in vain for any suggestion of sun. You knew it had to be there somewhere, but it had recused itself from any active participation. It was all these things and more.

Moreover, since as far back as he could remember, it had been the month of his father's unexpected death. His mother never let him forget that while the two of them were still here in this world, there was a third person who made up their family who was completely beyond their reach. Each year of his passing was marked with a simple ceremony in the front room, when they stood in front of what he had come to regard as the nearest thing to a family shrine, the sideboard with all the ormolu-framed photographs resting on the polished walnut grain. The time for commemoration and celebration was drawing near as the calendar turned full circle once more.

He was late again. A good start to the new week, he thought. He'd done his best to keep to what he'd promised Rosie in the morning, but again something had intervened and made him revise his to-do list for the day. He was slipping behind with some of the paperwork, and the part-time girl who dealt both with the accounts and some of the correspondence, as well as looking after the office in his absence, had called in sick for the second time in as many weeks, leaving him to cope on his own. Natasha knew what she was doing, but she was unbelievably slow at times, and as a single mother in her mid-twenties she had to balance child care and looking after a diabetic mother with the work she did for Laurence. He knew it was a struggle for her, just as it had been a struggle for his widowed mother all those years ago, and he was reluctant to see things solely from the perspective of a hard-nosed employer, but he knew that the limits of his patience were being tested.

When he got back home Rosie was in the living-room, wearing a knitted top in a mélange of earthy shades, one leg dangling above the fitted carpet, the other resting on one of the silk sofa cushions. On the coffee table was a tall crystal vase enclosing a generous spray of coral and lavender gerbera. She was feigning utter indifference to the cares of the world flickering across the television screen on the news. Laurence gave her a quick peck on the cheek before collapsing into an easy chair opposite.

She met his eyes. 'Is there any chance we might actually be able to sit down together – all four of us – at an agreed time?'

He wasn't quite sure how to react. He valued punctuality and strove to manage his schedule with as much efficiency as possible, but he had no control over outside events. Rosie knew that. They had been there endless times before. Why was she making it an issue now?

'Where are the kids?' he asked.

'Estelle didn't want to wait. She said she was famished, so she's had hers. Now she's upstairs doing her homework. And Kieron's gone into town to watch Pompey play.'

'Pompey playing on a Monday? Is that what he told you?'

'Laurence, he wants to be out and about doing things. That's perfectly normal. When did you last go and do anything special with him? Even teenage boys, or should I say especially teenage boys, need their dads.' There was more than a hint of reproach in her voice.

He rapidly went through his personal hard drive, trying to retrieve the appropriate file with the necessary information. It was true that he and his son hadn't actually done anything on their own for quite a while. He vaguely recalled an ill-fated attempt at fly-fishing a good two years ago, when Kieron was recuperating from a viral infection and Laurence had reluctantly made time for him one weekend. It occurred to him as they both stood side by side on the river-bank, while casting their lines across water that refused to stand still but skipped away with the capriciousness of youth, that he ought to seize the opportunity to exercise some of his parental responsibility. An ideal situation, or so he thought, to raise the matter of contraception and the significance of STIs. But Kieron only cried out in exasperation, 'Dad, there's no need for that. I'm completely clued up about all that stuff. Just leave it.' After that Kieron had spent most of the afternoon in a quiet sulk, while Laurence had busied himself with disentangling twine caught up in the shrubbery, gently blowing drops of water off the silken flies and trying hard not to feel and look disappointed.

'I don't think he's at an age when he wants to be doing things with me,' he said.

'Laurence, that's a cop-out. You never even make the effort now. I've told you that there's something going on, I can sense it. It's either drugs or girlfriend trouble, but he won't open up to me.'

'So what makes you think I'm going to be any more successful at finding out what the problem is? He's always been closer to you anyway.'

They were close to bickering. He wondered why their evening conversations were beginning to have elements of recrimination woven into each routine. It was almost as though Rosie was searching for something she could confront him with. Something he had failed to do, failed to notice, failed to comprehend. Not very different from the pattern of his own childhood, in fact. It had taken one of his early biology lessons about mycorrhiza in the soil for him to fully understood the significance of a symbiotic relationship. 'We have to support each other, Laurence. Please don't make me cross and then I promise I won't make you cross.' There were times when he had struggled to meet his mother's expectations. He was beginning to want things for himself, to see himself as a separate organism, to pull away, and yet she would constantly reel him back on the threads that held them together. When the days lengthened after the monotony of dark winter evenings, broken only by the occasional TV shows they watched together or by visits to the Bagshaw boys at the end of the lane, he'd be outside, kicking a football around with all the local lads, until his mother suddenly appeared from nowhere, admonishing him that he still had homework or other chores to attend to. And then he would be upstairs, hunched listless over his schoolbooks, willing time to march on and take him with it, or carrying the bucket with kitchen swill to the compost heap at the bottom of the garden, or filling the coal scuttle in the shed outside. And always the question that followed was, 'Laurence, have you washed your hands?'

He returned to the present. 'What about Bonfire Night? That's the day after tomorrow. How about having a barbie in the garden before we set off the fireworks? That'll make it more of a party. After that I can try and have a heart-to-heart with Kieron.'

Rosie looked across at him with a mixture of bemusement and resentment. 'Laurence Stewart, you really are impossible! Why do you always come up with these last-minute ideas? That means

I'll have to do some extra shopping tomorrow morning. If I want to marinade the meat, I can't leave it till Wednesday. I'm due to see Lee in the afternoon, anyway.'

'Why do you still need to see him? I thought you'd discussed everything. You've been to see him so many times already.'

'You're not keeping up, are you? There are dozens of small details to consider and the opening night isn't all that far off.'

He decided not to engage with the intricacies of the Callas operation and how these affected Rosie's schedule or the uncertainties of arranging a last-minute home feast.

'Come on, love, let's eat,' he said. 'There's something else I want to talk to you about.'

She headed off into the kitchen to put two plates of lasagne into the microwave, sensing that any new topic of conversation could only arise from the intricacies and uncertainties of Laurence's business world.

6

Laurence stood in front of the bathroom mirror, mowing his cheeks with deft movements of his razor. He pulled at his sagging jawline in order to deal with the uncompliant stubble that nestled in the folds beneath. The same ritual over and over again, and each time it required all his accumulated skill to locate, isolate and remove every patch of roughness, so that he wouldn't be cursing himself mid-afternoon for failing to carry out the perfect shaving routine.

It had taken him much longer than usual to nod off last night, and as he went through his morning ablutions, the rewind button on the previous evening's conversation with Rosie kept re-engaging. Fragments buzzed around his head like angry bees as he struggled to piece everything together. Why had she been prepared to pour such scorn on the idea? Why hadn't she realised it wasn't all about himself; he was doing it for the entire family. Why had she been so unreasonable? And the same loop continued, over and over again.

You must be mad. It's like watching a locomotive and the never-ending succession of freight waggons that you pull behind you. You never stop. You always have to find something new. You're like a rolling stone. A kid in a candy shop. All the sweeties at once. Why can't you be happy with what you've got? No, not another wave of disruption, not now with Kieron and Estelle at such a critical stage in their lives. You always want to be the first to find the next star at the end of the galaxy. Do you honestly think I want to live on a building site for weeks and months on end?

From his perspective it had all been relatively straightforward. Four thousand foot of living space. An Italianate front. A balcony with tiered pews. Oak panelling. Eight original stained-glass windows. A mezzanine floor. Character. Bags of charm. Period features, Rosie, period features. Remember what you said you were missing when we first moved here? Heritage in spades, and yet incredibly not even a listed building. This is called making a statement. A golden opportunity to realise a personal, no a family vision. The prospect of adding value over time. Potential, potential, potential. And yes, it would be the forever home. No more moves. Promise. Scout's honour.

Where he had seen the positives, she had only seen negatives. *Just look at the falling property prices. The whole world's in a mess, not just this country. What about possible dry rot, a leaking roof, the costly restoration work to the stained glass, the inevitable cracks in the masonry?* At times she was talking just like a surveyor. *Camping out on the land behind the building while the conversion was taking place? You have to be joking. Where's the nearest loo in the middle of the night? Where do you think we would all wash? Where could the kids conceivably do their homework? How long do you think we could endure the noise, the dirt, the mess, the ever-expanding budget and the over-run, the contingency funds drying up, as they were sure to do, the rows with the builders, the delays in the supply chain, the setbacks, the compromises? Think about those high ceilings and the costs of heating such spaces. You can't be serious. You need your head seeing to. You've taken leave of your senses. A bottomless pit. A white elephant. A pig in a poke. A scourge. Seven years of the plague. A ziggurat of false hopes.* No, he must have made that last one up. She couldn't possibly have said that. But he did remember seeing not so very long ago a picture in a glossy architectural magazine of a ziggurat block of new luxury apartments. How the mind and memory can so easily play tricks.

Rosie returned to her dressing table after seeing Laurence off. They had spent the night with their backs turned to each other, no stray hand reaching out for reassurance. He'd grabbed a quick coffee, mumbling that it was going to be an especially busy day; she'd had to repeatedly knock on Kieron's door before she could rouse him and then eventually he had stumbled off to school, half-awake as usual. Only Estelle had lingered, her rambling comments constantly revolving around the iniquities of being singled out for punitive biological treatment. Why did Lizzy have such beautifully rounded breasts, and perfect skin to boot? Why was becoming a woman made so difficult in her case? Why was nobody else in her class, at least no one she felt she could talk to, experiencing what she was going through? Life was so unfair. Boys didn't know how lucky they were.

Rosie sat her daughter down and gently squeezed her hands. She promised a joint consultation with her GP and indicated a possible referral if an expert opinion needed to be sought, and hoped this would soothe Estelle's concerns. She felt sure it was just a phase, just like the blotches on her daughter's oily skin. They would pass. In time. And then she moved swiftly from her daughter's concerns back to the worries she had about her son. Nobody could persuade her that there was not something deep down which had to be brought to the surface, but how could she sensibly get to the bottom of it without driving him further into his shell? Yes, puberty was an utterly rotten time – thank God it only happened once in life. A generation ago she'd had Lucie and very occasionally Dulcie for reassurance. Her own two parents had been so wrapped up in running the family business that adolescent anxieties in their youngest daughter were deemed to be entirely trivial, and at best an opportunity for outsourcing to the other siblings.

Rosie viewed her hair critically. Having succumbed to the latest advertising wheeze, she'd taken to using a new shampoo rich in caffeine, hoping that her hair would acquire even more of a magnetic sheen and that Laurence would notice it too. But after six weeks the difference was only marginal. She picked up her hairbrush and scraped down to the scalp with purposeful flicks of her wrist and then slowed the movements so that the brush merely rippled through the long glossy folds. This was what Laurence had loved to do in the early days of their marriage, running his fingers through the cascades of her hair, then gently massaging her scalp while gradually pressing her close, gripping her nape between his two thumbs as he sought admission to her mouth with the tip of his tongue, holding her captive between his strong arms as he rocked her body, first from left to right and then backwards and forwards. Those moments of tenderness and slow arousal – where had they all gone? What did she have to hold onto now? A peck on the cheek in the morning and on his return in the evening, the occasional cuddle in bed after a hard day, and the odd burst of mechanically-induced passion, leading to a rare penetration when he was up to it. She was conscious of an unsettling transition in her body, of unwelcome signs of dryness between her legs which meant that when they did make love she never quite felt fulfilled in the way she used to. She worried that she was heading for an early menopause like Lucie, now in her mid-fifties, who'd had a torrid few years before the flame in her was finally extinguished. Not just the everlasting time of the month but now the prospect of an all-flattening time of life.

She'd never even raised the matter with Dulcie, whom she called much less frequently than her eldest sister. And what did she know about her mother's own experience? While she was alive she had never talked about anything over and above the bare practical necessities. She had never once opened up to her youngest child about matters that had been bothering her (and Rosie counted herself lucky if Dulcie gave her a condensed version much later), nor did she ever inquire too deeply, after Rosie got married, into her relationship with Laurence. Any problems there might be would just sort themselves out. Northern grit would see to that. On the rare occasions when the two of them did meet she would beam at her new son-in-law, but produce much less than that for her youngest daughter. A big smile for some, a lesser version for others.

Rosie smoothed out the skin over her high cheekbones and reached for her grandmother's sewing-box, which had pride of place on the left of her dressing-table. She remembered like yesterday the moment her gran had presented it to her on her eleventh birthday, her first welcoming gift to the adult world, and the way she had gasped at the mother-of-pearl detail on the lid and the smoothness of the emerald green satin lining. She had lingered over the slightly musty and intriguing smell of past objects that had left their individually-scented traces, mingling with the fabric and the DNA of past family generations. She wondered how many unspoken thoughts the box had absorbed, how many projections of future happiness the precious stones had received, how many secrets had been locked away in its cavities and recesses by women who had something to hide. 'Rosie lass, when my mum gave it to me I started to use it for all my sewing. It was always used as a jewellery box before that. Look, I've put a necklace and a brooch and two ear-rings and an embroidered handkerchief inside for you.' Nothing changed, everything changed.

What had been handed down to her was still all there at the bottom of the box. Above nestled the items of slightly gaudy costume jewellery she had loved to wear in the early days of her working life, a little bit of glam to make her think she could be like any of the princesses she used to read about while growing up in Huddersfield. Higher up lay the more valuable pieces, like the arm-bracelet in rolled gold Laurence had given her to celebrate their first wedding anniversary, adorned with seven small enamelled roundels of individual roses ranging from an angelic white to a mysterious purple. 'Roses for my sweet Rosie,' was what he said as she opened the presentation box. It must have taken him ages to find it. How lucky she was to have somebody like Laurence, she had thought at the time. Was she still lucky right now?

She thought back to the previous night's confrontation. Why was he so obsessed with pushing through something he'd already decided on without even consulting her? He'd gone through all the architectural features of the Wesleyan chapel with almost forensic care, reading out to her the particulars in the agent's description, showing her the exterior photographs he'd taken with his new digital camera, insisting they'd be able to live on site while all the refurbishment and renovation was undertaken, reeling off ideas for turning the vast interior space into something approaching a modern palace. But she didn't regard herself as a princess, nor did she have any personal connection with the place. Like Laurence she wasn't particularly religious, and even his silly joke about the building putting her in the fast lane to paradise didn't correspond to any ideas she might have had of going up in the world. But he had persisted, reacting to her rejoinders with the slick determination he'd spent years developing in order to persuade sceptical clients that he had their best interests at heart. *Let me try again, love. Rosie, you're not listening properly to me. You've got it all wrong: I want to make this work for all of us. Rosie, I know we can be happy there.* In short, he wanted to make it the most desirable project on the planet. Yet she failed to be lured by the prospect of a pot of gold behind the next corner. She was unable to share his unique vision for their common future together. And she had felt a wall of frustration building between them.

She looked around their bedroom, with the custom-built wardrobes and their duck-egg blue surrounds, the moiré silk of the button tufted headboard in old gold and the mock Louis Quinze chair with its caramel-coloured worsted upholstery. Of course she liked beautiful things, but to her having a nice home was never about filling it with displays of deliberate ostentation. Laurence had left her to make all the decisions about the interior design, confident that after finding them the right exterior shell, she would then be able to fill it with all the patterns and colours and objects that made visitors to their home swoon in admiration, so that afterwards he told her how proud he was to have such a talented wife. And, to be fair, he never once interfered in some of her more extravagant choices, like the embossed purple wallpaper that covered the two side walls of the entrance hall. 'Interesting, Rosie, very interesting' was how he usually reacted whenever she asked him for a comment on domestic matters outside his purview. Nor did he find it easy expressing anything approaching antipathy towards any of her decisions, which was why he expected her to respect his judgements. 'But I know what I'm talking about,' was almost the last thing he'd said to her before she'd taken herself off to bed the previous night. He'd been talking about the property market; she'd been talking about their family.

Rosie sighed and wondered whether she was being unnecessarily difficult. There had to be some method of making clear to Laurence that he simply had to take a step back, reset the dials and see the bigger picture. As far as she was concerned, what mattered more than anything else was the restoration of domestic harmony and making certain that Kieron and Estelle were given all the support they needed. She wanted to feel that Laurence still respected her and valued her opinions, even if she couldn't hide the fact that she was diametrically opposed to his latest scheme.

There had been a similar stand-off three years previously, when Laurence had insisted that taking the entire family off to Morocco for a summer holiday made perfect sense. One of his contacts in the travel industry had offered them a two-week stay in a villa on the outskirts of Casablanca. 'But why not go through a travel company? That way they look after all the organisation and we don't have to worry about any of the details,' she had said, trying to persuade him to the contrary. And just as she had feared, when they got out of the airport there were problems sorting out a hire car. It was already quite late, the kids were getting fractious, and on arrival at the villa it hadn't really come up to their expectations with none of the promised food waiting for them in the fridge. The intense heat enervated her, whether she sat perfectly motionless or tried to create swirls of air by gently moving around. She spent the next fortnight making half-hearted compromises in order to stave off further conflicts, willing the clock to tick faster so it would soon be time to fly back. Then, at the airport just before their return flight was called, Laurence gave her a silk and leather antique purse he had managed to purchase in one of the souks without her realising what he'd been up to. He was like that, as she well knew. Relentless in his pursuit of an aim and resolute in discounting all opposition, and yet as soon as he realised his own single-mindedness was driving those he loved against him, he did his best to make amends. Sometimes there were little gestures, sometimes big ones: you could never tell with Laurence.

While she was pondering the merits of humouring him about the absurdity of his latest project, the words of a hymn she remembered having to sing with her parents at her side came into her mind – 'Nearer, my God, to Thee'.

She was alerted to a sudden clatter downstairs. It was too early for the post, but it might just be one of the deliveries of junk mail that were tipped with mind-numbing regularity through their letter-box. How was it that with money increasingly so tight, legions of companies had such huge amounts of cash to spend on mountains of randomly-targeted advertising? 'Crisis? What crisis?' they would have said if asked. If only they knew how often she picked up the piles of paper and quickly consigned them to the bin.

Then she heard some further unexpected movement below, so she went onto the landing and stood at the top of the stairs. Looking down she saw Kieron, his satchel flung into a corner, his long arms hanging like the wilting stems of an underwatered plant.

'Kieron, what are you doing at home? Why aren't you in school?' She hurried down the stairs.

He avoided making eye contact with her. 'I don't feel well. I want to lie down.'

'What is it, chick? Where does it hurt?'

He resisted her attempt to clasp his head closer. He was already quite a bit taller than she was and would soon be taller than Laurence.

'Look, just tell me what you need from the medicine cabinet and we'll put it right.'

'I don't need anything. I just want to lie down. Please, mum, just leave me be.'

She was still trying to work out why he wouldn't open up to her. Her gut instinct was to rule out drugs. She knew all about the dangers of teenage party drugs from conversations she had had at work as well as what her hairdresser Mandy and her friend Chantal from the basket-weaving class had told her. But even if she'd got it wrong and this was indeed all about drugs, she couldn't see how he could possibly afford to indulge in anything approaching a regular habit, since she and Laurence made a point of exercising tight financial control. To keep it going you needed lots of money. However, she was aware that getting teenagers hooked was part of a long-term investment strategy and credit for new customers was often readily available. On the other hand, she hadn't noticed any violent swings of mood and energy in the past few weeks. It wasn't impossible that his disengagement with the world in general and whatever else she happened to be saying to him in particular were indications of withdrawal symptoms, but he'd been in this state of suspension for a few weeks now, with little or no variation. It was as if the theatre curtain had descended and the interval kept stretching into infinity. Already weeks before she'd noticed how he'd been struggling with some of his schoolwork, and Laurence piling on the pressure hadn't been a smart move either, but she'd made every effort to reassure him that as far as she was concerned he didn't need to be anywhere near the top of the class, just as long as he wasn't right at the bottom. In any case what was cause and what was effect?

She suddenly remembered her own list of commitments for the rest of the day. 'Look Kieron, I still have to do some essential shopping for tomorrow night's barbie and I'm not sure I can be back before the late afternoon. There are things I really must discuss with Lee and Matthew at the Callas. I'll text or call you though, as soon as I have a minute to spare.'

'You can't.'

'What did you just say?'

'You can't.' And then, after a pause, 'I've lost my phone.'

'Kieron! Your new phone! You've scarcely had it half a year. It was your birthday present. How on earth did you manage to lose it? Where were you? Did somebody steal it? Did it fall out of your pocket? Have you tried ringing the number from Estelle's phone?'

The questions were rattled out like darts speeding straight for the board. She knew she always did this with the children when she wanted to get to the bottom of something. The waves of energy that built up inside her then became reflected in her over-active arms and hands and an effusion of words. When this happened she knew that both her children would stand quite still and impassive while the salvoes were fired off, willing her to increase the levels of intensity. It was the only way she felt she could give expression to her annoyance and show them how deeply she cared about something.

As she expected, Kieron said nothing.

'I don't believe I'm hearing this. That was a jolly expensive phone. You must have some idea of where you lost it.'

There was another silence and then she saw the first tears forming in one eye. He stood in front of her without moving, trying to keep the lid on the bubbling cauldron she imagined inside. She was reminded of overhearing Laurence's instructions to him on handling a crisis. 'The moment you allow others to see your true feelings, you're lost, son. You always need to keep everything under control. Never allow your defences to falter.'

She tried one more time. 'Look Kieron, I have to be going in a moment. Won't you just tell me what's bugging you? Let's sit down and have a chat. You'll feel better for letting it all come out. It can't be that bad, can it?'

He shook his head. 'I want to go to my room. Please, mum, please.'

'Kieron love, whatever it is, we're on your side. I'm going to help you pick yourself up. Don't fret. Don't brood. We'll have a chat about it tonight as soon as your dad gets back.'

She noted a look of alarm on her son's face just before he charged up the stairs. A few minutes later she was in her runabout heading for the shops.

7

Laurence was sitting in a corner of the Parisian-style bistro Steve had chosen. They could have gone to a number of other coffee shops where the baristas offered you fifty-seven varieties of a humble cup of coffee, but this was the most convenient for Miriam Bartrop.

'She told me she works as a dental technician and she doesn't have a long lunch-break. It needs to be more or less on her door-step,' was how Steve had explained the arrangement on the phone. 'She said she'll be there for half-one.'

Laurence looked at his Rolex. 'Well, if you've got it, I suppose you might as well flaunt it,' was Rosie's reaction when she first saw it on his wrist, and deep down he knew she probably regarded it as an unnecessary extravagance. It was almost half-past now. He hated being late for anything and he hated having to make allowances for people who were. Miriam wouldn't be able to blame it on the traffic. He wondered where Steve was.

He waved the waitress away when she tried to take his order. 'No, no, I'm still waiting for two other people,' he said.

And then he saw them both at the door. Steve gave a cheery wave and propelled Miriam towards the corner table. It was over a month since Laurence had last seen her, but he would have recognised her again without hesitation. She wore large, owlish glasses behind which two generous eyes surveyed the world with an openness Laurence found appealing. She was a little older than he remembered her, probably on the wrong side of forty, and as before no lick of paint had been applied to the exterior to hide signs of the passage of time. She was plain and unvarnished timber, but the warmth in her voice reminded him instantly of his own wife. What you see is what you get, he thought as she started to speak. No pretence, no side.

'I felt I had to say thank you properly to the two of you,' she said. 'And the coffees and anything else you'd like are on me. I insist.'

'There wasn't an awful lot we were able to do,' Laurence replied. 'It all happened so quickly, and thank goodness the ambulance arrived without much of a delay.'

'Your presence was very reassuring. At the time I felt I'd been turned upside-down. Completely disoriented. I was in another world.'

'But you're absolutely OK now, are you?' Steve enquired.

'I think so. Yesterday was my first day back at work. I'm still easing myself slowly into my old routine. They kept me in hospital for a few days till they'd carried out various tests and checks. And then I had time off.'

'Are you any closer to understanding what exactly happened?' Laurence asked.

'Yes, indeed I am. Do you know what a TIA is?'

'You're surely not going to tell us it's the first part of an alcoholic drink,' Steve volunteered facetiously.

She laughed and Laurence noted the same unforced charm that Rosie had. 'Even though I've got a scientific background – well, it's technical, to be more correct – I'd never heard of it either. It's short for a transient ischaemic attack. The more common way of describing it is a mini-stroke.'

Laurence looked startled. 'Goodness, that sounds serious.'

'I actually can't recall those last few seconds before the crash. I know I was driving along and then the next thing I remember was hearing the two of you at my side. I'd obviously had a complete blackout. It was all very disconcerting. I know I couldn't see properly while I was in the ambulance.'

'Aren't you rather young to be having something like that?'

She gave another laugh. 'I'm not coy about my age. I'm 51, I'm pretty sure I'm on the verge of the menopause and I know I'd been working too hard in the days before. It all added to the pressure, I suppose. The doctors said it was almost certainly age-related.'

They talked at length about her stay in hospital and how the NHS was still capable of delivering excellent care in her case, and how unfair it was that the media spent so much time reporting the under-funding as well as the scandals resulting from negligence and incompetence, rather than the success stories. Laurence drew a parallel with the over-dramatisation of the financial crisis; Steve winced in silent disagreement. Before they broke up, Miriam turned to Laurence.

'That's one reason why my brother's coming back to this country. He's actually my half-brother and a good bit older than me. He's spent most of his life abroad teaching English, but he's got health issues now and he'll have to fall back on the NHS for support. Thank goodness it's there for everybody. He can stay with me for a while when he gets back, but he'll need something more permanent, a place he can call his own. Steve tells me you run a letting agency.'

For a moment Laurence wasn't sure why he was being undersold. Laurence Stewart Management was more than just a lettings agency. He was a property developer first and foremost; he had plenty of other strings to his bow. Perhaps Steve was simply trying to bring custom his way.

Miriam's lunch-break was over. On the understanding that she would get in touch with Laurence as soon as her brother's needs became more apparent, she left them sitting over the remnants of a croque monsieur.

Laurence turned to Steve. 'Why did you make out I was a mere lettings agency?'

'Sorry, mate. I thought that bit would be more relevant than anything else. You're not becoming touchy in your old age, are you?'

'Watch it, Steve! It's bad enough if others get the idea that I'm just a one-trick pony.' He half-hesitated, but then decided to recount his discovery of the Wesleyan chapel and his attempts at persuading Rosie that this was a property dream about to come true.

This engine has restless amounts of energy, Steve thought. There was always some new destination that would be flashed up on the screens and an additional platform for the next relief service.

Laurence was looking expectantly at him, as if prompting him to board the train and take the ride.

'Who am I to tell you what to do?' said Steve. 'Never come between a man and his wife, as they say. But if I were in your shoes I wouldn't want to take on anything too big at the moment. I thought you painted too rosy a picture to Miriam. Just look at what's happened to the entire financial sector. All those banks having to be bailed out. That's going to have a knock-on effect on mortgages. Patrick's already talking about a noticeable downturn in the market.'

'That's precisely my point, Steve. You buy when the values are below where they would normally be, and you sell later when the market correction's taken place and the upswing is in progress.'

'I thought you said you wanted this to be your last move.'

'That's what I told Rosie, yes. And that's the general plan. But the principle behind making any good profit is to get something under the market price.'

'But isn't there a serious flaw in that argument? You won't be able to do all the renovation and refurbishment yourself. OK, you'll be project-managing most of it, but you'll be in the hands of builders and tradespeople. Those costs certainly aren't going to be heading down.'

'Wrong again, my friend. If the market begins to clam up,

there'll be much less work around and much more pressure on the building trade to cut their margins. I can't see there'll be too much of a risk. And if we get the project just right and everything done to spec, think about what it'll be worth five or ten years down the line.'

Steve could see he wasn't making much of an impact on Laurence's self-confidence. And who was he to argue anyway? More experience, more success, more assets to fall back on, more nous, more chutzpah. More everything, in fact. And, unlike Laurence, he didn't have a warm and supportive domestic situation to boost his own mojo. In his case, when he looked down the track there appeared to be an obvious delay. The train was never on time. When it did arrive and he found an attractive young woman sitting opposite, he could never maintain the conversation long enough to have a proper set-to with her. Some people had all the luck.

8

Before Rosie arrived at the Callas, she deliberated whether she should call Laurence to tell him about Kieron. She still felt sore about his intransigence, the way he again had the bit firmly between his teeth, but she knew she was the one who would have to make the first move at patching things up. The bickering was already beginning to sap at her own self-esteem. If she couldn't restore harmony, what did that say about her role as a domestic peacemaker? Perhaps it would all blow over far sooner than she imagined. That was Laurence's stock response to any sudden blizzard that halted his progress. He either got onto his snow-plough immediately or dug himself into the ground and waited for the storm to pass. *Perhaps I'm just making a mountain out of a molehill,* she thought. *Things will sort themselves out and Kieron will slay whatever demon happens to be riding him.* She quickly stuffed her purchases from the butcher's into cool-bags and placed them in the boot of the car.

When she got inside the Callas, she could see that the transformation was well underway, with a fresher, cleaner look to the place, the kitchen now separated from the rest of the space and sporting an array of stainless steel units and counter tops. She was disappointed to learn that Lee wasn't there. Matthew was the quieter one, the back office to Lee's front-of-house, and she hadn't yet had anything approaching an extended conversation with him.

He stroked his beard as he apologised. 'I'm sorry, but he's had to sort out a problem with the signboards,' he said. 'Never deal with people over the phone, if it's anything important. Otherwise you end up with a car crash. Do you have any idea what was on the original signboard when they delivered it yesterday? "Class". Class, I ask you! They obviously thought that was the right and proper name for a high-end restaurant.'

Rosie couldn't suppress a giggle. 'Well, you have to see the *funny* side of it.' The flat northern 'u' had a homely feel to it. 'And it could have been much worse,' she added. 'They could have spelled it c, a, double l, o ,u, s".

It was his turn to laugh. 'You're not from these parts, are you?'

'No, I haven't lost my accent, if that's what you mean. Even after living down here all these years.'

'What took you away from the north in the first place, if that's not a rude question?'

She laughed. 'I can think of lots of questions that are rude, but that's not one of them. Actually, I followed my childhood sweetheart down. He trained as a primary school teacher and his first job was in Chichester.'

'That's Laurence, isn't it?'

Her delight in communicating suddenly abated and her words became more measured. 'No, no, no. It's strange what a few years of living together but having differing priorities can do to you. Adam and I quickly drifted apart. I wouldn't have thought that could ever happen to us, but it did. I met Laurence some time after that when I was working at Florabellum.'

'Well, we all have to meet somewhere, don't we? With me and Lee it was a chance meeting in the street. I was right behind him, he dropped his wallet and I picked it up for him. In the normal run of things I don't suppose we'd ever have met. Two different worlds really. He's much cleverer than I am.'

They were standing at one end of the kitchen and Matthew

pointed to a hob where he had various pots on the go. 'I'm trying out a few things in advance. Come and see,' he suddenly said. 'We open on the seventeenth.'

'So that's a definite date then.' On one side of the hob Rosie caught sight of bowls of micro-herbs and small flowers. 'Is this what you're trying out?

'No no. These are some of the garnishes. They're all part of high-end cuisine these days. What it looks like on the plate is almost as important as the taste. Presentation matters.'

'Sweet as they look, can you eat all of them?'

'Of course! Everything on the plate is edible. Here, try this yellow one. It's wood sorrel. It's got a lemony flavour, but it's actually related to the broccoli and spinach family.'

She allowed the taste to linger on her tongue before commenting, 'I suppose I should know all this really. After all, I work in a flower shop.'

'I guess florists are like hairdressers. We all need them from time to time.' Then she noted a slight edge in his voice. 'Well, not like restaurants,' he added. 'You can happily get through life without once eating out.'

'You're not having doubts at this late stage, are you?'

'We didn't have any at all when we committed to the project in the summer. Mind you, it's been much more difficult for Lee than for me. I know the food side of the business inside out, but he's had a steep learning curve. In the meantime he can throw terms like "dynamic pricing" and "psychological pricing" at me. But a couple of things have happened recently which would probably make us want to reconsider if we had to start all over again.'

'But Matthew, that's awful.' Rosie touched his arm in support. 'The restaurant is such a nice idea. Why wouldn't it work?' The concern in her voice was palpable.

He sighed. 'It's the changing business climate, not the idea itself. In the past few weeks there's been a noticeable shift in the mood music everywhere. You won't have heard of the name, I suppose, but there's quite a famous chef in London – I met him once – who had to close his restaurant last month. His debts just piled up. He's actually left his suppliers almost a million out of pocket. They're all hopping mad. I can understand that. But the banks just wouldn't bail him out. And he's not the only one. These are tough times, believe me.'

'Yes, I keep hearing these stories about people being in trouble. You can't escape them really. They're on the radio and TV and in the papers. But Laurence says there must have been a flaw in their business plans for everything to go so badly wrong, and if they can just hold on things will pick up again in time.'

'But that's precisely the point. Some people can't hang on. There's nothing in reserve. I mean, Lee and I have ploughed our life's savings into this, and we still had to take out a small bank loan. If it all goes pear-shaped, we're done for.'

Rosie blinked. She could relate to uncertainty. She thought back to her early years of adolescent indecision when she had been more wrapped up in the heady feelings she was developing for Adam than in her schoolwork. She was unable to make up her own mind, moving from an eagerness to do something in rural studies without knowing exactly what, to a sudden desire to follow Lucie's own career path into interior design, all the while listening to her parents' constant exhortations to do something practical that would ensure a steady income before she inevitably became a wife and mother. And now here she was, having made all those fateful decisions what seemed a lifetime ago, choosing ultimately to open some doors and leave others closed. The unopened doors could wait until later, she had thought at the time. Except that as the years flitted by, she couldn't find the keys to most of the doors she still wanted to open. She was finding that Laurence's stubbornness was increasingly affecting the domestic sphere, where for so long she had felt secure and at ease. The man with all the wonderful ideas about what he wanted to do and how he planned to do it, who had swept her off her feet and within months proposed to her, now left her with virtually no more doors to open and no conveniently-forgotten cupboard drawers to pull out. And, after all, what had she done with herself, apart from drifting in and out of jobs after the break with Adam, getting married at twenty-eight and bringing two children into the world, becoming a junior partner in a floristry business and managing the occasional floral displays at local exhibitions? She let out a sigh.

'A penny for your thoughts?' Matthew had turned from stirring his aromatic sauces to look into her vacant eyes.

'I'm sorry, I must have been miles away. I don't want you and Lee to think I can't appreciate what you're going through. I know what it's like to have worries. With me it's family problems. Babies are a whole load easier than teenagers.'

'Care to talk about it? We can't take any final decisions until Lee gets back, since he has the last word about the business side, so we might as well find something else to chat about.'

She wondered for a moment how a gay man could have any inkling of what it was like having to be parent, friend, counsellor and arbiter all wrapped up in one to a fifteen-year-old whose own doors were not only bolted and padlocked but secured with access codes. The two of them were an odd match, she thought. From what she'd seen so far, Lee obviously wore the trousers in the relationship and looked quite a few years older than Matthew, but it was when she first saw them standing side by side that the incongruity was most pronounced. The tall thin Lee with rapidly receding hair, cultured and eloquent, negotiating the spreadsheets on his laptop with ease as he spoke to her and then pausing to gesticulate energetically; in another life he'd have been a dead ringer for a bank manager or civil servant. Whereas Matthew was much shorter and bulkier too (thanks no doubt to the need for constant samplings in the kitchen), outwardly more masculine with his cropped gingery hair and hirsute face and the tattoos she noticed around both wrists, but also with a kind and patient air she associated more with a philanthropic than a culinary occupation.

Initially she had wondered why somebody whom she felt looked more like a Lee had ended up with a name like Matthew. She had no problem imagining a chef called Lee. But Matthew? Names had a habit of surprising you.

Strangers in Huddersfield would constantly remark on the perfect symmetry of three young ladies called Lucie, Dulcie and Rosie, as if their parents had known well in advance that they would end up with three such girls. She had always regarded herself as an afterthought, even though her parents never for one moment let her think she wasn't as wanted as her two much older sisters. However, names were important. She and Laurence had deliberated for ages over the right names for their children, he insisting there could be no obvious shortening and she determined on something out-of-the-ordinary.

Suddenly she was back in the present. 'Have you ever considered becoming a parent yourself?'

Matthew rubbed his cheeks mechanically. 'It's not an option we've ever considered, no. It wouldn't work anyway. We're committed now to this project, and that means we both have to be here for most of the afternoon and in the evening too. You couldn't sensibly foster any kid with that kind of schedule, never mind look after a new-born properly.'

She was happy that the spotlight had moved away from her preoccupation with Kieron and she could now find something outside her immediate range of experience to focus on. She struggled to recall the last gay relationship in her circle of friends and acquaintances. It wasn't a world she had ever thought much about.

'But if things work out here, is it something you would contemplate? I mean, loads of people pay for childcare these days.'

'I don't think Lee and I are really family people. Work has always come first for both of us, and you need somebody in a relationship who's going to make parenting a priority. We're committed to the Callas, as I said, but it's still a risk. Plenty of businesses fail. More go under than stay afloat. I know I'm confident about the food side of things, but the test will be getting the punters inside if in future they have less money to spend on non-essentials. I think about that a lot. But Lee's far worse, he's a real worrier. He tosses and turns at night – that's how I know. I've left nearly everything on the business side for him to sort out. He doesn't like to talk much about what could go wrong and he won't exactly open up about it. It's almost as though talking about it makes the possible catastrophe seem much closer. And that's strange 'cos you normally can't stop him talking. Me, I'm a doer. I just get on with things.'

Rosie suddenly realised that she and Matthew were wrestling with an almost identical problem. 'I suppose most women, and certainly most mothers, are born worriers. Laurence is more like you, he's a doer too. I just like to know where I'm going and want to be able to see several steps ahead. And if there's anything or anybody close to your heart, I think you'll always end up worrying. I'm absolutely convinced my son has got something serious that's bothering him. What makes it doubly difficult is that I just don't know what that is, and I've tried my level best to get through to him. I just find myself standing in front of a blank wall. Again and again.'

'How old is he?'

'He'll be sixteen next March.'

'And it's not girlfriend trouble?'

'There isn't one particular girlfriend. Not as far as we know, anyway. He's brought several back to the house over the years, but it's not as though the same name has kept popping up more recently.'

Matthew pulled on the lobe of one ear. 'Hmm, I don't want to alarm you, but you need to approach this carefully. If you're finding it too hard to handle, get somebody else in the family or close friends of his or the teachers involved, otherwise it could all go pear-shaped.'

She saw his eyes narrowing and a frown forming. 'How do you mean?'

'Well, how shall I put this? I've got a younger brother, that's Jason. I was away at catering college when it happened, so I know most of this only second-hand. He was dumped by his long-term girlfriend and he felt he couldn't talk about it to anybody. He just bottled up. Luckily, my mum found him soon after he'd taken an overdose.'

Rosie stretched out an arm. 'But that's terrible, Matthew. It must have been a huge shock to you.'

'They say men are the stronger sex. But we have a habit of going to pieces when relationships break down. There are more suicide attempts amongst young men than you might think.'

'And your parents had no idea about what was going on?"

'My mum brought us up on her own. She was out at work all day and Jason was on his own most of the time. Considering we're brothers it's odd, but we didn't talk very much. Nothing very deep anyway. We went to different schools too. He was the clever one, I just bumped along. He came through it eventually though, had therapy and all that. He got married last year, so I'm hoping he's properly sorted now. But you're right, it was a shock at the time.'

The voices that frequently danced through her mind whenever things seemed out of kilter, offering one view and then another with little care for either the accuracy or the consequences of their counsels, were suddenly converging on an obvious conclusion. No, it wasn't drugs. It couldn't be drugs – where was the hard evidence? No, it wasn't the new English teacher who'd taken against Kieron and was threatening to derail his GCSE coursework. No, it wasn't some teenage prank that had gone wrong and which he didn't want to own up about. It was none of those things. Instead it had to be some little minx who had ensnared and then rejected him. Poor lamb, he'd have been left utterly defenceless. No wonder his world was in a spin; no wonder he couldn't cope. Somebody had played havoc with his feelings. Her immediate instincts were to rush home and protect him from further damage.

'I'm sorry, Matthew. I thought Lee would have been here by now,' she said, glancing towards the entrance. 'We were going to go through all the final costings and settle on the displays for the opening night. But it doesn't have to be dealt with this afternoon. It can wait a while. Give him my love and tell him I'll give him a call this evening.'

'I haven't given you the wrong idea about your son, have I?' he ventured.

'No, no,' she protested, 'but it's reminded me I still have something to attend to.'

She hurried out of the Callas, her cheeks hot with concern, and drove back in the gathering gloom of an early November afternoon. By the time she reached the house, having listened to the mindless chatter of the Greek chorus camped out in her brain during the entire journey, her heart was pumping. She heaved the cool-bags out of the boot and let herself into the house. The hall lights were on as were those on the landing.

'Kieron? Kieron, are you there?'

She pounded up the stairs and without pausing to knock flung open his bedroom door. She was met with a well of darkness. Trembling, she pressed the light switch. But if she'd been expecting reassurance, she was in for a disappointment. The bed had clearly not been slept in or lain on, the usual jumble of teenage clutter all over the room seemed no different than on any previous occasion. She scanned the bedspread: there was nothing approaching a letter or note.

She turned on her heel towards Estelle's bedroom, from where she heard the steady beat of instrumental music. She knocked firmly and walked in.

'Hiya, love. Where's Kieron?'

Her daughter was lying on her divan and playing with the Burmese cat. Before she had begun to lavish her attention on the feline world she had surrounded herself with a motley collection of fluffy animal toys, with Laurence indulging her whim for increasingly life-size creations. Then she had passed from the synthetic world to the real one. Laurence argued that having a proper pet would develop a sense of responsibility in her, and so the first of a succession of hamsters moved into her bedroom as sub-tenants. Despite her assiduous care, the life-span of each one could be counted in months, so that she eventually ran up against the buffers in her choice of names. Starting off with Dick, she'd proceeded to Nick, then Mick and finally Rick. When Rick expired, Kieron playfully suggested his successor could be called Vic and there then followed an argument over whether Rick was the diminutive form of Eric or Patrick, with Estelle taunting her brother over his deficient spelling. 'You say that, but Vick's the name of a company, isn't it?' To which she merely retorted, 'Oh shut up, clever-clogs.' Finally, she decided that a cat was likely to provide a better long-term emotional investment. Unable to see the anxiety in her mother's face, Estelle was still giving the cat her undivided attention.

Rosie tried again. 'Can you turn that music down, love. Where's Kieron?'

'I dunno. He wasn't here when I got back from school. Doesn't he have footie practice on Tuesdays?'

'No. That's on Thursdays. Are you telling me you haven't seen him since this morning?'

Estelle noted the hint of impatience in her mother's voice, but struggled to see why Kieron's whereabouts were suddenly being dramatised. Like her father, she wasn't easily fazed. 'Mum, it's not even six o'clock. He'll be back in time for tea. Anyway, what are phones for?'

'He said he'd lost his. How do you think I'm going to be able to reach him?'

'Lost? Are you sure it wasn't stolen? You've no idea how many phones get nicked at school. And everybody wants one of these new smartphones anyway.'

Rosie leaned back on the bedroom door and drew in a deep breath. This was a new factor which the dancing voices in her head hadn't yet considered. Kieron a victim of something approaching organised crime, too ashamed to admit to his own culpability? Wait a minute, said another voice, where's the difference between losing a phone in a moment of mindlessness and being the victim of some kind of racket? It amounted to the same: no phone. In any case, hadn't he said he was feeling unwell? Maybe he was sick with worry or the shame of having done something stupid. But then, why was the bed perfectly made up? It was obvious he hadn't even lain on it. Had the alleged malady merely been a ploy to bunk off school? Above all, why wasn't he home, for heaven's sake? It was dark outside. What on earth could he be doing on the streets? He'd be hungry by now. Wouldn't he?

Rosie tried a new tack. 'Where does he normally hang out after lessons?' The advantage of having both children at the same school was that you weren't dealing with two completely different parallel worlds. Estelle would surely be able to tell her.

'How do you expect me to know that? He's two years above me, after all,' and then, as an afterthought, 'Ben and his gang, I suppose.'

Rosie thought she knew who Ben was, the one with the sandy hair and freckles who'd been to the house before. 'And what's his family name?'

'Mum, why are you asking me these things? Ben Lowbell or Lowberry or something like that.'

Rosie retreated and closed the door behind her. Estelle was always more responsive to Laurence, especially if she felt she was being interrogated. Rosie knew that she was unlikely to get much more out of her, so there was no point in antagonising her right now. She hurried down the stairs and tried Kieron's number from the landline in the hall. She hadn't even thought to question the veracity of his earlier claims, and in fact the call went straight to voicemail. She tried Laurence's mobile number, but it was engaged. She rang the office number, but that was on voicemail too. She sighed. Perhaps she was jumping to conclusions, like the time she thought he was having an affair with Shaheen, the girl before Natasha, and Laurence had laughed in her face at the absurdity of the idea. There was nothing to do except check that the fish pie she'd taken out of the freezer that morning was properly defrosted, lay the table and hope it was all going to be merely a storm in a teacup.

9

While Rosie was trying to contact Laurence, he was busy dealing with a plumbing crisis in an old Victorian mansion split up into six flats for which he'd recently assumed responsibility. Since such maintenance issues, especially in older buildings, could occur at any time of day or night and at weekends too, he knew he was going to be the first port of call if a crisis occurred. He was already cursing his readiness to take on additional property management in this case without having carried out a thorough survey of this particular building beforehand. There was he, a qualified chartered surveyor, breaking one of the golden rules in the book. It was one thing to sit back and levy management fees on the residents and expect the coffers to swell still further without expending too much energy and effort; it was quite another having to ring round local tradespeople and organise emergency call-outs, particularly since he was legally obliged to go to the property and carry out an initial assessment of the problem as soon as he was informed. It had all come at the wrong time: he'd made a promise to himself that he was going to be home on time and he wasn't going to raise the matter of the Wesleyan chapel. Not just yet anyway; he still wanted to talk to his bank manager about a further mortgage. He quickly texted Rosie the briefest of messages – *Sorry, going to be late, property crisis* – before facing the ire of the ground-floor residents.

When he got back to Marlborough Close he found Rosie and Estelle together in the kitchen. Two plates lay on the kitchen-table, one already cleared, the other still bearing a forlorn-looking wedge of fish pie.

Approaching, he saw that the worry lines on Rosie's forehead were furrowed more deeply than usual. Even Estelle's welcome hug was less effusive than normal.

'What's up?' he asked.

Rosie's voice was a tad softer and darker than usual. 'We don't know where Kieron is. I haven't seen him since this morning, I can't contact him and we don't have a clue where he could be.'

She was almost invariably heart to his head. That was one of the things about her he most liked. Almost a decade earlier she had lost first her father and then within a year her mother, the woman whose eyes twinkled every time she saw Laurence. On both occasions she'd hurried north grief-stricken for the funeral, with the rest of the family following on. He'd had to take charge of managing family affairs while she stayed on in Huddersfield, parking the two children on his mother and sailing through each working day quite unperturbed by the disruptions to the regular family routine. When she came back again she immediately burst into tears, pressing herself against him and whispering 'I'm so glad I've got you'.

It had taken her several years to properly get over both deaths; whenever she heard about a family being bereaved as a result of a killing or an accident she was unable to contain her grief. Some years after that there'd been her sudden outburst one weekend, her fists pounding his broad chest in fury because she'd found a small box covered in expensive wrapping paper tucked away in the glove-box of his car, intended as a thank-you present to Shaheen for helping him to organise his new office so efficiently. For some strange reason he was never able to work out she had assumed he was having an affair and told him so, bursting into tears again when he laughed in her face. He always found it much easier if the window to his wife's soul was flung wide open and he could immediately look inside. Most of the time it was, since deception had never been part of her personal make-up. Once or twice though, her moods cast a cloak of deliberate or accidental concealment which he found difficult to penetrate.

The altercations of the previous night, the soured atmosphere of the morning, his wounded pride at having been misunderstood and his exhaustion at having to deal with an angry group of tenants now all suddenly receded. 'Come here, you two,' he said, putting one protective arm around his wife and the other around his daughter. 'Let's sit down in the living-room and have a council of war.'

Before Laurence's arrival Rosie had called Conny Andrews, whom she remembered meeting briefly at a parents' evening, and established that Kieron wasn't there. Nor did Ben Lovelle have any notion of where Kieron might be. The three of them pooled the names of all possible contacts, including Kieron's year tutor, but ultimately drew a blank.

'Let me call all the local hospitals and, if that fails, I can always give the police a ring,' said Laurence.

The way Laurence set out his plan of action, moving quite reasonably from exhausting their known individual contacts to appealing for help from a higher institutional level, merely made the knot in Rosie's stomach tighten further. *There's something horribly wrong*, the voices began to murmur. *We can feel it. He's been kidnapped, he's being held against his will somewhere, he's all alone in a cold dark room, they're doing nasty things to him, they're hurting him.*

She blinked silently at Laurence and the small flame of constancy within her began to flicker once more. He could infuriate her at times, but she knew there were always situations when she could rely on him. It was the only rock she could lean on.

An hour later they were none the wiser. The police hadn't exactly been unhelpful, but they saw no cause to trigger a missing persons search at this early stage, and using their past experience of erratic teenage behaviour they argued that there was almost certainly a simple and harmless explanation as to why this particular fifteen-year-old boy hadn't returned home. If, on the other hand, he hadn't turned up by midday of the following day, then they were told to get in touch again.

Rosie insisted on sitting up, long after Estelle and then Laurence had made their way upstairs. She was making herself ill with worry, that much she knew, but how else was she supposed to behave? Kieron was her son and she was his mother. When she finally crawled into bed in the early hours, sleep came only fitfully, and intermittently she heard Laurence throwing himself around on his side of the bed. In the silence of the night the dancing voices seized a fresh opportunity. *You're a bad mother, you should have seen this coming, you've been neglecting your duties, you should not have left the house this morning. It's all your fault, you've been too wrapped up in this Callas thing, your job is to look after your children and see that they don't come to any harm. That is what you should have been focusing on. You're to blame and now you will have to suffer for it. Bad, bad, bad.* And then they linked arms and danced a merry jig around her, cackling like a coven of witches.

10

Rosie was up just before six and crept downstairs to make herself a mug of strong coffee. She sat for a moment in the pale glow of the concealed lighting below the wall units of her kitchen, contemplating the grain of the oak cabinets, the way it wandered this way and then that, as unpredictable as the circumstances she now found herself in. Before they had even moved in Laurence had tried to persuade her to go for the glossy brilliance featured in the catalogue of kitchen options, but she had put her foot down. 'It's going to be my kitchen, and I want to be happy there,' was how she fended him off. So it was dependable oak that won the day rather than the sheen of something more superficially exciting.

She opened the back door and peered into the pitch dark of the garden she had laid out, a triumph of freedom over formality. Behind it lay fields that glittered in spring with the splashes of celandines and primroses, and later the flowers of rapeseed, and behind those came the stretches of open countryside that led eventually to the stone cottage where her mother-in-law lived, far enough away for her not to interfere on a daily basis but close enough for Laurence to get to her in case of an emergency. She switched on the patio light. The stalks and stems of the border perennials, blackened by the first autumnal frosts, stood lifeless in the chill air. Nothing moved. Next she went into the hallway and opened the front door, looking up and down the street, catching the sound of the first cars on the small estate as they fired into life, ready to carry their occupants off for another perfectly normal day. A curtain of light drizzle was beginning to descend. In the far distance she could hear the steady hum of traffic on the M27 sloughing off its way across the chalky downs. She hugged herself in her grey fleece against the morning cold and then returned to the kitchen, where she switched on the radio. More financial worries and concerns. More details of massive bankers' bonuses. More reports of the spivs still at work in the financial markets. More talk of a country in debt. More condemnation of excessive retail spending that was pushing people over the edge. More speculation about where the entire world was heading. This business news first thing in the morning was just too depressing, a constant drip-drip-drip of warnings and woes.

She switched stations and listened instead to the wail of artificial optimism coming from the sound of sharp and metallic instruments hammering out a repetitive rhythm, stirring the nation out of its sleep-deprived torpor. The utter banality of it all. This was no perfectly normal day. Not for her. All her washing had been ripped from the line and lay in a heap on the mucky ground.

And then, as the host of the breakfast show intervened to give a time-check, she thought she heard a different and more familiar sound, the sound of the front door closing. Before she could reach the hall, a bedraggled, rain-soaked and shivering bundle of flesh fell into her arms.

'Kieron, my lamb! My goodness me! Have you been out all night? Where on earth have you been?' She folded her arms tightly round him, releasing her hold only as the shuddering slowly stopped.

'Mum,' and as he looked at her she could see his eyes brimming with tears, 'I'm being blackmailed.' And then, a couple of sobs later, 'I know it's all my fault. I've been so stupid.'

An hour later, Rosie and Laurence were still trying to build a bigger picture from the fragments of unconnected details Kieron was blurting out.

'I don't get it,' she said. 'If it was all round the school yesterday morning, why didn't Ben say anything when I called last night? And he's supposed to be one of your friends!'

'Nobody wants to be a snitch.'

'But this isn't just a foolish prank.'

'We need to go to the police about this,' Laurence said. 'This is nothing short of criminal activity. There was something in the paper the other day about how this sort of thing is taking off. You only need a few nasty individuals to succeed and then the copycat brigade gets in on the act. Apparently it's being steered by people in the Philippines. Deliberate entrapment to start with and then this slow slide into blackmail.'

'I knew this Tweeter thing was a step too far. Isn't the internet enough on its own?'

'Mum, it's not Tweeter, it's Twitter.'

'Same thing. People twittering on about completely irrelevant things.'

'But Mum, I told you, it wasn't Twitter. It all went via Facebook.'

Laurence was trying to reconstruct causal links. 'And you say they got your mobile number from your Facebook page. And they kept sending you text messages with the demands? But why did you throw your phone away, son? That's valuable evidence we could have shown to the police.'

'I chucked it into a skip. I wanted it all to stop, I didn't think.'

The words opened a door in the long corridor that reached back into Laurence's childhood. *I didn't think, mum, I'm sorry.* His mother had glared at him with the sharpness of hard-edged steel. *You didn't think! How can you say that? You didn't think!* And her blows had rained down on him until he fell to the floor, a heaving tangle of young limbs. And the ritual had repeated itself until he was too big for her to physically assault and she had then used the whiplash of her tongue to underline her displeasure.

What was the point, he thought, in compounding the shame and anguish of that critical fallacy of childhood, the fallacy that presumes actions will have no consequences and that individual errors and failings will never come to light? What was the point of being a parent if you ended up behaving like a teenager yourself? What was the point indeed of repeating the errors of a parent?

When things go wrong, his mother used to say, it was always somebody's fault. Things didn't just happen. They happened because somebody did or didn't do what they were supposed to do. Actions had consequences. But then whose fault was it that Miriam crashed her car? Did she do something she shouldn't have done or fail to do something she should have done? Whose fault was it that Kieron had come off the rails? Was it fair to blame him alone for everything or were others equally responsible – the father who should have been monitoring his child's passage through adolescence more closely, those who operated particular websites and targeted vulnerable teenagers (and why were they vulnerable in the first place?) or society as a whole for allowing the early sexualisation and commercial exploitation of minors? All day he had batted such thoughts away, knowing that to every question once raised there had to be some kind of an answer.

Later, as he lay on his side of the bed, underneath the white shroud of his duvet, calling on distant sleep to carry him off and relieve him of any direct obligation to respond, Laurence saw the night sky reappear with its unfurled banners of soot and charcoal and pitch; he glimpsed the great banks of ominous cloud moving across the sea of darkness, their seething surface made momentarily visible by the explosions of lurid colour above; the taste of the dank bitter air of Bonfire Night still on his tongue, the acrid smell of fireworks still in his nostrils. The evening that should have been a welcome distraction had not delivered on its promise.

The avalanche of images continued to roll towards him, a summation fifteen years in the making. He saw his son, his precious new-born son, whose umbilical cord he had helped cut while Rosie lay back exhausted in the delivery room. A naked pink body with those fat little legs that his mother claimed were a chip off the old block, then cradled in Laurence's arms, gurgling contentedly as Rosie gently rubbed nappy ointment into the redness of his groin. Much later, standing on the edge of a three-metre diving board, his thin milk-white body about to fly through the air, the arms pressed together like an arrow, calling out 'Dad, watch me! Watch me now!' Later still the cheeky schoolboy face contorted in pain as he was stretchered off the football-pitch with a broken ankle. More recently the fingers that plucked and caressed the strings of his electric guitar, gripped the console of his PlayStation, tapped out messages on the face of his smartphone, stroked his keyboard, released buttons from their secure anchorage, zipped open what had been zipped up.

He acknowledged that at some point all children speculated about the sex lives of their parents, either in bewilderment or in disgust, or both. He had often wondered in his own case why there had never been another man in his mother's life, why in addition to losing out on the father he'd never really known he had never even come close to having a substitute father-figure, someone who would have initiated him into the man's world he was about to inhabit more successfully than his mother had been able to. If children speculated, parents did too. He had noted the physical changes taking place in his son, as he did with his daughter. He had heard Rosie talking about the Bernadettes, the Kayleighs and the Nuulas; he had occasionally seen the Ainas, the Jennas and the Rizwanas that made fleeting transitions from the kitchen to Kieron's bedroom and back again. Nothing regular, nothing permanent. Who was to say whether any of these entanglements had crossed the line between boyhood and manhood?

As he struggled with the blizzard of new images his brain was inflicting upon him, he saw his son in front of a small screen, doing what teenage boys do in the privacy of their own four walls, unaware that behind the screen there was an ocean of deep and dark water with eyeballs that floated in ectoplasm, suddenly emerging out of the murk, glinting and shimmering and flashing and winking. Eyes leering at him, at Kieron. Here he was. Young. Sexually mature. Under-age. And available. Then came the lips, primed and full, with reptilian tongues that flicked from side to side, with gobs of saliva that oozed and trickled and dribbled. In the background, rows of hollowed-out pumpkin gourds from the previous week's Hallowe'en celebrations, the flickering eerie candlelight twisting the painted expressions into life. And an accompanying soundtrack of maniacal, hysterical laughter. Utter distortions, one and all.

Laurence clenched his fingers together in frustration. The fascination with porn he could understand; he knew there were increasing amounts of it on the internet. It was ubiquitous; most young people, even those of a tender age, had seen examples of it, no matter how often they might deny having done so. The option he and Rosie had signed up to was designed to block all access to precisely those websites they wanted to protect Kieron from. But clearly there were mechanisms once installed that could be neatly circumvented by anybody determined to do so. Putting up barriers represented for most young minds a constant challenge to pull them down again. That was all part of growing up. He'd obviously underestimated his son.

At some point Kieron would have needed and wanted to seek relief from the tyranny of his teenage hormones. That was what porn was for. But he'd then gone one stage further and engaged in sexual activity in front of his webcam, staring no doubt with growing intoxication at some image on the screen of a mere slip of a girl, fresh and dewy-eyed, stretching her breasts towards him, her lips pouting in simulated desire, gyrating her lower body in his direction, uttering a succession of trite and lewd phrases intended to spur him on. And he had no longer been standing alone in his secret garden, naked and hard, communing solely with this little angel of temptation. Instead, she had opened the concealed gate at the end of the garden and the whole world had come flooding in: hidden and calculating eyes that were busy surveying and recording each line, fold and aperture of his body, registering each act of the manipulation of his own flesh. Contracts were being signed, money was being made, copies were being passed electronically through a vast distribution network, trailers and marketing slogans were being prepared. His son available for instant gratification. A piece of meat on the slab. A tasty morsel for the paedophiles out there. A commodity packaged for the rest of the world. And Kieron hadn't once stopped to think. The stream of urgent text messages willing him to commit to further online sessions, the sweet simpering siren voice of the girl professing undying love and complimenting him on his size and burgeoning manliness, the passion, the ecstasy, the thrill of it all. The prospect of the two of them soon to be together had driven him on. The virtual excitement soon to be made tangible in the real world, an imminent assignation with real flesh. And even then he hadn't stopped to think, engulfed in the tide of arousal that swept aside any remaining doubts and disabled all the warning systems. Hyperreality.

After that had come the demands, the unmistakeable tenor in the carefully chosen words, the steady whine of persistence culminating in a simple quid pro quo: cash in exchange for deletion. A ransom payment for erasure. No time to think, instead a sense of mounting panic. Teenage terror versus cold calculation. Finally, the trump card. A specific deadline, otherwise publication via Facebook.

He tried to imagine what it must have been like for Kieron, having failed to lay his hands on the sums being demanded, walking through the school gates yesterday morning and then suddenly being surrounded by jeering, giggling faces, pointing at the videos on their phones. *That's you, isn't it? Nothing but a stinking fucking perv. Who's the lucky girl then? Big boy now, aren't you?* No wonder his world had fallen apart.

On the other side of the bed Rosie was struggling to lay to rest the pictures that were flooding her mind. Kieron, her one and only son, wandering the streets on his own, with nobody at his side to offer a protective arm of support or lend a sympathetic ear, curling up on a bench in the local park as night began to compound his misery and anguish. She thought back to those heady moments after giving birth to him one sun-filled day in March, lying utterly exhausted in the sterile surroundings of the maternity hospital, hearing machines humming and whirring and seeing an army of arms and hands constantly in motion, but then clutching the little bundle of joy in her arms, gazing down at his shrivelled pink limbs and eyes still clamped shut, wondering what would become of him in the years ahead. Would he grow up to be like his father, tall and ample in all departments, with the nutty warmth of his brown eyes and the unruly scalloped locks of hair that constantly had to be held in check, or would he have his mother's aquamarine eyes, her dimpled chin and round bright features, and the neatness of her hands? And where would he be twenty years down the line, following in his father's footsteps and building his own business empire or aiming for the law or medicine or, who was to say, something equally as grand? And where would he be another two decades on from that, married (happily, she hoped) and with children of his own? Or perhaps divorced or maybe still single? How could she even begin to tell just by looking at the tiny features in his tiny body?

Memory now took her back to when he had still been a toddler. One afternoon she had been out with both her children, Estelle strapped securely in the baby-buggy and Kieron constantly pulling at her side and testing his strength, digging his heels in, then breaking free, only to fall over and badly graze his knee, so that his howls of pain could be heard at the bottom of the street. There was the time when the originally prescribed antibiotic hadn't assuaged an attack of tonsillitis in his young body and she and Laurence, desperate with worry, had taken him in the middle of the night to the nearest A & E. And then the pride she felt at his first sports day at primary school when he not only came first in the egg-and-spoon race but was narrowly pipped to the post in the sack race.

The images in her inner world switched from the bright sunlight of that June day with its beams and smiles and shouts to the gloomy uncertainty of their barbecue earlier that evening, waiting for what seemed like an eternity before the sausages, lamb chops and medallions of pork loin were properly cooked, not being able to gauge how Kieron would react to anything she or Laurence said, walking on imaginary eggshells around the patio where everything had been set up, busying herself with the bowls of salad and bread-baskets so she could avoid embarrassing eye-contact, and then willing the minutes to pass so that they could all be distracted by the fireworks. For what seemed like a few fleeting moments they had stood looking up at the vast backdrop in search of the distant stars, tiny pin-pricks of expectation in a sea of doubt, Estelle's whoops of delight cutting through the stillness of the air while Kieron's collapsed face remained pinned against the saturnine sky like a paper moon. She relived the display, the sudden explosions of energy, the spikes of brilliant colour dissolving above their heads into hundreds and thousands, the reds, the oranges, the purples, the garish greens and the brash blues, apparitions that had vanished as quickly as they had come. Was this what happened to all one's hopes, she wondered, moments when doors were thrown open into the intense beauty of another world, only to be slammed shut before you could properly reach out? Was adolescence destined to end in sordidness? She rolled over and sighed.

Laurence turned towards her. 'Can't you sleep either?'

'Laurence, what are we going to do now?'

'I can't get over the thought of all this criminal and commercial activity. Nothing but a bloody racket. I'm actually quite angry that Kieron threw away his mobile. It's not so much what it cost. It just makes it more difficult when we go the police tomorrow. We don't have that much in the way of hard evidence.'

'Are you sure the two of you want to pursue matters with the police tomorrow? I'm glad you didn't want to go down to the local station today. Not in the state he's still in.'

'But you can't let these bastards get away with something like this. Blackmail is a crime.'

'I know. But have you really thought this through? Once the police are involved, everybody at school will get to know about it. You have to think of Estelle too.'

'I bet it's already round the whole school, judging from what Kieron was saying. If it was on just a few phones this morning, think how many others will have seen it and downloaded it by now.'

'You know, it must have been so hard for Kieron to admit to us what he'd done. Poor lad, I've never seen him looking so ashamed before. He could hardly get the words out. If you take him down to the police station, they'll want to know everything. All the gory details. I'm not sure that'll be good for him.'

By now he was wide awake, the adrenaline pumping the fatigue aside. 'But what's the alternative? If we do nothing, those shitbags win. And school management are bound to have picked up on what's happened, so they will want to know all the facts too. And expect Kieron to dish the dirt. We can't simply pretend all of this never happened.'

'I'm just trying to make sure he doesn't have to get hurt any more than necessary. We can't let him go back to school tomorrow after you've been to see the police. We've got to keep him away. And Estelle too. I've been thinking about taking the two of them up to Lucie's. It'll take them out of this constantly sniggering and whispering environment. And all the finger-pointing. You know what kids are like.'

'That's not going to go away, is it?'

'If I take them away for a week or so, at least there's a chance that the dust might settle somewhat.'

'Hmm. I'm not convinced that's really necessary,' he replied. 'You'll be back for Mum's birthday though, won't you?'

'I forgot to tell you. The Callas opens on the seventeenth and I've got to be there, helping with the last-minute arrangements. I spoke to Lee just before we had the barbecue and they want me to be there in the evening too, as an honoured guest.'

'Rosie, I can't believe I'm hearing this. The seventeenth is mum's birthday.'

'So? Tell her we'll come round the following night. One day isn't going to make a big difference.'

'But we've always gone on her birthday. She expects us to. She'll have a meal ready for us in the evening. You know how she likes to cook for us.'

'Look Laurence, you know how much time I've already invested in helping Lee and Matthew. They've got to make a success of it. Their livelihood depends on it. You know how tricky the economic outlook is. I have to be there.'

'Christ, Rosie, they're not even family. Why the hell are they more important than my own flesh and blood?'

'I don't know why you're making such a fuss. It's an unfortunate clash of dates. It can't be helped. You can go with Kieron and Estelle. Tell your mum I'll pop in and see her when I can.'

'Bloody hell, Rosie. It's her special day. She'll be seventy-eight. She deserves us all to be there.'

Rosie switched on the light on her side of the bed. 'I hope you're not going to tell me she cares that much whether I'm there or not.'

'What a nasty thing to say. You're her daughter-in-law. She doesn't have any other. Why wouldn't she want you to be there?'

Rosie's face was already flushed, the wellsprings of sudden subterranean heat pumping up from below. 'I don't want to have another argument with you about your mother, not after a day like this. You know she's never really liked me. I've never been good enough for her. She's made that plain time and time again. Anyway, I've made my mind up. I'm going to be at the Callas on the seventeenth.' She glared across at Laurence, switched off the light and turned her back on him.

Laurence lay quite still in the dark, fighting the waves of resentment within. 'When you have these dark thoughts, Laurence, you just have to bat them away,' his mother had told him repeatedly in childhood whenever his temper tantrums had threatened to overwhelm both of them. And when her warnings failed to work, her hand would be there to underline the point. Dark thoughts had to be ignored, repressed, consigned to the deeper chambers of his existence where they could do no harm. That was how he maintained control. The gale outside was rattling the windows of his inner retreat, bellowing its rage through the cracks in the frame, calling for all resistance to end. He had to maintain control. Fighting battles on two separate fronts was a recipe for disaster.

When sleep reclaimed him an hour or so later, he was still lying on his back with clenched fists, determined he was not going to be beaten.

11

Despite a reluctance to admit it to herself, Rosie believed in family rituals as much as her mother-in-law did. Breakfast was one of hers. At the start of the day she wanted to have Laurence and the children close to her, not only sharing a meal together but hearing their individual concerns about the day ahead. Yet of late it had become something of a struggle to bind her menfolk to her in this way. Laurence now rarely sat down, impatient that his hot drink was taking so long to be drinkable, never short of a reason why he needed to be on his way. It was either the renewed absence of Natasha in the office, or a steady stream of auctions he had lined up, or assessments and valuations he urgently had to carry out, or viewings he had to schedule and attend.

Kieron was proving to be a particular problem. The provision of several alarm-clocks and repeated shouts from the bottom of the stairs failed to rouse him. As the clock moved mercilessly on, Rosie resented having to go up to pound on his door in an effort to drag him from the depths of a sleep-territory which only he seemed to inhabit. When he eventually surfaced, bleary-eyed, it was usually already time for him to set off for school. Which meant that very often she and Estelle were left on their own.

If there was one thing that Rosie had come to appreciate, it was being entertained by her daughter. True, the jokes that

Estelle told were sometimes corny, but they provided a welcome counterpoint to the bleak state of the world as reflected in the morning's news headlines. Above all, she was developing her comic talent in different ways, adding funny voices and mannerisms, cultivating dramatic pauses and sensing from her mother's reactions how to vary the pace of delivery. Whether it was something that arose naturally from the previous day in school, or the content of a website which she had come across, or her own innate theatrical flair, the material she chose never failed to make Rosie laugh. Only a few days previously, having cleared the breakfast-table before stacking the dishwasher, she had heard Estelle call to her from the passage.

'Before I go - have you heard the one about the pregnant woman…?'

'Young lady, you are far too young to know anything about pregnant women!'

'No, no, mum, this one's really funny.'

'Well, if that's the case you'd better tell me. I can hardly wait,' she added, mimicking her daughter's style.

'Anyway, she went into labour and then – would you believe it? – she started shouting at the top of her voice. Out came all these words. "Can't! Couldn't! Didn't! Shouldn't! Won't! Wouldn't!"'

Estelle paused, knowing she had her mother's full attention. 'Simple, honey (the initial two words were delivered in a *faux* American accent), she was having contractions.' And then they had both roared with laughter.

But nobody was laughing around the breakfast table that Thursday morning. The god of thunder was enjoying his special day. Rosie attempted a weak steady smile, Laurence sat stony-faced and Kieron stared gloomily ahead of him, while Estelle was moving her head rhythmically to the sounds of a tune only she could hear.

'You know, you don't have to go down to the police station with your dad if you don't want to,' said Rosie. 'We can just say it was a silly prank and others somehow took advantage of the situation.

We don't have to make a big drama out of it.'

'We agreed something different, Rosie,' replied Laurence. 'Kieron's the victim of a criminal conspiracy. It's not a prank at all. Anybody who hurts my son is going to pay for it.'

Estelle suddenly stopped jiggling her head. 'I don't know why you're making such a fuss. I know what a boy's willy looks like and in any case there's a girl in my class whose boobs are all over the internet. It's no big deal, we're not living in Victorian times.'

Laurence glowered. 'There is a reason why private parts are called that. It's an absolute disgrace if your classmate thinks that by exposing herself she's being smart and liberated. I hope you wouldn't even dream of taking off any of your clothes in public. And certainly not in front of any camera or phone.'

'But Dad, what about nude bathing? You make it sound as though there's something smutty about a naked body.'

'I'm not saying that at all. Where I draw the line is when naked images are exploited for commercial gain. There's too much pornography that is now readily available. I thought we'd managed to stop you viewing this stuff online. It's not good for Kieron and it's not good for you.'

Kieron continued to sit in silence, while the two adults and his sister continued to sit in judgement, albeit on three different cases. Estelle could only regard learned counsel's submissions as unworldly. 'You are so old-fashioned! Nearly everybody I know has seen some kind of porn. It's not the big taboo thing it might have been for your generation.'

'Estelle,' countered Laurence, 'I've already said it's about criminal acts. You and your brother are under age. Have you any idea what nasty people are out there, just waiting to use the bodies of young people for their own filthy purposes? We have to protect you from paedophiles and gangsters. I'm kicking myself that I couldn't even keep my own son safe from this kind of thing. And I'll do anything I can to stop this kind of thing happening to you.' His voice folded on a note of exasperation.

Estelle bit her lip. She was furious at the implication that she needed to be protected from something she had no intention of ever doing herself, even if she felt her brother was merely unlucky in being found out. It was just as well her parents had no idea what else was doing the rounds in her class. Rosie in turn was annoyed at the way Laurence insisted on turning the whole affair into issues of law and morality, when she could see that her son's immediate needs were for emotional reassurance. That was what mattered above everything else. Laurence was seething that holes were being picked in an agreed line of defence instead of a united front being maintained. Meanwhile Kieron sat in his private dock, waiting for an invisible jury to deliver its verdict. Yet he knew already what that was. Guilty as charged. What else could it be?

Laurence looked across the table at Rosie. Why were they increasingly pulling in different directions over matters of discipline? He had tried hard yesterday not to compound his son's anguish by beating the moral drum, not to act the censorious parent but to put himself in Kieron's shoes, not to underline the crass stupidity of what he had done but to offer encouragement and support. He had assumed Rosie would be fully on side, would want to see retribution and punishment for those who had turned their son's body into an object of voyeurism, only to discover that her preoccupation was not with putting the world to rights and securing justice but administering palliative solutions closer to home. It was ever thus. There was the time the eight-year-old Kieron had been caught puffing on a cigarette behind the apple tree in the Gosport Road garden, and Rosie had focused on the dangers of smoking instead of stressing the breach in trust Laurence had keenly felt. And the time when Estelle had come back from a sleepover and the host parents had angrily demanded to know why she had brought bottles of vodka and gin for the other girls to consume. Once again Rosie had relativised the issue, insisting that the blame lay with all three of them since there was clear evidence of collusion. Bad cop, good cop, that was the typical response, and he was tired of being accused of overreacting to each incident. Somebody had to make clear what was acceptable and what was not, otherwise where would the whole world be?

Parents couldn't just abrogate their duties. That was what his mother had instilled into him from an early age. 'Sometimes I can't just be your best friend,' she had said. 'I have a different role in life. That's the way things are meant to be.' Smarting at the absence of Rosie's unqualified support, he was certain he knew best how to guide Kieron through the current crisis. If they couldn't reach a consensus together, it would fall to him to ensure justice was upheld.

'Come on, Kieron, put your coat on and then we'll set the ball rolling. Rosie, just give the school secretary a ring and say that for family reasons Kieron and Estelle won't be in school today.'

Rosie stretched out across the table to squeeze the hands of both her children. She still wasn't reconciled to the formality of the process Laurence was now embarking on, but nothing would be achieved by prolonging the discussion. And if she was sure of one thing, it was that keeping Kieron and Estelle away from school was in everybody's best interests. She would call Lucie during the course of the morning, feeling sure her sister would be more than happy to accommodate the three of them for a short while, to give them the space and time they needed in a different environment in order to reflect and take stock. She knew that Lucie's own children were out of the house so they'd each have a separate bedroom. She would then call Lee and let him know she'd be away during the coming week, but that she'd place the orders for the floral arrangements and be back at the weekend before opening night in time to take charge of last-minute preparations.

Above all, she wanted to take herself and her children off for a breath of good North Country air, rejecting Laurence's silly and grandiose scheme for moving the family into a derelict chapel. She wanted to blot out memories of the room in the house where she now knew her son had stood naked, playing with himself for the benefit of what he thought was a teenage hottie who had befriended him on the internet, when in fact she had been nothing but a puppet, with the strings being cleverly pulled by others behind the scenes. She wanted to forget for a while the house in which her sense of well-being and security was anchored and the room in which her son's privacy had been violated. It was like being burgled many times over. What she couldn't know was that by willing her escape from the scene of the crime, by attempting to expunge all thoughts of how her domestic harmony had been shattered and defiled, she was actually much closer to the thought processes Laurence had been wrestling with only hours before.

12

It took Laurence much longer to reappear with Kieron than Rosie had imagined. She spent a desultory hour leafing through fashion magazines with Estelle, trying to distract herself from the details of an interview process she knew Kieron would find difficult. But then, she reasoned, if what had happened was already out in the public domain and there could be no pretence about it not being her son in the videos that were now circulating, wouldn't it slowly become easier talking about it?

She saw again the stooped figure of her first-born in the hallway, his hair matted and damp, his clothes reeking of sweat and the misty murky air of the early morning, his eyes bloodshot and scarcely able to make contact with the three of them, his head bowed over the kitchen table, feeding them fragments of information that others might have found titillating but which she found repulsive. For years she'd seen the evidence of Kieron's wet dreams on his bedsheets. She had often wondered how he was coping with the hormonal surges she knew all teenagers went through, but she'd left Laurence to be the first point of reference for something she couldn't possibly relate to herself but supposed all men could. Her son, though not yet a man, was no longer the innocent child she loved unconditionally. The thought of him losing his virginity to one of the fleeting female visitors he occasionally brought home with him had a habit of resurfacing with every sign of his growing physical development. They had talked together in general about sex and the importance of relationships, more frequently she supposed than what transpired between father and son, but she never for one moment imagined that he could or would do anything quite so sordid and sinister as exposing himself on the internet.

How thankful she was that she and Adam had waited years before giving in to their desires. She remembered the furtive fumblings and gentle stroking while they were still in the sixth form until one day, during his first vacation from training college, it had happened, quite naturally and unplanned. She looked across the table at her daughter, a composite image of two separate people with her mother's eyes and her father's unmanageable hair, her talent as a stand-up comic momentarily in abeyance, and hoped that the moment she fully became a woman she would be absolutely in control of any situation and not at the mercy of others. *Please don't let any of this happen to her*, she thought.

Judging by the coarse laughter of some studio audience she could hear in the background, Lucie was in the middle of watching daytime television when Rosie got through to her, and she needed to wait until the volume had been turned down. These days her sister depended on commissions for interior design projects and was home more often than not. At the phrase "family crisis" she simply said, 'Say no more. Come whenever you want.'

Rosie started to think about what she would need to pack and take with her. She still had to give Lorna a call at Florabellum and tell her she couldn't possibly do her scheduled shift that afternoon and would be away the following week too. For family reasons. Why go into precise details? She'd make it up later as quickly as she could. Extra shifts in the pre-Christmas rush, for instance. After all, she was a junior partner and surely entitled to some leeway.

It was midday by the time Laurence arrived with Kieron in

tow. Rosie was desperate to hear how it had all gone, but Laurence pleaded that he had wasted enough time already and still had many other things to attend to. They would talk in the evening, he said, and disappeared. She felt a sourness rising in her craw after his immediate departure and wondered why he found it so difficult to make time for his family at home. She herself had no doubt at all about where her first priority lay. In the early years of their marriage he'd regularly taken her out to see the latest blockbuster, and they'd spent weekends beachcombing on the coast or exploring the gastro-pubs springing up in smaller towns and rural backwaters. Then in the lazy days of summer they would roam the Hampshire countryside with foraging baskets, and even after the arrival of Kieron there'd been plenty of family outings, to theme parks, stately homes and trips across the water to the Isle of Wight. They had done things together as a family. They were still a family, she thought, but now their lives frequently ran in parallel lines rather than intertwined in a harmonious circle. She tried to locate in her memory the stage at which the dials had started to point in different directions instead of remaining in sync, but there were too many conflicting ideas vying for attention. It couldn't really have been the birth of Estelle, the daughter Laurence loved, at least initially, with an intensity she hadn't noticed with Kieron. And it surely wasn't the death of her parents, one after the other within a year, since Laurence had quickly adjusted his mood to hers, displaying his over-protective side and getting up even earlier in the mornings to bring her cups of tea in bed and cuddle her on the sofa in the evenings.

She had chosen to spend more time at Florabellum after she'd become a junior partner there, not only interacting with customers as in the past, but now also negotiating with suppliers and attending to back-room matters, and this had given her an additional focus in life. That in itself couldn't explain the subtle shifts in the patterns of her life. Was it the fact that she was sensitive to any sign of Laurence enjoying his flirts with passing trade – the demure wives who accompanied their forthright husbands to Patrick's agency where Laurence had once laboured to be star employee month after month, or later, once he had set up his own business, the single women in search of rental accommodation she'd seen fluttering their eyelashes at him? And then her own anxious peering into the mirror, the discovery of wrinkles and grey hairs, the gradual acceptance that no matter how hard she tried she would never be able to conquer time itself.

With Shaheen, the woman with the smooth dark-olive skin and supplicant eyes, she'd been prepared to think the unthinkable. Shaheen this, Shaheen that, the late nights, the sudden calls telling her about important business that simply had to be seen to, the lack of sex between her and Laurence; it all added up to an affair, didn't it? After all, despite his ample love-handles, Laurence was still an attractive man and potentially a good catch. No, it didn't all add up, as she was soon forced to realise. Sometimes the voices in her head were not fighting her corner, they had their eyes elsewhere.

But hadn't Lucie told her more than once over the phone, during their weekly chats, that men had a habit of straying, especially in middle age, and that she needed to take care of all of Laurence's needs? That was as far as she'd gone, but Rosie understood immediately the oblique references to the string of affairs Lucie's husband Ian had been having. He'd even attempted to grope her, just after their mother's funeral, but she'd kept the matter entirely to herself, even after Lucie's first warning. Yet Lucie and Ian, her fifty-six-year-old eldest sister and her libidinous sixty-year-old mate, were still together. So perhaps sex wasn't everything, perhaps there was another kind of glue that kept a marriage together. And if it wasn't any of that which gnawed away at her sense of contentment, perhaps it was the way Laurence wrapped himself up in his business world, pursuing one project after another, sometimes with a ferocious single-mindedness that unsettled her. 'Are you trying to reach for the stars?' she recalled once asking him, to which he'd responded with another question, 'And what's wrong with that?'

Ultimately she couldn't see how running after more money was making individuals like Laurence any happier. For that to be true she would need to see a face wreathed permanently in smiles and blessed with the sunniest of dispositions. Nor did the pursuit of material gain seem to be making the banks or the politicians and the national governments of the Western World any happier either. They all seemed to be stewing together in their collective mess, spouting their empty clichés and hiding behind walls of deception.

13

The first thing Laurence did after sliding back into his BMW was to ring Kieron's headteacher. He was annoyed there was no direct line, but it didn't really surprise him. Headteachers, like all modern CEOs, were shielded by an elaborate front-of-house regime, gatekeepers that knew how to wield their power. If you could grovel and make all the right noises you were in with a chance; if you adopted anything approaching an aggressive tone or were already on the blacklist as "one of those difficult parents", you faced several rounds of tortuous negotiations until you got what you wanted. All Laurence himself wanted was a quarter of an hour of Mr Sumner's time – was that too much to ask?

'If it's about Kieron and Estelle, Mrs Stewart has already rung this morning,' said the disembodied voice at the other end of the line in measured tones. 'Mr Sumner is informed, if that puts your mind at rest.'

'No, it's about Kieron and it's urgent,' Laurence responded.

'How urgent might that be?'

'Very.'

'Well, would you like to tell me what it's about?'

Laurence recalled that the last time he had cause to ring his GP's surgery he had needed to parley with an officious practice manager pressing him for clinical details.

'It helps if Dr Wallace knows why you're coming in,' added the voice.

'Thank you, but I prefer to discuss the matter with my doctor.'

Sumner, unless he was completely deaf and blind behind the moat that separated him from the outside world, would by now be clearly in the picture about recent developments, and presumably his gatekeeper would have been in possession of all the details the moment Sumner passed her the individual pupil case file for safe keeping, but Laurence resented the notion of having to forswear the final stage of confidentiality. For a moment he toyed with the prospect of giving a one-word response. Pornography. Masturbation. Voyeurism. Deception. Blackmail. He pictured the scandalised expression, the mouth awry at the other end. Whichever keyword he chose to use, he knew there'd be a follow-up question. And another. So he paused before saying in the sweetest tones he could summon up, 'This is such a delicate matter I couldn't possibly give you more information over the phone.'

'Well, Mr Sumner has a very busy schedule for most of the afternoon. If it's really as urgent as you say it is, I could ask him if he could spare you just a little time at the end of the day.'

'When would that be?'

'I don't know until I've spoken to him.'

Laurence had spent too long ringing potential and existing clients while still working for Patrick not to see through this ruse. The gatekeeper managed Sumner's diary, so she would know exactly what his afternoon looked like and whether there was a time slot just waiting to be filled. He decided to feign innocence.

'OK, please go ahead and I'll hold the line.'

There was the usual click on the line while he drummed his fingers on the padded steering-wheel, hoping Rosie wouldn't glance out of the window and see him still sitting in the road outside, having just told her how pressed for time he was.

'Hello?' said the disembodied voice. 'Mr Sumner can see you at 4.30, but please don't be late.'

If Laurence took objection to anything, it was the way some people talked down to him, chastising the adult schoolboy in advance for errors yet to be committed, telling him things any simpleton would already know.

'Thank you. I'll be there,' he said. He turned the ignition switch and pulled away from the house.

Before turning into the main road he glanced again at his mobile phone. Several missed calls and about a dozen text messages, two of them from Steve, the second of which read *Can we meet this lunchtime, say at the Drum and Monkey?* The earlier one had stated *Something's happened, need to chat to you.* Laurence was supposed to be relieving Natasha at one o'clock, and if he met Steve at the pub first the office wouldn't be manned during the lunch-hour, which was often a convenient time for business clients to call. On the other hand, if Steve was now jittery there had to be a reason for it. He never liked disappointing anybody, least of all Steve, who was one of the least pushy people around.

He pulled in, texted Steve, called Natasha and then his solicitor, who was handling a case in which a tenant in one of Laurence's buy-to-let properties had trashed the place and then disappeared without trace, still owing three months' rent. Then he noticed his mother had called twice that morning. She never texted him, arguing she couldn't be bothered to learn new technology at her time of life and that the keys were too small for her increasingly arthritic fingers.

He rang his mother's number. 'Hi Mum, what's this about me forgetting something?'

'You know, the shopping. Why didn't you come round this morning?'

In the days when she'd still been relatively mobile and content to drive herself to the nearest superstore to pick up her week's shopping, he hadn't seen her more than once or twice a month unless there was something urgent that needed fixing in the house. Tradition dictated he had to bring the whole family round to the house on the outskirts of Horndean, on "feast and family days" in her parlance, so on his birthday in April and hers in November, as well as on Boxing Day and at Easter, she would always cook a three-course meal, refusing all offers of help in the kitchen.

When he once enquired, shortly after his marriage, why Rosie wasn't included in the list of important feast days, she had dismissed the idea by arguing that the second day of February was just a few weeks after Boxing Day, conveniently overlooking the fact that the seventeenth of November was quite close to Christmas and that Laurence's own birthday on the twenty-fourth of April was often just a couple of weeks after Easter.

A year ago she'd given up driving, after being involved in a minor collision for which, in his own estimation, she was as much at fault as the other party was. That had dented her self-confidence and he had immediately offered to step in and deal with all her bulkier shopping needs. Since then Laurence had called first thing each Thursday morning to collect her shopping list, aiming to drop off the items that same evening or on the Friday. With all the other matters on his mind he had completely forgotten about her weekly shopping.

'I'm sorry Mum. I'm very busy at the moment.'

'You always say that. You always tell me you're very busy. It's not as though I need you every day of the week. For just one day in the week couldn't you think of me for a change?'

He'd been through these rituals many times before. He would fail to carry out her wishes exactly as she'd determined, like the time she'd asked him to repaint her bedroom and he'd mixed up the two shades of light green under discussion, only for her to berate him. 'Do I matter so little to you that you can't pay precise attention to my instructions?'

Long before that, while growing up in the house just outside Horndean, he'd felt her displeasure whenever her authority, and the "Gospel according to your mum", as one of the Bagshaw boys once put it, was challenged. One day, after he'd been out playing with other boys in the neighbourhood, she heard them call out 'Bye, Larry' as he walked up the short garden path. 'Larry? Larry?' She had looked at him fiercely. 'Why did you give those boys permission to call you Larry? Larry's not your name. Laurence is. Have I made myself clear?'

This latest outburst merely added to the overall tally. 'Haven't I always told you how important it is to stand on your own two feet and never depend on others? I've done my level best to show you through everything I do that actions speak louder than words. So, on the rare occasions when I do call on you for help, you can be jolly certain that it's important and I'm not just making a silly fuss.' The words were articulated with a fierceness which betrayed the last vestiges of a Glaswegian accent. And then, as if to mitigate the force of the verbal assault, she added: 'You do understand that, don't you? I would never want you to think I was being difficult.' All he could do, now as back then, was to apologise profusely for failing to match her expectations of him.

'Mum, I've got to see the school head late this afternoon, but I'll be with you this evening, as quick as I can make it through the traffic. I'll let you know I'm on my way. That's a promise.'

'The school head? Is it something important?'

'No, no. Nothing to worry about.'

For now he decided not to call Rosie but to wait until he'd got through the rest of the day before letting her know he couldn't avoid being late again.

On arriving at the Drum and Monkey, he found Steve sitting in a corner by himself, staring morosely into the near distance, his pale complexion set in sharp relief by the neatly-combed black hair. There was just a flicker in his eyes as Laurence drew near.

'Steve, my old friend, what can I get you?'

'I need to drown my sorrows. Can I have a double whisky?'

When Laurence returned with the drinks, Steve was chewing his lower lip. 'Patrick called me in this morning. It's all the fault of the banking crisis and what's happening to the economy. As you know, property sales are declining and prices falling. That means lower commissions. If things don't pick up soon, Patrick says he'll have to let me go.'

'But that's terrible, Steve. Why doesn't he get rid of the guy who replaced me before he thinks of giving you the chop?'

'Adrian's going anyway. He comes from a family of auctioneers and his dad wants to retire. His future's made, mine isn't.'

Since their meeting with Miriam Bartrop the previous week Steve seemed to have visibly shrunk, the eyes in their deep sockets retreating still further. From their very first interaction across the desks in Patrick's agency, Laurence had come to the conclusion that many of Steve's assessments of market conditions tended to magnify the risks and minimise the opportunities. In his world the glass was always half-empty.

'Well, it's not definite yet, is it? Come the New Year we could easily see the market bouncing back. I wouldn't zoom in on the worst possible scenario just yet. If you get yourself into a negative mode as your default position, you'll struggle to get out of it.'

'Christ, Laurence, just look at what's going on!' His hands were now constantly in motion. 'The whole state of Iceland is virtually bankrupt. And if I get made redundant, there's nothing else I could do. I've never been anything other than an estate agent. There'd be no point in me going to other agencies looking for work. They'll be in a similar mess, especially if things get worse.'

'Mate, if I had work to offer you, I'd certainly help you out. As you know, I do most of the work myself and Natasha's only part-time.'

Steve downed the remainder of the tawny liquid. 'I was hoping to persuade Linda to set up home with me in the New Year. She won't want to shack up with an unemployed loser.'

'Nonsense, Steve. If you really love each other, you'll find a way through the problems.'

'But that's just it. I can't be completely certain, and I don't think she is either.'

Laurence was reluctant to pull himself away and to leave

Steve wallowing in more self-pity, but he needed to get back to his office and then head off for Kieron's school. 'Cheer up, the heavens won't fall in. I'll catch up with you later,' he said. And with that he was gone.

The rest of the afternoon was a blur. The gentle drizzle that had started just after lunch was picked up by a moderate wind blowing in from across the Channel and flung against the window-panes of Laurence Stewart Management, providing a steady counterpoint to incoming phone calls and the rustle of paper as Laurence clawed his way through post-it notes left by Natasha, invoices, quotes for future maintenance work, complaints from residents about faulty doors and inadequate fire precautions, and a collection of bank statements. The software on his computer system was again playing up, so he was unable to navigate around his spreadsheets. 'But when the chips are down, you have to press on regardless. Keep calm and carry on,' his mother had drummed into him whenever homework assignments had built up to a point where they threatened to engulf him. 'I'm not going to help you. It's your problem. You let it get to this stage. You have to sort it out. This is what is going to make you strong.' He pressed on as the rain increased in intensity, slowly disappearing into the creeping shadows of a November afternoon, yet always audible in the background.

With a start he realised he needed to set off for the school. The rain was slowing down the traffic across town and he tried calling the school number at the next junction, where the lights were against him, only to discover that the line had gone to voicemail. Too bad, he thought, she's either gone home already or she's so snowed under with business herself she's not reacting. Rushing into the entrance of the school building, he noted that he was ten minutes late. 'Please don't be late,' was how she'd ended their telephone conversation earlier in the day. Laurence hated arriving late, not so much because he could foresee the levels of disappointment in people close to him like Rosie, but because it was a form of capitulation in the face of superior forces, an admission of defeat. Those same forces that resulted in him losing out at auctions, those same forces that were pushing him in directions he didn't want to go and prevented him from being where he wanted to be at the appointed time, and above all those same forces that had insidiously taken over his son's life. The times he had measured himself against them only for them to come out on top. And the top was where he wanted to be. Why should they deny him that?

There was no response when he banged on the door of the school office, and nobody responded when he thumped the headteacher's door. 'Never give up, Laurence, never give up,' the maternal voice said through the imaginary ear-piece. He walked down the corridor, past the walls with displays of child art, and found another door with the name-plate of the deputy. He tried his luck again. 'Come in,' resounded from within, and he found himself looking into the eyes of a Harriet Jones, her mounds of frizzy hair held back with a purple bandanna.

'I'm sorry to bother you. I'm looking for Mr Sumner, but he doesn't appear to be in.'

'Oh, he's around. I spoke to him only a few minutes ago. He said the person he'd arranged to see hadn't turned up, so he's gone off to meet the caretaker.'

'That was me. I'm sorry I'm late. The traffic's been absolutely hellish this afternoon. I did try to alert the office, but I couldn't get through.'

'Mrs McMahon's only here on Thursdays till 4. That's when she goes to physio.'

'How long do you think the boss man will be?'

'I can call him on his private number if you like, and find out.'

'Tell him it's Laurence Stewart and I'm sorry I couldn't get here on time.'

Harriet Jones looked at him more intently. 'Are you by any chance the father of Kieron?'

'Yes, I am. I suppose you've heard about what's happened.'

The face relaxed into a wan smile. 'Yes, these things have a habit of spreading like wildfire. You know what young people are like. They feed off every latest sensation. It can't exactly have been easy for you.'

He was glad not to have had a finger-wagging face of authority thrust in his face. Harriet Jones looked like a person you could lean on in a crisis, someone who would take the sting out of a confrontation with a few choice words, in short someone you could do business with.

She soon turned out to be the good cop to Richard Sumner's bad cop. When Laurence was at last admitted to his office, after a further delay of fifteen minutes, the dark clenched brows signalled the gravity of the situation. Mr Sumner didn't take kindly to the reputation of the school being sullied in this way, to which Laurence countered that the "crime" hadn't taken place on school property at all. Instead, on school premises, pupils had delighted in humiliating his son and circulating obscene material.

But that had been entirely Kieron's fault, countered Sumner, he had brought it upon himself – surely Mr Stewart would concede that?

The sparring went on for several minutes, Sumner aiming his accusations at Laurence with the skill of a prize fighter, secure in the knowledge that no matter how hard an irate parent tried to land a killer punch, such amateur attacks were no match for the pugilism of professionals. What was the point in being a teacher, and especially a headteacher, Laurence thought, if you can't understand the problem at a human level but are much more interested in the blame game? He'd only spoken to Sumner once before, at a parents' evening just before Kieron moved up from his primary school, and he hadn't warmed then to his rat-like demeanour, with the close-set unforgiving eyes and the thinning greying hair combed back in the pretence of a mane.

Laurence's encounters that day with officialdom had been less than satisfactory. At the police station he had been interviewed at length by a sergeant, and then was present while Kieron faced questions from the sergeant and a family support officer. Kieron had a good idea where the skip had stood into which he'd flung his mobile – and that was the only device which contained any hard evidence, apart from the browsing history on his computer – but if it had already been taken away to a landfill site, the chances of them ever being able to find the mobile were extremely remote, especially since the effort that this would entail could not be justified by the seriousness of the offence. The police could contact the phone company involved, but data protection laws would make any detailed disclosures difficult, and the Home Office didn't currently have any powers to compel compliance. Above all, in all probability those organising the text messages to Kieron's phone were almost certainly using burner phones (Laurence had to ask what these were and how they differed from pre-paid devices), and therefore the individuals could never be traced. Kieron was unable to remember whether the messages had come from the same number or a series of different ones. Hacking into a Facebook account raised the question of jurisdiction, since the UK authorities could only become active if the crime of blackmail had been planned and carried out on British soil. Pornography was only illegal if it involved the participation of minors, and although there was circumstantial evidence that the gang knew Kieron's real age, even if they were ever caught they could pretend otherwise. It would be equally difficult to establish who the ringleaders were who had downloaded the offensive videos from Facebook and circulated them amongst sections of the school community, although police support officers would certainly be happy to visit the school and carry out further enquiries there. They would also arrange to view the browsing history and investigate details of the individual websites.

Each of the individual strands that made up the sordid little saga was carefully pored over and analysed, but at every twist and turn any putative connection was left hanging in the air, with little or no resolution. Laurence's initial determination to unleash the forces of retribution on the brains behind the operation – which was why he'd gone to the police in the first place – had by then been superseded by his resolve to punish the perpetrators of his son's humiliation at school. No, things had not gone to plan, they had not gone well at all. It was understandable that the police would want to place this particular incident in context, drawing attention to the huge variety of scams being carried out on the unsuspecting, from the young to the elderly, directed from the four corners of the planet and not just within the UK, and stressing that at the heart of every scam, not merely the one of which Kieron had been a victim, there was the desire to extract money. Laurence knew that already. He wanted more than small doses of tea and sympathy. He wanted action. That was what he expected as a taxpayer, as a husband and father, as a responsible member of the community. Once again, the forces on the other side turned out to be much stronger and more resilient than he had allowed for.

There was something else Laurence learned from the hours he spent at the police station. In the midst of all the talk of deception and false identity, the phrase "sock puppetry" was used, and it had to be explained to him.

As Laurence left Sumner's room, he mused on the irony of having learned nothing at all from a key representative of the teaching profession, those very people who were supposed to know it all and put it all to good use. Nothing new there, he thought. Just like his own schooldays; if you played the game and did what the teacher told you to do, rather than what you wanted to do, you were fine. But if you flexed your muscles or stood up for what you believed in, they would always find some way of not giving you the same amount of attention in class and marking you down, or picking you up on petty technicalities. No wonder he'd struggled there for most of the time; they had rarely been on his side. Well Laurence, these mock results aren't particularly good. This piece of work isn't good enough, is it? If you don't pull your socks up, you won't be going anywhere at all. And they believed in their smug way that they were always right. A plague on all your houses, he thought.

Back in the school car park he discovered that a maintenance van had partially obstructed his exit, so he trudged through the rain that was now dripping from the sky like a gigantic leaking cauldron back to the school entrance, and then once more to the helpful Harriet Jones, who was still mercifully in thrall to her laptop and who obligingly put through a call to the caretaker. By the time he got back onto the main road it was well after six. He headed for the M27, which would – so he anticipated – get him along the coast quite quickly before he needed to turn off and head into the Hampshire countryside towards Horndean.

But it was a day when nothing was going quite the way he had expected it to, and just after he reached the junction for Cosham all the lanes of traffic on his side came to an abrupt halt. The rain was making it difficult to see ahead, the intermittent swipe setting of the window-blades just about able to cope, the red tail-lights of the vehicles in front like blobs of congealed blood on a corpse sprawled before him. He climbed out and peered into the distance; he could just make out flashing blue lights. It was bound to be some kind of accident, caused by the usual impatience of drivers anxious to get home combined with tricky driving conditions and a momentary lapse in concentration. That was what had brought everything to a standstill.

He phoned first his mother and then Rosie to explain the situation. He had no idea how long he'd be stuck there and he was still only about half-way to his mother's. In any case, as he'd forgotten to call round that morning, he thought he should deal with her shopping list before returning home.

Rosie thought he had his priorities all wrong. 'Why on earth couldn't you have waited till tomorrow morning to do that? Is it so urgent that you have to go there now? I've been waiting to hear what happened with the police this morning. I can't get much out of Kieron. When are you going to be back? What have you been doing all day? What do you want me to do with your tea? You do realise that I'm taking the kids up to Huddersfield, don't you?'

He listened while she piled one question on another, garnishing each comment with thistles of reproach in her voice. She didn't often put him under pressure like this, but because such a flurry of questions had been hurled at him so many times in the past whenever the heat of a moment intensified he knew he could choose which particular one he wished to respond to. 'If I could tell you when I expect to be back, I would. Honestly. It's really not my fault. I didn't plan this.'

She was clearly not satisfied with his excuses, and after his long and tiring day the last thing he wanted was a slanging match with his wife over the phone. 'My signal power's going,' he said and cut off the connection.

He reflected on her recurring lack of sensitivity towards his mother. No, it had never been a particularly happy relationship, and his mother's attitude towards Rosie had softened only slightly after the arrival of her two grandchildren. It was two years into their marriage before Kieron had been born, four weeks premature. Just a few months after the ceremony in Portsmouth registry office which his mother had done so much to prevent, claiming that a church wedding would have been so much nicer for everybody concerned, she had prodded him with questions. Is everything all right with Rosie? Is Rosie eating well? Is Rosie looking after herself? Has Rosie had all her check-ups?

When the family came to visit for one of the periodic feasts, his mother would never put any such question directly to her daughter-in-law. Instead she chose to quiz him on the phone or when he came by himself. At one stage he wondered whether his mother would find a new variation to her questioning and come up with something along the lines of 'Is everything in the bedroom department all right?' Except she never did. Later, when they had moved to the Gosport Road house just before the birth of Kieron, she had visited their new home only once, a visit which Laurence regarded more as an inspection. Personal questions were eschewed; it was all about the number of power points in the Victorian house and whether the wiring was still up to the job; how much the curtains had cost and whether they were washable or had to be dry-cleaned; if the neighbours were noisy and whether they had any young children; what the local shopping facilities were like.

It had been no different when they had moved to Marlborough Close. She had waited almost a year before she had agreed to come, and then looked critically at each room as she was taken on her guided tour, stressing in her comments the regrettable absence of character and period charm (which pleased Rosie) but also how four bedrooms and an en suite plus a downstairs utility room indicated how far they'd moved up in the world (which pleased him). All attempts to get her to make further visits to either house ended with 'But I've seen where you now live. I have a very good photographic memory. I don't need to keep reminding myself of how you live. You come to me. It's much easier that way.'

Whereas all four of them were expected to come for the periodic feasts, Laurence saw her more frequently, especially after she gave up driving. Thus the regime of the weekly trips was instituted, designed to enable him to pick up the shopping list and return a day or so later with whatever she needed to see her through the coming week. Over and above that there was always Mary Rees, her closest neighbour, whom she could call on in case she unexpectedly ran out of basic essentials. Mary, who was some years younger and had by now availed herself of the delivery service run by one of the major supermarkets, offered to include Roberta in the orders she placed. However, his mother was quick to make her objections clear to Laurence. 'You know what I've always said. Never be beholden to anybody. I don't mind asking if I need extra eggs or sugar, but I wouldn't want her to know precisely what I'm putting in my larder and fridge.'

Even when Laurence offered to buy her a computer and teach her the essentials of ordering online, she remained adamant. 'But it's not the same. If I tell you exactly what I want, I have a better chance of getting it. How do I know they won't mix up items or give me a different brand to what I want?'

She had always been very particular about the way she did her shopping. Once, while still a teenager, Laurence had seen her picking off individual grapes from a large bunch in a supermarket before putting them into the cellophane bag. 'Mum, what are you doing that for?' he had whispered, aware of the queue that was building up behind them and the strange looks coming their way. 'Well, I'm not paying for the stalks,' she had snorted.

They had moved from the house in Stubbington when he was just three, shortly after the death of his father. He vaguely remembered the generous entrance-hall together with its wide staircase and the back lawn from which he could sometimes see masts and funnels. Those early impressions were later reinforced by the books of photographs his mother sometimes pulled out to show him. She'd repeatedly told him that money was now going to be tight and they'd no longer be able to live in the detached Georgian house that overlooked the Solent, and so the rest of his childhood was spent in the house that faced Butser Hill on the outskirts of Horndean, a stone-built former farmworker's cottage which had just the two bedrooms upstairs, meaning that when his Auntie Joyce came to stay he was given a small camp-bed in his mother's room.

When he was much older he had started to probe the circumstances of his father's early death and the consequences for the two of them. He was told there was a widow's pension but that it was far less than his mother had expected, and that although his parents had apparently discussed the benefits of a life insurance policy, no further action had been taken. He sometimes wondered whether his mother's primary motivation for the move was not so much financial as a desire to get away from the sea. She could have taken in lodgers or turned their house into a B&B, he later thought in his early days as an estate agent. That would have brought in quite a bit of money, especially since the house occupied a prime location. Then she wouldn't have had to start her cleaning business. But that was just the way he saw things; she clearly saw things differently.

'I got married when I was twenty-three, so I didn't have a career,' she had once told Laurence. 'Before that I spent most of my time looking after your granddad. Right up to his death. It was your Auntie Joyce who waltzed out of the house at the first opportunity and went into nursing, leaving me to do all the caring. She was the one who was best qualified to do that. Instead, as the younger sister, I had to do it all.'

'But why did Granddad need looking after?'

'Have you forgotten? I thought I'd explained that to you. Your grandma was killed in the Clydebank air raid in 1941 when I was only ten. Your Auntie Joyce must have been about thirteen. We had to get through that terrible war entirely on our own. And then your granddad Fergus was badly injured in the last year of the war – I wasn't even fifteen when it ended – and he was in a wheelchair until he died.'

Details of the Stewart family history revolved like the figures in large medieval clock towers viewed through a tourist's binoculars, disappearing whenever the desire for enlightenment had been satisfied but emerging again whenever the trigger was activated, as it so often was when Auntie Joyce or the occasional very distant relations on his father's side of the family came to stay. 'Never forget that you're more than half Scottish,' he recalled his mother saying. 'We Scots don't stand for any nonsense.'

Not that he ever felt much connection with Scotland now. For reasons he could never quite work out, his mother spoke little of her own upbringing and frequently changed the subject whenever he tried to delve more deeply. He knew she intensely disliked tartans and any Paisley pattern, and shook her head at him when he once wanted to be given porridge for breakfast.

When Kieron and Estelle were still quite small, he and Rosie had decided to take the whole family on what he hoped would be a nostalgic return to the land of his mother's birth. It had taken all their combined efforts to persuade his mother to come. They spent a fortnight touring the Glasgow area, peering at the small house in Paisley which once housed the entire Clunie family, and then standing amidst modern blocks of flats in Clydebank imagining what it must have been like with bombs raining down on the local population. 'This was where your grandma died,' she said to Kieron. 'She didn't deserve to die when she did. Never forget there were evil people who killed innocent lives. Those who kill must be made to pay.'

A gloom had quickly descended on that conversation and they had struggled to find much else to talk about. Shortly afterwards a period of persistent rain had set in, making the planned trip to Loch Lomond a complete wash-out. Thereafter Laurence associated Scotland with grey skies, dour faces, the musty damp smell in the rooms of their holiday accommodation, and unhappy memories of the past.

The traffic was lessening as Laurence approached Horndean. In a few months he would see the young lambs again, forming islands of cream with their mothers in the grassy fields of early spring. Now he was merely conscious of the black expanse to either side of the road. It was still dripping with rain as he reached his mother's house, with just the single porch-light to guide him towards the door. Although he had a spare key, he rang the bell as he always did. He had spent nearly his entire childhood living there and the back bedroom upstairs was technically still his, but it was his mother's house, and she it was that decided who was admitted and who was left standing on the step outside.

For someone who regarded retirement not as an opportunity for endless socialising with other retirees or volunteering in the local community in order to keep boredom at bay, but rather as an opportunity for extended contemplation and reflection during which the shortcomings of the world could be assessed and solutions pondered over, Roberta Stewart still took extraordinary care over her appearance. The short silvery-white hair was combed back like plumage and her long straight nose and sharp grey eyes gave her an unmistakeably avian look. Her lean body enclosed in a neat woollen twinset, the hands gripped the front-door as if to signal solidarity with the building.

The first thing she said after their usual hug was 'Laurence, you need a haircut.'

He felt the unruly scallops of hair bristling about his ears. 'Mum, that's what you said last week. I told you, I've been busy. Very busy.'

'That's no excuse. You've had a whole week to do something about it. What are people going to think?'

Every visit to his mother's house was simultaneously a return to his childhood. The years when she would send him back upstairs to brush his teeth, polish his shoes, comb his hair or rectify lapses in school uniform policy – his first attempts at sartorial rebelliousness – and the years when she would criticise his choice of casual wear at weekends. Later he came to see his time at university as a period of liberation, when colours and textures and patterns, individually and in combination with each other, all became utterly irrelevant, only to discover when he landed the job at Patrick's agency that there were clear expectations of how he should dress. 'We're not an advertising agency, we're more like a bank. We need to project complete and absolute professionalism.' Out went the bold stripes and jazzy designs for his ties, in came the white and pale-blue shirts. 'We have a message but we are not *the* message, if you get my drift,' was how Patrick had put it. Even if he now allowed himself the occasional touch of adventurousness, Laurence never forgot that manners and appearance mattered. His mother had drummed that into him. Why else had New Labour made a point of not just jettisoning unwelcome ideological baggage from the past but making certain all its representatives looked smart and serious in the television studios and stayed relentlessly on-message?

'Where's your list?' he asked his mother.

'Goodness, you've only just arrived. Let me put the kettle on and make you a cuppa. Then you can tell me why you've been so busy.'

In the front room Laurence sank into one of the soft easy chairs with the Laura Ashley covering and looked across at the large sideboard made of solid oak, at what had come to be known as the shrine, on which stood all the family photographs, the metal frames polished until they gleamed and the glass so spotless it seemed to be missing. The largest of the frames on the left had him sandwiched as a toddler between his parents, firmly grasping their hands, his father dressed in his Merchant Navy uniform, his mother in a serge blue overcoat, both standing upright and eyeing the camera with quiet authority, while he was chuckling contentedly to himself. Whenever he was in the room he always felt those two sets of eyes following him round, his mother's in order to ensure he maintained a righteous course and his father's exercising a protective spirit from the past.

Everything he knew about Keith Stewart had come mediated through the recollections of his widow and what she chose to tell their only child. His father had come up to visit his Scottish grandparents from way down south in Sassenach country and on a night out in one of the Glaswegian dance-halls he had charmed the socks off first his Auntie Joyce and then her younger sister, so much so that when he went back to Southampton for his next scheduled tour of duty on board an ocean-going liner he could only long for the next spell of land-leave, writing a stream of love-letters that he posted when he next went ashore. Admittedly, the fact that he was the sparks and therefore responsible for radio communication had made it easier to arrange for an occasional phone call from out at sea, though private arrangements of this kind were normally frowned upon. His father was the man who knew all about the big wide world and had seen a decade more of life than she had, the man who had a fund of amazing stories to tell and who made her laugh and looked so handsome in his dashing uniform. The man who enchanted her with descriptions of exotic places in the long letters he continued to post to her while he was away. The man who would take her off in his bright red MG sports car up and down the south coast and through the New Forest and across the Cotswolds and then up to London and Oxford and Bristol, filling her mind with the pictures and landscapes she carried around with her when he was out at sea again. The man who would take her to gaze at the Georgian terraces in Bath and Cheltenham and promised that one day she would have a place of her own fit for a queen. The man who had found them the big house in Stubbington just before the child who had been an eternity in coming was born and where for a few brief years they had been a blissfully happy family. The man whose memory was kept alive for him by all the things his widow remembered and by all the things she knew he would have wanted Laurence to do.

What that meant in practice was a string of admonitions. 'Laurence, that's not what your father would have wanted you to do.' 'Laurence, your father always had high standards. You need to live up to them.' 'Laurence, if your father could see you now, he'd be far from happy.' 'Laurence, think of your father. Honour his memory.' And the picture of the father he never really had continued to radiate its commanding authority.

He quickly learned to fill the gap that fate had torn in his young life. It hurt most when there were events like annual sports days or Saturday morning football matches between local youth teams, when the other boys had two parents cheering them on, and his mother, who had never hollered in her entire life, showed her support only with polite applause. On those occasions when he and the other boys were asked what their fathers did for a living, his self-esteem would inevitably have been bolstered had he been able to say that his dad sailed the high seas on luxury liners and was responsible for all radio communication. He might have revealed in a dramatic flourish that he was at the bottom of the sea, which is what his mother tended to say as the critical day in November approached, but instead he always uttered the two simple words "He's dead" and waited for the expressions of embarrassment or blank incomprehension that invariably followed. The framed photograph was his only remaining link with a world to which he had never even been given access.

'Here we are,' his mother said, returning from the large

kitchen at the back of the property and setting down a tray with the willow-patterned tea-cups and a plate of the chocolate biscuits she knew he couldn't resist. 'Now, tell me all your news.'

Laurence decided to withhold details of Kieron's exploits, sensing that would simply eat up more time than he had at his disposal. He also feared this could trigger a spate of moral strictures, though he knew how careful she was never to interfere with any decisions that affected the upbringing and education of her grandchildren. 'I'm always here to help,' she once told Rosie. 'After all, I brought up Laurence in difficult times and so I know what it's like. There's heartache as often as there's joy. Never forget that moments of real happiness are like gold-dust.'

He focused instead on his discovery of the Wesleyan chapel, regaling her with the architectural details and illustrating his pitch with the photos he'd taken. The moment he mentioned its location, however, she appeared to lose interest. 'Are you sure this is the right kind of thing you should be thinking of doing in the current climate? There's no immediate need for you to move again, is there?' When he didn't immediately react, she went on: 'You've never shown that much interest in religion yourself. What could possibly be the attraction in going to live in a disused church?'

For a split second he wondered whether Rosie might have phoned her up to warn her about his latest project, but she hardly ever initiated communication with her mother-in-law in this way, any more than Roberta Stewart would dream of picking up the telephone on an impulse to talk to her daughter-in-law. Instead Laurence was more usually the intermediary, conveying requests, snippets of information and indications of intent in both directions, and tempering the occasional expressions of forcefulness on his mother's side with diplomatic sensibility.

'Look at the time,' he suddenly said. 'I have to be going. There are things I need to discuss with Rosie.' He avoided any reference to the possibility that his wife wanted to remove herself and his two children to Huddersfield for a week or so. 'I'll bring your shopping round tomorrow.' He wrapped his strong arms around her and kissed the top of her head. 'See you!'

Once back inside the BMW he quickly texted Rosie that he was on his way and pressed down on the accelerator as soon as he was onto the dual carriageway.

It was almost nine o'clock by the time he let himself into the house. Rosie was upstairs in the process of repacking a suitcase, with items of clothing scattered over the bedspread.

'Where on earth have you been?' she snapped. There was a new note of harshness in her voice. 'I'll be needing to make an appointment to see you next. Laurence, this really isn't good enough. Why do I have to wait for hours and hours to hear from you about what happened at the police station? Kieron's not been saying much. Why am I always last in line to be told about important things?'

He looked at the open suitcase. 'Rosie, I'd rather you didn't go north with the kids. It's important that we stay together as a family, especially now.'

She glared at him, her good humour now elbowed aside by the bully-boys of resentment she had been secretly mentoring. 'You've got a cheek talking about "family". We never come first as a family. There's always somebody else or something else that you decide is more important. Well, nothing is more important to me right now than our two children. My two children. It's all been arranged anyway. We're off straight after breakfast. It's a long drive and I don't want to arrive in the dark.'

Direct confrontations with Rosie were comparatively rare and he didn't at first know how best to respond. It wouldn't have mattered quite so much if she'd been more amenable to the prospect of living in the Wesleyan chapel and if she hadn't been spending so much additional time at the Callas. She was his wife, she was the mother of his children, she didn't really need to go out to work, he provided them with everything they needed, why on earth shouldn't she remain in the family home when there was a crisis? It had been a very long day and although his mother's tea had revived him, a sense of fatigue was now gaining the upper hand. Nor was his brain coming up with a sure-fire stratagem which didn't end in him having to back down and eat humble pie. *I'm the head of the household, I make all the important decisions, I can't be seen to be weak.* That was the default mode into which he now retreated.

'It's not a good idea for Kieron to go away right now. The police may need to talk to him in the next few days. They can't do that if you're away in Huddersfield. And what about the school anyway? Even if they might make an exception in the case of Kieron, you can't just keep Estelle away.'

'Well, it's a pity you didn't have time to discuss all of this earlier today. It's all fixed, Laurence. I've phoned the school, I've let them know Kieron and Estelle won't be back until the seventeenth, I've phoned Lucie and she knows we're coming tomorrow. It's too late to change any of this. Just accept you don't have a power of veto in this house.'

Was that how she saw him? A man with a power of veto? She was making him out to be some kind of hard-nosed power-broker intent on getting his own way not just once, but every time something came up for discussion. She'd got him all wrong. He wasn't doing any of this because he wanted to exercise unlimited power. He had their best interests at heart; it was only natural that somebody had to be in charge. You always had to obey the captain of the ship or the pilot of the aircraft, otherwise where would you be?

For a moment he wondered how his father might have approached such a situation, had he still been alive. How would he have kept the vessel away from the rocks, always assuming he'd been the officer on the bridge? Would he have steered a course that enabled both parties to maintain face and claim a win-win outcome? He had no way of knowing. Rosie had laid down what she was proposing to do and short of locking her away in a cupboard, how was he physically going to stop her from going ahead with her plans tomorrow? Damage limitation was now imperative. There was no point in metaphorically stamping his foot and saying 'No, no, no', especially since she could as easily laugh in his face as prostrate herself before him. Perhaps there was an area of compromise. There nearly always had been when he was stuck in the middle between a greedy vendor determined on not budging from the asking price and an over-confident cash buyer who believed they held all the right cards. Was there some kind of sweetener that could be arranged to bring the two parties together or some other way of scaling back on maximum demands without compromising on substance?

'How about just a long weekend then? You don't need to be away for a whole week, do you?'

Her cheeks were flushed at the verbal exertions he was putting her through. He simply wouldn't give up, he wouldn't leave her be, he had to come out on top, he wanted things to go his way, he wanted to make the decisions. Always. 'You are bloody impossible,' she said. 'This is not a weekend break somewhere, we're not jetting off to see the sights and coming back with a few knick-knacks as souvenirs. I want to put time and distance between what's happened before the kids have a sensible return to their schooling. If I could, I'd keep them away for longer, just so that it all blows over. But I've already said I'll be back for next weekend. You'll see.'

Laurence spotted the flaw in her argument. 'But you're not coming back next weekend because you think that's the right time to return, are you? You're only coming back because you want to be here for the opening of your precious Callas. And that's more important to you than my mum's birthday.'

Their positions were now entrenched. There was his needling again. He had taunted her once more with what he regarded as her false sense of priorities. She brushed away a few tears.

'There are times when I don't recognise the man I married,' she said fiercely. She felt both cheeks were burning. 'You'd better accept you're not going to change my mind.' She hadn't quite finished with him either. 'I think for both our sakes you'd better sleep in the spare room tonight.' And she went on repacking her suitcase.

As he lay on the hard mattress in the spare room, trying to focus his thoughts on what appeared to be an errant moth on the ceiling, Laurence was beginning to wonder whether he'd been pulled back into the past to the point where some super-matriarch had just smacked his bottom. He was in the wrong role in the wrong film. Why was she treating him like this? Why had she suddenly become so unreasonable? He was used to the odd swings in mood at her time of the month, but she had never put him on the equivalent of the naughty step before. What he found equally strange was the fact that he'd accepted his punishment without protest, withdrawing meekly from the conjugal bedroom where hitherto he'd always been the final arbiter in any dispute. She had got her way; he hadn't.

14

Laurence was awake early. The thin duvet that covered him in the night had glided off his ample frame like a reptile seeking a warmer and more hospitable location and his neck, accustomed to the downy softness of his usual pillow, felt uncomfortably stiff. He was conscious of the hearth at the back of his throat being fed with large quantities of combustible material. Extreme tiredness had quickly overcome him after the previous night's confrontation and he had slipped into a pattern of deep sleep punctuated by moments of shallow consciousness in which he vaguely recalled the crazed workings of his feverish mind. Cast into a subterranean dungeon, he had rattled his chains in fury, hurling imprecations at the silent walls, drawing in deep mouthfuls of putrid air and spitting out his phlegm in rage. Adrift on a bare mountain, his balance constrained by the biting winds around him, he clutched at each outcrop beneath him to steady his passage while he contemplated a possible descent to safety. And then he was drowning in the icy waters of a huge ocean, in which gigantic leering eyeballs drifted slowly past him before swivelling and spinning to track his progress through the murky depths. What utter rubbish his grey matter deemed important enough to set before him...

A few hours later he was sitting in his BMW, once more

heading in the direction of Horndean, the bags of supermarket shopping resting on the back seats, slowly sucking blackcurrant pastilles in an attempt to damp down the fires of hell that were licking around his throat, while the early-morning half-light fought to break free from its cocoon of swirling mists that had drifted in off the sea. He tried to make sense of that morning's brief encounter with Rosie. He had been willing her to walk into the kitchen and give him a warm hug, murmuring a 'You big silly bear', as she had done on the few occasions when they'd previously had a serious falling-out, and ask whether there was enough tea for her in the pot. Instead, she'd looked at him somewhat wearily, annoyed to see that somebody else had shifted the house from its nocturnal to its diurnal phase, switching on lights, the radio and the electric kettle, pulling back curtains and feeding the cat. She said she needed the AA book and atlas, so he'd gone out into the street to retrieve it from a side pocket in his car. She said the window-cleaner was due to call on the Monday and could he remember to leave the right money with the neighbour two doors down. She said that the meatballs and coleslaw in the fridge wouldn't keep indefinitely and needed to be used up. He'd said very little, lubricating his throat with small sips of his tea, hoping she wouldn't raise any of the previous day's events that might lead to the need for extensive discourse. She clearly wasn't interested in any further confrontation, but as his eyes followed her round, with Cupid and Mars struggling within him for the upper hand, he realised she wasn't paying him any attention. It was as if she'd thrown a cloak of invisibility over him.

He hated these odd spells of frostiness in their relationship. She was his wife, she was there to support him. He was her husband, he was there to protect her. Why did they have to pull in opposing directions, when for most of their marriage they had seen eye to eye on most matters? He would phone her that evening, just to make sure they'd arrived safely and she didn't still have any hard feelings.

His mother was delighted to see him at the door when he rang the bell. 'Why, it's my wee one,' she said in mock surprise, as she sometimes did when Laurence appeared before her. 'I wasn't expecting you to call quite so early.' As she stretched up to kiss his cheek, the crackle on the skin of her long neck gave it the appearance of an antique porcelain vase.

'I thought I'd get it out of the way, seeing as I messed up yesterday. And the supermarket's not so full in the early morning, even on a Friday.'

'You won't forget to call next week, will you? I'll have a much longer list since we've got the next feast coming up on Monday week. I'll need quite a few extra things.'

He hesitated. He could delay giving her the bad news until closer to the day, but by then she might have prepared some things in advance that wouldn't keep. Better to enlighten her now as to the need to consider alternative arrangements.

'Mum, there's something I have to tell you,' he said, while she was stacking tins in her larder and placing packets in the freezer.

'Oh, you're not going to tell me you'll be too busy to come. Not on my birthday!'

'No, no, I can come, if you want me there on the day. It's Rosie. She won't be able to make it.'

He was dreading yet another confrontation, especially since in addition to the ticklish soreness that had taken hold in his throat, he felt the tiny sledgehammers at work in his temples.

'Why's that then? She has a calendar surely, she knows the key dates. Or is she turning out to be as forgetful as you are?'

'Mum, that's not fair. I don't usually forget things. She's been busy helping to get this new restaurant up and running and the seventeenth just happens to be their opening night.'

'But how has she found time to do this? I know you mentioned it the other day, but I didn't realise she was one of the leading players there. I would have thought that being a partner in a business and working part-time, and having a husband and two children to look after, would have been more than enough to keep her happy and occupied.'

Laurence was torn. He could understand his mother's disappointment. He could make allowances for her heavy irony. It was the usual way in which she reacted whenever she was frustrated. On the other hand he resented the little barbs of criticism she was now directing towards Rosie.

'That's not fair either. This is a big step up for her. She'll be doing all the floral arrangements. She told me she just has to be there. There's only one opening night, after all. In any case, it'll be Christmas soon. Time for another feast.'

'Are you saying the whole family can't come before Christmas?'

'Oh no, they'll be back by then.'

'Back? Back from where?'

Laurence realised too late that the combination of too little sleep and too many incursions within his defences had caught him off-guard. Fighting a war on two fronts was sapping far too much vital energy.

He sighed. 'Mum, we've had a disagreement. Rosie's taken the kids to her sister's.'

He saw the raised brows, a questioning glint in the steel-grey eyes, the mouth open in surprise, the thin lips disappearing into her gums.

'Why has she taken Kieron and Estelle with her? If she wants to go off in a huff, why does she need my grandchildren to go with her?'

It was all beginning to unravel. Whatever he now said would lead to further questions, territory that he had no intention of entering.

'Mum, I'm under the weather. I'm running a cold. I'd rather not go into any details.'

'But Laurence, this is important. What's been happening? Has she left you? Tell me, please.' She was like a terrier at times like this. She would grip the bone and pull and pull until it was hers. She wanted to know everything.

When it came down to it, this was what he most feared; having to make a choice between the two women in his life, being forced to put one before the other. If he refused to come clean to his mother now, she might never forgive him for his betrayal of a trust that had bound them together all his life, a feeling rooted as far down as he could divine that she would always be on his side, no matter how many times he had disappointed her in the past and failed to measure up to her expectations. Sooner or later she was going to find out anyway; the whole family would simply not be able to maintain a wall of silence over what had happened. Yet if he bowed to the inevitable, what was Rosie going to think and say when she discovered that he had been discussing intimate family matters with the one person who had never completely accepted that she was a good and proper wife? How could he explain away what he still viewed as the kind of trivial tiff all married couples went through without going into details of what Kieron had done in front of his webcam and why that had led to the kind of situation Laurence now found himself in? With his head pounding and his throat raging, how was he going to be able to think strategically and find the right flow of information which gave his mother all she needed to know without making Rosie and Kieron and above all himself look foolish in the process? Having to admit to her a loss of control – not having prevented the sexual exploitation of his son in the first place and not being able to keep his marriage together either – was the worst of it. But he'd also failed to protect his son from harm and was therefore a failure as a father.

One natural consequence was that his wife could now use the argument of protection to remove the rest of the family from his direct harbourage. If he chose to run away and plead extreme pressure of business this would only make him look weak. In any case, he'd already played that particular card in the last few days; it was no longer available to him. 'Lying is the coward's way out,' his mother had repeatedly told him in childhood. He didn't have any other options left. Above all, he didn't need to put himself through the humiliation of admitting to moral bankruptcy in the presence of his own mother.

15

The only driving Rosie did on a regular basis was local. She drove herself to and from work; she ferried her children around when they required transport; she piled the boot and sometimes the back seats full of bags of shopping and the special offers Laurence directed her towards in out-of-town retail outlets. On the rare occasions when they didn't have foreign holidays but spent a few weeks in Cornwall or in Wales, Laurence did all the driving in the BMW and she was happy for him to chauffeur them wherever they needed to go. The hatchback runabout Laurence presented her with when they made the move to Marlborough Close was more than adequate for Rosie's short trips. The farthest she'd been in it was Chichester Harbour, when Kieron had wanted to see a sailing regatta there two summers ago.

The vehicle didn't really need the satnav Laurence had given her the previous February when she had reached her forty-fifth birthday. 'But they're all the rage. You won't have to worry about maps or directions ever again,' was the way he had sold the idea to her. Initially she'd been sceptical about yet another piece of technology claiming to make life easier, but after programming it successfully her own confidence had received a welcome fillip. When Kieron was given his iPhone a month later she felt able to talk all kinds of technical details with him. But the device had gone wrong on two separate occasions and she was becoming less convinced of its reliability, which was why she'd asked Laurence to dig out the AA book that morning. She told Kieron to sit beside her in the front of the car and act as her navigator, though most of the journey involved long stretches of motorway, M3, M25 and then the M1.

The car, her 'motor-buggy' as she called it, was due for its sixth MOT and its annual service in a couple of months. Given the choice, she would have preferred something a little more comfortable for a journey of several hundred miles. The engine produced an irritating whining noise at high speeds and the hardness of the driving seat was becoming an issue by the time they reached the orbital motorway round London. The expectation that she would simply need to maintain a cruising speed and keep steering ahead was quickly dispelled. She had to keep her wits about her when faced with countless contraflow systems, as there were heavy goods vehicles which would suddenly emerge from feeder lanes forcing her into split-second decisions either to stamp on the brakes to or press her foot right down if the overtaking lane was blocked. A succession of sharp showers was making visibility an additional problem and the upsurge of unwelcome heat was causing little beads of perspiration to form on her brow.

However, the driving relieved her, at least in the early stages, of having to return to the drama of the previous night. Once her bedside light was switched off, the voices in her head that had been especially active in the past few days swung into action once more. *Was that really necessary,* one of them wanted to know? *You have a tendency to blow things up out of all proportion. Sending Laurence into the spare room really takes the biscuit,* another opined. *Whatever next, will you be throwing all his clothes onto the street like a fish-wife?* The chatter continued. *There you go again, overreacting just like every other emotional woman. Is that a picture of yourself you would care to have framed? You are silly to think you could ever take Laurence away from his mother. You will never be able to drive a wedge between the two of them, even if you give it your all. Just grow up and accept that the two of them together will always be far stronger than you could ever be.* Then, however, the over-confident protagonists in the front row were pushed to one side by the counter-insurgency forces. *Let's get one thing absolutely straight. This is the twenty-first century, he has got to understand that women are no longer men's chattels. You are not an appendage in this marriage. Rosie, you have a perfect right to your feelings. Brushing them aside as though they were of no consequence just shows what a little tyrant he's becoming.* What was that phrase Lorna had recently quoted from a book she'd been reading? *Don't let the bastards grind you down.* Quite right, you have to stand up for yourself. If you don't, nobody else will. Except that Laurence wasn't really a bastard. Not that kind of one anyway. But, but, but. The fact that he can't understand why you feel so strongly about that wretched ruin of a chapel and the regularity with which he always puts his mother first simply demonstrate to those who have eyes to see how self-centred he's become.

By the time she switched off the alarm that morning, her mood had softened. She wanted to go downstairs immediately, make them all a cooked breakfast and consign the catalogue of disagreements to Room 101. Instead, she found that Laurence had beaten her to it and taken possession of her kitchen. The way he had stood there with his two feet planted wide apart made that absolutely plain to her. He'd upset her natural morning routine. He'd countermanded her plan of action. Quite deliberately. Obviously and intentionally. And then he had stared expectantly at her, with a coffee mug in one hand rather than a teacup, as if waiting to hear an apology or, at the very least, an expression of regret. It was all too much. She couldn't be expected to jump to attention and perform according to the dictates of his team of scriptwriters. To compound matters, she'd been unable to rouse Estelle and Kieron promptly. Neither of them had packed all the things she'd said they would need to take with them, so she was shouting instructions from the hallway while the clock was ticking away. Laurence was mumbling something at her which she hadn't really understood, and if she'd queried what he'd said, it would have been clear that she hadn't been listening to him properly, which would no doubt have triggered another jibe, so she let him slink out of the house like a wounded animal.

It was much later than planned when, with the luggage safely stowed in the boot, and Thermos flasks filled with strong sweet tea and a clutch of hard-boiled eggs in a plastic container keeping Estelle company on the back seat, she had steered her hatchback out of the close at roughly the same moment that Laurence was ringing his mother's doorbell. In the early part of the journey there had been plenty of distractions to keep them all amused. They played the usual quiz games, they commented on the passing scenery, they discussed the dreary weather and they whistled their disbelief at the poor quality of the other road-users. But after a while each new activity lost its novelty value and quickly exhausted its potential. Both children were becoming fractious. The tailbacks on the M25 were slowing their progress and the drizzle was increasing in intensity. Her attempts at blotting out memories of who had said what the previous night and then the following morning, together with her interpretations of the words used, were creating an uncomfortable head of emotional steam for her to deal with. All she really wanted was for them to put this unpleasantness behind them and for the whole family to come together. And then, much to her distress, she began to hear strange popping noises from inside the engine compartment, accompanied by a loss of power.

16

Predicting what your client would do next was a game Laurence had quickly learned to play at the outset of his career. It was a bit like playing a game of chess. If you hung onto the other person's words and responded accordingly, matching each question with an appropriate answer, adjusting tone, attitude and content to whatever was being said, you would certainly be able to establish a rapport and have a good time in the process. If you chose to concentrate on each individual moment, the figures on the board might move up or down or diagonally, some might be lost and some might be gained, but the king and queen could be left to enjoy the trappings of power behind an impenetrable fortress at the far end of the board. Just like a soft sell, in fact. Much less wearisome, and it left no distressing shards of glass on the floor either. However, if you failed to keep the main objective within your immediate sights, there was also a real prospect of the entire interaction ending up as a tattered heap of unfulfilled expectations. If you needed a cheque as confirmation of the deal being closed, if you had to get a signature on a piece of paper as your guarantee of success, warm words on their own would never be enough. A promise or a smile-wrapped 'maybe' wouldn't cut the mustard. And if – God forbid – you ever lost sight of the two prime targets at the opposite end of the board from where you were sitting or your own prime movers were left exposed to a sudden ambush, it would be impossible to recover.

Applying the same principles to long-standing family relationships might be thought easier. There were the traditional patterns of attack and defence, the set pieces which lived off an intricately-designed choreography and the long rallies in which the ball was kept in the air without either party seemingly able to gain a decisive advantage, as well as the moments of repose which allowed both sides to consider, reflect and revise their positions before victory was declared, defeat conceded or a truce to hostilities agreed. After seventeen years of observation and evaluation with Rosie and well over double that number with his mother Laurence knew he could never be regarded as a mere novice at this game. Yet Rosie had temporarily floored him with her unexpected intransigence and, as if that were not enough, his mother was about to play him a blinder.

She looked at him with palpable concern, the eyes flickering occasionally, the mouth set in earnest concentration as Laurence began at the beginning. She listened and didn't once interrupt. When he reached the end of what he wanted to say, she laid a thin bony hand with the immaculately varnished fingernails on his arm. Even in the days when she went out cleaning for others, the hands and fingers would be well protected with lined plastic gloves and massaged with lanolin at the end of the day. Now, as so often in the past, the nails glistened. She let out a sigh.

'My poor wee boy. Poor wee Kieron. Poor wee Rosie. This is quite dreadful news. You must all have had sleepless nights.'

She appeared quite unfazed at the thought of her grandson engaged in auto-erotic activity in front of a webcam which, despite her only rudimentary knowledge of how modern computers worked, she correctly took to be a secret eye capable of spying on the unsuspecting.

'They used to call it entrapment when I was much younger,' she said. 'That was in the days when proving adultery was so difficult and there were such strange rituals you had to go through if you wanted a divorce. And people were no longer individuals, they merely had functions. You were a co-respondent, for instance. There were a number of instances where hotel managements were offered backhanders to facilitate everything and cameras were installed inside the bedroom wardrobes. I even remember, just before you were born in fact, a famous case where the Russians did something similar to a homosexual member of the British Embassy in Moscow. Then they blackmailed him into spying for them.' She sighed again. 'Laurence, dear, it's all been done before. They might have changed the methods they use, but the basic principle is as old as the hills.'

As if to lift his own sagging spirits she went on, 'It's funny, you know. Just after your granddad died, your Auntie Joyce and I were so in the doldrums. We were left all on our own. There were some neighbours of ours who were the first on our street to own a TV set. They told us straight to our faces – it's no joke – that they wouldn't dream of undressing in front of the TV for fear they'd be seen by people on the other side of the box.'

Laurence was visibly amused. He wondered why his mother was so sparing in the stories she told of her early years, stories which clearly had the power to entertain.

Nor did she find the notion of Rosie taking her two grandchildren out of the immediate range of fire at all unacceptable. 'I'm sure I'd have done the same. In a situation like that your instincts as a mother just kick in. You want to look after your babies and keep them from harm. I'm sure a completely different environment will help them all to gather their thoughts.'

Gather their thoughts. Gather your thoughts, Laurence, was what she had told him to do after he outgrew the power of her hand to chastise him. Code for coming to one's senses. More than a hint that one needed to change direction.

She hadn't taken his side, but nor had she criticised him directly. Where was the unbending moral severity he'd expected to encounter, the talk of declining standards in public and in private behaviour, the displeasure at a lack of control, disbelief at the infantile actions of nominally adult beings, the general drift into decadence? He had totally miscalculated her possible reactions. She had more than surprised him.

As he pulled away from his mother's house and headed towards his office, the sledgehammers paused for elevenses and the stokers in his throat temporarily ran out of combustible material. He felt a quiet sense of satisfaction. As he never stopped telling himself, it would all blow over. It would all come right in the end. Now that hostilities had ceased on the maternal front, he only had to bring Rosie back on side. Given time, all would be well again.

But all was not well in the office. Natasha had rung and left two voicemail messages to say that she was terribly sorry but her seven-year-old had twisted her foot and she'd had to take her to the local A&E, so she wouldn't be in that morning. A contractor who was supposed to begin work on an extension to one of Laurence's newly-acquired properties had been declared insolvent, and he would need to start the process of getting quotes all over again, with the inevitable delays. Plus the fact that the contractor had already received an advance from him for the purchase of building materials and that payment would now be irrecoverable. Then there were still problems in the block that had been affected by the plumbing crisis a couple of nights previously. The emergency plumber had obviously been in too much of a rush to finish: the water pressure was much lower than it needed to be.

The phone rang. 'Hi Laurence, it's Steve.'

'Morning, my friend. What can I do for you?'

Laurence listened to Steve reeling off details of a refurbishment property in one of the town's back-streets which the Costley-White agency was marketing.

'It's not shifting, Laurence. I thought you might be interested. After all, it's one of those projects I thought would be just the ticket for you.'

Laurence was reading between the lines. 'Has Patrick put you up to this?'

There was a hesitation. 'No, not exactly. But you know the pressure we're under. We've got to sell the stuff. I have to sell the stuff. Laurence, I'm worried about losing my job here. Getting the commission on another deal would help us out.'

There was no deviousness to Steve; he wasn't very good at spinning yarns. Yet there were simply too many other projects at the moment that were creating unexpected difficulties, in addition to the turmoil on the home front, and he wanted to maintain a degree of financial flexibility for the Wesleyan chapel. 'I understand, Steve,' replied Laurence. 'I don't think I can take on any more renovations in the current climate. I might not get the expected returns.'

'So you don't think this is all a minor blip on the horizon after all?'

'There are worrying signs, I grant you that. Those bank bailouts last month are clearly going to have a knock-on effect with liquidity. But you knew that already. I just don't see why everybody needs to talk about a major crisis. Actually, all this over-dramatisation is making things worse.'

'But I'm really worried, Laurence. There's a report in today's FT about a quarter of a million Yanks who lost their jobs last month. It'll be a re-run of 1929. That's what I'm afraid of. They sneeze and we all catch a cold.'

Laurence was glad he'd stopped off at a chemist on the way in. The tablets were helping to deal with the sledgehammers and the fiery furnace. 'Wait a moment. That's all bullshit. You're letting yourself get panicked into a really downbeat assessment of the situation. Nothing's shifted in the fundamentals. Property is still a sound investment.'

'Well, I think you're missing the point. It's the economy as a whole that's the problem. It's going to shrink, Laurence. There'll be much less money available, people's living standards are going to drop and they won't have the spare cash to put into the housing market.'

Laurence had been there before. This melody was nothing new. He wasn't prepared to listen to another of Steve's jeremiads. At least not today, with a cold and a mini-crisis in his own office to contend with. 'OK, mate, I understand,' he said. 'I'm sorry I can't help you today. We'll have a drink sometime. Take care.'

Meeting a brick wall meant you reversed and went down another street. Simple. There was no point in clogging up his mind with matters that would struggle to find an immediate resolution.

He decided to call the police station again. The sergeant he'd spoken to the previous morning was out on an urgent call and his colleague had little to add to what was already known. They hadn't been in touch about viewing Kieron's computer either.

Laurence put the phone down. He considered ringing the helpful Harriet Jones, but he could anticipate what she would say and knew she would refer him to the unhelpful Sumner, and he didn't really want to speak to him. He put his head in his hands. There were some days when everything was rotating, the floor was slipping beneath him and nothing settled the way it was supposed to. But this was a phase, he thought, as he looked out onto the grey sodden streets and the grey spray-can in the sky that seemingly still had so much to give. All this will pass. Eventually.

17

She'd never had a breakdown before. She couldn't recall Laurence ever having had one either. He was too smart for that. He knew what to do. He traded in year-old cars for the newest model, everything on guarantee, and of course he was a dab hand at fixing things. Here she was, on the hard shoulder of the orbital motorway, not yet on the M1 heading north and nowhere near where she'd expected to be by lunchtime, with intermittent drizzle dampening her spirits, forced to listen to a succession of sibilant sounds coming from the wires plugged into Kieron's ears, and waiting for the AA recovery man to arrive.

'Mum, I need the loo!'

'I'm sorry, Estelle, you'll have to wait.'

'I can't. It's urgent.'

'Just sit on it then. There's hardly a bush in sight. If you can't hold it in, you'll have to crouch down in full sight of everybody.'

'Mum!!!'

'Oh don't worry, at the speed they're flashing past they won't notice you.'

It hadn't helped that Kieron expected her to know the entire inner workings of a combustion engine when they finally came to a juddering halt in the slow lane. Working all the electronic gadgets in the kitchen and putting them right, for instance when the whisk of a mixer jammed, was one thing. But she'd never been taught which bits of the engine were likely to be at fault when a car unexpectedly and spectacularly lost power and how to carry out mechanical first-aid. That was what the AA was for. Thank goodness she'd had the relevant details in the glove-box and hadn't needed to ring Laurence.

When the recovery man eventually arrived, he was most apologetic. 'I'm sorry, love, but it's the mother and father of all disaster days. So many breakdowns today. And the weather doesn't help.'

One unclogged fuel filter and a replaced set of spark plugs later, they were on their way again, with strict instructions to keep the engine running and to seek a proper overhaul at their journey's end.

'Mum, I'm starving!'

'Me too!'

'What? Have you eaten all the boiled eggs?'

Having made a promise to stop at the next suitable service centre while she remained in the vehicle, Rosie pressed her foot down on the accelerator. Along the south coast she rarely had the need or opportunity to drive up to the speed limit, but now she was even prepared to exceed it, keeping a wary eye on the fuel gauge as the car ate up the miles. The moment she saw the turn-off signs for Mansfield and then Chesterfield she began to relax. It wouldn't be long now. The Yorkshire she'd grown up in would soon be within reach.

In the distance she glimpsed the tall structure of the Emley Moor TV mast winking at her in the twilight and saw herself again as a six year-old, sitting on the floor of their sitting-room, wondering why the family TV set – as well as all the television screens in their street, as she later discovered – had suddenly gone dark. It was left to Lucie to explain to her the next day that the huge mast had collapsed through the pressure of packed ice. Over to her left were the bleak areas of Pennine landscape barely discernible in the fading light, and ahead the still and brooding silence of the moors, which Dulcie had taught her to regard as Wuthering Heights territory. She shuddered at the memory of the murders on Saddleworth Moor and the notion that as a teenager she might have been hiking with schoolfriends near to where bodies were buried close to the surface. After the long drive she was weary and dehydrated and it was all becoming too much for her. Kieron and Estelle had been arguing about acts on *The X Factor*. The only thing that kept her going was having to concentrate on the driving and not think about Laurence.

By the time they left the motorway it was already dark, and then they got caught up in the rush-hour around Huddersfield. When they finally got to Lucie's place it was no longer raining, but there was an uncommon chill in the air. She felt utterly drained.

Then her mobile rang. It was Laurence. She batted him quickly away. She couldn't face talking to him right now. He'd have to wait.

Lucie was standing in the door as they climbed out of the car, her short grey hair framing a full round face, with the clear bluish-green eyes all the Wingfield sisters had. She pressed them in turn to her ample bosom and gestured them to sit down around the log-fire that was burning. 'You must be clemmed. I've just made some parkin. It's that time of the year. Would you like some?'

Kieron and Estelle exchanged looks of incomprehension. Rosie stared at some of the memories of childhood: the polished brass instruments lying in the hearth, the upright piano in the corner that only Lucie had been pressured into learning to play, the antique card-table with its green baize lining, the big Rowntree presentation tin with colourful scenes from the dales, all rescued from the family home when it was sold. 'I was beginning to think you'd never get here. It's been a reight long time.' The accent was pronounced and she continued to pepper her sentences with words that Kieron and Estelle struggled to understand. 'It's gone proper parky. Still you're in the warm now.'

Rosie's mobile rang again. Once more she batted Laurence away. She needed to unwind first. She looked at her big sister and recalled how once, as a child, she'd misbehaved and Lucie had put on a posh accent, saying very deliberately, 'What do you think I'm going to do with this child?' And then they'd both laughed, the eldest and the youngest of the Wingfield sisters, bound together by a sense of impish fun.

'Where's Ian? Is he still out?' Rosie asked.

'He's away on a fishing trip. He's in Canada with some pals of his. Search me why they had to go there. You can fish in these parts. You can fish in the Lake District. You can fish in Scotland. No, it had to be Canada. So we've got the whole house to ourselves.'

The ringtone on Rosie's mobile seemed more insistent than ever. Lucie looked across at her, willing her to answer. Rosie reluctantly pressed the button.

It was Laurence. 'Hi love, you had me worried. Not answering. Did you get there all right?'

'Sort of. We've only just arrived. I haven't had time to recover yet.'

'Can we talk?'

'About what?'

'Everything. You know.'

'No, I'm sorry. Now's not a good time. Ring me tomorrow evening.'

Lucie's smile faltered. 'Hit a rough patch?'

'You could say that. Let's talk later when the kids are in bed.'

Several hours later Lucie opened a bottle of vodka to go with the lime juice. After Rosie finished explaining what had happened to Kieron, Lucie said, 'I just don't get this new Facebook stuff, petal. Jane told me it gives young people all these extra friends, but they never get to see them, do they? Invisible friends, what good are they? It's like all these fat cats having loads of zeros in their bank accounts. Looks fine on paper, but what can you do with it?'

Rosie twisted the eternity ring on the third finger of her left hand with its cluster of diamonds, the one Laurence had given her on their tenth wedding anniversary. More was not less in most cases. More was more, and that was good. That's what a lot of people thought. People like Laurence. There always had to be the prospect of another couple of zeros, another clutch of properties in your portfolio. And for the younger generation addicted to this Facebook thing, a few more friends, and then more clusters of friends. Not just dozens but hundreds, thousands even. That was the way the world worked for some people. You couldn't easily undo the thread that made up the cloth. The fabric was woven and the garment finished.

'I just felt I had to take Kieron and Estelle out of that hothouse and give myself some breathing space too.'

'So what's not quite reight on the home front?'

Rosie sighed. When she'd talked to her sister the previous day, she indicated that the reason for getting away was all about Kieron. 'It's Laurence. He's got this crazy idea of wanting to buy a chapel and restore it so we can move yet again.'

'Did he discuss it with you?'

'Discuss?' She clicked her teeth. 'He never does that. He makes all the decisions by himself and expects me to follow suit. I don't think he really listens to a word I say.'

'You haven't mentioned this before. How long has this been going on for?'

'Quite some time, I suppose. You know, in a funny kind of way that was one of the things that first attracted him to me. He was always so decisive, knew exactly what he wanted, had a clear idea of where he wanted to go and how to get there. So different from Adam, who used to brood for weeks on end before making up his mind. I think that's probably why we split up. I couldn't get him to commit. He kept saying he needed more time. Men!'

She looked across at her big sister. The lips, once full and given to displays of striking shades of lipstick that Rosie sought to emulate in the way she painted her nails, had now grown in on themselves. A thin line of colour around the mouth no longer made any sense.

'You said it, petal,' replied Lucie. 'Just be thankful you're not married to a bloke like Ian. It's the fatal combination of a roving eye and wanting to do his own thing.'

'You mean like this fishing trip to Canada?'

'Yes, but I can handle that. What I find much more difficult are all the lies and deception about his affairs.'

Rosie paused. 'But you still want to be with him?'

'You know, I've often thought about that. Would I be better off on my own? I'd have nowt to rub against and challenge me. There'd be nobody to question whether I was doing the right thing. I'd miss that.'

'I wouldn't mind so much if Laurence took an interest in the work I'm doing. I've told him about the Callas but apart from grumbling about the time I spend there, he doesn't really want to know. But when I told him that the opening night there clashes with his mother's birthday, oh that's a reight old calamity.' She lapsed back into the vernacular, echoing the warmth and homeliness coming from her sister's northern inflections.

'He expects you to put his mother first?'

'That's exactly it. That's one reason I'm still so furious with him. She comes first all the time. We don't.'

'Well, I don't think I ever got on with my own mother-in-law either.'

'I bet she was never as disapproving as mine. I remember the first time Laurence took me to see her. She kept staring at my fingernails – I'd painted them in different colours, you know the way you used to do your lips – and then she'd extend her own hands in some kind of gesture and display her own beautifully varnished nails. As if she was saying, that's the way to do it properly, dear.

'All la-di-dah, eh?'

'No, that's just the point. When she disapproves, it's not so much what she says, it's all in the body language. But when she speaks you can still hear the Scottishness in her voice, and it's

Glasgow rather than Edinburgh, if you see what I mean. Don't forget, she had a cleaning business, so I don't think she's really a snob. She just doesn't like me. Doesn't think I'm ever good enough for her Laurence.'

'The daft a'porth! Remind me again, why did she have a cleaning business?'

'Laurence says she didn't have much choice. When his dad died, they didn't have a lot of money. She had to sell up the home they had and move somewhere smaller, and she wasn't really qualified for anything either. There wasn't much she could do except clean people's houses. Later she got into the office cleaning business.'

'And now she lords it over my little kid sister?'

'I keep away from her as much as possible. There are these set days in the year when she expects us to come round for a family meal. I don't mind telling you, I'm always counting the seconds before we can leave. But I have to hand it to her, she's a much better cook than I am.'

They went on talking long after midnight, the clock on the mantelpiece ticking purposefully away in the background, the dying embers of the log fire producing an occasional spark and hiss. Left to her own devices Rosie would probably have collapsed in a heap through exhaustion, but the combination of her sister's animating presence and the generous quantities of spirit she was being plied with dissipated her sense of extreme fatigue.

'Let's talk again in the morning and then we can decide how you'd like to spend the rest of the week,' said Lucie. 'It's not as though I get to see you and my nephew and niece all that often. Let's enjoy ourselves. No point in pulling long faces, eh?'

18

Laurence had another uneasy night. He was back on his side of the marital bed, but there was no soft arm or buttock he could stretch out to fondle and no warm voice to whisper in his ear. There were only a few occasions when they'd been apart: the time Rosie had gone up north after the death of her parents and more recently when Dulcie had broken a leg and Rosie had spent a weekend away, plus the odd conference which had meant overnight stays. Other than that they'd always been together, he and the other Mrs Stewart. He let her be for most of the time. He hadn't raised any objections when she'd said she wanted to go on working at Florabellum after they got married, and he hadn't tried to stop her investing in the business with her inheritance money, though that would have been more useful in kick-starting his own career move. He hadn't even suggested she was perhaps taking on too much when she got involved in the Callas project. Nor had he ever demanded too much in the way of sex from her. After the birth of Estelle she'd said she didn't want any more children, and though he would have liked another child, he never once pressed the issue. He wasn't such a bad husband, was he? All he wanted to do was provide for their little family and go on working towards a better future. What was so wrong with that?

And then tonight when he'd called her, she hadn't even been

prepared to talk. They could have taken stock and he would have tried to smooth down her ruffled feathers and give her the feeling he understood her concerns. But the voice at the other end of the line hadn't had the smile tucked inside it that he longed to hear. He'd done his level best to sort out the problems with Kieron, take on the representatives of officialdom and stick up for his kid, and how had she responded? Her first thought had been to take him away with her. Away from his own dad. And why the hell had she taken Estelle as well? There was no reason to have done that. Estelle could have coped with the banter and ribbing at school, and the two of them could have had a wonderful weekend together, just the two of them, father and daughter. Instead, here he was, on his own in an empty house, with nothing to look forward to other than a lonely weekend and a lonely week to follow. Shit!

He turned over to grip the other pillow for support. At least his mother had been an unexpected rock at the start of the day. He was convinced that telling her about Kieron would have automatically ended in lamentations about his own role as a father and his inability to shield her grandson from harm. She was always so good at that: finding somebody to blame when things went wrong, making clear that when wickedness triumphed it was because of individual culpability. When bad things happened, it had to be somebody's fault. Accidents were simply euphemisms for a failure to admit responsibility. The disasters and calamities that befell the world were nothing but a consequence of human error. Nothing ever happened by chance and nothing was ever pre-ordained either. He wondered what she'd make of one of those Americanisms increasingly doing the rounds, the idea that "shit happens". Not in her world-picture, that was for sure.

He still couldn't quite work out why she'd behaved in the way she had. Was she perhaps getting a bit soft in the head in her old age? Was that why she hadn't berated him or Kieron, why she hadn't been revolted by the thought of what her grandson had been up to in his bedroom and why she hadn't for one moment implied that Rosie was acting against the best interests of all the family in driving them up to Huddersfield? He couldn't imagine getting off quite so lightly had he done anything remotely comparable at Kieron's age. By then the verbal lashings had taken over from the violence of the hand. And had either of these measures done him any real harm? Were there scars he could point to which proved the deeds? Was he a worse individual today for having had such a strict and censorious mother? But sleep was already overcoming him as he struggled to make sense of his philosophical musings and the ceaseless questioning inside his mind.

19

The next morning, after arranging for the younger of her two grown-up daughters to take Kieron and Estelle off their hands for the day, Lucie was in the kitchen with Rosie. 'I'll do two different tray-bakes and some tarts', she said, 'and then when they come back later this afternoon we can all stuff ourselves with cake.' Their mother had taught Lucie and Dulcie how to cook and bake, but by the time Rosie appeared on the scene she'd lost interest in teaching culinary rudiments to the latest member of her brood and moreover had far more pressing things to attend to in the family business. Rosie was left to pick up the few skills she had by observing her eldest sister at work in the house.

As she watched the assorted packets of ingredients being mixed, whisked and kneaded into the right consistency, she sighed and said to Lucie, 'I do wish I had your talent in that department. I just make do with shop-bought stuff and it's never as good as the home-made thing.'

'We all shine in different ways, petal. For me it's always been about two things. Interior design to get me out of the house and then putting good food on the table to get me back inside. It's the one thing I know that keeps Ian close. You know what they say, the shortest way to a man's heart and all that.' The chuckle at the end seemed almost ironic.

Rosie remembered her brother-in-law's attempted grope just days after their mother's death. 'What is it that keeps you together? It's not just food, is it?' she suddenly asked.

'Well, after thirty years, you might well ask! It's certainly not sex, we have nowt of that these days. He's been going elsewhere for his bit on the side. I sometimes think it's a sort of mental illness that some men develop. You know, they need to do it with loads of other women in order to feel reight in themselves.'

'Does he know that you know?'

'The funny thing is we've never actually talked about it. Not openly anyway. I've dropped hints and he's said stuff in a roundabout way. That's putting it politely though. Another word would be lies. The thing is, if it's all out there in front of you, you can't pretend any longer. That's worse, I suppose. Pretending is better. You kid yourself, you paint a smile on your face as part of your make-up, even though it doesn't stop the pain. Dulcie's known for quite a while too. It's OK for family to know. But now, how about yourself? Is it just a rough patch you're going through with your master-builder or do you think it's more serious?'

Rosie was picking at a loose thread in her jumper. She must have snagged it on something sharp that morning. If she pulled it any further she would risk damaging the pattern.

She looked at her sister in weary resignation. 'Is this the way all marriages end up? You run along in close parallel lines for so many years and then one day the trains are shooting off in different directions. I really wanted to get out of the house to sort out in my own head what's happening to me, but I guess I know already. He doesn't want what I want and I don't want what he wants.'

'Are you missing him?'

'You mean now, right now? No, I don't think so. But if I was away for more than a week I think I might.' Then, on an impulse, she asked Lucie, 'Do you think a separation would help?'

Lucie wiped her hands on her apron and placed them on her wide hips. 'Petal, I don't think I'm the right person to answer that.'

'But you're my big sister, Lucie. When I was growing up and our mam was busy, as she nearly always was, if I needed help you were the only one I could turn to. There was no point going to Dulcie. She would have left me to stew in my own juice. She always had her head stuck up in the clouds or her face buried in books. For a long time I think she was really jealous of me being the baby of the family. It's only recently I think I've been able to understand her better.'

'I don't think any of us have ever completely understood Dulcie. She was always so strong-willed, and even our mam couldn't get through to her at times. You were probably too small to remember, but she went through terrible tantrums if I didn't let her play with my dolls. She threw one of them out the window once. She twisted the head off another one. It's just as well she married this drip of a husband she's got. I reckon, if she'd married your Laurence, that would have been the perfect car crash.'

Almost instinctively, Rosie recoiled from the notion of anybody else taking Laurence away from her, even if she sensed Lucie was trying to make a joke out of it. 'Do you think I'm a drip then?'

'You wazzock! What a question!'

'But you seemed to imply that if there's one very strong element in a marriage, it can only work if the other element is a drip.'

Lucie burst out laughing. 'No petal, I'm not saying that. Really I'm not. But you can't have two big personalities living happily together for long under one roof. Sooner or later one of them has to go.' She went on kneading her dough and then suddenly asked, 'Do you still love him?'

Rosie couldn't recall when she'd last been asked that kind of question about Laurence or even when she'd consciously thought about it herself. She'd accepted that the natural corollary of being married to him for seventeen years was that of course she loved him. Now she wasn't so sure.

'Do you still love Ian, knowing what you know about him?'

Lucie's face tightened. 'But that's just it, isn't it? I couldn't swear to it in a court of law that he's been having all these affairs. I couldn't give you names or places. And I haven't hired a private detective either. What good would that do? But everything points in that direction. I can just feel it in me bones.'

Lucie had side-stepped the crucial question. There was the pretence again. For a moment Rosie wondered whether that too was part of the thread that made up the warp and the weft of the Wingfield sisters; you couldn't have openness and honesty without a degree of hypocrisy and deception. Too much bright sunlight meant there were no areas of shade for more tender plants to develop.

She went out through the back door into the long garden that afforded glimpses of the hills in the distance, standing proud against an easterly wind that was rolling in off the North Sea. Just as in her own garden, early frosts here had turned the dahlias into blackened hulks and the withered seed-heads of the old man's beard were clinging to their stems in a last act of defiance. Laurence would be ringing in the evening, at least she'd told him to. Would he actually do it? As she gazed into the ripped shreds of cloud in the late autumnal sky, she couldn't be completely certain.

20

On the Friday evening of the following week Laurence was sitting at home with a takeaway in front of him, watching a sports channel on satellite TV. It had been a productive week in some respects and a disappointing one in others. He'd found the time to go a local barber shop and have the length of his hair reduced by almost half, so that his head looked smaller than before. Above all, he was feeling much better now that his cold was finally on the wane.

When he arrived on the Thursday morning to pick up his mother's shopping list, she approved the cut. 'Your father always kept his hair quite short. "Less bother all round," he used to say, and it's good that you're following his example. Back then all the men had short backs and sides.'

Since there was no reason to hurry home to Marlborough Close after office hours he worked on through the evenings in and out of his existing renovation projects. He always needed to call on qualified plumbers and electricians for the complicated technical side of things, but apart from knocking down walls he was up for a number of less demanding tasks such as plastering walls, basic joinery and fitting kitchen cupboards, as well as all the interior painting. Nobody would have been able to persuade him to take a back seat. When he was project-managing a refurbishment, the more jobs he could do himself the easier it was to maximise his profit.

He'd also had a heart-to-heart with Natasha and made it clear that he couldn't run his business without full and committed support from her. He even went as far as offering her additional hours, but it quickly became apparent that she'd been making her own alternative plans and wanted to start an entirely fresh job in the New Year. That meant he would have to draw up a new job specification and arrange for a corresponding advertisement to go into the next edition of the local paper. He also decided to contact the Job Centre and let them have all the details.

The auction of the Wesleyan chapel was scheduled for the twenty-fifth of the month. He'd had a meeting with a distant friend, one of the architects in the Southampton office where he had once worked straight after uni, and asked him to prepare initial plans for a conversion. Another meeting with his bank manager hadn't gone so well. As he suspected, there was a general reluctance to fund any new projects without a very large percentage of available ready cash and sufficient collateral offered as security. 'We are not going to burn our own fingers, Mr Stewart, not after what has just happened,' was the unyielding response he got.

Even though his mother had been distinctly cool towards his latest grand project, he thought the funds she had received on selling her cleaning business a decade ago might be available to him in some form or other, if the bank wasn't prepared to lend him the money. It all depended on where his mother had invested her capital and how quickly it could be withdrawn. She would surely help him out, if nobody else was prepared to back him. After all, what was so risky and reprehensible about investing in your own family, in your own flesh and blood?

His own family was turning out to be less dependable. When he'd managed to reach Rosie on Saturday evening, she'd been perfectly civil towards him but had reiterated her wish to go into purdah for the next few days. 'Laurence, I told you I thought it best to take a big step back from everything that's happened and not to pick at sores until they've had time to heal,' she had said. 'I'll be back on Friday night and until then I just want some peace and quiet. For myself and the kids.' That had been pretty much all she'd said, and when the short exchange had ended he'd felt he was none the wiser as to the true state of her emotions. Even though he'd offered to tell her more about the meeting he'd had at the police-station, her lack of apparent interest had merely succeeded in pushing him away.

At least Estelle was quick to respond when he reached her mobile on the Sunday. He could tell from her excited chatter that though she was missing him she was enjoying her trips to local shops where Rosie had bought her two new tops. He also managed to speak to Kieron on the same mobile, although their conversation was much shorter because he was being called away by somebody in the background. He wondered how far the emotional state of his own children's lives was now being conditioned by Rosie's own priorities. *It's all wrong*, he thought. *They should be here with me, talking through their problems with me.*

As the days of the new week went by, however, he quickly lost himself in his usual full schedule. On coming home after the additional hours he had put in labouring on site, he fell into bed drained of all physical energy and slept relatively soundly.

Hoping he would have something significant to report back to the rest of the family, he rang the police again on the Thursday. Yes, they'd been investigating a number of leads, both at a national and an international level, and were in close touch with a variety of stakeholders. Yes, it was clearly the tip of an iceberg and the existence of what was called "the dark web" was making it easier for paedophiles to organise criminal activity and to distribute highly pornographic material. Yes, they were doing everything possible to deal with those who had initiated the blackmail attempts, but without hard supporting evidence this could only be part of a long haul. Yes, they'd been in touch with the NSPCC to press their own concerns about online safety. Yes, it was a complication that the original website had been taken down so quickly, thus shutting down that line of inquiry, but then these websites were like mushrooms, popping up all over the place and disappearing without warning once they'd served their purpose. Yes, they would advise closing the Facebook account which had been hacked into and from which the offensive videos had been posted. And no, they couldn't do anything to stop the stories that had already appeared in sections of the press and they certainly wouldn't release any personal information, but ultimately little could be done to stop the investigative actions of a free press in a free society apart from applying for injunctions through the courts in the usual way.

Listening to the inspector overseeing the case, Laurence struggled to remain upbeat. 'What you have to understand, Mr Stewart, is that these days anything that is put out on the internet becomes virtually indelible. Whole generations to come will have to wrestle with the problem of saying and doing things which can't be unsaid and undone once they are circulated on the internet. It's the way society is moving, I'm afraid.'

Against his own better counsels, he decided on the Friday morning to try the school head, Sumner, once more. Nothing positive had yet come from the police, but maybe at school ringleaders had been identified and culprits punished. That would surely reassure Rosie and the kids on their return as well as easing the transition to a new week of school. But even though Laurence managed to get past the gatekeeper, Mrs MacMahon, without having her water-cannon or tear gas trained on him, the conversation with Sumner was just as frustrating as his earlier meeting with him had been. If students chose to engage in extremely foolish activities on the internet, schools could not be held directly responsible. This was where parents had to step up to the plate. The whole episode was indeed highly regrettable, but it was pointless trying to shut the stable door at this stage. The school was currently reviewing the methods it used to alert young people to the many kinds of danger they faced from those who wished to exploit their vulnerability and cause them harm, and it would continue to maintain the closest contacts with parents so that matters could be addressed at several levels. Mr Stewart would see that school management were taking their responsibilities very seriously. At the next governors' meeting this would be a major item on the agenda. Naturally the school had cooperated fully with the police liaison officers, who had interviewed a number of individuals, but there could be no question of any sanctions being applied since the material had been freely available on Facebook and no technical offence had been committed.

Laurence did his best to remain in control while listening to the robotic voice at the end of the line mouthing what sounded suspiciously like pre-rehearsed formulations, all designed to shift the blame and responsibility away from the fine institution whose name – through no fault of its own – had been sullied in this quite reprehensible way. *You jerk, you moron, you piece of shit*, he thought to himself as he put the receiver down. That would not be the end of it. If so little support was forthcoming from that quarter, there would be other good schools in the area who would surely be able to offer Kieron, and perhaps Estelle too, a place. Rosie would doubtlessly see things that way too.

At last there was a text from Rosie, telling him they expected to be back within an hour or so. Cold had been sweeping down the country during the past week and even on the south coast people had been describing the mornings as quite nippy. Rosie and the kids would be bound to appreciate hot mugs of cocoa when they arrived. He pattered into the kitchen and started to make the necessary preparations.

21

On the way back in the car, Rosie did everything she could to deflect her thoughts away from what she knew would be a difficult encounter with Laurence by focusing on what she thought she'd achieved after a week with her sister in Huddersfield. At the end of each day, with Kieron and Estelle safely out of earshot, they had returned to the state of Lucie's marriage as well as to her own. Whichever way they looked at things there seemed to be no easy resolution, no sudden Houdini-like twist which unknotted all knots and left both victims feeling free and fearless about the future. Rosie was left with the impression that it would take something very dramatic for Lucie to give Ian his marching orders. And he clearly saw no reason to disturb the existing domestic arrangements. The thing about lethargy, she thought, was that the longer it went on, the more it clung to your way of thinking. She saw it in others, and she was increasingly conscious of it in her own life.

It had been good to go back to the world of her upbringing, to hear once again the homely earthiness of common speech, the flat vowels and elided consonants. On the Sunday morning as she lay in bed she heard church bells ringing in the distance. As part of the weekend ritual their mam used to drag them to the place of God down the road, all kitted out in similar outfits and carrying little posies, smiling sweetly at Mr So-and-so and Mrs So-and-so as past business was reviewed and future business contemplated. Throughout her childhood she had never been able to escape the feeling that shopkeepers and their families were part of the process of ceremony and circumspection in the local community. You had to keep up appearances, and when the chips were down you had to put on a good face for a bad game. If you wanted to be a rebel, you were asking for trouble.

It was clearly the wrong time of the year to explore the countryside and to keep two teenagers actively occupied. There was a limit to the amount of retail therapy Rosie herself felt comfortable with, though Lucie and her niece clearly had very different ideas. Kieron was frequently left out of things. With no other males in the household and nobody he knew to talk to in the neighbourhood, he'd been pushed back into his shell and was altogether uncommunicative, choosing to spend hours in front of the television set or walking the streets on his own, a hooded figure wrapped up in his own impenetrable thoughts. Rosie's attempts to plumb the depths into which he'd retreated would have required far more energy than she was able to summon up. If she had thought that a week in a different environment would bring about a transformation in the situation, she'd been seriously mistaken. Having come clean about the episode in front of his webcam, her boy was unwilling to elaborate any further. Admitting to the act did not mean he would open up his mind to further close inspection.

If it was the wrong time of the year to be roaming the Yorkshire countryside, it was clearly not the wrong time of the year for Rosie to go with Lucie to the local cemetery and visit the graves of their parents. The two of them stood in their woolly hats and with their collars turned up as icy winds blew papery yellow leaves and fragments of twigs around the gravestones. They looked down at the two small headstones of pale marble, the once shiny surfaces now etched with traces of airborne city grime and marked with the trails of earthbound insects.

Both sighed almost simultaneously. 'Don't you think,' Rosie said to Lucie, 'that our mam and our dad worked themselves into an early grave? Neither of them got to seventy.'

Lucie took Rosie's hand. 'I sometimes think money was more important to them than their own kids. For them it was always about expanding the business.'

Rosie felt a little shocked. 'But we never wanted for anything, did we?'

'It was all right for you, petal. You were the baby of the family. They expected me and Dulcie to help serve the customers after school and on Saturdays. You had your free time, we had to work.'

Not for the first time Rosie was hearing something transmuted from the past, other recollections of childhood than her own seen through a different prism, other realities to set against her own.

Dulcie being the only sister who still worked full-time, a further family reunion had had to wait until later in the week. This had involved a long drive to Beverley and back again, Lucie and Rosie sharing the driving. Kieron and Estelle had scarcely been able to disguise their awkwardness in the presence of their bookish Aunt Dulcie, whose universe revolved largely around the local library where she worked and whom they scarcely remembered from their previous encounters. Her children, their cousins, had long since flown the family nest, and having to listen to three grown-ups endlessly reminiscing about their childhood, the local landscape and the peculiarities of Yorkshire folk made Kieron and Estelle sullen and fidgety. At one stage they both wondered whether the others were talking about somebody called Hayley and then somebody else called Ellie or perhaps it was one and the same person.

'They don't have very much to say for themselves, do they?' was Dulcie's pointed comment to Rosie as they were leaving.

The week had not been an unmitigated success, Rosie thought as she joined the anti-clockwise weekend tailbacks on the M25. At least, she hadn't been worrying about the danger of another mechanical breakdown. The car had been checked very thoroughly by one of Lucie's friends in the motor trade and after a series of additional minor repairs the vehicle was deemed fully roadworthy. That was welcome news ahead of the next MOT. If only fixing marriages was as straightforward as fixing cars. When you worked at a garage you had a set of diagnostic tools that gave you instantaneous readings, output levels and efficiency ratings. Then you knew what you had to do. You cleaned a few bits that were full of unwanted gunge and put them back, you fitted replacements for parts that were worn out, you filled up sumps that needed filling up, you applied lubricants and silicone to metal components, and after that you declared the motor to be almost as good as new. Checking to see if both halves of a human relationship were still in good working order was a much more daunting task. What would you look at first? How did you determine what needed fixing and what could be left as it was? Where would you find the qualified mechanics? Even if you thought you were up to completing the analysis yourself, how would you know which parts to replace, which to discard and which merely required a little fine tuning?

As she swung into Marlborough Close, Rosie was determined she would not engage in any new confrontation with Laurence. It was clear that if the past week had done nothing to banish the troubled state of her marriage – and this was certainly the worst patch she could recollect ever hitting – there were no grounds for thinking that threats, ultimatums or even a decision to waltz off like a dancing queen would leave her better off. There were the children to consider, for a start. One could naturally presume a degree of resilience on their part, but subjecting them both to the major upheaval that a separation, not to mention a divorce, would bring, especially with Kieron facing his GCSEs in half a year's time, would be quite irresponsible. And yet she'd also become aware of the fact that she had a perfect right to set her own red lines, to indicate to Laurence what she was prepared to accept and what not, and to fence off territory where she wasn't prepared to accept any interference from him. She had a right to live her life as she saw fit. But there would always be limits. That much had emerged from the extended conversations she'd had with Lucie.

At first, when Laurence put his big hands around her waist and pressed his lips to her forehead, she wasn't quite sure how to react. Too much in the way of an emotional display might lead him to think that all was forgiven and they could simply turn over a new leaf in the book. Restrained coolness wasn't really in her nature though; she only had to see her mother-in-law to realise how different a person she considered herself to be. She put her hands round his neck and hugged him, without giving him a kiss.

'I've made you all some hot cocoa,' he said. 'And there are ginger biscuits as well.'

She remembered her sister's parkin. 'That was thoughtful of you. I'm not sure I need anything right now. We stopped for a meal just before we got to the M25. But Kieron and Estelle will probably jump at the chance.'

While the children were in the kitchen with their father, Rosie made her way upstairs with a suitcase full of dirty washing and foiled expectations from her week away. She noted that Laurence hadn't bothered to make up his side of the bed. For an orderly man, she thought, that was worthy of a black mark. His orderliness was one of the things she had liked about him when he had first walked into the shop, and she had felt his eyes following her around until she was ready to deal with him. He was always so well turned out – that was his mother's doing, she was sure of that – and she'd never once seen him dress scruffily or inappropriately. No designer beards for him: he would shave assiduously every morning and ensure that his skin was smooth to the touch. When she hugged him there was invariably a whiff of welcome astringency coming from his after-shave or cologne which overlaid – but did not completely conceal – the strong scent of masculinity. She never had to tell him about wrongly-squeezed tubes of toothpaste or leaving the toilet seat up or putting his dirty laundry in the proper basket, unlike Kieron, whose items of clothing she frequently found scattered over the entire first floor. Not that these were ever cardinal issues for her, but it made for less trouble all round. Laurence was good to look at and, whenever they were in company, unfailingly polite to everybody else. But all these things were superficial; they didn't mark out the substance of the man. And that was where the certainties of the past were giving way to the anxieties of the present.

When she returned downstairs, Laurence was sitting with his back to her on the sofa, an arm around each of his children, watching a DVD of some comedy series, all three responding in unison to the rib-tickling moments. Kieron and Estelle had clearly missed him during the week. He could so often be a good father, she mused, when he put his mind to it. When there weren't other things that took precedence.

As she stood looking at them, she struggled to recall what it was that Dulcie had said to her during the week. That was it: 'The way we feel today is only really measurable in terms of the way we felt yesterday.' In other words, Rosie thought, the reason I'm feeling so unhappy right now is because I know I wasn't feeling like this a short while ago. And, knowing that human emotions would be far more difficult to negotiate than inanimate objects, she turned her attention to the week's soiled laundry.

22

One of the few things Rosie felt she had learned from her week away was that blotting out the uncomfortable past and uncertain present and replacing them with an expectant future helped to draw the sting from recent confrontations with Laurence. Excising unpalatable elements from her consciousness also meant she could be selective about where and how to invest her next surge of emotional energy. If she believed that part of her husband's job was to make and keep her happy, just as she would surely have acknowledged a reciprocal role for herself, then instead of dwelling on his failures she needed to focus on opportunities still to come when he might be expected to deliver on his side of the bargain.

Those were the noble sentiments she carried around with her like a lodestone. The reality was different. Long after the children had gone to bed that Friday evening, she busied herself in the kitchen, examining her stock cupboard and making mental lists of shopping she could attend to the next day, inspecting the working surfaces and the fridge to see if Laurence had done anything untoward in her absence (he hadn't), and if he'd bothered to replace the bit of strip lighting that had gone on the blink (he had). She rather hoped he might disappear off upstairs without any further discussion, but just when she had run out of things to do and was considering how she could prolong her pack-load of displacement activities, he appeared in the doorway.

'Hello, love. Can we talk?'

'What about?'

'Everything.'

'I'm quite tired. It's been a long day, especially with all that driving. We might not be able to think straight.'

'I'm tired too. Not just because it's the end of the week, but because I've been busy all week working on that refurbishment in Lindon Road.'

She had a fundamental choice. She could ignore all his approaches, pleading fatigue, and hope he might leave her in peace over the weekend. That would forestall any additional confrontation. All transmissions temporarily suspended, normal service to be resumed later. Or she could yield to her curiosity, having put Laurence off during the week, and discover what exactly the police had said to him and what progress, if any, had been made, after which they might work together on ideas for helping to get the children through the coming week in school. In other words, combining the past and the future but sidestepping the immediate present. Wouldn't that be a much better option for you, her brain appeared to be saying.

Moreover, she didn't want to get into the ins and outs of his fanciful plans for the chapel or any other refurbishment projects, knowing how easily she'd be drawn into making comments about how he saw the world through the prism of his purely selfish priorities. That would have returned her to the here and now. She decided to head for the past.

'What exactly have the police achieved?'

Even before he said anything, she didn't think he'd have very much to report. He was the one who'd been pushing to take what was initially a private family matter into the public domain. He had gone against her declared wishes and better instincts. She had left him in no doubt about that.

She listened to what he had to say with a growing sense of

frustration. Here he now was, with little to show for his misplaced efforts. It was all very well for him to act like a government spokesperson at a press conference, mouthing the ways in which the internet was increasingly being used for criminal activities of all kinds and stressing the number of cases that had come to light about the "grooming" (terrible word, she thought) of under-age children. She didn't need to listen to the voice of officialdom, she didn't need to hear about any national or even global perspectives, she didn't need to be given statistics or trends. All she had in mind, all she wanted to concentrate on, was the welfare of her own son. And she told Laurence as much.

'I've already been thinking about that. We've got to take him away from his school and enrol him somewhere else.'

She was aghast. 'Why would you even think of doing that? That would involve far too much upheaval and disruption. There's his GCSEs to think about. Never mind the loss of all his friends.'

'Friends? Fine friends, if you ask me. They didn't exactly stick by him when it all came out.'

'You don't know that. You only know what some of the others in the school did. You can't tar everybody with the same brush. And what about Estelle anyway?'

'Well, we can move her too.'

'We? Have you actually stopped to ask yourself what our children might want? Here you are, deciding things again without consultation.'

She felt the sharp words ringing like loud bells in her ears. She had declined to follow the course outlined by her brain; she had opted to remain in the present; gut instincts had overridden counsels of caution. It was well past midnight, but the night shift hadn't been properly briefed by the daytime staff.

Still standing in the kitchen doorway, across the table from her, his eyes had sought the warmth of a smile he knew was hers to give, a confirmation in her voice that all his efforts had been worthwhile, that they shared in wanting the best for their two lovely children. But it was like looking at a different person.

Something had driven her away from him in the past seven days. She was imputing motives he didn't have. In suggesting they move Kieron and Estelle to a different school he had been guided simply by the belief that this would lead to far less distress than leaving things as they were. A parent with little sense of responsibility wouldn't even have considered a change to the status quo. If he hadn't cared what happened to his kids, he'd have told them to ride out the ribbing and the bullying on their own, casting them adrift on the high seas of an unhelpful school environment.

'I don't think we can expect any support from Sumner.'

'Sumner?'

'Yes. I went to see him after I took Kieron to the police, and I phoned him up yesterday.'

'You didn't tell me about that.'

'You didn't give me a chance, did you? You kept pushing me away.'

So that was how he saw things. She was pushing him away. She was the one who wouldn't let him do what he wanted to do. She was the bad cop. Her entire energies had been directed towards giving them all a proper breathing space as far away from the scene of the crime as possible and without her having to listen to accounts of his tit-for-tat encounters with players on the periphery. Apparently, he was hell bent on justifying every single action of his.

'I can't deal with this. Not now. I'm going to bed.'

They undressed in silence and once in bed she turned her back towards him, clutching her pillow with her left hand. Sensing the right arm by her side, Laurence stretched out an exploratory hand. She feigned sleep and made no response.

23

While he was shaving the next morning, Laurence examined the face in the mirror. Did he really have 'I am an ogre' stamped on his brow? Was that how his wife now viewed him? What had she and her sisters been up to in the week? Why had she come back with the needle still in the same groove, producing the same niggly undertones he'd heard a week ago? All he wanted was for them to put the recent storm-clouds behind them and to focus on returning the craft and all its passengers to a safe and welcoming harbour. All week he'd missed the warmth coming from her side of the bed, the touch and scent of her hair when he kissed her face in the morning and at night, the sparkle of the blue-green eyes and the brightness and openness of the face that had first captivated him, something so different from what he'd seen in his previous girlfriends. When he looked into it, it was like gazing down at the bottom of the swimming-pool where as a nine-year-old he had first learned to swim. The water was clear, there was no murkiness, the floor was unmarked, there were no dark corners where sirens might lurk, ready to pull the unsuspecting swimmer below the surface. He never for one moment believed she could be capable of any deception. Honesty was one of her defining characteristics. If there was something in their relationship that was now clouding that water, she'd surely tell him. He needed to have it out with her over the breakfast-table before he went off to the Lindon Road project.

Laurence rarely had much to eat for breakfast, tending to pile up the calories later in the day and especially in the evening. The effects of the burgers or meat-filled sandwiches at lunchtime and the crisps and sugary snacks together with the beers in the evening were visible on his waistline. Once the calories had set up permanent camp there, they could not be shifted. His physical exertions on site did little to change that. The children had always been fickle about their requirements. Estelle, like her mother, confined herself to a bowl of cereal, although she'd gone through a phase of wanting eggs prepared in a variety of different ways – boiled, fried and poached – before instructing Rosie when she entered secondary school that she now expected grown-up food, with a preference for Eggs Benedict every morning. When he was younger Kieron had munched his way through endless slices of toast, with each of the four quadrants covered in a different-coloured and different-flavoured jam or marmalade. For some time he'd been finding it increasingly difficult to match his body rhythms to circadian conventions, sleeping so long in the mornings that he often stumbled off to school without having eaten or drunk anything, so that with a cry of anguish Rosie would tear after him before he could cycle away and push an apple into his satchel. At the weekends, however, all four of them sat around the kitchen table together. There would be glasses of freshly-squeezed orange juice and a cooked breakfast which Rosie did her best to vary in its constituent parts, leaving Laurence and the children to guess without looking at the frying-pans which combination of the variables they could expect. Bacon was a staple and eggs too, though here the presentation might vary, but then more often than not the plates would contain at least three other items: tomatoes, mushrooms, black pudding, sausages, baked beans, grilled peppers, hash browns, fried bread. Even if she wasn't quite as good a cook as his own mother, Rosie was determined to dish up a lot of colour on the plate. She always made an extra effort.

'Kieron, chick,' Rosie suddenly said while the others were still eating. 'We need to talk about next week in school.'

Laurence looked across at her. She'd pre-empted him. 'If anybody wants to be nasty to you, you can be much stronger in your responses if you think for a moment about how you're going to react.'

Kieron said nothing. Laurence cut into the silence. 'Son, there's something else you might like to consider.'

Rosie gave Laurence a sharp look, interjecting quickly, 'My lamb, you and Estelle can give each other all the support you need. It'll be difficult for both of you, I know. That's why we should talk about it now.'

Kieron turned to his father. 'What's the "something else"?'

'Look, there's no reason why you need to remain at that school. It's not just the – you know – the blackmail thing and the videos, there's that English teacher who's making life difficult for you. A fresh start would mean you could wipe the slate clean.'

Laurence could tell from the way she was eyeing him that Rosie was not prepared to let him have a free run. 'We want you to decide what you really want to do,' she said. 'It won't be easy having to find your footing and settle down in a new place. Anyway, you'll miss all your friends if you move from Moss Hill.'

Kieron looked from his mother to his father. 'What other schools are there?'

'As far as I know, we're in the catchment area for two other places. If you like, we can look at their websites and I can take you to look at them from the outside.'

'Laurence!' He was hearing his mother's admonitory tone in what Rosie was saying. 'One of your reasons for getting us to move from Gosport Road was so we could be close to Moss Hill. You said it was the best school in our area.'

'Back then perhaps. But it's rather gone downhill under Sumner. I wouldn't be confident of the same ranking today.'

They usually tried not to argue in front of their children,

especially where matters of discipline and upbringing were concerned. But Laurence knew from past instances that Rosie was much less keen on taking a hard line than he was. She saw in any of her children's transgressions the opportunity for rehabilitation. Moreover, she was particularly good at exposing inconsistencies in any arguments he might advance, with or without the children in earshot, so he could almost have predicted what kind of intervention she would make next.

'I thought you wanted our children never to run away from a problem but to confront it head-on,' she said. 'If Kieron leaves Moss Hill, how does that demonstrate backbone?' And as she saw his mouth beginning to form a rejoinder, she quickly added what a short while later he acknowledged to be her final killer thrust. 'And let's get one thing straight. Don't think for one moment that in a town like this what happened at Moss Hill can be kept in a vacuum. People have a habit of talking. Sooner or later the kids in any new place will find out why Kieron moved schools half-way through the year. And then we'd be back to square one.'

Kieron's eyes went from his father to his mother. 'Mum's right, dad,' Estelle suddenly piped up. 'When he goes back they might give Kieron a hard time to begin with, but they'll quickly find something else to bang on about.'

Laurence attempted to conceal his astonishment. Here was his own daughter saying what he would have expected to say himself in the self-same circumstances. *It'll all blow over, things are never as bad as they seem, don't make mountains out of molehills.* All sentiments close to his own heart, principles that had held him in good stead in the past, phrases he would have been happy to voice now as a descant to the tune Rosie was playing. So why hadn't he done so? He could find no explanation.

'Kieron, son, it's for you to decide,' Laurence said after draining the last of his orange juice. 'Whatever you want to do, your mum and I will support you.'

Rosie avoided any sense of triumph at halting Laurence's steamroller approach. She only wanted what was in Kieron's own best interests, playing games was what others might do.

'Why don't we sit down later this morning and chew over everything together?' she said as she squeezed Kieron's hand. 'And if you want to stay where you are, we can think of ways to get you through the coming week.'

'That'll have to be without me, I'm afraid,' Laurence said. 'I need to be working at Lindon Road for most of the day. But we'll catch up again this evening.'

He was quickly gone, having no desire to linger after a defeat, wanting only to move on and put the unpleasantries at the breakfast-table behind him. So typical, Rosie thought. He puts himself first and his family comes second. She hurried to find a warm coat to shield herself against the adversities of a cool morning and then hopped into her hatchback before heading off to stock up with supplies for the weekend.

24

When she awoke early on Monday the seventeenth, Rosie's first thought was her determination to make a success of the day ahead. Laurence had come back on the Saturday evening with a new mobile phone for Kieron, not another top-of-the-range smartphone but a basic device that was eminently serviceable. That meant he could again be reached and he in turn could keep in touch by texting. Before Laurence rushed out of the house on the Saturday morning a similar idea had occurred to Rosie, yet somehow she'd neglected to mention it to him and as the day progressed the idea drifted down her list of priorities. Secretly she was pleased he had thought ahead and acted for once with the family's interests in mind. As soon as the new school week started, she would insist that Kieron keep her updated during the day and would ask Estelle to keep an eye on him in the breaks and over lunch.

She spent a couple of hours after returning from her shopping expedition coaching both her children on how best to deal with what she was convinced would turn out to be a tricky situation. She also made a mental note to ring the school office and, despite Laurence's reservations about their ability to do so, remind all concerned of their duty to administer appropriate pastoral care.

She was finding it difficult to view Kieron as a sexual being.

For fifteen years he'd been her little lamb, her chick, and she wasn't quite ready to relinquish her maternal desire to protect and possess. Deep down, however, she knew that the gradual transformation from boyhood to manhood would soon be complete. The world of innocence was a thing of the past. She could never stop loving him, regardless of what was to come, but she accepted that her love for him would have to be shared one day with the woman he chose to be with. He was just a few years from disappearing off to college and then the process of cutting the links to hearth and home would accelerate. The family would be in retreat.

She made another mental note to raise the matter when she next spoke to Lucie on the phone and find out how she coped after her own two daughters had flown the nest. Being somebody's child was difficult; being the parent equally so. She remembered how, as the headstrong but naïve individual she had been at eighteen, she had flouted all the warnings her parents had issued about needing to safeguard her own future and the dangers of rushing off down south to be with Adam as he started his teacher training. All she remembered were the energy-sapping rows and the fact she had nobody to turn to, Lucie and Dulcie having already escaped into the big wide world that she herself couldn't wait to explore. Then, years later, as the caprice she had taken to be everlasting reality slowly fell apart, the realisation took hold that all her parents had really wanted to do was to protect their little baby from the setbacks and disappointments of a world infinitely more complex than she had imagined. Yet, as she thought again of Kieron, Rosie also knew she would be powerless to shield him entirely from whatever awaited him at Moss Hill.

The next morning she was once again awake before the alarm told her what to do, feeling the mysterious waves of heat rippling through her body and making her want to throw off the bedclothes in a calculated act of defiance. She heard the slightly irregular breathing coming from the other side of the bed, the way in which Laurence seemed to gulp in the air around him and then pause, sometimes almost interminably, before releasing it again in fitful spurts. She'd only seen him briefly on the Saturday evening, having spent the rest of the day at Florabellum, working in the shop and making final preparations for today's big event. Yesterday had again seen a clash of sorts after Kieron and Estelle disappeared for the day. Laurence told her his mother would be happy to postpone the feast until the Tuesday evening, so that they could all go as one family.

'I don't think that would be a good idea. Not at the moment.'

'Why's that?'

'There's enough frostiness all round. Kieron isn't going to be a bundle of joy, you and I still need to sort out some issues and your mother and I don't exactly cut it either. In case you hadn't noticed.'

'Rosie, Rosie, what's happening to you? What's happening to us?' Laurence had said, and the slightly patronising tone had immediately put her back up.

She had wavered for a moment, as uncertain as before about the emotions that were competing within her, unwilling to declare a new offensive while still considering the effectiveness of the more recent skirmishes. But then the floodgates had opened.

'It's always the same with you, and I'm getting tired of it. It's one scheme after another, one big idea after the next that you seem intent on pushing through, no matter what the rest of us think or want.' And then, fighting back a few tears, 'I'm beginning to think there's no more point to this marriage.'

She had stunned him into utter silence. She in turn was incredulous that he didn't immediately set about justifying his every action and making it clear to her why he was right and she was wrong. That was what she had expected him to do. Eventually, after they had glared fiercely at each other across the kitchen-table, he had quietly said, 'I think you're being ridiculous.' That had merely made matters worse. The one thing she was becoming increasingly sensitive about was his tendency to patronise her. She had stood up without a word and gone out into the back garden. It was a windy day, with blotchy clouds billowing across the sky like endless lines of washing that had failed to pass the Persil test. She hated having to admit to herself that the seventeen years of this marriage might yet turn out to be another caprice, that perhaps her whole life was destined to be a succession of caprices, extended moments when her heart was full of warm desire followed by the bitter realisation that nothing was forever, that the day would always give way to the night, and that no matter how hard she tried she couldn't will herself into a permanent state of happiness. Or, at the very least, contentment.

Only the previous morning she had gazed at the withered signs of life in her garden, at the browns and yellows and ochres, memories of what had once been. She knew that a few months from now little spikes of green would once again be pushing up from inside the brown earth, overcoming all the resistance from above, and that the dry bare limbs would eventually be crowned with tiny buds swelling and filling with energy until they burst open in explosions of vibrant spring colour. That was nature. What could she expect from what she took to be the desiccated stalks of her own marriage? She simply didn't know. She only knew that deep down she wanted to be lifted up and transported to a different landscape, where things were green and fresh and not brown and stale. At the same time she wasn't prepared to put her children through any unnecessary upheaval. That wouldn't be right.

25

On the other side of the bed, Laurence was beginning to stir. The previous night he had lain awake for some considerable time, willing his mind to shut down and accept the inevitability of sleep, but it plainly had other ideas. Fragments of their conversation over the kitchen-table had made an unwelcome return, lining up like members of a Greek chorus to chant in unison, "No more point to this marriage." No more point, no more point. She was over-reacting, she must be, he thought. Marriages don't break apart because of disputes over the children. A relationship doesn't automatically collapse because it is put under strain. He had hoped she would have returned from Huddersfield refreshed and keen to put their disagreements to one side. Instead, the once bright face with its ready smile looked tired and drained of vitality. Whatever he said during the day seemed to consist of the wrong words or the wrong tone or both, judging by the reactions he was getting.

By the time he got back on the Saturday evening it was clear that Kieron had made up his mind to stay where he was and face the music rather than make a fresh start elsewhere. He wasn't sure whether Rosie had applied much pressure while he'd been out, though he sensed from Kieron's face over breakfast that his chances of ever winning the basic argument were slim. On his return he therefore saw no reason to re-open the discussion and accepted his defeat with good grace, enjoying the hug Kieron gave him and the moment of delight as he handed over the new mobile. That should have been the end of it. He'd lost, she'd won. Kieron and Estelle knew how they were going to get through the coming week. Move on, don't pick at scabs, look to the future. And then on the Sunday morning, with just the two of them left at the table after breakfast, the face no longer glowed in his direction. All he really wanted to do was take his whole family with him to celebrate his mum's birthday on the Tuesday, to bring everything and everyone together again. Instead, Rosie had spoken of frostiness and had once again brought the antagonism with her mother-in-law into play. Nothing new had happened to affect that relationship; they hadn't spoken on the telephone (no surprise there), nor had he introduced any additional element into the proceedings. He wasn't the one upsetting the apple-cart: they always went to his mum's for their regular feasts, save the one occasion when Rosie was laid up in bed with flu and the time when Kieron was still in the middle of a school exchange to France. These rituals were one of the things they did as a family, it was what helped to define them. None of the goalposts had been changed, so he couldn't understand why she was making such an issue of it.

Women were funny, he thought. Such beautiful creatures with such adorable personalities, but they were hard-wired in different ways. After almost eighteen years he thought he knew his little Rosie inside out, knew her little ways, knew how he could tease her and then enjoy their moments of happy communion afterwards, knew how to look into the openness of her gentle face and feel his own optimism reflected in her constancy towards him. After all this time he thought he had worked out which buttons he needed to press to be certain of her response, only to discover that the batteries in the remote control had gone completely flat.

He moved onto his side. He felt a familiar ache between his legs, the ache of desire for this woman lying just inches away, so tantalisingly close. He could smell her more keenly in the mornings than at any other time of day, the smell of familiarity and longing that was drawing her closer to him, despite all their differences. He stretched out a hand and found the small of her back. He rubbed it gently.

'Laurence, what are you doing?' She was clearly awake.

'Rosie, love, can't we just forget our differences?'

'It's not as easy as you think. Too much has happened recently.'

'But we can work through all that. We've got so much together.'

'I'm beginning to think there's more that we don't have.'

He rolled towards her and placed a hand on her breast. She twisted away from him.

'There you go again. You think I'm available to you whenever you want it.' The moment she said it, she regretted it. She realised she couldn't remember when they had last made love, yet she wasn't prepared to surrender to further intimacy merely because he believed that would automatically put things right again. Part of her yearned to feel the strength of his limbs enclosing her body, his teeth nibbling at her ears, the warmth of his cuddles. But the other half resisted, arguing that she would be utterly powerless to deny him whatever he wanted, that she would be a mere puppet in his hands, speaking the lines he wanted to hear and moving in tune to his own rhythms.

'Rosie, Rosie.' He placed a hand on the nape of her neck.

'Not now, Laurence. I have too many things to see to. Today's a big day.'

Later that morning he texted Kieron and received an immediate response. The rumpus surrounding the circulation of videos that showed a pupil of the school performing sex acts in front of a camera had subsided during the intervening ten days. Teenage exploits were clearly like so many news stories in the media: blanket coverage with an obsessive interest in every minor detail, and then the caravan simply moved on to the next best thing. Perhaps the prurience was understandable: which teenager was not interested in sex? Perhaps those who had stored the material on their phones would soon find something else to titillate the toxic mix of hormones, immaturity and inexperience swilling through their minds. Perhaps his son would not be remembered months later as Wanker Stewart. But perhaps also the world would always need its daily fix of sensationalism, perhaps there would always be victims, just as there were always winners and losers.

Perhaps, perhaps, perhaps. Perhaps Rosie wouldn't be so sore with him by the end of the month. Perhaps she would slowly come to realise that the chapel project was the kind of fresh start they all needed. Perhaps then it would be much easier to consider alternative schooling for Kieron, assuming the environment at Moss Hill was still a concern. All he had to do was to hold fast to the course he had set. Given fair winds and a good sprinkling of fortitude, things would come right in the end. They always did.

He rarely liked doing any physical work prior to an evening engagement, unless he was able to freshen up afterwards. Getting hot and sweaty a few hours before his mother's feast was not a course of action he would normally have considered, but the Lindon Road project was in its final stages. There was only the one back bedroom with the rotten floorboards that still needed sorting out. The replastering of the walls was finished, the painting in the other rooms only required last bits of touching-up, the electrics and plumbing were in place save for the new combination boiler that was due to be installed later in the week. All that was still left on the agenda were the fitting of the new kitchen and the laying of the carpets. The sooner he finished off what he was able to do himself, the closer he would be to putting the house on the market or advertising it as a rental. Turnaround times in this business were key. Any initial delays in the paperwork or sorting out and supervising the contractors, or the emergence of hidden problems in the fabric of the property once the refurbishment was under way, put back the point when he could look at the total spend and see what kind of profit he was destined to make. During the previous week, with Rosie and the kids away, he'd worked flat out and made good progress. Now he just needed to assess the damage to the wood and measure up for the replacement timber. It would take at most an hour, he thought. Even though there was no hot water available in the property as yet, he would change from his suit to the overalls he kept on site and then scrub up in cold water afterwards before setting off for Horndean. No time to double back through rush-hour traffic to Marlborough Close and shower there, though that option would have enabled him to see and talk to Kieron.

But when he got to the end-of-terrace property in Lindon Road, just as the street-lamps were being switched on in the fading afternoon light, he could see that the front door had been forced open. His heart sank. The street had two opposing terraces of Victorian two-uppers and two-downers, some of which had been forcefully dragged by their new owners into the twenty-first century so that little of the erstwhile period charm remained. Double-glazing had largely replaced the sash windows, concealed porches had been closed off and given tiny ante-chambers to the outside world like excrescences, and in a few cases pale render had been applied to the attractive red brickwork. However, the street was conveniently located for the motorway and a train station and it was in an up-and-coming area. That was the reason Laurence had immediately sensed potential when he had first come across the property and he was particularly pleased to have cut a deal with the two heirs who owned it before it even went to auction.

He had wanted to retain the original front door, so it had been sanded down and repainted, but the existing frame was unsuitable for a modern five-lever mortice deadlock system. He could see that jemmies had been used to drive into the space between the door and the frame. He pushed his way into the hall and felt for the light-switch. In the gloom he could only feel a tangle of wires. Christ, he thought, that's all I need right now. He went back to his BMW, fished out a torch from the glove-box and then surveyed the damage.

The new switchboard had been dismantled and the mains supply cut off. All the light-switches, power-points and door-handles had been removed. More was to come. The kitchen units and the new appliances still in their packaging which he had taken delivery of on the Saturday and placed in what was intended to be the kitchen-diner at the back of the property had vanished. The copper pipes for the new heating system that he had already painted together with the radiators they were designed to service were nowhere to be seen. *Fuck, fuck, fuck!*

His first thought was that this had to be an inside job. No simple cat-burglar would have had the skill to fiddle around with the mains supply or been in possession of the blowtorches needed to uncouple piping from radiators. This could only have been a team, presumably working in the night, either on the Saturday or the Sunday, whose main aim was to strip the property of anything that could be passed on within the trade or sold cheaply as job-lots. Laurence knew all about the increasing instances of metal thieves operating under the cover of darkness. Not only railway tracks were being targeted but wrought-iron railings and gates outside residential properties. And then off to the nearest scrapyards or metal specialists with the booty, no questions asked. If the bankers were stealing assets from the people, the criminal under-classes were not far behind. People were desperate to make a fast buck.

He took out his mobile and called the police. Next he walked down to the adjoining house in the row and rang the bell. After a long pause a wizened old figure opened the door, blinking at him as if from another world.

'I'm sorry to bother you,' Laurence said. 'I own the property next door. You may have heard some of the refurbishment work going on. I was last here on Saturday and I've just come back to find the place burgled. Well, stripped of most of the interior fittings, to be precise. I was just wondering whether you might have heard or seen anything.'

As he spoke, the old woman edged closer cupping her right

ear. She straightened up and then shook her head.

'That's awful. I don't know what the world's coming to.'

'So you didn't hear or see anything,' Laurence repeated.

'No dear, I am sorry. I hope they catch whoever did it.'

So do I, thought Laurence, so do I. You spend almost every day of the week working your fingers to the bone in order to give yourself and your family a better life, and then before you know it there are others who make a mockery of all your hard work. Something for nothing was the name of the game they played. Except there were no rules, they just took any chance that came their way, leaving you to pick up the pieces (if there were any left).

In his mind he ran through the list of contractors who'd been to the property in recent weeks to carry out essential works, people he'd worked with before and who'd given him a fair deal this time round. But he quickly remembered that he'd never actually been there while any of the labour was being carried out. He could get in touch with his associates and quiz them about which individuals had been sent to Lindon Road to do the work. But how would that look, casting aspersions on the integrity of other people's staff? And what if the gaffers themselves had been responsible? Where would that leave him?

It was over half an hour before the police arrived, but Laurence was no clearer about what else he needed to do. The formalities though were rapidly concluded, photographic evidence taken and official tape secured around the front door. There would have been no point in him attempting to deal with the floorboards in the gloom of a house without electricity. Not much chance of any forensic evidence either, one of the policemen had commented. Virtually all the metal parts in the house had been purloined, and given the fact that those involved were all professionals the gang would have been wearing gloves anyway.

As he drove out towards Horndean, Laurence could feel a head of steam building inside him. Repeated instances of injustice and him right in the middle of it. First one criminal gang making

Kieron's life hell and now another determined to cash in, albeit in a different way. And then there was Rosie playing up, making him feel that somehow he was the one who had done wrong and needed to be punished. For fuck's sake, what had he done to deserve all this?

His mother was beaming at him in the open door. 'You are more or less on time, my wee one.'

'Happy birthday, mum. I haven't brought you any flowers this time, but I've got you a present. I hope you like it.'

Laurence handed over the box in its black-and-gold gift wrapping. She shook it gently, then sniffed. Her eyes lit up. 'I think I know what this is.'

He had grown up with her cleanliness, her mania for scrubbing. It was one of his first impressions of childhood. If he left any tide-marks in the wash-basin or bath-tub, or allowed any water to spill onto the floor, or the careless spray of toothpaste from the act of brushing his teeth to mist the mirrored wall cabinet, she would be on to him. And if he ate messily and failed to contain the crumbs from his toast within his plate, or clumsily sent dollops of gravy from the Sunday roast onto the table-cloth, she would remind him, 'Somebody's going to have to deal with that. Now who might that be?' And as he grew older, she would again repeat the very same words with an ironic smile playing around her lips, as if they both knew it was all part of yet another family ritual.

There was always the scrubbing and the polishing in addition to the hoovering. Everything had to be spick-and-span, objects had to be tidied away whenever they were not needed, and yet order was important because you always had to be able to find things when required. It was always the same when she came home from her days spent cleaning for others. He knew she wore plastic gloves to protect her hands from the sharp disinfectants, detergents and other cleaning materials, but no sooner was she back in the house than she would wash her hands with scented soap at the kitchen sink. Then she would spend several minutes rubbing the lanolin lotion over her palms and the back of her hands as well as between her fingers.

He had once asked her, 'Mum, why is it you always have to wash your hands when you come back home?' She had looked at him as though he had questioned her very own existence and replied firmly, 'It's to remove all the traces of grime from this ugly world of ours and take away the smell of plastic on my hands.' It was yet another of her rituals, one of the many that marked the different stages of her waking day but which he knew made her life more controllable.

Her grey eyes softened and twinkled as she opened the box and took out each cake of soap from the cushioning surrounds. 'Mmm. Tea rose, jasmine and lavender. My favourite scents. You are such a considerate wee boy.'

He followed her into the kitchen. There was an enticing smell coming from the oven. 'What have you been cooking?'

'Because it's only the two of us tonight, I haven't pulled out all the stops. You've had this main course before, though it's a long time ago and you've probably forgotten. It's Chicken Provençale, an Elizabeth David recipe. Come on, let's have our starter.'

Between bites of the pie with a filling of goat's cheese and red onion, he told her about the break-in. She looked at him with a face of motherly concern. 'I hope you're properly insured.'

He shook his head. 'I don't think the house insurance policy covers the fittings, though I'd have to check that. It certainly wouldn't include the boxes with the kitchen units. That would be household insurance. Even if I'm fully covered, there's still an excess waiver, and afterwards they'd have good reason to put up the premiums. And do you know what's even worse than having to clear up all this mess? I'm beginning to think I can't trust people. Why was the place targeted when it was? Knowledge must have been passed on through the grapevine. It can only have been someone who was already working there. There's no other explanation. And who do I point the finger at?'

'Do you think somebody might have borne you a grudge?'

'Me, mum? I've always tried to be fair to the guys I work with. Always. We all want to get on.'

'Aye, but if you put temptation in front of people, not everybody can resist. Your dad always used to say that they could never stop even the stinking rich from nicking things from the cabins. Towels, bathrobes, tooth-mugs. Anything that wasn't screwed down solid. I suppose for some it must have been the thrill of walking off with things that didn't belong to them, even perhaps the thrill of the fear of getting caught.'

'I bet nothing much happened to them even if they were.'

'Your dad said that liners were a bit like luxury hotels. You wanted repeat business, so you couldn't really afford to annoy any of the customers. But then it's a bit like supermarkets these days. They know they're going to lose stock through shoplifting, so they take account of that when they do their prices.'

'It seems to me that if you're a small-time criminal or just a housewife in need, if you end up nicking from a supermarket you don't get treated the same way that people in five-star hotels or on cruise-ships do.'

'Yes, Laurence, but why do people find themselves in need in the first place? You have to pay your way, you don't have an automatic entitlement to goods just because the advertising industry tells you so. Cut your coat according to the cloth you have. Plain and simple.'

Laurence immediately knew where the discussion was heading. She must have been soaking up every single negative story in her favourite tabloid without much critical reflection, as she often did when she watched the television news. With very few receptive ears to harangue during the daytime, the presence of her son provided Roberta Stewart with a welcome opportunity to comment on the unacceptably high levels of personal debt, the unacceptably high bankers' bonuses and the unacceptably high sums of money Brussels was again wasting. Laurence sat and allowed the tidal wave of agitated voter fury to wash over himself. He knew she needed to get it all out before they could turn their attention to other matters.

At last his mother remembered the casserole steaming away in the oven and returned to place its contents, with their heady sun-drenched aroma of herbs, on the table.

'You haven't told me yet why you didn't all want to come tomorrow.'

Laurence looked down at his plate and avoided his mother's watchful gaze. Every stepping-stone in their conversation had taken him merely from one instance of perfidious human nature to the next, examples of the world slithering around in a morass. He sighed.

'Mum, did you ever go through a really difficult phase with Dad? You know, a point when you felt you weren't really getting on?'

Her eyebrows indicated incomprehension. 'Whatever put that idea into your head? Your dad was the most wonderful man you could ever hope to meet. He was such a loving father to you too. We never had so much as a cross word together.' There was now a mistiness to her eyes. 'Even now, after all this time, I still don't know why our lives had to be torn apart. You and I didn't deserve this. We could have been so happy together.' He wanted to reach out and comfort her in their joint sense of loss, but before he could react she went on, 'There's something wrong with Rosie, isn't there?'

Again he felt torn. He hated the idea of being disloyal to Rosie by admitting to his mother that his own marriage couldn't compete with the idyllic memory she had of her own, and he could not knock on the head the current worries that clung to him like burrs after a walk through scrub vegetation. His energy levels were at a low ebb, compounded by the grey and gloomy days of the month and the cold that had left him feeling drained and strained. The circles of his professional and personal life, which he had sought to keep within neat and delineated boundaries, were beginning to coalesce. Neither of them could be seen as a refuge from the other. There was only one person who knew him better than he knew himself. It was to his mother he felt he now had to turn.

'Nothing I do or say at the moment seems right to her,' he told her. 'It's as though she no longer trusts me. And I can't see that I've changed at all. Mum, why do I do what I do? It's not just for me, it's for her too. For all of us.' He stopped suddenly, beginning to feel he was the patient on a therapist's couch. He was no longer in control. The raw emotions inside were bubbling up to the surface, deflecting him from the course he had set.

'Laurence, you know I really don't want to interfere. It's your own life and you have to lead it as best you can. You stick to your principles even if...' She paused and in turn he looked questioningly at her.

'Go on.'

'I was going to say,' and she paused again. 'Even if others don't stick to theirs.'

It was a coded message, that much was clear. She'd avoided mentioning her by name. That was what she nearly always did. The roundabout way of indicating that two things were not as perfectly aligned as they needed to be. That two beings were not properly matched, as the natural order of things would have dictated. The consequences, however, were for others to draw. Sooner or later it had to happen: a cloth that had been stitched together at speed without due care would begin to come apart at the seams. You couldn't yoke different threads together and expect them to form the yarn that produced the perfect material. He knew what she was thinking; he'd heard the same fragments of speech before, evolving and revolving in so many of their conversations, spiking each past homily with the forcefulness of her inner convictions. Having made one message clear, she would move on seamlessly to the next subject she had in mind.

'I hope you've now given up on this chapel idea of yours. There wouldn't be any point, would there? Not now. And you've never been remotely religious, so where would have been the attraction in living in a place where they used to sing "Nearer, my God, to

Thee?"'

Another coded message. Why pursue the notion of moving the family from one place to an entirely different one, if the fabric was already coming apart? Good old Mum, at least she was being consistent.

'Mum, I don't think you understand. It's a wonderful opportunity for development.' Then in an attempt to confront her thought processes, 'It really doesn't matter who ends up living there. It would make a fantastic home.'

'I hope you don't overstretch yourself. That would not be a good idea at all. These are risky times.'

He considered asking if he could count on her financial support if the need arose, but decided that the moment was not yet opportune. She, meanwhile, had decided to move the conversation on yet again.

'How's my grandson, how's Kieron? I was so looking forward to seeing him this week.'

'Well, he's texted me twice today and it seems as though he's managed to keep the demons at bay. I think he was most worried about facing more humiliation in front of all his mates.'

'Is he still playing on his computer?'

'Rosie and I haven't stopped him using it. There wouldn't have been much point anyway. Now he's had his fingers burned he won't go near the fire again.'

'But you said he'd been watching pornography. That cannot be the right thing for him to be doing. Can't you put a stop to that?'

'We did talk about that briefly. It's every parent's nightmare. But it's not as easy as you might think. Kieron's a savvy kid and there are ways of getting round all these parental blocks. That's not the main problem though. It's the availability elsewhere that matters. That's one of the things the police were quick to point out. You know, it's a bit like access to alcohol. You can ban all that stuff from your own home, but there'll always be a kid somewhere that can lay his hands on enough booze for a wild party the rest of them end up going to. We've warned both Kieron and Estelle over and over again about all these dangers. Banning things won't always work.'

'Well, it wouldn't have happened in my time. And even if it had, I'd have made sure that sanctions were in place.' With that she pushed back her chair from the table and announced she was going to bring in the dessert.

When they'd finished their Eton mess, she reminded him of the last ritual of the day. They went into the front room, where she poured out the Drambuie into the crystal glasses, pointing hers towards the shrine on which the golden-framed photographs were displayed. He looked across to the faded sepia photograph of the young Paterson family with the two little daughters in the middle, to the solitary figure of his grandfather Fergus, standing with a pipe clenched between his teeth at his garden gate, to the much bigger one of his Auntie Joyce perched on a wall and swinging her legs at the camera, and then to the heart of the collection which showed him on a local beach, a few months after his third birthday, tightly gripping the hands of his mother and father as they gazed absent-mindedly into the distance.

'To absent family,' his mother said.

While he gently sipped the warming liquid, he couldn't help thinking that at this stage his own Rosie would almost certainly have been far from her mind.

26

When Rosie left the house, long after she'd kissed and hugged Kieron and Estelle goodbye and somewhat sheepishly pushed a birthday card for her mother-in-law into Laurence's hands, she went straight to Florabellum to start work on the individual table arrangements and the large display intended for the reception counter. Lorna was busy in the front of the shop, but whenever there was a lull in customer traffic she came into the stock-room where Rosie was busy sorting and selecting from the array in front of her.

'This is looking good,' she said. 'I'm sorry I can't come to the party tonight, but Pete and I are taking the kids to a concert in Southsea. A family treat we arranged some time ago.'

Treats, Rosie thought, are for other families, not for mine. She wanted this to be a day when she wouldn't have to confront any of the problems in her own family, when she could join Lee and Matthew and everybody else and share in the anticipated joy and enthusiasm of a project being set on its way. Bright colours to replace the domestic monochrome. Even if she couldn't weave happiness into her own family, she was determined to make use of the threads elsewhere.

'Once I've got this out of the way, I'll make a start on the Advent wreaths, if that's OK with you,' she told Lorna.

After a quick bite to eat in the deli across the road, she carefully packed all the items bound for the Callas into her car, putting a box of back-ups onto the front passenger seat. When she walked through the new double doors at the entrance to the restaurant, she saw the whirls of activity that were part of the final rush to complete. Somebody called Tony was fiddling with the sound system and trying out volume levels for Lee to approve; somebody called Kevin was adjusting the spotlights on the ceiling; somebody called Amy was polishing the cutlery on the tables and somebody called Anna was carrying boxes of fish packed in ice from a small van parked outside. The transformation of the interior space was virtually complete: the walls, resplendent in the soft apple-green she had finally persuaded Lee and Matthew to accept as the ideal background for the black-and-white blow-ups that showed Maria Callas in her leading roles; the subtle geometric design of the carpeting in three shades of grey, which she argued would be much better at disguising spillages than the original plain colour they had wanted; the mirrored tiles on the four supporting pillars, designed to reflect as much light as possible; the hints of earthiness coming from the iroko frames of the dining-chairs; the sparkle of the crystal candle-holders on the tables; and the elegance of the sheer black marble on the reception counter.

Lee stopped what he was doing and gave her a peck on her cheek.

'You wouldn't believe how nervous I am,' he said. 'All these weeks of preparation and planning, and we're just about to open!'

'Lee, it looks absolutely wonderful. If the food is as good as this place now looks, you'll have the customers pouring in.'

'Let's hope so. We're opening to the public at eight-thirty tonight, after we've had our own celebratory meal at six, so poor Matthew's going to be really busy. But he's got help in the kitchen and we've got two waitresses from an agency, so there's not much that can go wrong there.'

'I'll just pop and see Matthew before I start bringing all my stuff in. Is that all right?'

'Hi there Rosie,' Matthew called out, a hand on a gigantic blast chiller as she walked into the kitchen. 'How are things?'

She gave him a weak smile. There would be no point in enlightening him about what had really been on Kieron's mind and the consequences which that had set in train for her family, and no point either in touching on any of her marital concerns, though she instinctively felt Matthew would have lent a sympathetic ear. 'Fine, thanks,' she replied. 'Have you got everything under control?'

'Hope so. If I've forgotten anything, it's a bit late now anyway. We're giving you all a set meal at six, the à la carte choices are only for the punters later on. Otherwise it would've been too complicated.'

'But Matthew, finger food was all I was expecting. You said it would be a reception for invited guests at six.'

'I know, but we wanted to do it in grand style. And if everybody comes, we'll have forty-eight people here, so then there's the multiplier effect.'

Rosie blinked in mock surprise. 'Wow! That is a lot. Who else have you invited?'

Matthew smiled at her. 'It's a bit like wedding receptions. You know, the guys you just have to invite because they're family or whatever and the friends you really want to be there.'

'So who's family tonight then?'

'Well, the editor of the local paper, a representative from the local radio station, somebody from the tourist office, the bank manager who gave us the additional loan, a couple of food critics, and then we've got quite a few other people coming down from London as well.'

'That sounds fantastic. You'll have everybody seated for the words of welcome, I guess, or are you are going to push the tables to one side?'

'No, no. That would cause too much confusion. Lee's handled all the seating arrangements. If you look closely at the individual tables you'll see that they all have name cards. Yours is on one of them too.'

She went back outside to her car and started carrying in the first boxes with the table displays. 'Do you want a hand with any of that?' Lee called out.

'Thanks, they're not too heavy. I can manage.'

The composition of her table displays had been a labour of love. Lee had told her about one of Callas' signature roles as Violetta in *La Traviata*, and explained that the opera was based on a play in which the leading character wore white and red camellias in her hair alternately. Rosie originally planned to have the same flowers as centrepieces, despite her reservations about sourcing them at an acceptable price, but after discussions with Lee she was convinced that roses would do the lady equal justice.

'It wouldn't have been a good idea to have anything too fragrant, like lilies,' Rosie pointed out. 'For a start, some people are allergic to certain kinds of floral fragrance and then there's the added problem of pollen. That's a complete devil to get off clothing once it's been marked. You can get some really outstanding roses all through the year which keep for quite a while. And there's no scent either.' Aware of the incongruity of what she'd said, she added with a laugh, 'That's fine for the people with allergies, but perhaps not for the traditionalists.'

'Almost an argument for using plastic flowers,' Lee joked.

'Silly, that would do me out of a job.'

So she had come up with a simple design of three rosebuds in the centre, surrounded by a miniature garland of alstroemeria, with assorted maple leaves around the edges. To overcome any sense of uniformity she had opted for four basic variations of colour in the roses, ranging from soft pink through crimson and scarlet to a sunny yellow, so that each finished centrepiece would be repeated just three times throughout the tables in the restaurant. For the display on the reception counter she had chosen something rather more flamboyant, strelitzia and ornamental grasses with sprigs of bright-red rowan berries. 'There's a reason for those,' she told Lee. 'They're for keeping the evil spirits away. That's in country folklore. I hope they'll have a similar effect here.'

When she'd finished putting the final touches to everything, she surveyed the entire space from a corner. On the reception counter to one side of the velvet-lined entrance portal lay a neat stack of menu booklets with the name of the restaurant picked out in gold lettering. She glanced briefly inside and noted the small but distinctive range of dishes.

Suddenly she felt two arms around her back. Even before she twisted round to see, she knew it could only be Lee and Matthew. 'Rosie, well done. It all looks fabulous,' said Matthew. Her cheeks glowed at the appreciation they were giving her, and she soaked up their warmth and kindness like a dehydrated pot-plant that had been standing neglected in a corner.

She pointed to one of the pages. 'I'm impressed with what you're planning to offer your guests. I've never had roast quail before.'

'You will, Rosie, you will. Only a matter of time,' said Lee. The three of them laughed heartily, sharing the moment together.

Shortly before six, the first guests started to arrive. Rosie was glad she had changed into something more formal, having chosen a black woollen shift to go with a contoured multi-coloured tunic, since half the people that she saw walking in had made an effort to come in their finery. Lee made a speech in which he thanked all their backers and friends, in which she was included, and there followed a champagne toast. She found herself at a table with three other guests, an attractive-looking man opposite with just a hint of grey around the temples, a much younger man who turned out to be the electrician and a woman Rosie took to be about sixty who soon introduced herself as Matthew's mother. Immediately behind her there was a rather noisy table where people were discussing novel and amusing names for enterprises, from "Junk and Disorderly" (for household clearance) to "Curl Up and Dye" (apparently a hairdressing salon) and "In Cod we Trust" (a fish-and-chip shop somebody had spotted in a seaside resort). For a moment she was torn between listening to the raucous sounds at her rear and the chatter that was just starting at her own table. The middle-aged man turned from Matthew's mother and gave her a friendly smile. She leaned forward to escape the hubbub.

'I'm John,' he said. 'John Bibby. I gather from Lee that you were responsible for all the floral arrangements.'

Rosie felt another warm glow to her cheeks. 'All in my line of business. I'm a local florist.'

The way he looked at her with his warm brown eyes reminded her of Laurence, but he was slimmer and she supposed him to be less tall. 'That's good to know,' he said. 'My younger daughter is getting married next May and I promised her she could have the reception in a garden marquee. I've already spoken to Matthew about doing the catering and it would be nice to have somebody with your talent doing the flowers.'

Rosie was surprised there was no mention of a wife, but noted that this John obviously had the means to finance a garden reception. Not wanting to be considered a flirt by the others, she refrained from uttering what she was thinking: *you look too young to have grown-up daughters.*

She turned to Matthew's mother, who was as quiet and unassuming as the elder of her two sons. 'Have you come far for the opening?' she asked, and then quickly realised she must have sounded like the Queen making small talk.

'I came down on the train this morning,' she said, and the accent was unmistakeably London in origin. 'I'm staying with Lee and Matthew overnight.'

Rosie found it much easier engaging the electrician in conversation. He was local and happy to talk about his business, but as they chatted she was acutely conscious of another pair of eyes following every movement of her expressive hands: those of the man opposite her. Then the first course was served, a ballotine of rabbit with braised fennel and celery.

As the first bars of an operatic aria emerged from the swell of human voices around her, she found herself drawn to the eyes of the man opposite. *Stop it,* she thought, *I don't do flirting. I never*

have done. I'm a married woman. I'm old-fashioned. I'm not like
my brother-in-law. I don't have his roving eye. Can't you see, I'm
wearing a wedding-ring. What must the other two be thinking,
they must have noticed how you keep looking at me. You can't
seriously think I'm at all special. I only did the flowers.

Before the main course arrived, Lee tapped on his glass. 'I
hate interrupting your conversations because from the sound I
guess you're having a good time, but I just wanted to say a few
words about why Matthew chose the next dish. We felt it had to
be something Italian because Maria Callas had her first major
successes on the operatic stage in Italy just after the war, so we
decided to give you a rose veal stew that's called *osso bucco*. And
at the risk of throwing too much Italian at you, here's the first line
of a key aria in one of her greatest roles, in Puccini's *Tosca*.' He
hesitated for a moment and there was a sudden hush in the room.
'In a sense I think it sums up what we're both about and I think it
sums up Matthew's role in the kitchen too. She sings *Vissi d'arte,*
vissi d'amore, which means "I lived for my art, I lived for love." I
can't think of a better piece of music on this our opening night.'

Rosie knew little about classical music and even less about
opera. She liked to listen to Kieron's electric guitar, but given
the choice she would opt for undemanding, easy-on-the-ear
listening, so she was uncertain as to what to expect. Yet as the
voice began to open up and the strings began to surge, she sensed
a vulnerability in the singer's voice and had a sudden urge to
discover more about the work itself. She found herself looking
once more into John Bibby's eyes. When the aria was over and the
next set of plates began to appear, she asked him, 'Do you know
anything about that opera?'

'It's beautiful music, isn't it? Something for true romantics.
Unfortunately, like real life itself, it all ends tragically. The
heroine – that's Tosca – kills herself after her lover has been
murdered on the orders of the chief of police.'

Her face clouded over. 'How can wonderful music like that
have such a sad background?'

He smiled at her. 'That's what defines true art, or that's what they say. It's about bringing extremes of emotion together.' As the plates with the *osso bucco* were placed in front of them he declared, 'Wow, that certainly smells good. I can't wait to taste it.'

Rosie's senses were being gently aroused and she was soon back in her childhood dreams where each individual sensation gave way to the next and the ripples of warmth they produced started to radiate from deep within her until it felt almost as though her fingers and toes were tingling with the excess energy. There on the plate in front of her was a garland of saffron risotto ringing the rich dark-looking pieces of meat flecked with emerald-coloured herbs. How had Matthew known, she wondered, that her floral arrangement would mirror the design of his main dish – or was that just coincidental? The succulent veal fell apart in her mouth and she allowed it to linger on her tongue, revelling in the depth of flavour. Opposite her she was aware of another mouth moving in time to hers.

Rosie turned to Matthew's mother. 'Did you teach him to cook? His talent must come from somewhere.'

'I've never understood it myself. There's no history of it in our family. When he was fifteen he suddenly said he wanted to become a chef.'

'Well,' John said, 'talent like that deserves to flourish. I think we can all agree on that.'

They were equally appreciative of the dessert, a clementine posset with triangular-shaped pieces of hazelnut shortbread. By the time the espressos arrived, Rosie felt the belt of her dress pressing against her waist. She hadn't intended to eat quite so much, but her appetite had yielded to the stimulation, her stomach failing to send urgent signals to the brain to stop.

She looked at her watch and thought of her children at home on their own. Laurence would be with his mother until late and she needed to get back. Other guests had already started to say their farewells and she quickly stood up from the table. She was still glowing. At the door she hugged both Lee and Matthew, declaring the evening to have been one of the most enjoyable she could ever recall. Just then she felt a gentle hand on her arm.

'Forgive me,' John said. 'I didn't quite catch your name at the table.'

'It's Rosie,' she said. 'Which I suppose is a pretty obvious name to have if you're a florist. Except my parents didn't know that when I was born. Mind you, I could have been called Daisy, or Lily even.'

'Oh, Rosie's much nicer.' He handed her his business card. 'Can I give you a lift at all, or do you have your own transport?'

As she looked at the embossed lettering and saw his job title, the connection with Lee and Matthew suddenly became clear. 'I meant what I said about the wedding reception for my daughter. Will you get in touch? Please.' Then he added, 'In case you're wondering, I'm divorced. My part of the deal with my ex is that I get to organise and pay for this reception. I want it to be a success.'

She smiled nervously. 'I'll certainly bear that in mind. I'm sorry, I have to go. My children will be waiting for me at home.'

'No husband?'

She hesitated. The last time she recalled having that kind of instant connection with a man was when Laurence had walked into her shop and swept her off her feet. She was experiencing a similar reaction to this man, the man she now knew from his business card must have provided some of the financial backing for the Callas. There was something about the way he looked at her that made her feel special, desirable even.

'He's not at home at the moment. That's why I've got to get back. I'll be in touch.'

She realised she was trembling as she walked back to her car. *This is all wrong,* she thought. *How can I have any kind of feelings for another man? I may be having problems with Laurence, but I'm still married to him. Why should this bank manager think he can just flirt his way into my life? No wonder though, if he's divorced. He obviously believes he can pick up any woman he comes across and fancies.* And she attempted to put all thoughts of John Bibby out of her mind as she drove home, thinking only about the wonderful aria she had heard Maria Callas sing and the wonderful food which Matthew had cooked for them.

27

Rosie felt Laurence crawl into bed well after midnight and wondered in her semi-sleepy state what he and his mother had found to talk about all evening. Any conversation she had with her mother-in-law hardly ever strayed beyond the familiar. She could almost predict the patterns of dialogue whenever they were together. She often had the idea that she was performing in a play where the characters on stage had mastered their lines perfectly and there were to be no sudden surprises or deviations from the playscript.

The next morning Laurence told her about the break-in, and she noted once more how sanguine he appeared to be when considering the consequences. She knew she would have been boiling with rage if anything similar had happened at Florabellum.

As the week progressed, she believed she was witnessing a slight improvement in Kieron's mood when he returned home from school, though she wasn't entirely sure whether he was merely putting a brave face on things. Perhaps the dust was beginning to settle.

She saw little of Laurence. In the mornings he was quickly out of the door, and in the evenings he frequently didn't return home until after nine. She was beginning to wonder whether he was deliberately finding additional things to do elsewhere. When she asked, he was never short of an answer. It was either the office paperwork that was getting behind, or residents making trouble in some of his management portfolio properties, or the aftermath of the Lindon Road break-in, or further trips to the police-station to press home his demand for retribution. She too was out of the house for most of the day, working off the extra time she'd taken during her week away. As each day stretched from the morning darkness to the dreary gloom of the evening, they both found more than enough to keep them occupied.

This was her favourite time of the year in the shop. Earlier in the calendar there had been the heady scents of jasmine, gardenias and stephanotis and the brilliant splashes of colour in the pot plants, with cut flowers and boxes of bedding plants displayed outside on the pavement to delight her senses. For most of the time all she had to do inside was unpack, select and discard, sift, strip and trim, arrange and re-arrange, mop, sweep and wipe, actions she could accomplish virtually on auto-pilot while chatting to the customers or to Lorna. By late October, however, she was busy hand-painting the glass baubles, or winding thin satin strips into miniature globes that would be sold as additional Christmas decorations, or selecting the most suitable candles to be placed in the storm-lanterns that stood on sentry duty in the large shop windows. Then, as the Advent season approached, it would be time to start preparing the wreaths, the moment when she could direct her hands and fingers to work in bursts of intense concentration at her little pieces of art. She and Lorna always waited until the last possible moment before assembling so that the elements remained as fresh as possible. When she was on her own in the shop, she would segue from her place at the long table in the stock-room to front-of-house as soon as the chimes on the door went, and then return with keen anticipation to where she had left off, drawing in the slightly sharp smell of the pine and fir needles as she bound the assorted berries and nuts into the sprigs of holly and ivy, threading and weaving the elements together with expert ease and finishing off with neatly cut ribbons. This was where she could lose herself, responding to an inner rhythm that governed the binding of bouquets at other times of the year, that dictated the way her hands shaped and formed what was destined to merge and intertwine. Her nimble hands moved gently over the sea of materials, feeling the rasp and sting of the textures against the skin of her palms and fingers, tying and twisting until she was satisfied that each wreath was uniquely different.

As she worked, her memory would throw up episodes from her childhood when she used to sit at the kitchen-table, an earnest expression fixed firmly to her face, assembling structures made of plasticine that would then be adorned with gaudy buttons or hat-pins from her mother's sewing-box, or working with swathes of raffia or balls of string, cutting shapes from coloured paper, or taking twigs, leaves and grasses from the garden and stuffing them into tiny jam-jars which she would place on the window-sill in her bedroom. Sometimes she would merely sit gazing through the big panes of glass into the long garden beyond, until Dulcie came up behind her and tickled her ribs or clamped her hands over her eyes.

It was always Dulcie who pulled her out of her periods of contemplation, the eight years which separated them a constant reminder that she needed to snap out of her constant reveries, leave her childhood behind her and catch up with the real world. One day when Rosie was still only eight Dulcie was incredulous to hear that she still believed in Santa. Later, after she'd started secondary school, Dulcie would sometimes catch her reading the romantic novels she regularly sought out in the local library, and she quickly learned to shut her ears to the snorts of disdain that came her way. 'Are you still reading that trash? You need to read proper literature for a change. Never forget, this is Brontë country.'

Adam too found it difficult to accept her fascination for the sickly-sweet plots she would regale him with when he returned home from teaching practice, the endless permutations of a girl from a poor background at odds with the world, yet nevertheless endowed with a firm belief in the constancy of true love, finally being rewarded with the fine figure of a stereotypically affluent professional man who managed to combine swashbuckling adventures at large with a dedication to hearth and home.

As she worked on her Advent wreaths, her fingers moving over the materials like bees' feelers, the memories of the warm dark eyes opposite her on the Monday night began to surface again. She had dispelled all thoughts of John Bibby on her return to Marlborough Close, but now on her own, in the back room of the shop and surrounded by the touch and smell and promise of the approaching festive season, she was finding it hard to ignore them. Why should she feel embarrassed if she wanted to relive those moments? The eyes like coals at which she felt she could warm her hands, the greying temples that offset his youthful features, the carefully manicured fingers with a dusting of fine dark hair, the voice so soft and deep that she sometimes strained to hear his exact words, the way he had complimented her on her name. There was nothing wrong in acknowledging the existence of an attractive man. That in itself didn't imply anything of significance. The world was full of attractive men. She'd seen them in the glossy magazines she loved to dip into while Mandy was doing her hair, escorting the brave and the bold to film premieres or lounging near pools in the company of models and starlets. She'd seen them in the soaps she watched most evenings, except that on screen they had an irritating habit of cheating on their wives and girlfriends or getting caught up in dodgy deals. Not much constancy there.

She wondered why John's marriage had fallen apart. Had she cheated on him, spurned his love and affection and abandoned her role as wife and mother, or had he cheated on her, behaving just like the cads she had grown to recognise on the small screen? Or had his marriage slowly disintegrated in the way that a carefully-fashioned piece of oak might succumb to woodworm until the outer shell collapsed, leaving a hollowness within?

She knew that some things didn't last, no matter how solid the outer appearance might be. She and Adam hadn't been able to steer their relationship away from the rocks; Lucie and Ian were merely keeping up appearances, but ultimately living a charade; Laurence was kind and generous, but was that enough, was that sufficient to keep the show on the road? She no longer felt the old tingle when he touched her. The nagging and persistent feeling that she had stopped being the most important thing in his life troubled her whenever her thoughts turned to him. Hadn't she earned the right to experience a thrill at the idea of another man expressing an interest in her? What could possibly be wrong in that?

She heard the chimes on the door and got up to attend to her next customer. When she returned to her bench several minutes later, her thoughts drifted back to the table at the Callas and the smile again curling upwards from the corners of his mouth before spreading to the slightly puckered skin around his eyes. That smile, she felt, was genuine.

28

'Just put your head down and do what you believe to be right.' That was one of the things Laurence's mother used to say to him when he told her about the conflicts he was experiencing at school, the teachers who kept pushing him in directions he didn't want to go or the classmates who refused to accept the lead he was prepared to give. Getting on with the job in hand was what he quickly learned to do; excessive inner reflection leading to paralysis might be fine for academics, intellectuals and philosophers who surveyed the world from their ivory towers, but then they never needed to point to any practical achievements, which were the things that really mattered. These luminaries might describe all the finer points of pure theory, offer you a range of options and debate at length all the benefits and shortcomings inherent in any number of positions, but if you then challenged them and asked, 'So what would you do?', you invariably got an evasive answer that began with 'Well, it all depends.' Like the politicians he heard squabbling on the few news programmes he managed to catch, there was a lot of hot air around. Just get on with it, he thought. That's what you're there to do. Fix the problem.

If sticking to his principles was the mantra he grew up with, it didn't take him long in his first job after university to realise that if he wanted to succeed, and especially if he wanted to succeed financially, conflict resolution was just as important. You had to work towards that all-important win-win situation, even if you believed deep down that you were going to come out on top. No point in acting like a bull in a china shop, no advantage whatsoever in revealing your hand too soon. You had to keep in mind your ultimate goal, even if on the way there you knew there had to be an element of give-and-take. That was all fine and dandy when money was involved, when you could haggle over figures on a sheet of paper or work out net interest on a proposed investment, but emotions couldn't be quantified like that. You couldn't offer someone an increased percentage of future bliss in return for an excessive amount of current suffering.

Or could you? He'd spent long enough selling people houses and flats to know that his chances of closing a deal were much higher if there was something for both head and heart. But then nothing could trump the purely emotional aspects that swayed a potential buyer, the kerb appeal of a property or the intangible wow factor.

He knew he could harry the guys at the police-station and keep pressing them about the state of their inquiries. He could ring round his usual list of contractors and casually drop into his conversation the notion that the Lindon Road break-in must have been an inside job, querying whether they had heard or seen anything of relevance. He could also continue to ask the financial experts among his contacts how the national economic situation and the local housing market were likely to develop in the coming months. He could do all of this and more. What mattered in the end, however, was what he had to show for his efforts. He, Laurence Stewart, had to point to something and say, 'Look at that. I've made a real difference today. Things are a little bit better now than they were when I first decided that something needed fixing.'

Although he spent most of the week chasing professional matters up on the phone or in person, pleading, cajoling and at times insisting with varying degrees of success, when it came

to the relationship with his wife, and especially the new project
he was determined to proceed with, he was none the clearer
about how to achieve perfect compliance. Having a minimalist
version of marriage thrust at him at either end of the day held
out absolutely no attraction whatsoever; he wanted his old Rosie
back.

Kieron and Estelle were already picking up on their reduced
levels of communication and the strain of having to maintain a
semblance of normality. 'Dad, have you and Mum been having
words?' Estelle wanted to know midweek, while Rosie was busy
in the utility room with the laundry.

'What makes you think that?'

'Dad, you are funny at times. You think we don't notice when
you behave differently. You seem to be avoiding each other too.'
She looked at him quizzically with a pained expression. 'Is this
all about what happened to Kieron? Have you been arguing about
him?'

'Sweetheart, there are always ups and downs in any
relationship. You don't always feel the same every day of the
week, do you?'

'So this is not about Kieron? He's been getting really worried.
He told me so.'

'Good lord no. We're not happy about what's happened. I think
we've made that clear to both of you. But what's done is done. We
have to move on. It's more important to punish those responsible.'

He could see she wasn't satisfied with his explanation. She
had something of his dogged terrier-like persistence about her.

'Why aren't you getting on then?' she asked.

'Look, Estelle, I'm not going to talk to you about your mum
and me, and certainly not behind her back. That wouldn't be fair,
would it? I'm sure you wouldn't like it if people behaved like that
to you.'

'But you talk about us all the time. We know you do. And
behind our backs too!'

'That's enough, young lady. You and I don't want to have

a falling-out, do we?' Yet the moment he uttered the words he realised that he had given Estelle the confirmation she had sought.

Driving back to Marlborough Close on the Friday evening, he kept telling himself to tread carefully. He did not want to be disappointed again. In a briefcase beside him lay the plans his architect friend had drawn up for the chapel and delivered just a day previously. Also inside was a gift-wrapped box of the most expensive Belgian chocolates he'd been able to find. Comfort food, he thought. She'd surely appreciate those. At least he hoped she would. But the new Rosie who was emerging from her chrysalis was quite different from the Rosie who used to entwine him with her soft expressive hands and press herself against him during the early days. The infinite trust she had once had in him, in his judgements and decisions, in his total commitment to her, some of that trust had been ebbing away. Why else would she have raised the point of their marriage? The words had not been spoken in jest or in fury; they sounded like a statement of the blatantly obvious uttered in the cold light of day.

When he arrived she was in the kitchen chopping up fresh basil, the knife being thrust this way and that, the soft leaves bruising and wilting under the pressure of her hands.

'Hi there, love. I've brought you something.' She glanced at the black-and-gold wrapping paper and quickly said, 'Thanks, but I'm a bit messy at the moment. I'll open it later.' In the past she would have stopped whatever she was doing, curious to discover what he had brought her, her eyes misting over in anticipation before tearing open the folds of paper.

'Had a busy day?'

'Yes. You know what it's like, this time of the year and all that.'

He tried again. 'How's everything at the Callas? Are expectations being fulfilled?'

'I phoned Lee again yesterday. They're very happy with the way things are going.'

After each prompt he expected her to behave the way she always did, pouring forth a flurry of details in a rush to draw him into the experience, so that he could share and partake in her world. Now every question seemed so effortful and her replies were pared back to the barest of essentials.

'I'll just take a quick shower.'

'OK. It'll be ready shortly.'

Under the shower he pondered his next move. With the auction now just a few days away he wanted to see if her attitude had softened in the meantime. If he broached the matter again over the evening meal, and in the presence of Kieron and Estelle, she wouldn't be able to close down completely. They would be looking at her to gauge her reaction, as he would. There'd be no escape from that. If she had any concrete objections, he would address them; if the kids were at least open to the idea he would see how far they might go in applying some pressure on their mother to give up her all-out opposition. It was a project for the whole family, but one in which there had to be winners. It was all a matter of presentation.

'Do you remember Clive Nolan?' he asked, as they were half-way through a hearty stew.

'No. Should I?'

'We go back a long way. He started as a young architect in Southampton just before I joined the firm as a surveyor. I'm sure I've mentioned him before.'

'You may have, but I can't remember now.'

'I asked him to draw up plans for the new chapel.'

She clicked her teeth. 'You're not going to start on that again.'

'Rosie, this is for all of us. It could be our new future together.'

Estelle gave him a questioning look. 'Dad, what are you on about?'

'There's an old chapel coming up for auction next week. I've been trying to persuade your mum that this could be a wonderful new home for us. There'd have to be a proper refurbishment and it'd take a while to get everything finished. But just think what it would mean, living in a grand old building with plenty of history. We'd all have more space than we have here and...'

He didn't manage to finish his sentence. Rosie had already cut in. 'We're in the middle of a meal and I don't want to hear any more about these ridiculous fantasies you keep having.'

There was a stunned silence as Kieron and Estelle looked at both parents, their knives and forks clattering onto the plates.

Estelle was the first to react. 'Mum, why is it a fantasy?'

Rosie found herself on the defensive. Her intention had been to halt the discussion, but now she was being challenged to explain her choice of words.

'Laurence, I said no and I mean no. I am not going to move from here.' She had wanted to include the children in her ringing refusal to discuss his plans, but now saw there was more than a flicker of interest from both of them.

Estelle's terrier-like grip was there again. 'Dad, where is it? Can we go and see it?'

Rosie was beginning to feel arraigned, pinned to the wall with the rest of the family circling. 'Laurence, don't push me too far. You might live to regret it.' The words were out before she had time to think properly. She could see from the horrified looks she was getting that the threat was being taken seriously. The heat that had been welling up inside her cheeks had made her eyes smart, a reflux from her stomach had caused the meal to go sour in her mouth.

Suddenly the dam wall crumbled. She burst into tears and left the table.

'Dad, what's going on? Why is mum reacting like this?' This time it was Kieron who was demanding answers.

Laurence stood up uneasily and followed Rosie upstairs. He found her lying on the bed in a heap. 'Rosie, love. What is it?' He touched her on the shoulder and she turned to face him, her face flecked with blood vessels close to the surface, her eyes brimming with tears.

'How many times do I have to tell you this? No, no, no! Go

ahead with this stupid idea of yours and that's the end of our marriage.'

He sat down on the edge of the bed. This was the second time she had crossed the line verbally. He couldn't believe what he was hearing. She was distraught and unreasonable. Something must have happened during the week to poison her mind towards him. There could be no other explanation.

'Rosie, why are you being like this? You must know I'm doing this for all of us.'

'There you go again. Nothing makes you stop to consider whether other people might want something different. It's only ever about you. I've had enough. I deserve better than this.'

He moved towards her again, but she thrust him away. He held onto her and she lashed out with her fists. It was like the time she had accused him of an affair with Shaheen. She was becoming utterly hysterical.

'Rosie, look, we can talk this through.'

She twisted herself free and raced down the stairs. With a growing sense of disbelief he saw her grab her car keys and her coat and disappear out of the door.

Kieron and Estelle were immediately in the hallway. 'Dad, dad! What have you done? Where's mum gone?'

29

She drove through the darkened streets trying to regain control. She knew this wouldn't have happened a few years ago. There was something inside her that needed repair, a thread that had snapped without warning. Things were unravelling. 'Metal fatigue' was what they called it when parts of a fuselage broke up. It felt much the same right now. The wholeness that was part of her being, the wholeness that defined her marriage, appeared to be little more than a chimera.

She was hot and beginning to perspire, so she stopped the car to remove her coat. Waves of unexpected and unwelcome warmth were sweeping through her body. She gripped the steering-wheel and tried to make sense of it all. Why did Laurence have to spoil it all? A week that had started so well in the Callas, the joy she had experienced during opening night, the satisfaction that had suffused her while she worked on her Advent wreaths. And then she remembered the ardour in the eyes across the table, the eyes that had promised understanding and comfort.

She took out her purse to see if she had placed his calling card inside one of the flaps. She had. There were two numbers: the landline was obviously the bank's, but there was also a mobile contact. She hesitated. What would she say? What would he think? What would be the point?

She considered ringing Lucie. She could almost anticipate what she would say. Men are all the same, big, foolish oafs. But perhaps this one might be different. How would she know if she didn't at least try?

The number rang out and went to voicemail. He was obviously unavailable. Spouting her frustration and blubbing to a wall of silence at the other end would just be silly. She ended the call and considered who else she might contact. She knew she needed to talk. She didn't want to be left on her own with her feelings twisted and contorted.

Suddenly her mobile started ringing. It was the number she'd just called.

'Hello, John Bibby.' The voice was as consoling as she remembered it.

'Oh hello, I'm sorry to bother you.' She steadied her voice. 'This is Rosie. From the Callas on Monday night.'

'Well, this is a nice surprise. I'm sorry I didn't get to my mobile in time when you rang. I was just seeing one of my daughters off.'

She wondered where he was and what he'd just been doing. What would he think of her if she said she needed a shoulder to cry on? How would that look? She didn't want to appear like a little child.

'Is there something I can help you with? Did you want to talk about the wedding reception?'

She hesitated, uncertain how to proceed. He wouldn't know unless she told him. There'd be no point in faking it.

Her courage faltered. 'I'm sorry, I really don't know why I phoned your number. I was at a loose end.'

'You'd be surprised how often bank managers have to listen to confessionals. That's what priests used to do. Now it's people like us and the family doctors who help to pick up the pieces.'

How had he sensed she was having a personal crisis? Was he telepathic?

'Where are you anyway?' he asked. 'I'm at Portsmouth Harbour train station. Pascale and I have just had a meal together and she's off on the ferry now to spend the weekend with friends on the Isle of Wight.'

So that's what he'd been doing. 'Er, I'm on the main road heading into Gosport.'

'Wrong side of the water, aren't you? And he added with a laugh, 'I'm just on the other side: Not a million miles away.'

He had to wait for the next ferry across before he found her sitting in a little Italian café he'd told her to head for. When he arrived he briefly touched her cheeks with his lips and she felt the kind of tingle that she used to feel when Laurence touched her. Soon they were sipping hot chocolate and telling each other their life stories. He'd followed the love of his life, Yvonne, to her home town of Avignon before bringing her back to England after finishing his studies. Their first daughter, Elodie, was born soon after they got married and then two years later Pascale had appeared. The rows had started shortly afterwards. There was always something that Yvonne found fault with, whether it was the climate, or the food, or later the educational system and what he was prepared to offer her. Nothing he ever did seemed quite good enough for her. Eventually she had gone back to France, and after the divorce the two girls had decided to remain with their father. Now Elodie was happily married and living in London; Pascale would be next to leave the family home, with plans already well advanced for the ceremony in May.

Clearly, she thought, getting married at the age of twenty-two with a child already on the way was not in retrospect the smartest of moves. That was the position she'd almost found herself in, except she'd made it clear to Adam that she wouldn't have children without his commitment to marry her, and that hadn't been forthcoming.

As the chocolate released its power and made her cheeks glow again, she began to loosen up. The block on her desire to communicate, so evident with Laurence, was now lifted and the details streamed out of her. Like strangers in the night who meet and know they will never encounter each other again, she was telling him about her husband, her children, her sisters and her mother-in-law, her frustrations and her hopes. He listened, intent and focused, with a gentle prodding whenever she jumped too many stiles at once and left him slightly bewildered in the field behind her.

'You must think I'm utterly crazy, telling you this crap about people you've never even met,' she said at one point.

He laughed. 'Well, you listened to my crap, so why wouldn't I listen to yours?'

She looked at the dregs at the bottom of her cup. It was getting late and there was only one other couple in the café, young and tactile, their heads almost touching across their table.

'I think I need to go,' she quickly said.

'If you want some space you can always come back to my place.'

She began to tremble. This was all moving much too fast for her. She knew that if she acquiesced she wouldn't be able to avoid the intimacy she felt he was craving. He had been a reassuring presence, he had offered the shoulder she desperately needed and she knew he promised more. She was finding it difficult to separate the face, the eyes and the voice from the idea of a rock. Everything was becoming an intoxicating blur. *Stop it*, she heard the voices say. They had been silent for a good while, but now they began their internal dialogue again. *You are a married woman, you have never once cheated on your husband, you know you should have slapped Ian hard as he attempted his grope, you have responsibilities as a wife and a mother, you are not some cheap slut that lets herself be picked up on the street for a sleazy night of sex only to be cast out with the empty milk bottles the next morning.* The opposing faction was not holding back. *Remember that one novel you once read in feverish haste, while your teenage fingers raced to turn the next page, the one where the kindly aunt says to the heroine, "You only experience real love once in your life". Remember the sad tale of the princess in her gilded cage, the hopeless figure of a husband playing the field, the only solace*

coming from her two children and a few trusted friends, and her
desperate desire to be loved for who she was. Remember that at
least one-third of all marriages end in divorce, and that trend is
rising. Remember that over time people change and that the person
you marry is not the same person seventeen years later. Remember
that you too, Rosie Stewart, have a right to experience happiness.
The chatter was becoming insistent, the increased volume was
drowning out the message on John's lips.

'It's just a bed for the night. No more.'

She wanted to feel another body warming hers, holding her,
comforting her, promising that her inner weather would change,
but she knew that Kieron and Estelle would be wondering where
she'd disappeared to and why at this late hour she still hadn't
returned.

'John, I appreciate the gesture. But I have to get back.'

'Can I see you again?' His eyes had a sudden fiery intensity.
'Please.'

'We can keep in touch. Yes.'

She drove home slowly, savouring the moments that had
passed, looking sideways at the illuminated shop-fronts, the cafés
and bars inside of which faces nodded and joked and touched, the
houses where elderly couples sat in silent communion on sofas
staring at images on the television screen, the young men and
women on the pavements with their arms gently entwined, all
threaded together with the silk-strong strands of a spider's web.
She wanted to live again.

It was just after midnight when she got back. She could see
from the porch that the hall lights were still on. She fished out
her keys and purse. Then she saw that her mobile had gone dead.
The battery obviously needed re-charging – like her own. She
climbed the stairs, expecting she would have to creep into bed.
Inside the bedroom it was dark. She switched on the small side-
light. Laurence was not there.

30

It was the day of the auction and Laurence had to drive into Southampton to get to the venue. When Rosie rushed out of the house on Friday evening, he considered going after her in pursuit. She was clearly upset, that much was obvious. She had never done anything like this before, although her impetuosity occasionally broke through the still surface of the water. He knew instinctively that it was simply a matter of time before calm descended, before he could hold the old familiar Rosie in his arms once more.

Seeing the concern in the eyes of his children, he worked hard to assuage their fears. 'Mums and dads don't always see eye to eye about things. When it's about something really important, like a new house, their feelings take over. Mum will be back, just give her time,' he'd said.

'Dad,' Estelle had asked, 'you wouldn't do anything like that, would you? Running away like that?'

Laurence's smile was unforced. 'I hope not, sweetheart. Why would I want to run away from you?'

They had sat until eleven, all three on the sofa, channel-hopping and bingeing on packets of crisps, before the accumulated exhaustion of the past week had taken control. Laurence decided to retire to the spare room again, hoping his absence from the marital bed would help to de-escalate the tension. In that he'd been wrong. The following morning, after the children had disappeared from the breakfast table, her only comment to him about the matter was: 'Thanks for moving into the spare room. I think it's best for a while.' She had said nothing further about the chapel and nor had he.

The auction, however, was a fixed date. Since there wasn't the slightest chance of having that postponed, stepping back from the fray would have meant him losing all chance of possession. She might continue to be difficult, but come the New Year she would surely be much more amenable. Even if she refused to give up her opposition, this was an ideal candidate for refurbishment, with the prospect of a sizeable profit on completion. As he'd told himself so often in the past, it was simply too good a prospect to walk away from.

He tried to get Steve to come with him, but he was too busy trying to impress Patrick with the number of viewings he had lined up on a particular property. Laurence was delighted that at the last minute Clive Nolan had managed to make himself free to accompany him to the auction rooms.

'It'll certainly make somebody a wonderful home,' Clive said, after Laurence had told him about Rosie's lack of support, 'but you'll need to keep on top of the costs. Otherwise you could quickly end up with a money pit.'

The chapel was the first item on the agenda after the lunch break. Laurence was surprised that there were so few people in attendance, so his hopes rose for a quick and easy sale. He scanned the room, trying to work out whether any of the faces he saw posed a potential threat.

'Have you set yourself a limit, Laurence? How far above the guide price are you prepared to go?' Clive wanted to know.

'It's on at one eight five and with a bit of luck the auctioneer might even start below that. I don't really want to go above two hundred, because of the fairly whopping restoration costs we both calculated,' Laurence replied.

But the opening bid from the floor was already at the guide price, and before he even joined in he could see with some consternation that there were two other bidders who were inching the price up. He hadn't spent all that time and effort, in addition to Clive's professional fees for the plans, to be thwarted on the home straight. When the older of the other bidders dropped out at £225,000, he looked across at his only other remaining rival, a man in a bomber jacket with large rubbery lips and a fixed expression. Go on, yield to me, Laurence was thinking, I want this more than you do. But he'd underestimated the other man's tenacity. Who and what was he, a builder or a religious fanatic, he wondered? He had to go on wearing the other player down with his will-power and determination; he had no intention of capitulating. Eventually, with the price at £248,000, the hammer came down.

Clive was looking sceptical. 'Are you sure you've done the right thing? You're way over!'

'Thanks for the moral support. It'll be worth it in the end. There's a sizeable bit of land to go with it, after all.'

After he'd written his cheque for the deposit, he took Clive off for a celebratory drink. This was going to be the start of something special, he thought as they downed their pints.

31

Rosie was sleeping badly. She would lie on her side of the bed and listen to the voices squawking away in her head. There were now so many of them, all refusing to take their turn before speaking, that it was becoming a cacophony. In one sense she found that easier to handle than one voice giving out the same unwavering message: so much white noise that filled the spaces of her mind instead of individual sirens with a set agenda who might have lured her onto submerged rocks. Yet the path ahead was not at all clear. John had been comforting and understanding, but there was no way of telling what his deeper motives might have been. The acceptance of his offer of a bed would have placed her in his debt. There's no such thing as a free lunch, her dad always used to say. That was the problem with affairs, she thought. You gave up one kind of dependence for another. Which was why some people went for one-night-stands: no strings attached. But that was not something she had ever been able to understand. The whole point of having sex was that it was part of a loving relationship. Just like the messages in all those novels of her teenage years. You waited until Mr Right came along and then you stayed faithful to him until your dying day. Simple, really.

What was much less obvious to her now was whether Laurence really was her Mr Right. Once she had seen Adam as her white knight in shining armour, but after she'd followed him down to Chichester the relationship had slithered into a state of stasis. She would come back from her succession of mundane and trivial jobs with her levels of energy and self-esteem sapped, waiting for her knight to spirit the two of them away on common adventures. However, when he returned from his day's teaching he declared himself to be exhausted, yet spent hours preparing his next set of lesson-plans or endlessly reading books on teaching theory and practice. 'But I don't understand, you're qualified now,' she had once remonstrated with him. 'Why do you have to keep reading about what you already know?' And he had given her one of those withering looks that made her feel small and inadequate.

Their lovemaking too was nothing like what it had been in the early days. It was mechanical and increasingly infrequent, to the extent that she began to wonder if he'd found somebody else. Then, when she pressed him to commit to a date, so that they could formalise their relationship and she could begin to think about the family she'd always wanted to have, she realised that his retreat was already quite irreversible.

Dawn had not yet arrived to carry her into a fresh day. She stretched out an arm, but the warm folds of Laurence's body were not there for her to touch. Then she remembered John's eyes and the smiles creasing his face. It would be cold outside in the late November air and it was suddenly cold inside her. She wanted a glow of contentment to inhabit her own body, more than the occasional hot flushes that would suddenly surprise her with their intensity.

There was something else troubling her. Over the last few days, on lifting herself out of bed in the morning, it had felt like a swarm of bees dancing around the inside of her skull. Initially she thought the discomfort was coming from the inner voices in her head, that this was their form of protest at not being listened to, but the spasmodic activity subsided the moment she swallowed some painkillers. She'd experienced similar symptoms the night Laurence returned from his auction and told her that his final bid had been successful. She'd been aghast to hear that he'd gone ahead with something deliberately calculated to annoy her, and lightning streaks of pain had seared her temples. 'You really are crazy! I said I'm not moving!' she recalled shouting at him. 'Where's the gain, Laurence? Where's the added value that is going to make a real difference to our lives?' she had demanded to know.

He had remained totally unperplexed. 'We don't have to move. Not soon anyway. It'll be the next big refurbishment project.'

Her sense of fury had intensified at the thought that he was playing some kind of waiting game, that all he needed to do in order to secure her acquiescence was mark time. For a second she thought of getting up and rushing out again, ready to fling herself into John's arms. But then she saw the sadness in her children's eyes and she immediately drew back. Kieron was still spending long hours alone in his bedroom and Estelle was accepting every invitation that came her way for sleepovers at friends' houses. If she ever left Marlborough Close, could she count on being able to take her children with her? She couldn't just park them on John; that wouldn't be fair. If she went ahead with a trial separation – which was what some of the more persistent voices had been arguing – where would they live? Huge additional costs would be involved in setting up home elsewhere. Would that be worth it?

For the first time she felt trapped. Laurence was still sleeping in the spare room and she saw him only briefly in the mornings. In the evenings, if he was in the living-room with the children, she would find things to do in the kitchen or upstairs. The house was large enough to contain them both and to limit encounters to an absolute minimum. But she could see this was never going to be a permanent solution. Something had to give.

It was time to return to the Callas with the next set of fresh displays. She was looking forward to seeing Lee and Matthew again, reassured that nothing sexual could interfere with the warmth of the relationship she had with them. When she rang the bell, it was Lee who let her in, clutching a sheaf of papers in his hands. 'You'll know all about paperwork,' he said, as he planted a kiss on both cheeks. 'We've just got ourselves an accountant and he's insisting on very precise book-keeping. That's all new to me of course, so it's a case of learning by doing.' She touched his arm. 'Well, if I can help in that department, you're welcome to the experience I've got.'

She found Matthew in the kitchen, bent once more over his pots and saucepans. He looked at her keenly, his eyes alert and sympathetic. 'Hiya Rosie, you're looking a bit peaky today. Pre-Christmas blues, eh?'

She was concerned that her inner weather was so obviously on show. The effects of that morning's painkillers were beginning to lessen.

'I think it's more serious than that,' she said with a sigh.

'Still having problems with your son?'

She suddenly burst into tears. She hadn't done that with John. She'd been able to contain herself. Now, with Matthew, there was no need to do so. 'I'm so sorry. You must think me a terrible wimp,' she choked.

The sound of her tears had brought Lee into the room. 'Are you OK?' he said, putting his long angular arms around her. 'Whatever's the matter?'

'I think it's her son,' Matthew said. 'She told me about him disappearing.' On opening night Rosie had reassured him that everything was back to normal, without revealing the full extent of what had happened.

'No. no. It's not just Kieron. And I didn't tell you the whole story either. He was tricked into appearing naked on one of these internet livestreams and was being blackmailed. That was a big enough shock. Now I think my marriage is breaking up.' It was all too much for her: a failure as a mother, a failure as a wife and as if that wasn't bad enough, she was behaving in public like a completely emotional woman.

Lee patted her gently. 'Are the two things connected?' he asked.

Rosie shook her head. 'It's been like this for a while. Laurence just ignores my feelings and pushes ahead with his silly little projects. He's not interested in what I think.'

They sat her down and Matthew brought her a glass of sparkling water. 'This surely can't be the first tiff you've ever had. Everybody goes through a rough patch from time to time. We've both been there and done that.'

'This time it's different.' She was struggling to articulate her ideas. 'I've met somebody else and I don't know if I still love Laurence the way I used to.'

Lee held her hand. 'Give it time and it'll all blow over.'

She burst into tears again. 'That's exactly what Laurence always says. My feelings don't matter to him.'

Matthew was looking straight at her. 'Lee's right, you know. Everything blows over in the end. It's never a good idea to rush into something new.'

Later, in the car driving away from the Callas, she rapped herself across the knuckles. *Why did I have to behave like a silly little girl and make an exhibition of myself in front of Lee and Matthew? They're not marriage guidance counsellors. Why on earth couldn't I control myself and keep my love life private? There's no way they can help me with my current problems. I have to deal with this by myself.*

She looked into the rear-view mirror and saw that her face was a complete mess. She couldn't possibly go back to Florabellum in a state like this. That would be so unprofessional. In any case, though Lorna was a good friend, she didn't want to have to unburden herself to her. Anyway, Lorna never stopped talking about the fantastic relationship she had with Pete.

Yet within minutes she was floundering again. She took a deep breath and dialled a number.

'John, it's Rosie. I'm sorry I haven't been in touch for a few days. Can we meet up?'

32

It was the first full week of the New Year; the Christmas festivities belonged to the year that had departed. The deadness of the dead season was still holding everybody and everything in its grip: the riming of the trees overnight was the first thing Laurence noticed when he pulled back the curtains and looked out onto the fields of black earth beyond their house. By the time he left the house pale shafts of watery sunlight were lighting up the landscape. In a while the lemony globe hanging in the sky would be in retreat, as the air filled with sea mists creeping across the escarpments along the coast, like the onset of astigmatism. People crept about the streets muffled against the cold. It was the worst time of the year to do any business in the property market. People simply weren't interested.

Laurence was pleased in one sense that Natasha had chosen to go when she did. He now had time on his hands to induct her successor without any undue haste. There had been just a handful of applicants and most of them, judging by their letters, were totally unsuitable. He'd been left to interview a woman who had just gone through a divorce and was returning to employment after a long gap, and a fierce-looking Polish girl in her mid-twenties who had worked in real estate in Krakow. It was no contest really. Ilona was slightly off-putting in her old-fashioned spectacles and frumpish clothing, but even with her less-than-perfect English Laurence could see that she was determined to impress him with her skills and very quick on the uptake.

Getting her to manage his office was now the least of his problems. Before Christmas, when he was still expecting the acquisition of the Wesleyan chapel to go through smoothly, there had been unexpected setbacks. A meeting with his bank manager had exposed the precarious state of his finances. After paying the deposit to the auctioneer and successfully exchanging contracts he had planned to press ahead with the refurbishment. However, the existing revenue streams from his property management were deemed to be insufficient collateral for the bank loan he'd been hoping for. In addition, he had had to shell out extra money on the house in Lindon Road, and despite it having gone straight onto the market there was as yet no expression of interest. If on the other hand he turned it into a rental property he could not expect anything approaching the capital funds he needed. With six credit cards currently maximised there was nothing left with which to pay the first set of contractors. Even talking to other high-street banks had done nothing to revive his waning levels of optimism. It was true what was being whistled in the four corners of the land: there was something called the 'credit crunch'. It wasn't just affecting other people.

Then there was Rosie, his other major problem. In the run-up to Christmas Estelle had flung her arms around him one evening and asked him tearfully, 'Dad, why aren't you and Mum getting on?' Normally, in the early part of December, Rosie would have been busy transforming the house into a state of pre-festival anticipation, putting up washing-lines for the cards that had already started to arrive, hanging up sprigs of holly and mistletoe, displaying in large glass receptacles branches coated in silver spray with clusters of brightly-coloured baubles, arranging fairy-lights around the mantelpiece in the living-room and the frames of doorways, and lighting large scented candles in the reception rooms. Several times in the evenings she had returned late, just before he had turned in, without indicating to him – or to Kieron and Estelle, whom he later asked – where she'd been. The earlier frostiness in their relationship had gradually morphed into a state of indifference. There was no obvious hostility towards him, she didn't raise her voice or express her displeasure at anything he did, and essential family business was transacted without a hint of animosity. He was completely unnerved at the way she would now look through him, the face often expressionless and occasionally highlighted with flecks of red.

A week before Christmas she had said to him while they were both in the kitchen, 'Please apologise to your mother, but I won't be coming with you to see her on Boxing Day. I've already wrapped up her Christmas present. You'll find it in the hall. Oh, and I've just posted her a Christmas card from all of us.'

'What about Christmas itself? Are we to have anything approaching a normal Christmas?' he had asked almost plaintively.

'I've got an invitation for Boxing Day, that's why I can't come to your mother's. But there's no reason why we can't have a traditional dinner here on Christmas Day.'

There seemed little point in having another confrontation with her. He didn't for one moment suppose she would begin to justify her actions. He was grateful she wasn't going to abandon all semblance of normality during the Christmas period, at least for the sake of the kids. The fact that she often withdrew when he entered a room where she happened to be, and he was no longer able to touch her and drink in her scent were things he found more troubling. When he had outgrown his mother's capacity to render her physical punishments, she would sometimes withhold expressions of affection, so that he began to crave her closeness and waited for the moment when she would once again put her arms around him and kiss the top of his head. He had known such such moments would come, it was only a matter of time. That was what he clung onto now, though it was weeks since Rosie had embarked on this slow and sustained process of decoupling.

He wondered whether she might have formulated a New Year's resolution to put the past behind her, since he hadn't once mentioned the chapel refurbishment again in her presence, but there was no softening. He'd been disappointed too at her reaction to the Christmas present he had given her. He knew she had a summer frock that she loved to wear when it was warmer, the bottle-green background crowned with clusters of paler and darker pink roses. After searching online he'd managed to find a rucksack in an almost similar design. 'Is this a subtle hint?' she had wanted to know, without a trace of irony. He was initially nonplussed, but quickly attempted to placate her feelings. 'I just thought that once the season comes round again you might find it useful for carrying things in.'

Nor had his mother been able to help much when he took Kieron and Estelle to see her on Boxing Day. She had made a great fuss of seeing them again and had, in his opinion, behaved impeccably as a grandmother. After they'd finished their meal and the children were in the front room watching television, she had picked up on the look of sadness she had seen in their eyes. 'You don't look too good either, my wee one,' was her comment as she and Laurence did the washing-up. He was on the point of switching her attention away from the rocky state of his marriage to the pressing problem of having to find extra funds for the chapel refurbishment, but was keen to soak up her concern and sympathy.

'Mum, I don't know what else I can do to bring her round. It's almost as though she's become semi-detached. You know, not in the marriage, but not out of it either.'

'There are experts you can turn to. Marriage guidance counsellors. If you can't sort it out between yourselves, you will need outside help.'

He was surprised at her analysis. She'd spent all the years of his childhood telling him to stand on his own two feet and sort out any problems he had by drawing on his inner reserves, and now she was implying that if there was an impasse that was the time to employ others to do the heavy lifting. He wasn't yet ready to capitulate though, and in any case he knew that counselling could only work if both parties were committed to the process. He hadn't even hinted at this possibility to Rosie.

Above all, he was beginning to worry about the effects of the continued stand-off on his children. He spent several evenings talking to Kieron on his own, mostly about his schoolwork but also, without ever being specific about the difficulties between himself and Rosie, about the ups and downs in relationships. He told Kieron about the first proper girlfriend he ever had, just after he went into the Sixth Form, and how they had both been keen members of the photography club and revised together for their exams. 'And did you,' Kieron asked, and Laurence could see the effort involved in formulating the question, 'did you do it with her?'

His son had never before quizzed him about his own sexuality. He paused before answering, recalling the awkwardness of the original situation. His son deserved an honest answer.

'Yes, I did.'

Kieron wanted to know more. 'Was it OK?'

Laurence smiled weakly. 'No. No, it wasn't. We were both virgins and I think we both mucked it up. The first time is always difficult.'

One Saturday Laurence took Estelle to a local pony club because she had declared an interest in wanting to ride. He spent the best part of a morning watching her, clad in a smart outfit and relieved of the morose expression that now often darkened her face, trying out different animals and then soliciting his opinion. 'Dad, how about this one? He's much livelier than the last one, wouldn't you say?'

He talked to one of the trainers and quizzed her on the equine gender issue.

'All animals are different, that goes without saying,' she explained. 'But geldings tend to have a more even temperament, whereas mares can sometimes get very moody and are difficult to control, especially when they are in heat.'

Tell me about it, Laurence thought. *Why are female emotions so tricky to handle?* He went on eyeing his daughter with concern, as she went round and round the paddock on a succession of different horses, quite unable to make up her mind.

On a Wednesday morning, while he was peering at his spreadsheets in the back office, he heard somebody come into the front reception area where Ilona was at work. A few minutes later she tapped on his open door and said, 'There's a gentleman to see you.' It wasn't clear why she'd been unable to deal with him, since he'd already instructed her how to access the database and provide information for new clients.

He soon found himself looking at a tall thin individual whose weather-beaten face extended far into the cranial area, the expanse punctuated only by a pair of bright blue eyes behind horn-rimmed spectacles.

'Hello,' he said. 'I'm Denis. Denis Meredith.' He removed his thick woollen jacket.

'I'm sorry,' Laurence said, as the man looked at him with a sense of expectation. 'Should I know you?'

'I'm Miriam's brother. She told me she'd already spoken to you.'

'Of course! The name... I didn't at first make the connection.'

'You weren't to know. My father was killed in a car crash when I was still a child and my mother later remarried. Her second husband, Miriam's father, died young too, so we've always been semi-orphans.'

'That's interesting, we have something in common. My father died at sea when I was just two. I don't really remember him. So you've just come back to this country?'

'Yes, I've been abroad for most of my working life. Thailand, Japan and for the last five years in China. Teaching English. You could call me a major export article. Or,' he added with a distinct chuckle, 'part of the brain drain.'

He looks old, Laurence thought, but the moment he begins to

talk his whole face lights up with vitality. He recalled Miriam's earlier reference to his health problems.

'I've been staying with my sister since Christmas, but she's only got a small flat and I want to find a place of my own. I was hoping you'd be able to help.'

'To buy or to rent?'

Denis laughed. 'If there's one thing you don't expect to make from teaching English abroad, it's a fortune. I have some savings but I can only afford to rent.'

Unlike other lettings agencies in the area, Laurence didn't as yet have a large portfolio of rental properties, but he called Ilona in and directed her to print out a few particulars. 'Take a look at these and if you'd like to view any of them, just let me know and I'd be delighted to show you round.'

Denis extended a hand at the end of their conversation in an old-fashioned way, saying with a ready smile, 'I'll be in touch.'

The gloom had lifted, Laurence thought. The fish were beginning to bite again.

33

In the run-up to Christmas Rosie would draw additional vitality from those around her. She was always fired up by the smiles of anticipation on the faces of people, and especially by the expressions of wondrous delight in the eyes of young children who gazed up at the colourful illuminations and decorations in the streets. She would share in the seasonal jokes of the customers who came to Florabellum, shake her head in mock horror at salacious details of office parties and listen to what they were planning to do in the company of their loved ones between Christmas and the New Year. When there was an occasional lull, she and Lorna would sip mulled wine and nibble gingerbread and mince pies to keep the cool freshness in the shop at bay. She heard the tales of what had gone wrong during the past year and how the new year was going to change all that. She saw her own life reflected in the thoughts of others.

This time the run-up to Christmas was different. The face that stared back at her in the morning mirror of retribution had only bad news for her: a few more grey hairs and yet another wrinkle that had managed to burrow its way into her skin. The twists and knots inside her stomach were dulling her appetite and the neuralgic twinges in her temples reminded her uncomfortably of the biting winds blowing across the North Sea during her childhood, which now seemed to be blowing their way into her hearth and home. She couldn't understand how Laurence had adjusted almost without demur to her new regime. Every morning he would emerge from the spare room, having made up his bed, and put his soiled laundry neatly into the laundry basket. He would place his used coffee mug in the dishwasher, and if it was already full he would gently set the programme in motion before going out to his BMW and driving away. When he came home in the evening he would park in the street so that she never had to move her car from the driveway. He would often spend an hour together with Kieron and Estelle on the sofa while they watched some insane comedy show, or she would hear his occasional peals of laughter when he was with them in their bedrooms. At the end of the day, before they went to their separate beds, he would ask if there was anything she needed doing in the house or any heavy items of shopping she wanted help with. He would inform her if he expected to be home late or was working at the weekend or was seeing Steve for a drink. There was nothing that drove him further away from her, but nothing that brought him closer either.

She wanted the emptiness within her to be filled and the tight coils of frustration to subside. Once or twice she thought of making an appointment to see her GP. Dr Famotibe had been really helpful over prescribing the right kind of medication to deal with Estelle's period pains, but that problem was specific and manageable. How could she begin to describe what was at the heart of her own discontent? Were the headaches and the hot flushes confirmation of an early menopause or merely temporary reactions to living in a difficult domestic environment? Was it just the onset of the dark season that was draining her of her usual vitality, or were the lower energy levels a reaction to a stuttering engine that needed to be fixed in a way she couldn't yet conceive? All she knew was that the prospect of seeing John again lifted her spirits. She craved the warmth coming from his eyes, the little smiles that would dance around the corners of his mouth and then spread across his cheeks.

When she phoned him after her tearful departure from the Callas, he'd been on his way to a meeting of local branch managers. His suggestion was that they meet the following evening. 'Don't worry,' he had said. 'I'm utterly reliable. Just like clockwork in fact.' And then he had added to her amusement, 'But unlike clockwork, you don't need to wind me up.'

She spent the minutes before his arrival looking around the splashes of red and yellow on the walls and tables in the little Spanish restaurant he had chosen, thinking about the plates of paella she had served up for one Sunday lunch the previous summer, as her children gazed in anticipation at the mix of peppers, prawns and saffron rice. The sunshine was in the food and in their faces.

'What you need is a complete break,' he had said half-way through their meal. She remembered her last break just a few weeks previously which had singularly failed to achieve any kind of breakthrough. 'Let me take you away for a few days between Christmas and New Year. How about Paris?'

'Oh no,' she said. 'I couldn't leave Kieron and Estelle. What would I tell them?' And then she thought of Boxing Day, and the ritual she knew would be re-enacted once more in her mother-in-law's house, the questions she wanted to avoid but which might not actually have been asked, the warmth that might have been there for others but which she would be unable to feel. So when he offered to show her where he lived on Hayling Island with the sea on his doorstep, and then also demonstrate his culinary skills, it was a temptation which she found hard to resist.

As she drove towards his house, a few hours after Laurence and the children had set off for Horndean, she again heard the voices in her head murmuring their scepticism. *Couldn't you have been rather more gracious in your reaction to Laurence's present? Why couldn't you be bothered to join in with the others while Kieron worked his way around his new video game? Was it because Laurence was clearly having so much fun?* After she'd engaged the handbrake outside the sleek modern bungalow, the chatter intensified. *Don't cross any boundaries, don't do anything you might regret, don't make a fool of yourself and spoil your make-up again, don't forget you are merely a guest in somebody else's house.*

When he opened the front door she could already smell something rich and meaty in the oven. He told her he had prepared a rack of lamb complete with herb crust and a fine parsnip purée to go with the sautéed potatoes. Laurence never cooked, but John said that learning to do so was an absolute necessity after his separation from Yvonne and later divorce. 'After all, I couldn't let Elodie and Pascale starve, could I?'

'We never talked properly about the food at the Callas on opening night,' she said, as she sipped her dry white wine. 'It was more about the music.' And then she quickly added, 'Not that I didn't find that interesting.'

'I was enormously impressed with Matthew's cooking,' he said. 'I might ask him for a master-class and improve my own skills.'

'But you're already a very good cook,' she insisted. 'If your bank ever goes bust, you could always start up a restaurant yourself.'

He returned her smile and she noticed for the first time a scar on his left temple, a slight blemish from his past. 'Thanks to our Prime Minister, I don't think there's even the slightest chance of my needing to do that,' he said. She recalled the media glee just before Christmas when the country's leading politician had accidentally claimed that he had saved not just the banks and the UK, but the whole world.

After lunch they went for a walk along the shingle beach. The sea breeze had picked up and was eating its way through her windcheater. She clung to him as they slowly picked their way across the uneven surface, with a handful of dog-walkers and beachcombers for company. Beyond them she caught sight of a few sails on the grey horizon. When she next looked across the expanse of water, some of the smaller boats had vanished completely and a few of the larger vessels were beginning to dominate the skyline.

'Are you happy with your job and with life in general?' she suddenly asked.

He sighed. 'Don't think for one moment that I didn't want to break out and find a better job with more responsibility. I did. But the girls were settled and at a good school and I had to be there for them. Their mother was more interested in herself than anybody else. But I never told them what I thought. I left them to work it out for themselves.'

'Have you never thought of remarrying?'

He turned to look at her flushed cheeks and the depth of colour in her eyes. 'You can't just slot a new figure into an established pattern,' he said. 'It has to be the right fit. That new person has to be really special.'

His lips were quite close to hers, but both held back, as if afraid to give in to the moment. She looked at the coastline ahead of them as it swept round to the left, leaving a continuum between sky and sea, one expanse of muddy-grey flowing into the other.

'Why do you think marriages go wrong?' she suddenly asked.

There was a long pause before he replied. 'I can't generalise,' he said. 'Every marriage is different in its own way. I can only speak about my own.'

'How long is it that you've been divorced?'

'It seems like an eternity now. Fourteen years it must be. Elodie was just twelve when the decree nisi came through. Yvonne was the one who insisted on her freedom. And of course, she missed France terribly. Or so she said.'

Rosie thought of Kieron and Estelle in her mother-in-law's house, together with the husband who had grown so distant, like some of the sailing-boats on the horizon. Then from the long corridor in her mind she remembered the dots that danced on the page as the story continued and the waves of passion became unstoppable. She suddenly wanted John to throw her onto the shingle and make love to her madly, irrespective of the people who might see them on the beach.

A moment later, as her cheeks cooled, she dismissed the notion that had once stirred her teenage passions. 'I need to think about getting back,' she said.

They walked back in silence. As he held her hand firmly in his he would from time to time squeeze it gently, and she would respond accordingly. They stood for a while outside the bungalow, with its neat white picket-fence and a slab of tired lawn that was waiting impatiently for the warmer days of spring.

'Can I see you again in the New Year?' he asked.

'Yes, yes,' she replied. 'Somehow when I'm with you I feel better.'

But two days later, their plan to meet again had to be abandoned. She started feeling alternating spasms of intense heat and intense cold which convulsed her body, accompanied by throbbing pains in her joints that made it difficult to stand up straight. She took to her bed, feeling utterly miserable. She told Laurence that it was the flu and he should stay away from her in case he caught her germs. Instead he brought her hot lemon and honey first thing in the morning and stayed home for the first few days of her illness.

'Don't you have work to do? she croaked at him.

'It can all wait,' he said. 'I've told Ilona to tell me if there's anything urgent.'

As she lay propped up on her pillows she wondered again at his capacity to deal with every crisis without a smidgen of doubt that things wouldn't improve. He reassured her that if the fever hadn't subsided within forty-eight hours he would be ringing her GP with an urgent request for a home visit. And the fever did subside as predicted, though she still felt very weak.

It was well into the first week of the New Year, with Laurence already back into the swing of things and out all day, before her thoughts returned to the bungalow on Hayling Island and the man who had cooked her such a fabulous meal on Boxing Day. She wavered before sending him a text, but she felt she had to apologise once more for the brevity of her previous message and its stark reference to the flu. All she'd received in return from him was a *Thinking of you. Get well soon.* She wondered why he hadn't sent her any other texts while she'd been ill. Had his ardour cooled, or was he just being considerate? Now back at work herself, she listened to Lorna enthusing about the film she and Pete had seen in the week after Christmas. In the early days of her marriage she and Laurence would spend at least one night a week at a local cinema and then talk about it over a meal. Unlike Adam, who had increasingly made her think her opinions were never as valid as his, Laurence always gave her the feeling that whatever she had to say mattered to him.

On an impulse she texted John. *Happy New Year! Lorna thinks "The Reader" is a great film to see. Would you be interested?*

When he responded a short time later it was obvious that he had misunderstood, interpreting her formulation as a suggested threesome. A few texts later it was clear that he preferred the theatre or opera, but was more than happy to go to the cinema with her. And then it was her turn to feel she had misunderstood. Lorna hadn't mentioned the Nazi death camps and the depressing historical background of the film, nor had she touched on Hanna's suicide. 'It's a love story between a middle-aged woman and a teenage boy,' was how Lorna had sold it to her.

By the time the film was over she no longer wanted to discuss it, as she might have been persuaded to do with Laurence. She had drifted in and out of concentration mode during the film itself, choosing to rest her head against John's shoulder, and by the end she was all too conscious of missing certain important connections. She also realised far too late that talking rather than watching something together in silence had been her primary motivation for contacting John again. What she wanted more than anything else was to be with a pair of sympathetic ears that would help her to make sense of the conflicts within her.

John pointed to a newly-opened wine bar on the opposite side of the street to the cinema. Initially he just wanted to have a quick look inside, but the place appeared sufficiently inviting for Rosie to react positively when he suggested a glass of wine. Their conversation turned to the perils of opening a new business in a difficult economic climate. 'You know, when times are tough you think long and hard about spending money on non-essentials,' he said. 'When the wolf's at the door you don't automatically think of champagne.'

She laughed at his ability to put things so neatly into a nutshell. 'I suppose there's not a great deal of difference between the Callas and this place. You certainly need the punters.'

'With any new venture there are only a few who succeed,' he said. 'You always have to take a calculated risk. You have to act like all big boys do, with bags of confidence. If you fail, it's people like us who end up having to scrape you off the floor. That's always messy.'

An hour or so later they were walking back to the side street where they had both parked separately, away from the bright sodium street lamps and the loud insistent neon lighting and into the semi-darkness of a residential street. She was startled to see they were in Lindon Road, where she knew Laurence had been busy with a refurbishment.

At that point she suddenly stumbled on the uneven pavement and John turned to catch her before she fell. As he held her in his arms she felt his mouth on hers. It was surprisingly fierce. She didn't fight against him but yielded, almost instinctively. It was as if two moths had both been circling a flame for weeks, resisting the light and the heat for fear they would both be consumed. Now the last walls of resistance had crumbled.

She couldn't quite remember what happened after that. Neither of them spoke, but she was conscious of being impelled towards the back seat of John's car, feeling him on top of her and then, while she was still trying to make sense of it all, moving inside her while his tongue invaded her mouth. When he was spent he kissed her gently and cradled her head in his arms. It was so dark in his embrace that he could have been anybody.

'Shall I drive you home?' was all he asked.

'No. I must drive myself back. I don't want any questions.'

As she drove herself through the same streets she had traversed just a few weeks previously, again seeing figures on the pavements weaving their way along, again hearing their excited voices and peals of laughter, she was acutely aware of the stickiness between her legs and the feeling of emptiness that had taken possession of her entire body.

34

Laurence came downstairs the next morning to find a note on the kitchen-table: *I've gone to spend a few days with Lucie. I need time to think. Love to Kieron and Estelle.* He couldn't imagine how early Rosie must have set off. He hadn't even heard her come back the previous night. He'd spent the entire evening trying to distract his children from the absence of their mother. He'd even invented a story about an old friend of hers throwing an unexpected party to which she'd been invited, not knowing what kind of explanation they might have heard from her.

After they'd reluctantly gone to bed, he had sat on his own, gazing at the dying embers of the log fire they had enjoyed all evening. He didn't for one moment think she might be deceiving him. She never lied to him, even when she was cross. That was one of the things he kept coming back to: the fact that she would never keep things back from him, never put up a wall of pretence. He'd never once thought she might be seriously interested in another man. He'd done his level best to satisfy her in bed and spoil her whenever he could, and not only on her birthday and at Christmas. Why could she possibly think that any other man would give her more than he could? But her deliberate refusal to be part of the family celebration on Boxing Day and her unsettling reference to an alternative invitation, on which she refused to elaborate, and now a long evening which she said she'd be spending with friends, with no indication when she might be back, made him wonder if something might be afoot.

Or was her absence from home just a convenient way of reducing their contacts to an absolute minimum? And was it clear to her that by punishing him like this she was also punishing Kieron and Estelle? He found that especially difficult to reconcile with the picture he had of her. They might have disagreed over aspects of the children's upbringing, but he never once thought she could put her own interests ahead of all others. That too was one of the things he loved about her. In so many respects she was utterly selfless, ready to believe in the goodness of others and driven by a need to facilitate their happiness.

He waited longer than he would otherwise have done, ensuring that Kieron and Estelle had something warm inside them before despatching them off to school. The questions rang in his ears when he showed them Rosie's note: 'Why isn't Mum here? Where's she gone? Why does she need time to think? Why can't she think here?'

As he headed off from Marlborough Close he wondered whether he should have dished up another white lie. They knew he was sleeping in the spare room and that this was not a temporary deviation from what married couples normally did, and they had seen how she would suddenly withdraw if he walked into any room they were in. He in turn didn't need their reproachful looks to remind him that the needle of their internal barometers was signalling stormy times ahead. All he could do was to call either Rosie or Lucie or both later that day and ask for an explanation. That, he felt, was surely the very least he was entitled to receive.

For the time being he had equally pressing matters to attend to elsewhere. A final attempt to secure additional funding from his bank to put the chapel restoration project back on course had foundered. None of his protestations about the value of the collateral he was offering had made much of an impact. He had never seen the tap run so dry in such a short space of time. The money that had always been so freely available the moment it was turned was now beyond his reach. He'd had no difficulty in coming up with the deposit, but he was already seriously overdrawn after paying the remainder of the purchase price, and his bank hadn't accepted his repeated reassurances about the shortfall being a mere blip on the radar. He now had no alternative but to seek help from a source on which he had so often counted in the past.

It was a Friday, and a day later than planned he was going to pick up his mother's shopping list. This time he knew he wasn't going to be in and out in a matter of minutes. When she opened the door, he thought she was looking a little tired. 'It's my wee one again,' she said softly, as she put her arms around him.

After she'd returned from the kitchen with a pot of tea and his favourite biscuits, the first thing she wanted to know was 'Has Rosie completely recovered from her flu?' It was one of the things he vividly remembered from his childhood, her capacity to suddenly ask a question about the topic he most keenly wished to avoid. She had the homing instinct of a sophisticated missile. He knew that whatever he said there was bound to be a detonation.

'More or less, but she's decided to have a change of air. That'll really put paid to any lingering symptoms.'

He could see that his reply was not being taken as a signal to move on.

'Oh, really? Where's she gone?'

'She wanted to see Lucie again anyway.'

'Is that the air she wanted to have?'

He began to falter. The steel-grey eyes were locked into his gaze. 'It's, it's complicated.'

'Laurence, are you telling me everything? You said she needed this mysterious air after that unfortunate incident with Kieron. You implied much the same when she couldn't come on Boxing Day, and now in order to deal with these supposed lingering symptoms she needs the air they only have up north. What's wrong with the air where we are? There's nothing finer than sea air, surely.'

Damage limitation, he thought. I need to talk about my finances, I don't want to get any further into the state of my marriage. She probably suspects something and knowing her she'll worm it all out of me.

'Actually, my air could do with a little more oxygen,' he said.

He knew she would find some way of returning to an unwelcome subject, that was one of the things she was so good at. But for now her attention was being pulled away from matters matrimonial to matters filial.

'Please don't talk in riddles, dear. Out with it.'

'Mum, it's the chapel. I need extra funds. I was hoping you could help me out.'

'I warned you, Laurence. I told you not to take too much on. Even I could see the way things were heading last autumn. Don't tell me you've forgotten the first principle of good housekeeping.'

She was making him feel small again. He was her child and she was never going to let him forget that. He knew he had disappointed her. Yet he couldn't let her inconsistency pass unchallenged.

'You always taught me to go on striving and never to give up. All I've ever done was to keep that in mind.'

'There's a huge difference between being ambitious and being reckless. I'm beginning to wonder whether Rosie might not have come to the same conclusion.' The guided missile was back on course again.

'Can we please talk about the project without getting Rosie mixed up in it?'

'But Laurence, dear, you were the one who always insisted this was going to be your new home. Whether Rosie liked the idea or not.' The guided missile was now heading straight for him. 'I really don't want to interfere in your business activities, but if I were in your shoes I'd get shot of this mystical chapel of yours. Even if you only want to carry out a refurbishment, you won't get much joy out of it in the current business climate.'

'Does that mean you won't lend me any money?'

'I'm sure I don't have the sort of sums you'll need hanging around in my current account. But even if I did, I don't think I'd be minded to hand them over to you just like that. I say that not as your mother, but as someone who has her business hat on. It really isn't such a good idea, you know.' And then, as if deliberately wanting to compound his discomfort, came the rejoinder, 'Sort out your marriage first before you embark on anything new.'

It was uncanny, he thought, as he headed towards his office, that his mother could read him so well. Of course, observing a child over the course of forty-five years meant that you knew or guessed things which would be hidden well below the surface to nearly everybody else.

Suddenly his mobile alerted him to a text message. Keeping a cautious eye on the traffic around him, he noted that it was from Steve, wanting to know if they could meet up over lunch. Talking to Steve might at least give him some breathing space, a diversion from the uncomfortable matters that were teasing his mind.

But if he thought he could relax over a pint and a pasty in the pub, he was in for another shock. 'It's happened, Laurence,' Steve said, as soon as they had found a corner table. 'Patrick's getting rid of me.'

'Oh, mate, I am really sorry to hear that. Are you sure he can't be persuaded to keep you on?'

'No chance. The only other full-time employee he's keeping on will be Gemma. He needs some eye candy to draw the punters in, and I don't happen to be wearing a skirt. The whole sector's going tits up anyway. Nobody wants to buy or sell at the moment, Laurence. I might just as well emigrate. There's not much prospect of me finding anything else down here. Let's face it, there'll be dozens if not hundreds in a similar situation. Why should I turn out to be the lucky one?'

Laurence could tell from the heavy bags under Steve's eyes and the shadow across his face that any words of his would struggle to break through the carapace of despondency with which Steve had covered himself. It was Eeyore all over again, with burst balloons and empty honey-pots.

'Well, don't start moping, and don't forget that fear is a bad giver of advice,' said Laurence. 'Why don't you take yourself and Linda off into the sun for a proper holiday? That'll give you time to think. If I could offer you work, I would. But I've just taken on Ilona and in any case I'm paying her far less than I guess you've been getting from Patrick.'

Steve chewed on his lower lip before responding. 'But what do I do now, Laurence? My job is my life. It's the only identity I have. What can I possibly offer Linda without regular work? It's OK for you. You've got the whole package. Your own business, a lovely wife and kids. I've struggled all my life to get just a little of what you've got, and what have I got to show for it? Fuck all.'

'Steve, mate, I hear your pain. But wallowing in your misery isn't going to bring you anything new.' He paused before continuing. 'If it's any consolation to you, I've been going through a really rocky spell with Rosie. I'm beginning to wonder if she might have found somebody else.' He paused again and noted the shock in Steve's eyes. 'And I've got another problem too. I can't drum up the extra funds I need for the chapel project. But you know me: whatever doesn't kill you just makes you stronger.'

If only he had absolute belief in that, he thought to himself. He'd been struggling for a while now, fighting to keep the upper hand. He was becoming bogged down in trench warfare, not even gaining an inch of new ground despite all his efforts. Nothing like the battles that used to be fought in the past, with massed armies on either side. The arrows and spears flew through the air and in later generations the muskets were discharged, and at the end of each engagement, after hours of effort, the enemy was slain. There was a winner and a loser. So simple, really.

After paying for two rounds, Laurence made his excuses and felt the chill of the early-afternoon air on his face before slipping quickly behind the wheel of his car. The glum faces he saw on the streets did little to suggest that the new year had brought with it much in the way of munificence.

As he pulled up outside his office, a few huddled individuals were hurrying past the windows, their collars turned up against the wind, not pausing to look at any of the displays. He hardly had time to greet Ilona before she reminded him, 'You have Mr Meredith at three o'clock. He wants to see the flat in Winchester Court.'

He was glad to see Denis again. He didn't know many men of a similar age. True, Patrick was by now sixty, but there was little else you could talk to him about apart from the property business. Denis was somehow different, there seemed to be a vast hinterland waiting to be explored. He still had the vestiges of a deep tan into which multiple crevices had been carved that criss-crossed the surface, which reminded him of his mother's crackled neck. He was beginning to stoop, the first signs that his frame was yielding to the passage of time, though his handshake was firm and strong.

'I'm still having to adjust to the colder, damper climate here,' he said.

'What was it like, living so far away from your roots?'

Laurence could see an answer was slowly being prepared. He had no idea how many times Denis might have been asked a similar question, by people who would have regarded him primarily as an exotic foreigner. Unlike his own father, and despite his occasional forays abroad on package holidays, he had never experienced any desire to travel the high seas and explore alternative cultures. For a moment he wondered if his father might have looked like this in his mid-sixties and how many stories of a world beyond he would have to tell.

'You can try hard to integrate, of course. Indeed, up to a point you have to just in order to survive. But you will never completely understand the mentality and the perspective that others bring to bear on life in general.'

'Was there one part of the world that you enjoyed more than any other?'

Again, the answer was not a pre-formed response. It seemed to take time to emerge from the recesses of his mind.

'I suppose Japan takes some beating, though on a different day and in a different mood I might react differently to your question. There's a wonderful stone garden next to one of Kyoto's temples, with fifteen boulders representing the continents and oceans of this world. Wherever you stand in this garden you will only ever be able to see fourteen of them. This failure to see everything is part of the Zen belief in the unknowable and its awareness of the uncertainty in life itself. It represents human imperfection. We think we understand everything, but so much is actually beyond our comprehension.'

The conversation was beginning to draw Laurence in. He spent almost every waking minute of every day so deeply wrapped up in practical details, countering facts and assertions with alternative facts and assertions, obsessing about figures and yields, that the prospect of a philosophical excursion was like being offered an unfamiliar yet strangely appetising dish.

'Wasn't there some American politician who talked about the "known unknowns"?'

'Yes, I think a lot of fun was made at his expense by people who were all too certain there was nothing left to know. But the really frightening thing was that he also talked about the "unknown unknowns". Who knows where the human race is heading? We've made a pretty big mess of things so far.'

Laurence was tempted to cross swords. He wanted to say that societies paid too little attention to what had been achieved in terms of material progress, that people were far better off than they had ever been, but he sensed in what Denis was saying a world that he knew had always been there but which he had never bothered to properly acknowledge.

'Did you find it easier to think about all these unknowns while you were over there?'

There was another pause before Denis replied. 'I certainly had plenty of time to reflect. There's nothing really new in the job I had. You teach the same old things: the grammar, the spelling, the vocabulary, over and over again. That knowledge hardly ever changes, doesn't really need renewing. So I was able to think about other things. But I'm forgetting myself. As a teacher you learn to let others speak, especially if you're teaching a language. How about yourself? How do you view your own job?'

'You must have heard what's been happening in the last eighteen months or so. It's not looking good at all. In fact, a good friend of mine who also works in the property market was telling me over lunch that he's going to be made redundant. And he's not the only one.'

There was a wry smile on Denis' face. 'So I suppose everybody's now in a buyer's market, am I right?'

'Up to a point. You first need cash. And the banks are now very reluctant to lend. That's because they have hardly anything themselves.'

'Ah yes, there are limitations to the notion that risk is good. That is at the heart of this crisis, of course. I remember when I was still teaching here in the late sixties, before I went abroad, bankers earned no more than teachers did. But then taking risks started to drive profits and that became the name of the game. That happened all over the western world. Risks were taken with our debts and debts became a kind of social control for politicians. If people had mortgages they wouldn't go on strike, there wouldn't be any social unrest. If you're going to blame anybody, you first need to examine the degree of collusion that went on.'

Denis had clearly got things all worked out. Laurence was finding it hard to come up with a compelling alternative, and he hated getting into conversational territory in which he would struggle to make his points.

Taking a leaf out of his mother's book, he quickly changed the subject. 'I gather from Ilona that you're interested in the Winchester Court flat. Shall we take a closer look at it?'

In the car Laurence felt much happier pointing out the streets he remembered from his early days as an estate agent where redevelopment had taken place, contrasting these with those still caught in a shadowy existence away from the central thoroughfares. He needed no theories and no philosophical world-view to explain to Denis how money followed the first signs of investment in the infrastructure. Everything flowed from that crucial start. Anybody who had eyes to see could surely appreciate that.

For someone who had lived most of his adult life in confined domestic spaces, Denis was proving quite picky about the kind of property he was prepared to rent. On paper the Winchester Court flat seemed to tick many of his boxes, but the location was not to his liking and the rooms were much smaller than he had supposed. Laurence knew there was no point in labouring any of the issues; when a client was as quietly determined as Denis appeared to be, any additional push would have been entirely counter-productive.

'You've seen everything we currently have to offer,' he said. 'However, a tenant's just given notice on a property with a sea view in Southsea. That won't become available until March. It's not as big as the flat you've just seen, but the location would probably suit you better.'

'Thanks, Laurence. I don't need to rush into things. Never a sensible thing to do anyway, in my view. Please keep me posted. And I've really enjoyed your company this afternoon. If we could meet again soon, that would be splendid.'

After dropping Denis off near his sister's workplace, Laurence headed for the supermarket where he routinely dealt with his mother's shopping list. As he was repeatedly jostled by other shoppers plainly in a hurry who hardly paused to utter a word of apology, the civilised way in which he and Denis had parted stood out in sharp relief. If his mother hadn't devoted so much time to the cause of good manners, he wouldn't even have been in a position to notice any difference.

Little time had been available since that morning to consider which properties he would now need to sell, if his mother continued to maintain her uncooperative stance and refused to rescue him from his financial impasse. Giving up now on the entire project would not only spell out a personal defeat, it would also mean a failure to realise the potential in an attractive asset. It was all very well for his mother to imply that he needed to cut his jacket according to the available cloth, but it made no sense either to discard the material just because the buttons, the sewing-thread and the liner were missing. He would make one last attempt when he returned to deliver his mother's groceries.

But the butterscotch had hardened still further since their morning exchange of opinions. He had convinced himself that his mother would never sit idly by and turn a deaf ear to a desperate appeal for help from her only child. The outer severity had been employed so often to bring him to heel, but then she had always relented. On his arrival she held him quite firmly in her arms, but there was no smile as he placed the box on the kitchen-table. The voice was unwavering. 'I can't do it, Laurence. I'm sorry, but you're going to need a re-think. The last thing I want you to do is to climb deeper into a deep black hole.'

He found it difficult to suppress a feeling of bitterness driving through the deep darkness of the Hampshire countryside towards the twinkling lights along the coastline. He wasn't expecting any charity, his mother knew she'd get back every penny he borrowed from her, so why was she refusing to give him what he wanted and needed?

That same morning Estelle had warned him that because she was taking part in a Year 8 baking competition on school premises she expected to be home late; Kieron had texted him while he was still with Denis that he was going with a friend to the greyhound racing stadium in Tipner. Neither of them made any mention of their mother. If they were distracted from the unresolved domestic situation, so much the better.

On his return to Marlborough Close Laurence therefore found the house in darkness. Despite the heating being full on, it felt cooler inside than he was used to. There was no point in lighting another log fire just for himself, so he reached instead for a bottle of whisky which he normally kept at the back of the drinks cabinet. The sharpness of the spirit on his tongue gave way to a feeling of contentment as it descended, the warmth spreading slowly from his abdomen towards the extremities. A few minutes later, as the welcome tingling in his limbs began to subside, he reached for a second glass. His eyelids began to droop and he gave himself up to the headiness of the moment.

With a start he heard the front door crashing shut. It was Estelle. 'Hi, Dad. Have you been snoozing?'

On sitting upright he became aware of a slight dizziness. He heard the words issuing from his lips in a strangely dislocated state, as he responded falteringly to his daughter's questions. There was something else at the back of his mind he had wanted to attend to. Of course. He had a wife. A pretty little wife called Rosie. She wasn't here. She was somewhere else. Yes, up north. With her sister. He had wanted to call her. Really. He'd been busy though. All day. So many other things to do. A bit of a blur really. He'd do it tomorrow. Not now. He couldn't think straight right now. He couldn't talk properly either. The words, you see, wouldn't come out the way he wanted them to.

Leaving Estelle wondering whether he'd been talking to himself or to her, he struggled off the sofa and tottered up the stairs to bed.

35

When Rosie got back to Marlborough Close shortly after midnight, she sat in her car, hugging the folds of her coat and trying to stop the inner shaking that was convulsing her. The cooler night air was seeping into the fetid cocoon where she believed her brain to be. Her body was becoming a war zone for competing extremes of temperature: heat against cold, cold against heat. It was like standing on the rim of an erupting volcano in the middle of an icy northern expanse. She was trying hard to make sense of what she remembered. She had felt no pleasure, no release, but nor had she done anything to stop the sudden and completely unexpected invasion of her self. She had lain on the back seat of a car and allowed a violation to occur. She hadn't put up her hands to signal her opposition to the assault, hadn't aimed her fingernails at his face in an attempt to draw blood, hadn't thrust a knee into the softer areas of his groin, hadn't screamed or shouted or begged for help. She had caused it all to happen. Without a struggle. Perhaps she had secretly wanted it, using her eyes and lips to fire up his arousal to the point where he could no longer hold back. Either way she was guilty: cowardice or complicity. She had betrayed Laurence. She had betrayed herself.

Eventually she climbed out of the front seat, the only thing that had given her backbone support during her return journey, and let herself into the dark house. She made her way up the stairs and into the bedroom, pulling off the different layers of her clothing until she stood quite naked. She moved trance-like towards the en suite and the shower cubicle and stood for what seemed like an eternity feeling the stinging needles of hot water from the shower-head on her skin. Her hands moved mechanically over her entire body, rubbing and scouring the crevices and folds for fear she had missed even a tiny area of defilement. The water that ran off her body was transparent, but her eyes saw only self-renewing streams of brown liquid slowly draining away. She knew that she would not be able to face Laurence or her children in the morning. She also knew that she would not be able to face any customers in Florabellum. She knew she had to get as far away from the south coast as possible.

In the middle of the night, unable to sleep and hunched over her legs in bed, she sent Lucie a text telling her that something terrible had happened and she was travelling up to see her. Then she sent Lorna a longer message, expressing her profuse apologies for any inconvenience but claiming she'd had a relapse and would need to stay in bed for a few days.

A good hour before anything was likely to be stirring in the house, she picked up the heap of discarded clothing lying in a corner of the room and crept down the stairs. In the kitchen she squeezed it all into two large carrier-bags. She grabbed a sheet of paper and a felt-tip pen and scribbled a note for her family. She quickly filled a Thermos flask with strong black coffee. Then, clutching a small overnight case and the carrier-bags, she walked out into the frosty January air towards her car parked in the street.

Well before she needed to join the local motorway she noticed a builder's skip at the side of the road and stopped to cast her clothing into its wide-open jaws. She had considered going cross-country via Oxford, following what seemed to her to be a nearly vertical line through the heart of the country, but it was still dark and she would have had to contend with unfamiliar roads and fewer signs of life. Better by far to be tucked into well-lit motorway lanes, surrounded by constant streams of other people packed into their individual spaces but still close enough to be within touching distance. She needed to feel that she was not alone.

As soon as she was past London, she pulled into a service-station and made her way into a self-proclaimed restaurant, in which small groups of truckers were talking animatedly between mouthfuls of fried food and individual middle-aged men in crumpled business suits were staring into the middle distance. The smell of cheap frying fat and stale male sweat hung in the air, making her feel nauseous. She eyed the men nervously, wondering if any of them would get up and regard a woman on her own as fair game. She managed to find a quiet corner of the room and warmed her hands around a large cup of over-milked cappuccino.

She looked at her mobile. There was a *Mum, where on earth r u?* from Kieron and a *We're missing you. When are you coming back?* from Estelle. As yet nothing from Laurence, and nothing from Lucie either. It was just after nine o'clock and she was sure her sister would by now be up and about, yet she hesitated to call the number, believing that the explaining she had to do was best left to the intimacy of a domestic space. She sent her another text, saying she was on her way and expected to reach Huddersfield by lunchtime. If Lucie was away, she reckoned she would have to find herself a B&B; Dulcie was unlikely to provide a strong shoulder to cry on, even though she had made the effort to travel up and see her after the episode with her broken leg.

Back on the motorway she was surprised to see so much heavy goods traffic, especially the bunching of the larger vehicles that always terrorised her and made her drive faster than desirable, simply in order to escape the congestion. A short while later she found herself in the middle lane behind a car that was packed with children on the back seats and which suddenly decided to shear out into the fast lane to avoid a truck a short distance ahead. At the same time she was conscious of a sleek saloon that flashed past on her right. Almost immediately there was a vicious squeal of brakes and a honking that seemed to last forever. By now she had almost caught up with the slow-moving truck in her original lane. That could so easily have led to a nasty collision, she thought. It was just as well she had managed to reduce her speed, otherwise she would have run into the back of the truck. And what if she had done? That might have been the end of her. No more misery and unhappiness. No more stark reality in a world that wasn't even making the effort to be nice to her.

And then she thought of Kieron and Estelle and two other famous children who had lost their mother in an accident at high speed. How could she have been so selfish? They needed her, she was their mother. For a moment she considered turning off the motorway at the next opportunity and heading back to the husband and family she had left behind. And then she remembered that sordid back-street assault that was still haunting her. She couldn't look into their eyes and tell them everything was OK when it clearly wasn't. Not right now.

As she gripped the steering-wheel and peered ahead of her in the middle lane, aware that the traffic would suddenly creep up on her from behind and then race past in the overtaking lane, she realised there was too much over which she had no control and which threatened to pick at and pull apart the threads of stability and harmony in her life, just as the onset of a crisis in one of the books she remembered from her childhood would suddenly and unequivocally rip things apart. Even as she held tight to her course on the motorway, she accepted there could be no such thing as an auto-pilot in any relationship, there could be no coasting along. Nothing was fixed forever, everything was in flux.

From deep within her throbbing head she heard again the voices that started off with softly whispering, scarcely audible sounds, but which were gradually building into an insistent clamour for possession of her mind. *You are a bad person, you are no better than a slut, a cheap piece of flesh permanently soiled. You will never be able to erase the memory of what you have done, you will carry this stain with you until the day you die. You have destroyed any pretence of being a good wife and a good mother, you have cast your husband from your side, you have abandoned the family home and all your responsibilities. What a despicable advertisement for the human race.*

No sooner had the one faction with its rabble-rousing adherents to the Old Testament exhausted its armoury of rebukes and reproaches than the counter-litany set in from the New Testament. *Rosie, deep down you are a good person. You believe in what is right and proper. You have never deliberately done anything to harm your husband, your children, your sisters or any of your friends. You know that from time to time you have made mistakes, allowed your lofty ideals to blind you to practical considerations and in moments of disorientation have struggled to plot a sensible course. In all of that you have been no different than any other human being, so why be so tough on yourself? How could you have possibly known that a night out with somebody you viewed as a friend was going to end as it did? You behaved entirely appropriately, you weren't drunk or inebriated, he was the one who took advantage of you, there was no way you could have foreseen what he would do. There has to be salvation for you.*

The counter-insurgents were waiting to pounce again. *Rosie, you're kidding yourself. You led him on, with all those smiles you exchanged with him, the physical closeness you were party to, the attraction you felt for him, the signals you were sending out every time you were with him. I want you, I want your body, I want to yield to you, I want to feel you inside me. There you are, you've at last spelled it all out, you were complicit in what took place, you didn't push him away, you didn't once say no, you permitted it to happen. No judge or jury would believe a word you might say in your self-defence.*

She felt her eyes brimming with tears. It was getting too much for her. All she wanted was for the clouds of despair to give way to unbroken sunshine. But even as she indulged in her vain little fantasy, she realised it was no more than that. Nobody was going to intervene and wave a magic wand. Outside the wintry sky was hanging low, sagging with all the other cares of the world. Life in the other lanes was streaming purposefully past. The most she could hope for would be to see herself caught up in the slipstream of others.

Once off the motorway she decided to pull over and ring Lucie. There'd be no point in heading for the house if she wasn't there. The number kept ringing out and she was on the point of terminating the call when she heard her sister respond breathlessly. 'Didn't you get my texts, sis?' Rosie asked.

'Sorry, petal, I've been busy all morning with a leak from the washing-machine. It's flooded the kitchen.'

'You poor thing. I hope there's not too much damage.'

'I had it on overnight. It's never happened before, but no doubt we'll survive. Why are you calling?'

'I've just turned onto the A637.'

'The A637? What are you doing up here?'

'Lucie, something awful's happened. I – I, I didn't know where else to turn.'

'Lord almighty, you sound in a terrible state. Come on over. We're at home.'

As she headed towards the outskirts of Huddersfield, she was becoming unsettled at the thought that the "we" almost certainly meant Ian, the brother-in-law whose hand would have been between her legs had she not used her elbow to force him away. She didn't really want him to be around while she unburdened herself to Lucie.

'Rosie, love, you look all in,' Lucie said, as she opened the door. 'Come on inside, we've mopped everything up in the meantime. Let's go into the front room while things are drying out in the kitchen. Would you like some tea?'

Rosie was finding it difficult to articulate her thoughts. She had pushed the events of the previous night to the back of her mind while she concentrated on the driving, but now the absence of sleep and the swirling images that kept resurfacing were leading to a feeling of dizziness.

'Where's Ian?' She was expecting her sister to say that he was miles away as usual, servicing satellite dishes or installing aerials.

'Oh, he decided to take the day off. Wanted a long weekend for a change. He's just popped out to the off-licence. He won't be long.'

'How long?'

'Rosie, petal, whatever's the matter? Did you want us both to hear what you have to say?'

Rosie put up her hands. 'No, no!' The tears were welling up inside her. 'Can't we just go for a walk?'

'You daft a'porth! Just look at you. Your eyes are all red, your face looks a mess. It's bloody cold outside too. Why on earth do you want to be out in the elements when you can be here in the warm?'

'Because I don't deserve any better.'

'Oh lordie, what nonsense you're spouting. Look, let me make you a cuppa.'

'When is Ian going to be back?'

Lucie gave her a sharp look. 'Are you trying to avoid him? Is that it?'

Rosie nodded and then burst into tears. Lucie held her close, rubbing the small of her back. 'OK, Plan B. Let's take your car, but you're in no fit state to drive. I'll do that. We can always pull in and have a cuppa later. Let me just get my coat.'

As she sat next to Lucie, Rosie saw the glowering sky touching the crimped lines of the hills in the distance. The light remained an obstinate shade of grey. It seemed easier talking at the slightly misty windscreen than at her own sister.

'Lucie, I don't know if it's already my early menopause, but I've found it so difficult handling my emotions these last few weeks,' she said. 'I met someone on the opening night at the Callas and... I suppose I just fell for him.'

'You mean, you've been having an affair?'

'Not exactly. We haven't been together all that often. He's divorced and I suppose he must have been lonely, and me... well, I felt frustrated.'

'Does Laurence know?'

'I don't know. At least, I don't think so. Last night we went to see a film together. Lorna recommended it, but it wasn't really my cup of tea. Much too depressing and not really what I wanted. Anyway, it all happened when we were walking back to our cars.'

'What did?'

There was another flood of tears. 'I was raped,' she wailed.

'Good god. What a brute! Have you been to the police?'

Rosie took some time to reply. 'That's the point, Lucie. What evidence do I have? I scrubbed myself silly in the shower when I got back home. And it would be my word against his. What makes it worse is that I didn't resist.'

'You're not going to tell me that you secretly wanted it to happen.'

She blew into her handkerchief. 'I'm so confused, Lucie. I found him attractive, yes. He was kind and listened when I told him about all the problems I was having with Laurence. I thought that perhaps we might have a future together. But I don't think I was quite ready for sex just yet.'

They had left the built-up areas far behind them and the starkness of the wintry sky met the bleakness of the open countryside as it fell away to either side of the country road. 'You poor little sod, you've got yourself into a reight proper mess.'

Rosie turned towards her sister. 'I don't know what to do, Lucie. How can I go back and face Laurence and the kids? I just want things to be the way they were all those years ago.'

'You wazzock! How old are you? You'll be – what – forty-six in a few weeks' time. Have you learnt nowt by now?'

'But when you get married, you never think that so many

years down the line it'll all go wrong and begin to fizzle out. You just expect things to go on forever.'

After a while Lucie said, 'Dulcie was spot on, I'll give her that.'

'Why, what did she say?'

'While you were still a kid, she told me that you'd stuffed yourself full of too many romantic notions and that one day you were going to have to wake up to the real world. You know, she didn't for one moment believe that Adam was right for you. She didn't think it'd last.'

'Why didn't she tell me that to my face?'

'Oh Rosie, what am I going to do with you? Would you have listened to her? Would you have taken a blind bit of notice? Some of the hardest things in life you just have to find out for yourself. You're not going to take anybody else's word for it. Not even your own family's.'

Rosie fell silent. She had expected her sister to take out a lamp and point a way for her through the enveloping gloom, but on this raw January day there were no shafts of sunlight remotely sharp enough to prise open the banks of low-lying cloud. Nor were the spirits of the countryside she had grown up in and which now filled her with a longing for the untroubled years of her childhood close to whispering any advice in her ear. High above Huddersfield the air had grown imperceptibly thin.

She was suddenly back in her childhood, following her teenage sisters along the hedgerows and picking blackberries. 'We have to pick them before the first frosts,' Dulcie had warned.

'Why's that?'

'Because then the devil pisses on them and turns them bitter.'

In her eagerness to obey her sister's instruction she had pulled off the over-ripe berries in haste, crushing them between her fingers which she wiped clean down the front of her dress.

'Just look at the mess you've made of yourself. All that juice! Our mam will be furious.'

The blood-red juice of her childhood had indeed turned bitter. Lucie was patting her arm. 'Look, love. I know a super little teashop where we can have an early lunch. And then I must phone Ian and let him know where I am. He'll probably think I've been carried off by aliens.' Then she added, 'You didn't tell me why you weren't keen on him being around. He's not been up to his old tricks again, has he?'

Rosie froze in her seat. She hoped she would never have to admit to her own sister what had once happened. The last thing she wanted to do was to cause trouble for her, or her husband for that matter. 'How did you know?' she quaked.

'Oh Rosie love, you can't be married to someone all these years and not know what they're like deep down. They may think they can keep secrets from you and you'll never find out. It's the leopard thing and the spots. Or the woven figure.'

'The woven figure?'

'Yes, it's something Dulcie said a while ago. Some poet or other she came across. Life stitches us together in a particular way. That's what makes us unique. But you can't unmake the pattern, you can only follow it, it's part of you.'

Mercifully Lucie didn't ask for details. Rosie wondered whether this was a further act of self-preservation or whether she wished to spare her sister the anguish of recalling another unwelcome sexual advance. Lucie was married to a philanderer, yet she was still his wife. Her sister's marriage remained a mystery to her. How could she continue to live with him under the same roof?

Even as she wrestled with the complexities of another marriage, she was aware of the inconsistencies in her own. The thought of ever lying in the arms of John Bibby and expecting to exchange one lover for another without incurring any painful consequences now struck her as impossibly naïve. What was it he had offered her, apart from a sympathetic ear? Why hadn't she heard any voices in her head reminding her of the possibility of predatory male urges taking control, even as her own hormonal levels were on the wane? Was that all she had been in John's eyes, an opportunity for a quick lay and nothing more? He had known all along that she was married. Was that the special thrill he had got, and would he have been half as brazen had she been a divorcee? She simply didn't know. Nor did she know if she was going to be able to pick up any pieces from her relationship with Laurence. It might have been easier without the overwhelming sense of guilt. She fretted that she might not be able to conceal the truth from him and agonised at his possible reaction. One uncertainty merely replaced another. Whichever direction her mind took, she found herself in blind alleys or at best one-way streets with no opportunities for a sudden U-turn.

A short time later they were back in the real world. Feeling the waves of exhaustion that were clouding her thinking, she gulped down large sips of her sweetened tea. Their order of omelettes was taking some time to arrive. The old-fashioned little café with its chintz curtains and willow-patterned teacups and plates was filling up with elderly ladies muttering their cautionary tales in hushed whispers and casting their looks about them. She was beginning to think that the walls were closing in on her.

Lucie suddenly stretched across the table and gripped her hands. 'You're very welcome to stay with us for a few days, you know,' she said. 'I'll make certain Ian doesn't come too close.' How odd for her to make that kind of a statement, Rosie thought. She must have some strange power over this errant husband of hers.

'No thanks, sis. Look, I obviously need more time to think. I suppose I can do that better when I'm on my own.'

'There's a really good B&B this side of Grange Moor. You could stay there. But make certain you come over to us for a meal soon. You're my kid sister, remember.'

They parted outside the café, the two sisters heading off in opposite directions, the one turning back to her husband, the other turning away from hers.

36

When Laurence woke on the Saturday morning, the first thing
he was conscious of was a throbbing head. He liked his pints of
beer, especially if he was out with friends, and whiskies were an
occasional added extra, but he had always tried to pursue a course
of moderation in his drinking. He remembered the time shortly
before taking his A Levels when he and some of his schoolfriends
had spent the entire evening consuming a haphazard selection of
hard spirits and cans of beer. He had been violently sick all over
the furniture while the parents of another boy had been out for the
evening, and when they returned home he was taken, in a state
of dehydration and exhaustion, back to his stony-faced mother,
who had demanded to know why he had brought such disgrace
upon himself and caused her such unforgivable embarrassment.
All he could recall this time was drinking at least three glasses of
the hard stuff, but perhaps there'd been a fourth and a fifth too.

Earlier in the week, while the kids were upstairs, he had
spent a gloomy hour looking at the television screen as a domestic
drama unfolded. The husband was a tight-fisted control freak
who was married to a much younger woman, and there had been
endless rows about the household budget. 'Give me space, give me
space!' she had repeatedly screamed at him, as if that was all they
needed to solve their financial problems. When Laurence had read

Rosie's note on the kitchen table twenty-four hours previously, that was the litany at the back of his head. In November after taking herself and the children off to Lucie's for a week, she'd returned as she said she would. He felt sure this time would be no different, though he certainly couldn't help wondering why she'd come back so late after her night out and whether that had any connection with her sudden decision to disappear. Her erratic behaviour was clearly of some concern to their kids and he was finding it difficult persuading them that her mood swings, her coolness towards him and the various assignations outside the home on which she had refused to elaborate were within the range of normality for a middle-aged married woman.

Using television drama as a reference point for his own marriage was hardly a reliable guide, but there was almost nobody else he could turn to as a sounding-board. His mother's views about Rosie were ambivalent at the best of times and his friends in the local area were either younger and much less experienced, like Steve, or older, twice divorced and now single, like Patrick. His architect friend Clive was most probably gay and never talked about girlfriends. He had little contact with his two brothers-in-law in Yorkshire. The one spent more time away from home than Laurence regarded as acceptable and the other, Dulcie's dull and taciturn husband, reportedly spent more time in the loft ordering and reordering his collection of beer-mats and pub signs than anywhere near a telephone. All of Laurence's other acquaintances would be reluctant to open up about the state of their marriages and impart valuable advice about how to handle aberrant wives. Thus there appeared to be no alternative to relying on his own gut instincts to guide him on the path ahead, should Rosie's strange behaviour continue. In the meantime, the idea of giving her space, as presented in the screen drama, seemed his only option.

He should have called Lucie the previous evening. Just to find out if Rosie had arrived safely, just to be able to reassure the kids. He couldn't think why he hadn't done so on his return to the dark and empty house or why, for that matter, he had allowed his thoughts to be hijacked by the promise of easy access to alcohol. Now he was paying the price for his inexplicable over-indulgence. His head was sore. Truth to tell, his heart was sore too. Why was he lying on his own in the spare room and not alongside his wife in their double bed? Why had she turned away from him? What had he done to deserve this kind of treatment from her? And then he paused to remember the conversation earlier in the week with Steve, who had been dripping with self-pity. He had no intention of following suit. If their mother wasn't around, it would be his duty to look after their two children. Somebody had to. Who else was there?

He rolled out of bed and made for the en suite in the master bedroom. He could smell Rosie in the bedroom. He could smell her on the bedlinen, on the Louis Quinze chair and on her bathrobe that hung from the inside door. He was missing her touch, her smiles and the warmth of the flat vowels in her speech. As he stood in the shower, he felt the ache of desire in his body again. He wanted her so badly.

It was well after nine o'clock by the time Kieron and Estelle looked in on him in the kitchen. He had revived himself with a large pot of tea and was peering at a series of spreadsheets on his laptop, trying to finalise which items in his portfolio he would put on the market to stem his cashflow crisis.

'I was about to give your Auntie Lucie a call,' he said without much conviction. 'Have you heard back from Mum at all?'

They shook their heads. They hadn't quite shaken the sleepiness out of their teenage systems, but their eyes revealed a state of anxiety as they sat down opposite him. 'Dad,' Kieron said. 'Me and Estelle want to know if you and mum are getting a divorce. Do you still love her?'

Laurence hadn't expected quite so much directness first thing in the morning. 'Whatever makes you think we're going to split up?'

Estelle was looking tearful. 'Mums don't just disappear for no good reason. Not unless they're really unhappy. We can't see why our mum wouldn't want to be here with the rest of us.'

Laurence eyed the back garden through the large window. The murky greys of the past week were no longer in charge; a watery sun was beginning to filter through the thick lumps of cloud in the sky. 'Look,' he said. 'Let me phone Huddersfield and find out what's happening there. The weather looks much better today. How about if I take you to see the chapel I bought and then we can go down to the sea.'

'That's the place Mum said she wasn't moving to. That's what's been driving her away, isn't it?' Kieron said forcefully.

'No, son, that's not quite right. I never said we'd be moving there. Your mum made that clear. If it had been left to me, yes, I would've wanted it to be our new home. You'll see why when I take you there. But now my plans are to get a refurbishment organised and afterwards put it on the market.'

The scepticism was still there on Kieron's face, but Estelle pinched his arm and said, 'We hardly ever do things together now. It'd be good to see inside, even if Mum isn't here.'

'I'll phone your Auntie Lucie first and then we can get going,' Laurence said.

A few minutes later he was listening to his mystified sister-in-law. 'She's not here,' Lucie said. 'We parted yesterday lunchtime and she said she'd be heading for a B&B that I told her about. In fact, I tried to reach her last night but the call went to voicemail. An hour later I rang the B&B to see if she'd arrived, but they said they were full up and they'd had to turn away one woman who came mid-afternoon and wanted to stay the night.'

'I don't understand. Why isn't she with you? She said she'd be staying with you for a few days.'

'Oh Laurence, it's too complicated to explain.' And then she continued, half-jokingly, 'What've you been doing to my little sister anyway? She's not her usual self.'

You can say that again, Laurence thought, but he had no

intention of opening up to Lucie. He couldn't be sure what Rosie might have said to her, if she had indeed said very much. He wasn't going to pretend he was the little innocent, but any lengthy discussion now would delay the start of the planned outing.

'Keep trying her mobile and we'll do the same,' he said. 'The battery may be flat, who knows?'

In the car heading towards the chapel, Estelle seemed fired up with energy. 'Dad, Mrs Fentham says that the rich are getting richer and the poor poorer. Why is that?'

Laurence found himself using a series of generalisations to justify the iniquities of the world, only for Estelle to pounce. She was intellectually the sharper and more savvy of his two children. On she went with her questions. 'Dad, where's the dividing line between ambition and greed?'

'That's a philosophical question, if ever there was one,' he said, looking through the windscreen at the mottled sky.

'So you don't really know?'

'I think I do, but it's not so easy putting it into simple words.'

'Are you greedy?'

'No, I hope not.'

'But you are ambitious?'

'Yes.'

'What does Mum think you are? Greedy or ambitious?'

He was aware of how close to the bone his daughter's questions were getting. 'You'd have to ask her that. Look, why don't you give her a call and find out where she is?' They were just a couple of minutes away from Warsash, but once more, when Estelle tried, she only managed to reach the voicemail facility.

Completion of the purchase of the chapel had gone through at the very last moment after Laurence had succeeded in mobilising all his cash reserves. Yet the project had almost come off the rails and the path ahead still seemed very uncertain without the release of further equity. But as he stepped out of the car and stood in front of the imposing building with his children, the rebellious doubts that had started to cut through the firewall of his confidence were being repulsed. He hadn't come this far after so many business ventures only to make one catastrophic mistake in the absence of a favourable tail wind. Others might have baulked at the risks involved in committing to a huge budget with no guarantee of a full return, let alone any kind of profit, but he had never believed in half-measures or playing it safe. A grand roll of the dice might be too theatrical for some, but he wanted to be there on stage with all the big names instead of sitting passively in the auditorium hoping to bask in a few occasional rays of reflected limelight.

'Dad, if this was once a holy building,' he heard Estelle asking, 'does that mean that the people who might one day live here will be blessed for the rest of their lives?'

He was on the point of embarking on the principle of a deconsecration when his mobile rang. It was Lucie.

'Laurence, Rosie's just been in touch. It was like you said. Her battery was flat and the daft a'porth had forgotten to take her battery-charger with her. She's in a store in the centre of town waiting for her phone to be fully charged.'

'Well, that's a relief to know,' Laurence said after telling his children. 'Give her a few hours and then you'll be able to call her and find out when she's coming back.'

'Dad,' Kieron asked, 'would Mum still have been upset if you hadn't bought this place?'

'I've already said that we're not going to live here.'

Estelle pounced once more. 'That's not an answer to the question. Is Mum unhappy because of all the money you're planning to spend?' She had once hovered outside the kitchen door while her parents were in the middle of an argument about spending. "You can't have a champagne taste on a lemonade pocket," was what her mother had said. To which her father replied, "But we don't have a lemonade pocket."

The thicket they had entered as part of their conversation was turning up plenty of uneven ground, and Laurence had to pick his way carefully. 'It's all part of my job. You have to speculate to accumulate. That's what people like me do all the time. Mum knows that.'

He could sense that they were both unconvinced. He pointed upwards to the stained glass. 'Well, come on now. Honest opinions. What do you think of the building?'

'It's very grand,' said Estelle. 'Is that really us?'

'I've told you. There are no plans to move from Marlborough Close.'

'But if we did move, where would we go to school?'

He was about to reply that the distances involved would not preclude them from remaining at their existing school, but managed to check himself in time. Any reply he gave might fuel their suspicions that he was merely putting a potential move on hold rather than forswearing it altogether. He had no intention of making them think he was trying to exert undue pressure in their mother's absence.

'Just look at the time,' he said. 'You must be starving by now. Shall we go and find a nice place to eat somewhere along the Hamble River?'

He'd learned these ploys from his mother. If there was a subject she wanted to avoid and if any conversation was beginning to get too complicated to handle, she'd move off in an entirely different direction. And as he turned the ignition key, the amazing thing was that it nearly always worked with his own children too.

Over lunch the children brightened: Kieron was eager to discuss the Premier League and Estelle recounted the endless mishaps others had made in the recent school baking competition. When Laurence returned from the loo, he discovered that Kieron had put through a call to his mother from his mobile. At last she had got her phone recharged and was deeply apologetic about needing to take herself away from her children. At least that was the impression Kieron conveyed. There had apparently been no mention of Laurence, much to the latter's chagrin.

'Did she say when she's coming back?' he asked.

'That's what I wanted to know, but she didn't tell me exactly. "Soon" is all she said.'

'We all need time to ourselves every now and again,' Laurence said. 'Your mum's entitled to a bit of space too, you know.' But he was beginning to wonder where exactly he featured on her list of priorities.

They spent almost an hour walking along the river, pausing to identify different types of waterfowl that would suddenly appear from underneath the reeds or push out from unseen eddies. A flock of Brent geese quickly flapped over them, chattering in disgust. Life was there where you least expected it, Laurence thought. You could stand perfectly still on the riverbank and allow your eyes to travel over the surface of the water, but no fish would bob up to the surface and create tell-tale ripples, no dark and sleek feathered objects would slide into view from behind the next bend in the river. Then, a few strides later, there would be a rustle in the grass or a gentle splash in the water or a keening in the air above, or they would happen upon a small river-craft piloted by a wizened face wearing a beanie-hat and windcheater to ward off the cold. Whenever you thought that everything had retreated into a shell there would be brisk reminders of lives – small and large – being lived.

The watery sun was already low in the January sky when they returned to Marlborough Close. Laurence decided to put his car into the garage rather than leave it in the driveway, and as he walked towards the porch he saw Kieron waving a piece of paper at him. 'Dad, this was on the mat,' he said.

Laurence inspected the document; it was an official slip of police stationery that asked him to call the local station. His immediate thought was that they had at last made some progress in identifying the perpetrators of the internet outrage on his son. It had taken them long enough. Just before Christmas he'd been on the point of writing an official letter of complaint to the IPCC, but an inner voice had reminded him that this was the season of goodwill and kicking up a fuss might prove counter-productive.

There had been no progress either on establishing who the masterminds behind the Lindon Road break-in were; none of the stolen items had so far made an appearance online. Perhaps, just perhaps, there had been a tip-off and the boys in blue had been able to make an arrest. If asked, Laurence would have been the first to acknowledge that neither of the two incidents could be classified as major crime, and he knew that the local force struggled with its clear-up rates, so if some kind of progress had at last been made, so much the better.

Yet when he called the number no information was forthcoming about the reason they wanted to see him. 'We will send someone to see you shortly,' said the voice at the other end. 'Are you going to be in during the next couple of hours?'

'Yes, but can't you tell me over the phone?'

'No, sir, we would prefer to do this in person.'

Fair enough, he thought. If it was the blackmail against his son, perhaps they'd come with an explanation of why it had taken them over two months to get to the bottom of it and he'd be given a personal apology for all the inconvenience. If it was the burglary, they might arrive with photographic evidence and ask him to confirm that the recovered goods were indeed his.

When he opened the door less than an hour later, the two possible scenarios he had in mind quickly receded into the far distance. Outside stood a thick-set police officer and a much younger female colleague. 'May we come in, sir?'

Their grave demeanour as he led them into the living-room made him think of Rosie.

'It's not my wife, is it?'

'No, sir, it's not your wife. It's the one part of our job none of us likes to do. I'm afraid we sometimes have to be the bearers of bad news,' the older officer said.

Laurence's mouth went dry. He was already anticipating what would come next.

'We're very sorry to have to tell you that your mother has passed away.'

'What? How? I was with her yesterday.'

'We received a call from the next-door neighbour, a Mrs Rees. Mrs Stewart was supposed to go round today for mid-morning coffee and when she didn't appear the neighbour went to investigate. There was no reply when she rang the bell, but she had a spare key for any emergency so she let herself into the house. She then found your mother upstairs in bed, but very sadly there was no pulse. She immediately contacted us and requested an ambulance. She said she tried to get in touch with you, but there was no reply from your landline number. She didn't know where to look for any other numbers.'

The lips opposite continued to move, but Laurence was unaware of any meaning issuing forth. He was no longer sitting on the sofa in his living-room. Instead, he found himself looking at a primeval landscape. There was a sudden gap in the forest where a mighty oak had previously stood. He heard the echoing groan which seemed to emerge from the bowels of the earth just before the tree toppled over, sending ricochets through the undergrowth. When the last vibrations could no longer be felt, there was a stillness on the forest-floor. Everything had changed.

His ears began to tingle, his heart started to thump loudly. He became aware of his body pressed into the upholstery. His head was full of questions. Why hadn't his mother tried to reach him? Why hadn't the voicemail kicked in when Mary Rees phoned? Why had it happened right now? He continued to stare in disbelief at the two impassive faces in front of him. 'I need to tell my children. They're upstairs.'

'And your wife, sir. You mentioned your wife.'

'She's away at the moment.'

The female officer managed a weak smile. 'Would you like me to tell them for you?'

'No, no, thank you. I – I just can't believe what's happened. I really can't.'

'We are so sorry for your loss. Every life is precious, sir.'

Later that evening, as he sat with his two children on either side, gripping their young hands, Laurence returned to his primeval landscape, and saw himself again rooted to the ground, unable to move away from the yawning chasm before him. He remembered being a small boy, trying to stretch his thin puny arms around the massive tree trunk, feeling the gnarled ridges of bark as they pressed into his soft young flesh. That was where he wanted to be.

37

When the call came from Kieron, Rosie was sitting on the edge of the bed, nibbling at some spring rolls from a Chinese takeaway. Since arriving at her sister's house the previous day, nothing had gone according to plan. She hadn't realised just how uncomfortable it would have been to be in the same house as Ian. If she hadn't reacted so promptly to his attempted grope, who knows what he might have done with his rugged and powerful frame? She had been alone with him in the kitchen at the time. He might have pinned her against the wall, pushed his tongue into her mouth and cupped her breasts. No witnesses around and a slightly hysterical bereaved daughter given to flights of fancy – what chance would she ever have had if she had wanted to defy the odds and complain?

She couldn't have known then, as she did now, that the scales had already fallen from her big sister's eyes. The more she thought about Lucie's reaction yesterday to what she had hoped would always remain hidden away, the less she felt able to understand how her sister could remain under the same roof as her brother-in-law. Perhaps Lucie was a more forgiving individual than she felt herself to be, but there was little to make her think he had any intention of altering his ways. Hadn't Lucie implied that it was all in his nature and that she had learned to accept him the way he was? She shuddered at the thought that she might have been left on her own with him for even a short time.

She had driven for miles towards Kirkburton, pinning her faith on her satnav, in pursuit of the B&B that Lucie had so warmly recommended, only to find that all the rooms were taken because of some local agricultural conference being held over the weekend. Handed a list of three alternative places to try, she had set off in some haste and spontaneously opted for the second-named 'The Golden Apples' because it sounded the most romantic of the three. When she had arrived there, tiredness and growing hunger had made her legs feel heavy; a renewed stabbing pain in her temples was adding to her discomfort.

Once inside her room she had instantly felt better. It was comfortably furnished and had a generous en suite, in which she soon treated herself to a long bath using the scented oil so thoughtfully provided, opening the hot taps repeatedly as the water cooled. Then she had nodded off, realising this with a start as her head slipped towards the water and began to tickle her nostrils, after which she had sensibly retired to the bed that was dressed enticingly with a soft duvet in a fleur-de-lys pattern.

When she had awoken, it was after seven. The first thing she wanted to do was to let Lucie know where she was staying and then think about how she could sensibly respond to the text messages she'd received earlier in the day from Kieron and Estelle. They would be worried if she failed to react. As far as she could remember, nothing had come from Laurence, but she needed to check.

That was when she discovered not only that the battery was completely flat, but that despite searching through her overnight case she had clearly forgotten to pack the battery charger. She considered pulling on some clothes and going downstairs to use her landlady's landline, but fatigue and the promise of a comfortable bed proved stronger.

The next morning she felt suitably refreshed and rose early. After a full English breakfast she headed off into the centre of town to get her mobile recharged and buy a new charging device. While she waited for communications with the outside world to be restored, she wandered aimlessly through the streets she remembered so well from her childhood. Back then, the Victorian buildings had towered over her and the spaces seemed so vast and unbridgeable. Now, everything seemed self-contained and manageable. She was determined not to allow the painful memory of what had happened on Thursday night to overwhelm her. But perhaps it was easier to think like that hundreds of miles away from the cinema and Lindon Road, away from the bank where he worked and the bungalow he had on Hayling Island, away too from the husband who now seemed so remote and inattentive to her needs. Hearing the animated chatter on the pavements and the ensuing bursts of laughter, seeing the broad grins on the faces of people coming towards her and watching how hands and arms caressed other limbs took her back to the security of those early days, when Mum and Dad, Grandma and Granddad, Lucie and Dulcie, had been there to protect and nurture her. Kindness, the quintessential expression of the human condition, that was all people needed to live by, in order to feel safe and valued and respected. That was all she had ever wanted for herself.

When Kieron reached her at lunchtime, a new feeling of guilt immediately gripped her. She felt she was being entirely selfish, imagining that her needs were greater than those of the two people who unquestionably depended on her. They were still at such a vulnerable point in their lives and she couldn't be certain that Laurence, with all his other preoccupations, would be prepared to put their interests first. What if something else had happened during the time she was away which she knew nothing about? Kieron said they were out for the day and mentioned that Laurence had taken them to see the chapel. What was he playing at? Was he trying to create an alliance against her? Who knows, he might have seized his chance in her absence, determined as ever to get his own way. Perhaps he would succeed in selling the idea to them and then they would begin to apply more pressure when she returned. If she returned. Did she want to return? What a stupid thought. Of course she did, but it was all too complicated at the moment. The soreness she felt in her heart at how she had been taken advantage of would take time to heal. *Wait a moment*, said a voice. *You're not comparing Laurence with John, are you? There's a big difference between being raped in a car at night and feeling disrespected by a husband more intent on pursuing his own agenda. How could you even begin to compare the two?*

She mopped up the remaining crumbs of her spring rolls and sighed. Being by herself was now compounding the problem. The tendency to brood overcame her and the voices that had retreated to the far recesses of her mind scampered back towards the centre of the stage.

It was too late in the day to drive to Beverley and return by nightfall. Besides, she wasn't keen on another extended stretch of driving. She needed to talk and not just be talked at. At the other end her sister's voice, even if it carried those typically forthright, no-nonsense overtones, would be sure to provide an alternative perspective. Where Lucie was generally more emollient and protective towards her youngest sister, Dulcie never recoiled from calling a spade a spade. So she had taken herself away from husband and family. What sort of ego trip was that? All marriages went through difficult patches. Many such alliances were far from ideal; surely she could see that in the relationship between Ian and Lucie. She needed her head sorting out if she couldn't be happy with what life had given her. There were loads of abusive husbands who beat their wives black-and-blue, couples who couldn't have kids and families that didn't know where the money for the next meal was coming from. Here she was, trying to make out she could no longer put up with her husband's money-making activities and his insensitivity towards her. Call that a crisis? And then this menopausal weepiness. Good lord, Rosie, that's what happens to women. Wake up to reality! Beauty fades, fertility declines and is extinguished, dreams are consigned to the scrap-heap. You simply have to get on with the business of living.

She picked up her phone.

'Dulcie, it's me. Hiya, sis. Are you well?'

By the time she had finished talking to Dulcie, she was relieved she hadn't mentioned the rape. That would have been the last straw. Her sister would have condemned her for even agreeing to a night out with a man who wasn't her husband. It would have been her fault anyway. She must have led him on and made him think she was fair game. What other conclusion could he have possibly come to? No, it was good she hadn't driven all that way to Beverley and been forced to listen to such a dressing down at close range. Dulcie was probably the last person she could expect succour and sympathy from in an hour of need.

She considered going back into the centre of town and spending the afternoon in a cinema, sealed up in a world of make-believe and away from the painful realities outside, but with other sentient beings around her. But very soon what she had wanted to repress, the consequences of watching a film whose content she had so wrongly anticipated, bubbled back to the surface. A cinema was simply not the right place to be. She wondered if she should call Estelle, to whom she had hardly said more than a few words when Kieron called earlier. Estelle would surely have another joke or riddle or pun for her, and she could take delight once more in her daughter's powers of amusement. But what if she was on the receiving end of a flurry of reproachful remarks? How would her daughter react if she was unable to specify a precise date for her return?

Her thoughts kept drifting back to family. Family, not strangers, no matter how outwardly sympathetic they might be. She recalled the cemetery in Edgerton that she and Lucie visited in November, where they had stood in silent contemplation as the icy winds tugged at their clothing.

She picked up her thick woollen scarf and winter jacket and was soon back inside her car, heading for the northern reaches of town. It took her no time at all to find the two gravestones again, side by side. As the twilight began to creep round the hillsides, casting long shadows, she remembered the soft sticky toffees her dad would hand out to her with a nudge and a wink, saying 'Shhh! Don't tell anybody else!', and the way her mum would look critically at her clothing before she ran out to play in the street, 'Little Miss Muffett, you'll catch a cold dressed like that. Run upstairs and find yourself a warm jumper.' They never sat and moped, they were always on the go. Too much so, she thought. What was the point of working your fingers to the bone if you never even had the time to enjoy the fruits of your labour?

The armies of shoppers, the boots of their cars stuffed full of special offers and once-in-a-lifetime bargains, their children's faces pinned to the side windows, were clogging up the roads out of town. Where do they all come from, she thought? And then, as if from nowhere, the strains of *Eleanor Rigby* took over her cranial spaces. All the lonely people. Where do they all belong? How was it possible, she wondered, for so many people to be surrounded by so many other people and yet still feel lonely. Eleanor Rigby, the lyrics stated, lives in a dream, waits at the window. Much later, she died in the church and was buried along with her name. Then, with a shiver, she thought of the concluding lines. Nobody came. No one was saved. How terrible, she concluded, to live a life like that.

While she was standing at a set of traffic lights, with the darkness closing in around her, her mobile rang. Mindful of the danger of talking while driving, she pulled over at the first opportunity, but by then the ringing had ceased. It was Kieron. Why was he calling again just a few hours after she'd told him he would need to be patient a little while longer? All she wanted was a little more time to herself. She activated the call back option.

'Mum, you've got to come back. Dad's in a terrible state.'

'Why? What's the matter?'

'Granny's died.'

She didn't need to think twice. It was clear what she had to do.

'My poor lamb. I'm so sorry. Tell your dad I'll be on my way first thing in the morning.'

38

Laurence spent much of the following night lying on his back in the spare room. He had refused to let the tears come, willing them back into their sacs like an angry poultry farmer driving his fowl into the sanctuary of their coops. No tears now, please. One question was demanding to be answered. He knew that a seventy-eight-year-old had no indemnity against death, that every day beyond the biblical span was itself a minor miracle, one more brake on the Grim Reaper's advance. But why now? Why just hours after he and his mother had parted in a state of disarray bordering on hostility? He wondered with creeping unease if there was indeed a link between the two events. Perhaps he had unwittingly caused his mother so much anxiety and concern that her heart had been unable to cope. As yet he had no way of knowing. Since the death was unexplained and his mother had not been seen recently by her GP, there would have to be a post-mortem. But hearts don't suddenly stop beating without some kind of trigger, do they? Perhaps she had lain in bed preoccupied with the thought that he was pushing ahead with something far too risky. Not only that, she probably held him responsible for the fragility of his marriage. Her stern, disapproving look after he'd told her about Rosie's renewed absence from home had said it all. He was in danger of throwing the big dice and coming back with nothing to show for it; he couldn't even be a successful husband and keep his family together. Not measuring up to the high standards she always insisted on had blighted his childhood, his choice of wife and his business ventures. There was invariably something withering about the comments she made whenever he fell short. Not quite enough effort, must try harder. Like the comments on his early school reports. If she'd once said to him, 'Try your best and that will always be good enough for me,' it would have been fine, but she had kept pushing and cajoling and urging. Failure was never a random event to which even the great were occasionally prone, it was an admission that not enough heart and soul had been put into delivering the best possible result. Now she was gone and he would never again be able to show her that sometimes he did get things right, sometimes he did manage to pull off the deals that others envied him for, sometimes there were moments when she could be justly proud of him. Above all, he couldn't rid himself of the sneaking suspicion that he was to blame in some way for her death.

The only thing he clung to in the depths of his despair was hearing Kieron's triumphant cry, 'Dad! Mum says she's coming back tomorrow.'

39

Rosie set off early on Sunday morning. The absence of traffic gave her the illusion that she was making more rapid progress. She knew exactly what Laurence must be going through. In a few months' time it would be ten years since the death of first her father and then soon after that her mother. Neither parent had managed to get to seventy. She pondered the possibility that there was something in the Wingfield genes which meant that all the women had an early menopause and were destined to watch the sands in the hour-glass run out quickly.

She didn't find it difficult to assemble her feelings about Roberta Stewart. It was clear from the very beginning that her mother-in-law had wanted better for her son than a mere florist, but she supposed that when the moment came for Kieron to formalise an arrangement with a future girlfriend she too would be critical. After all, wasn't it right and proper for her to want the best possible wife for her son and the best possible daughter-in-law for herself? Her relationship with Roberta, or "Mother" as she insisted on being called, was always at arms' length, and that suited each of them just fine. She couldn't actually recall any fiery confrontations, if only because frostiness seemed to be the prevailing meteorological condition.

There was no getting away from the fact that Laurence's

mother had been a good grandmother to Kieron and Estelle, never forgetting their birthdays, and surprising her in other ways too. When they had each reached their tenth birthday she had set up a savings account with a five-figure investment to mature when they were eighteen. Not bad for a tight-fisted, mean-spirited Scot, she thought at the time. She knew that Laurence derived all his restless energy from her; she could see what a lack of ambition led to in the husbands of her two sisters. She also acknowledged that fate had dealt Laurence a weak card; at least she'd had two parents by her side and two siblings to grow up with. He had been forced in on himself, with only a single parent to rely on for support.

She was sensing that her own shocking ambivalence towards what had happened just a few nights previously and the uncertainties of any future relationship with Laurence were no longer uppermost in her mind. They had been displaced. Three people had just lost a loved one. A year or so before Lorna had hobbled into work after spraining her ankle, only to find that her remaining wisdom teeth started to play her up. 'The newer pain just pushes the older pain into insignificance,' she explained.

Even so, as she approached the final leg of her homeward journey she was nervous about the questions which she supposed would soon surface. There was no way she could magic away the curiosity Kieron and Estelle would be sure to exhibit about the precise circumstances which had led to her renewed flight from the family home. Much more daunting was the thought of how she was going to react if Laurence pressed her for an explanation. She knew everything would depend on how he asked. She could be economical with the truth if she had to be, but she would be incapable of lying to Laurence. He had once told her that he felt she would always be totally honest with him.

What worried her most was the thought that if she hit a low point when her guard was down, she would have to tell him about John and what had happened in Lindon Road, and then there would inevitably be questions about whether she'd been having an affair, and for how long, and whether she wanted a separation or even a divorce. But as the familiar landmarks along the south coast came into view and she smelled the sea air coming through the car's ventilation system, she realised that she was about to be tested. For a while she'd nurtured vague hopes that Lucie, and later Dulcie, would have pointed out which of the many doors along the corridor that she now found herself in she would be required to open. Which door promised the neatest and quickest exit from this mess of her own making? But these hopes had been vaporised. First, she alone would have to clear up the mess and only then would she be able to find the right door.

40

Laurence heard Rosie's car in the driveway before the children did and rushed to the front door. He so wanted to make a good impression and not to say or do anything that might antagonise her. He was in pain, and he didn't want any more.

'Hallo, love,' he said as she walked towards him, 'It's so good to have you back.'

She stopped and took his hands in hers. 'Laurence, I'm so sorry about your mum. Really I am. I know what it's like. I've been through it before.'

She moved closer to hug him and felt a strange sense of relief as he rubbed her back with his strong warm hands. *This is the man you married, for richer or poorer, for bad days as well as for good days,* she heard the voices saying in unison. As she clung to him she waited for the anti-chorus, but dissent came there none. And then Kieron and Estelle were flinging their arms around her.

Days later he still couldn't make up his mind whether she'd taken the snap decision to travel down again so quickly because she was concerned about the children or because of him. There was a wariness he detected in her eyes, as though she was weighing up whatever she said, and her movements through the house resembled those of a newly-born gazelle uncertain whether her thin legs might give way on the uneven ground. Their bodies repeatedly made brief contact, a steadying hand or arm for just long enough to provide reassurance but never long enough to imply any further meaning. Once or twice he wondered how she would react if he kissed her, but her face was never suitably aligned for long enough for an approach not to appear forced. He didn't ask if he could return to the master bedroom, nor did she offer.

He spent most of the Sunday afternoon in a state of numbness, glad that the children were around Rosie while he was left alone with his thoughts. Tomorrow was the first day of a new week, a chance to get back into the swim of things. Paper and computer screens were easy to deal with: they didn't answer back or display emotions that required a response.

Lying alone in his bed in the spare room, he struggled to find sleep. He was riding on a merry-go-round of images: the chapel and the plans for its refurbishment, the parts of his portfolio he would put out to market, the police who had arrived to deliver unexpected news, the estrangement from his wife that he was no nearer to comprehending, the welfare of his children, the prospects for his business. And as each image came round again, it was supplanted by the face of his mother looking straight at him. She was calling to him, but he was unable to hear what she was saying above the din created by the revolving machinery. All he knew was that he hadn't been able to hold her in his arms and say a final goodbye.

41

The next day, the start of a new working week, all four of them were sitting around the breakfast table. Rosie was surprised she didn't need to rouse Kieron and that Estelle insisted on helping her. She was secretly glad that both their attentions were focused so clearly on their father and that his practical mind had already turned to the practicalities of a funeral. The more she was able to talk about his mother and the state of his feelings, the less need there would be to talk about herself. The more she could direct their thoughts to what lay ahead, the less danger of them wanting to explore what was already in the past.

'Laurence, what would you like to do? Guys, what kind of a farewell would Granny have wished to have?'

Laurence allowed himself a rueful smile. 'Knowing what she did for most of her life, I guess the cleanest solution would be a cremation. When she used to polish the bathroom, she always told me, "Leave no traces behind."'

Placing a boiled egg in front of Laurence, Rosie touched his shoulder. 'Are you sure that would be a good idea? If you bury someone, you always have a grave you can go to, a place where you can be close to them.'

'And it makes it easier to remember somebody, if you know you can keep going back there,' Estelle volunteered.

Laurence cracked open his egg. 'It's tricky, isn't it. You've got to get that basic decision right. You can't go back on it later. I don't think Mum was very religious, but she loved ceremonies.' And then he added, 'There's not much to a cremation, really. At least with a burial you get to have a proper service in a church.'

'Think of your mum, Laurence. Think of what she would have wanted.'

'I've got to go to the house this morning anyway, speak to the neighbour, see if I can find anything among Mum's papers that would point to her wishes. In any case, we can't set a date for the funeral until the coroner has received details of the post-mortem.'

As soon as he had left and the children gone off to school, Rosie busied herself filling the dishwasher and organising the week's laundry. Work was therapy, work took your mind off other things. She had sent Lorna a text the previous evening, telling her that she was feeling much better and would be back at work today. There would be the next set of floral arrangements for the Callas to get sorted. She knew Lorna had already ordered spring bulbs which would have to be assembled in decorative pots. She would grasp any opportunity that presented itself to be with others and to talk about anything but herself.

'You're still looking rather peaky,' was Lorna's first comment when Rosie arrived at Florabellum.

'Oh, I'm on the mend, don't you worry. How about yourself? What's your weekend been like?'

Only much later, when she had completed the new set of table decorations for the Callas, did she mention that her mother-in-law had died, placing all the emphasis on how devastating it had been for Laurence and the children. It was easier sharing in the grief of others; her own grief at a relationship that had died so soon after its inception was already locked away in a drawer.

When she arrived at the Callas shortly before lunchtime, Matthew was on his own, heaving packets out of the freezer.

'Lee's out. He's taken our weekend takings to the bank and wants to have a word with John too.'

Rosie felt a sudden tightening in her muscles. 'John?' she inquired.

'Yes, you know. John Bibby, the bank manager. You met him on our opening night. Without his help we wouldn't have got off the ground.'

Ah yes, she thought, the Good Samaritan, the wolf in sheep's clothing, the angel of mercy. How she longed to erase that evening from her mind, to paint out the smiles she had put her trust in. If there'd been an ounce of decency in him, she'd have heard something from him in the past few days. 'So how are things going now?'

'Better than we had at first hoped, I have to say. There's been a bit of a post-Christmas dip, but we've still got our heads above the water.'

That was what she needed to do herself, keep her head above the water. She would not sink without a struggle. Meanwhile keep the spotlight on others, go on asking the questions. 'How's your brother Jason these days?'

Matthew was starting to peel and chop vegetables. 'Oh yes, I told you about him and his problems, didn't I? Well, there is some news. He and his wife are expecting, so I'm going to become an uncle.'

'I'm very pleased for you, Matthew.' It crossed her mind that Jason had gone to counselling for his depression. She wanted to know more, but if she dwelt on that Matthew would immediately sense she had a personal reason for enquiring further. He wasn't stupid. Sooner or later, wherever she went and whatever she did and whoever she spoke to, all her attempts to blot out the past would come back to haunt her.

42

Laurence made the office his first port of call. One of his tenants had just accepted a lucrative job offer overseas and would soon be moving out. After checking the details, Laurence told Ilona to contact Denis. 'It's a bit pricier than what he said he was prepared to pay, but it's in a very nice area. Ask him if he wants the particulars and if he's keen we can set up a viewing.'

He was almost embarrassed at her outpouring of emotion when he told her about his mother's death.

'Are you going to have the coffin in the house for three days? That's what we do in Poland.'

'No, no,' Laurence replied. 'As soon as the post-mortem is complete the body will be transferred to the undertaker's. They'll make the actual funeral arrangements, but we as a family have got to decide whether it should be a burial or a cremation.'

'So the whole family cannot come and say goodbye at the house?'

'That's not how we do it in this country,' he said. 'I suppose death is very much sanitised over here. Most people die in hospital, the relatives don't always get to see the body and then it's quickly put away.'

'But that's so sad. Don't you believe?'

'In God, you mean? I've had to believe in myself for most of my

281

life. There wasn't much room for anything else.'

Ilona looked crestfallen. 'Everybody should believe in God!' she cried. 'The world would be so much happier.'

Yeah, he thought. Lots of differing gods competing for attention, endless arguments among the believers and between the churches and sects. Religion was just a battleground for the hearts and minds of people. A bit like the market economy, in fact. Whose God is the biggest, who can point to a greater number of miracles, who can do the best pitch for paradise, he thought bitterly. No point though in antagonising Ilona, it's not her fault that too much is being over-promised and under-delivered. 'I'll be off then,' he said. 'See you later.'

Mary Rees, as far as Laurence was able to tell, had always been a good neighbour. While he was growing up, he had played with her only child, a boy called Martin and of similar age to himself. To begin with he had thought Mary was his much older sister, until his mother told him some years later that the child had been "born out of wedlock", as she put it. He often wondered whether that accounted for the distance between his mother and her nearest neighbour, no doubt compounded by the fact that there would always be a man around the place, sometimes for over a year, before he would invariably disappear and in due course be replaced.

'Her heart is in the right place,' his mother once confided in him, 'but she gets taken advantage of again and again. She's a lesson to us all, if you know what I mean.' Knowing what his mother meant was one of his first lessons in survival.

Mary was now in her mid-sixties, with two bright button eyes shining out of a full, red-flecked face and heaving bosoms that disappeared into huge abdominal folds of flesh. She'd always had a soft spot for Laurence on account of his good manners and his obvious devotion to his mother. 'I just wish Martin would care about me a little more,' she had said to Laurence on one occasion when he enquired after the erstwhile playmate he hadn't seen for years. 'I've got four grandchildren, and he's been with I don't know how many women altogether, so I hardly get to see them all. Not many people come a-calling these days, so it's a pleasure you're showing your face. I'm so sorry it had to be like this.'

'The upsetting thing is that Mum seemed all right when I saw her on the Friday evening. There was nothing to indicate it would be otherwise.'

'Laurence, I always say it's better to be gone in a puff of smoke than to have to watch a fire slowly eating everything up.'

'That's a very poetic way of putting it. The problem is that in such cases you never get to say goodbye properly. When somebody in the family goes, there are no more questions you can ask about the past, no more memories you can share. That particular door's closed and the key's been thrown away.'

'The funny thing is that for years your mum and I didn't chat very much,' said Mary. 'It was only when I stopped working a few years ago that we began to get close. As close as she would let me, that is. You know, I often wondered if the way she sometimes got so fierce was really a kind of mask. A way to hide something.'

Laurence looked surprised. 'How do you mean?'

Mary hesitated for a moment. 'Some time ago she told me she'd made a big mistake in her life. I'd just been telling her about the death of Martin's dad. He just scarpered when I fell pregnant at eighteen and I didn't see him again until just before he died. He had cancer, you see. It was eating him up. That's what I meant earlier about the puff of smoke. Anyway, I told Roberta that I never regretted keeping Martin, even though my parents said I should give him up for adoption.'

Laurence suddenly felt a need to probe. 'Did she say what her mistake was?'

'No, she didn't. As it happened, the phone rang just after she said that. In fact, it was you who was calling. By the time she'd finished talking to you the moment had passed. But you could never get her to open up about things if she didn't want to. Even if I'd asked her later I don't think she'd have told me. I couldn't imagine her ever making a big mistake, though. She wasn't the type. She always seemed to get everything right. Always kept her house spotless. Not like me!' She gestured at her domestic disorder, the piles of laundry waiting to be ironed, boxes of cat food and sacks of litter, a pair of mud-encrusted gumboots sitting next to fluffy carpet slippers. He wondered how his mother had been able to sit among so much chaos during her coffee mornings with Mary.

Eventually he made his farewell and headed down the lane to his mother's house. It was the first time since he had lived there that he had let himself in without ringing the bell. Nothing seemed out of place, everything was as spick and span as ever.

When he started on the process of turning out all the contents, he imagined it would be quick and easy. Something made him pause before climbing the stairs. Only two days previously she had trodden these stairs for the very last time, thinking almost certainly about the way they had parted, but not knowing that she would never see him again. He clenched his fists and pounded the wall: the grief he had refused to express in tears was coming out in fury. 'Why did you have to go like this?' he yelled. 'Couldn't you have waited to see me succeed again?' And then he heard her voice inside his head, calling from afar and saying what she invariably said whenever they had disagreed in the past, 'Not another word Laurence, not another word.'

The covers on her bed had been pulled back, and the pillow still bore the impression of her head. He opened the drawers of the two bedside cabinets where he knew she kept most of her personal things: recent council tax and utility bills, bank statements and investment portfolios, assorted keys, a small quantity of cash, her old driving licence. He was beginning to feel like a burglar in the hunt for valuables. There was no will here, no envelope with a declaration of her last wishes. For someone who was so particular about keeping her affairs in order, this was a surprising omission. She surely couldn't have supposed she would live forever. But then as with so many of the other remarks she had made in her life which inhabited the deeper recesses of his mind and waited to be brought out of cold storage, he recalled something she had said after selling her cleaning business. 'Solicitors are a pain in the neck. They remind you of your place in the queue for leaving the planet.' When he had pressed her to explain the cryptic comment, she had referred to the solicitor's recommendation that she should tidy up all her financial affairs in the form of a will. This was before the sudden death of Rosie's parents, and since she hadn't been quite sixty-eight at the time he had not regarded it as anything very pressing. He had never asked her about it and she had never volunteered any information. But on reflection he was sure she must have made a deposition and that at least one copy would be in the hands of the solicitor. Perhaps she had placed her copy somewhere else in the house.

He pulled open her wardrobes, thinking she might have kept things of importance in document cases. He saw only neat rows of dresses, blouses and skirts, jackets and winter wear, with her shoes and boots all lined up neatly on the floor. He moved to her dressing-table, inside the drawers of which lay her underwear, her boxes of jewellery, the still unused cakes of soap he had given her for her last birthday.

He went downstairs and stood in front of the shrine, the only window to the past from which he had come. The father he'd never really had, the aunt who'd been taken from him far too early, the mother whose heart had decided that enough was enough. He opened the sideboard doors and surveyed vases, dinner services, ornamental coffee cups, and then on one side files relating to her final business years, together with bank correspondence. Inside the top drawers he found silver cutlery, a ring-binder with shop receipts and copies of mail-order confirmations.

He looked under the stairs, where he knew she stored the huge albums with collections of family photographs, and found more bank statements and bills dating back decades, with the respective calendar years marked on cover-sheets. It looked as though she had kept everything of note that had ever been set down on paper from the day in the sixties when they moved in.

Meticulous as in all things. But he failed to find what he was looking for.

Then he remembered the loft, which he recalled last being inside just before leaving for college. That was the place to which she had occasionally consigned what he called her "junk", including a large radio-gramophone that he dimly recalled playing with before he even started school. Already he had spent over two hours searching through the house. He didn't have the time to go on sifting and searching; there were other matters he needed to attend to back at the office. The funeral arrangements were going to suck up a lot of time in the week ahead. The loft would have to wait. Any will would also have to wait.

43

In the days after her return Rosie concentrated on her own survival. Fight or flee, she'd learned in secondary school, were the body's primary defences. She'd twice tried to flee, but on neither occasion were the results conducive to her own well-being. It was so easy in story-books: something always happened to make the problems go away, like the miraculous cleaning agents constantly being advertised on television that would cause all deposits and encrustations to loosen their grip on existence, all germs to curl up and die, all stains to give up the will to live. But she knew she wasn't in the middle of some storyteller's little saga. This was real life. She would have to fight whatever problems came at her.

To begin with, the children were hugely relieved that she was back. Within a few days, however, she was conscious of their hound-dog eyes following her around, nervous of her movements, anxiously seeking reassurance. Whereas previously they often spent the best part of an evening in their upstairs rooms or with friends, now they would regularly weave into sight like sheepdogs guarding a flock and then pounce with questions about homework assignments to which she felt they already knew the answers, or jog her memory about family outings to which she attributed little or no significance. Later, when the sheep had been driven into their pens and there was no obvious escape, the shearing would begin. Instead of confronting her with direct questions about her own state of mind, they would frame their queries in a generalised way. 'Mum, what are the main reasons people stop loving each other?' 'Mum, are there always two guilty parties when marriages break down?' 'Mum, is a separation automatically followed by a divorce?'

Most challenging of all were attempts by the leading players to hide behind a cloak of anonymity. 'Mum, what are the consequences for the children when parents split up?' She knew what they were up to, but she played their game. The killer questions would be dropped without warning into a trivial exchange about the latest boy band or the dress sense of ageing teachers. Frequently she came close to revealing her exasperation and displaying her emotions like bare knuckles. Whatever they did and said, they knew, and she knew, that they were talking about the state of Laurence and Rosie Stewart's marriage and the fate of their two children, Kieron and Estelle.

Months ago she would have delighted in sharing evidence of her children's wiliness with her husband, but now she recoiled at the thought. The less they talked about her and the more about him, the easier it would be to airbrush the past few weeks from the record. When Laurence returned in the evenings, she would routinely take an interest in the events of his day. She'd only once spoken to Mary Rees, outside in the lane before they went into one of her mother-in-law's feasts, so she lapped up what he had to say about his long conversation with her. She asked him about his discussions with the undertaker's and for details of the funeral that had been fixed for the Monday of the following week; she insisted on looking after all the floral arrangements herself and offered him a range of options. She helped him draw up a list of people who would be invited to attend and told him she would make all the necessary contacts. She debated with him the merits of various venues for the wake and the funeral repast, she sat and held his hand whenever she saw the turmoil in his eyes. He was like a wounded animal about the house. Towards the end of the week, as the moment of official leave-taking began to loom, he turned to her and suddenly blurted out, 'You know she was the most important person in her own life.'

'Oh Laurence, don't say that. She made you what you are.'

'That's just it. She made me into a copy of herself. She didn't really let me become a different person.'

'Just look at you. How can you think that? You see the similarities, I see the differences. You're no carbon copy.'

When he squeezed her hand in what she took to be a show of gratitude, she wouldn't have resisted if there had been more to come. But the husband next to her was probably just as wary of exposing himself to rejection as she was of signalling rapprochement. She had been thirty-six when her mother died. Nothing would bring her back now. All she had of her were her memories. Nothing would bring her mother-in-law back either. She wanted Laurence to hold onto his happy memories of her. That was what Lucie and Dulcie had told her to do ten years earlier as they stood together at the graveside, her tears and theirs dissolving into the falling rain.

44

When clarity came within a few days about the cause of death, it was still something of a shock. Myocardial infarction was on the death certificate. It sounded less dramatic than a heart attack, but there was no way of concealing the fact that Roberta Stewart's heart had decided it had had enough.

On receiving the news Laurence buried his head in his hands. When things go wrong, somebody is always responsible. Things don't just happen. That had been drummed into him from an early age. If he hadn't pressed the issue with the chapel refurbishment, his mother might still be alive.

It was too late to turn the clock back, to reverse any of his recent decisions, to unsay any of the words that had passed his lips. Nothing, absolutely nothing, would now bring his mother back. There was therefore no need to delay the inevitable, the moment of official leave-taking, the point at which the very last of the formalities would be completed.

He was determined that the funeral was going to be a low-key affair. His mother might have revelled in festivities and celebrations, but she had expressed only withering contempt for the farewell given to one of Laurence's university friends after a fatal road accident; the mourners had been instructed to wear casual and colourful clothing, there was a jazz combo near the altar, and smiles, laughter and a buzz of excitement had filled the church. That, in her eyes, was pure sacrilege. Her funeral therefore had to be taken as seriously as much of her life had been. All those she had once employed were invited, together with Mary Rees and the other neighbours from their lane. Lucie and Dulcie both came, though their respective husbands did not, as well as two distant cousins from his father's side who lived in the London area. But if the number of mourners was modest, the number of flowers was not. Rosie had pulled out all the stops to fill the church with scent, binding lilies, hyacinths and lilies-of-the-valley into the wreaths. 'It's what your mother deserves, Laurence. You need to give her a good send-off,' she whispered to him just before the service started.

He closed his eyes for most of the proceedings. He wanted the service to be over and done with and then to be left in peace, so he could grieve and reflect on his own responsibility. The coffin was in his direct line of vision, the coffin in which his mother's body lay. He would never again witness those alert grey eyes meeting his gaze, willing him on. He pretended to be somewhere else, conjuring up images of holidaymakers on tropical beaches, palm trees swaying gently in the sea breeze. But if his eyes engaged in this make-believe and took him away from the source of his grief, his ears did not. He could not shut out the words coming from the clergyman, the fragments of a text which reverberated around the stone walls and continued to echo in his own interior spaces. *One generation passeth away, and another cometh: but the earth abideth for ever. That which is crooked cannot be made straight, and that which is wanting cannot be numbered. To every thing there is a season, and a time to every purpose under the heaven: A time to be born and a time to die. Vanity of vanities, all is vanity.*

Then Rosie was nudging him to stand up and join the rest of the congregation for a hymn. Again, the words resonated in his mind: *melt me, mould me, fill me, use me.* It was too much like the commands his mother might herself have used. That at least made it fitting.

After the burial they retired to a former coaching inn to which Laurence had taken his mother after scraping his way onto a university course of his choosing despite his disappointing A Level results. 'She was here with me once before at an important stage in my life and now I feel her spirit is with us here today,' he said in a short address before they all sat down for a meal. He didn't quite know how he managed to hold it all together, clenching his fists in resolution and staring over the sea of misty eyes trained on him. His mother had certainly made an impression, that much was for sure.

He walked among the group and overheard fragments of conversation. 'She either liked you or she didn't. There wasn't anything in between.' 'She used to intimidate me at times, but when I stopped working for her she never failed to keep in touch.' 'I've never known anybody like her for making you do things you didn't really want to do."

Out of the corner of one eye, Laurence caught sight of a luncheon party entering the lobby area, with a young boy clutching an oversized teddy, holding onto the hand of what looked like his grandmother. All the other grown-ups seemed to be elderly; a middle generation was nowhere in evidence. Then he was back in his own childhood, sitting up in bed while his mother read him one Paddington Bear story after another.

'What do we learn about Paddington?' she had asked him at the end of each story. 'He's polite.' 'He's got good manners.' 'He's a well-behaved bear.' He knew immediately what she expected him to say: the words might have differed slightly, but the sentiments were always the same. When for some unaccountable reason he had staged a fight with his own teddy and pulled off one of his ears, his mother patiently sewed it back on again, saying only, 'You have to repair whatever deserves to be kept together.' She must have loved him, he thought. It hadn't been plain sailing with her by any means, but while he was still small there were no comparisons he could have made. He only had the one mother, and she was the standard by which everybody else had to be judged.

He looked across at Rosie, talking animatedly to Steve. Now that his family had shrunk he desperately wanted to hold onto what he still had, his wife and his two children. He could see how Steve's dour features were slowly brightening. Rosie had that effect on people. It was in her eyes, the way they shone with the clarity of a fresh spring day when she engaged with you. It was in the tilt of her head when she mirrored your own movements. It was in her smile when it spread from the corners of her mouth upwards, lifting her features. It was in the chuckle with which she often framed whatever she said. Why, he wondered, had the bond that had once held them together so firmly become so frayed and tenuous? What was driving this unwelcome centrifuge in their relationship? Perhaps he was too focused on the things he could point to, the things he could hold and touch, the things that made him feel good about himself. Perhaps he was too ready to exchange one shiny new car for another, to discard the perfectly serviceable for the dazzlingly new. *You have to repair whatever deserves to be kept together.*

In the car on the way back home, Rosie was happy to do most of the talking. He was surprised, given her slightly morose manner in the recent past, that during the wake she had repeatedly drawn people close to her, smiling and even occasionally laughing at what they had to say. 'Your friend Steve seems to be in a right old state,' she said to Laurence. 'He was telling me about all the things he was trying to do to keep his girlfriend happy. As if money were the most important thing in the world. I'm sure he'll find another job soon enough. If she's really the right kind of person for him, she'll stick by him anyway. And he's not at all bad-looking.' To which Laurence initially wanted to say that looks alone weren't everything, but then thought better of it.

By now the sun had irradiated the overnight hoarfrost, like some gentle giant pulling the icy blanket back from its covering of the hedges and fields. 'You know, I was thinking,' Rosie said as the car left the rugged upland and moved within sight of the softer coastline below, 'there are three things a florist always relies on.' She had learned from Estelle the quality of inserting a dramatic pause. 'Births, marriages and deaths.'

Laurence turned to her and grinned broadly before commenting, 'And the one thing everybody needs is a place to live.' As if to reinforce what he hoped was now a common line of thinking he said, 'So I reckon that together we've probably got the two best jobs in the world.'

45

It was the day after the funeral. Rather than sit in his office and mull over features for a revamping of his website, Laurence decided to make a start on household clearance. 'This is the leanest time of the year,' he said to Ilona. 'Nobody buys houses or moves in January. Unless they're pretty desperate.' Then, remembering that Denis had expressed an interest in viewing the latest property to become vacant, he asked her to see if the following afternoon would be convenient for him, and made for his mother's house.

As soon as he was awake that morning his thoughts began to circle around what he needed to do. Her clothing and her cheaper jewellery would go to the local charity shops, unless Rosie wanted to keep some items for herself. He would order a skip to dispose of all the files and business records she had hoarded like so much treasure. He would check to see if any kitchen or household utensils or smaller items of furniture might be of interest to Mary. He had no intention of giving away the collection of glass ornaments; they were precious. He would make a start by creating different piles for the collection agencies. All of this would keep his mind focused while processing her possessions; this would be the perfect activity to staunch the wound that was beginning to open up again. He was aware that being in the house on his own would bring back a clutch of uncomfortable reminders from the past. But he had no other choice, this was his filial duty.

'Do you want me to come and give you a hand?' Rosie had asked over breakfast. He thought the offer had been made with genuine sincerity and he wavered before replying. 'Thanks love,' he had said, the first time in weeks he recalled using the additional endearment, 'but to be honest, when two people are involved there's always a lot of nattering and showing and comparing that goes on. It's quicker if I just deal with everything on my own.'

Once inside the house, however, he found himself drawn once more to the shrine. He was now the only subject in the photographs still alive, and yet the dead continued to exercise their influence beyond the grave. He looked again at the two sisters, Joyce and Roberta, the elder of the two slightly taller, but both with the same thin straight nose, slim waistline and tidy appearance. If anything there was an impish smile playing on the lips of his Auntie Joyce, as though she believed the taking of a picture to be an excuse for yet more fun, but then he remembered the last couple of visits to their house when she had looked forlorn and given him concerned looks. Or perhaps that was his interpretation now. Memory, Patrick had said to him soon after he had taken Laurence on, is such a fickle thing. It's not just about facts, it's about apprehensions and desires, which is why selling houses is often bound up with irrationality. Clients would claim to have seen the perfect property somewhere else, or would magnify shortcomings soon after a viewing, imagining faults and insisting that they were real. People saw in things what they wanted to see, just as they saw in people what they wanted to see.

He knew that even if he were to find an envelope in the loft with a specific instruction from his mother that she wanted to be cremated, it was way too late to reverse the course that had already been set. Some things in life and in death were irrevocable. Once done they were done. Nor did he for one moment regret listening to the family advice. The shrine would disappear, with all the framed photographs most probably ending up in a sturdy cardboard box in yet another loft. However, it was good that there was going to be a headstone with inscriptions in gold – and he had already decided it would have to be the best available Italian marble – around which he and others could gather whenever they wished.

In the meantime he had contacted his mother's solicitor and established that there was indeed a will and she had received a copy of it. Where she had deposited it for safe keeping was something he couldn't comment on, but Laurence would need to make an appointment for a formal reading of the contents to him. Even supposing he was the major beneficiary, it would take many months for the process of probate to be completed and he could expect to see an improvement in his financial situation. Pushing ahead with the sale of two smaller properties from his portfolio had therefore been only right and sensible. Money wouldn't bring his mother back and her money could not be his only salvation. But the clergyman's words that had made such a fleeting impression on him yesterday came back to haunt him. All is vanity, he had heard the man say. *What's the point? Why am I splitting in two, if it makes the lives of my loved ones no happier?* For the first time in his entire advocacy of the project, he fully accepted, and without any reservations whatsoever, that if Rosie wished to stay in Marlborough Close, that was where the whole family needed to be. He'd use all his knowledge and experience to turn the chapel into a desirable residence and give it high-end spec to increase its attractiveness, but it would be for others to live there.

He pulled down the step-ladder that led into the loft, not feeling he was likely to find anything of significance. On reflection, he couldn't see why his mother would have kept anything valuable or noteworthy in an area under the roof that wasn't readily accessible, especially for older legs like hers, that wasn't insulated against the elements and wasn't treated to a regular cleaning regime. However, when he peered into the loft area it all looked much worse than he had feared. At least the light bulb was still working, but the passage of time had left its mark. There was a thick layer of dust covering the floor-boards that rippled like sand dunes the moment he moved across them. Cobwebs criss-crossed the interior space, there were the remains of what looked like a bird's nest in one corner where a damaged roof tile had provided a small aperture from the outside world and in another corner piles of droppings that probably came from small rodents. Above all, a smell of mustiness and decay clung to the rafters and purlins.

He shook his head in disbelief. When he was showing prospective clients around unoccupied properties they would sometimes pull open the doors to pantries, under-stair cupboards, fitted wardrobes and other recessed spaces, only to expose multiple sins of omission. Cover up and scarper, as Patrick used to say. Paper over the cracks, stuff unwanted junk into the eaves, bury ironmongery in the garden: there was no end to which some people were prepared to go in order to hide the frowzy, the unclean and the ugly. No wonder fly-tipping was becoming a menace, especially in rural areas.

The throwaway society, though, was enjoying something of a boomerang effect. It had become domesticated: in houses and cottages where owners scarcely contemplated the idea of loft conversions, the roof space now served as a reverse disposal chute. Laurence was shocked, until he realised that his mother, for all her attention to scrubbing and cleaning and polishing, was no different from anybody else. Out of sight, out of mind. This was where she had consigned all the objects like toasters with frayed elements, defective curling tongs, broken carpet-beaters and collapsed ironing-boards for which she had no further use. This was where she could blot them out of her life and forget they had ever existed. He was amazed that the whole recycling revolution had clearly passed her by. His instincts had been right: there was nothing up here of value which he needed to sift through. He would simply instruct a company to clear the entire space and hoover up the mess before the property was put on the market.

But as he turned to go down the step-ladder he noticed a blue trunk, its top surface coated in dust. He didn't remember seeing it before. Roberta Stewart had never possessed a passport and had hardly ever gone away herself, although she had been happy to see her son go on organised camping holidays in the summer. From what he recalled, she had a small overnight case in one of her wardrobes, but he had never come across anything as big as this before. The trunk had clearly been assigned its ultimate resting place here in the higher regions of the house. But why? Amongst all the other paraphernalia and the jetsam and flotsam from her life, it stood apart. It was crying out for investigation.

The trunk was locked, and there were no keys to be seen in the vicinity, nor did it yield to the force he exerted on it. There had to be a reason why it was locked. He quickly clambered down the steps and went through the house to a small outhouse in which gardening implements and a small collection of DIY tools were stored. Wiping away the sticky candyfloss of cobwebs on his face and in his hair, and armed with some sharp instruments of his choice, he returned to the loft.

Minutes later he had prised open the two locks and was gazing at the contents inside. There were many bundles of letters, all neatly tied with different-coloured string, nearly all of them, as far he could see, in chronological order. Nestling in between the stacks there were slim pouches from which edges of documents peeped out. These, he felt, had to be the tickets to his mother's past, and he reckoned he had to be in there somewhere. These were the pieces of the jigsaw he had never seen. All he knew about his father had come filtered down to him through his mother's recollections; even his Auntie Joyce had hardly mentioned him when she came visiting from Scotland. So his mother had been something of a secret hoarder: he'd guessed as much on seeing all the files with business correspondence and the masses of utility bills and bank statements squirrelled away downstairs. But why had she pushed all these personal memories to the extremities of her house?

He realised with a start that he had already messed up his clothing. There were several specks of dirt on his suit jacket and arachnoid deposits around his shirt collar. His shoes resembled wrinkled sheets of sandpaper. In his eagerness to explore he hadn't paused to consider that stepping back into the past would inevitably leave unsightly traces. Moreover, the cold was beginning to get to him; he could feel the banks of frosty air pressing down on the roof tiles. If he was going to read any of the contents, it would have to be done somewhere warmer and somewhere cleaner.

Instead of manhandling the trunk down the steps, he gathered up individual bundles in his arms and placed them on the floor of the landing. There was no way his mother could have taken a full trunk up into the loft herself; his guess was that she or somebody else had placed it up there, and as the years went by all she needed to do was to tie up the most recent correspondence and deposit it with the other bundles. Luckily, not all the postmarks were smudged. It was like dating trees by examining the rings on their trunks.

The first set he took out to read were letters his father had written to his mother before their wedding, a few from Southampton but most from the ports at which his liners called, Cape Town, Kingston and other fleshpots in the Caribbean, Colombo and Singapore. It was becoming like an act of voyeurism: the effusive expressions of love from his father destined to be read only by his mother, but which now enabled the son to retrace the high points of their relationship.

In one of the pouches he found their birth certificates and marriage certificate. There was indeed almost ten years in age between them. Hidden between some of the letters were wedding photos, duplicates of which he'd seen in the albums downstairs. Then came more letters, often posted in the Mediterranean, in which his father was clearly pining for his mother, but which carried little detail of the cruises themselves, concerned as he mostly was with the emptiness in his inner life. From what he could tell his father hadn't been in the country for his birth in April 1964, so the first mention of himself occurred in a letter posted in Gibraltar two months later. His father must have held him in his arms during a period of shore leave before departing for the Mediterranean. *I know he won't be able to understand yet but please tell our Laurence how much his daddy loves him and how I can't wait to be back with you in our lovely new home.* This must have been the house in Stubbington. The very last letter in that particular bundle had been written late in October 1966, but it wasn't clear if this derived from an outward or return journey, except that it had been posted in Lisbon.

Tied to this pile was a large manila envelope which had been folded in half. Laurence's fingers began to shake as he pulled out details of his father's cadet training and conditions of service with the Merchant Navy, his wartime record and a King's Commendation for Brave Conduct awarded in September 1943. Then came a series of yellowed newspaper cuttings relating to the events of 20 November 1966, some of which didn't even mention the Radio Officer by name but confined themselves to a few basic facts. The man in question had been washed overboard in a storm in the Bay of Biscay, but despite frantic efforts by the crew no trace of him had been found. However, there was one reference to an allegation made by an anonymous member of the crew when the ship docked in Southampton a few days later that it was extremely unusual for the sparks to have been wandering on the deck in such high seas – quite inexplicable in fact. The inquest held some weeks later led the coroner to conclude that this was a case of accidental death rather than death by misadventure but, as he had taken pains to point out, that was purely on the basis of the evidence laid before him.

Laurence's mouth went completely dry. He closed his eyes for several minutes to take in the implications of what he had just read. It was by no means crystal-clear that the freak waves of a storm had suddenly enveloped his father and washed him overboard; there was a possibility, which would have been underlined by the verdict the coroner ultimately rejected as an alternative, that his father had known exactly what he was doing and that he might have calculated the obvious consequences of being on deck in the midst of towering seas. This was his father, the man who'd been presented to him throughout his childhood as a hero, with the monarch's commendation for bravery, whom he should forever look up to. But his father had been no novice; he was forty-six when he died and apparently in good health. Why had he done something which most sensible people would have classified as highly risky?

Nothing else in the trunk yielded any further information about his father's death. There was nobody he could now ask. It was all an unexplained mystery. Unless there was something in the other bundles of letters that might offer up pointers.

Laurence felt his heart beating faster than normal. He hadn't expected his emotional temperature to be stoked up again so soon after the funeral. He was stumbling from one furnace to the next. Above all, the investigation of the contents of the trunk was taking longer than he had bargained with. He was hungry and thirsty. He needed to take a break and he needed the loo urgently. But he also knew there were still more letters to be read.

The first thing Laurence noticed when he picked up one of the bundles from Joyce was the difference in handwriting between the two sisters. He'd always received a birthday card from her right up to and including his tenth birthday, but he'd quite forgotten how big and loopy the script was, compared to his mother's slightly crabbed and economical writing. There were a few bundles that dated back even before his parents' marriage to the time when Roberta was courting Keith. One or two letters hinted at a degree of envy on the part of the elder sister, since it was she who had first danced with the dashing young man from the Merchant Navy, but Laurence skimmed them rapidly, knowing he would not find any references to himself.

In the late fifties Joyce had responded to something his mother must have mentioned in one of her letters about her frustration at not becoming pregnant. Joyce attempted to reassure her that five years of waiting, especially when the couple were apart for several extended periods every year, was not at all unusual. His mother must have picked up the same theme in the early sixties, because Joyce, drawing on her medical expertise as a nurse, was making suggestions about what Roberta needed to do in order to increase her fertility and even described the position she should adopt in bed immediately after intercourse. There were occasional niggles that Roberta refused to travel up to Scotland to visit her sister and that Joyce was then forced to use up some of her holiday entitlement in order to come down to the south coast to see her.

Laurence reminded himself of the different time in which these figures had lived and moved. In the sixties people were not in the habit of phoning each other at length, and certainly not over long distances, unless the matter was urgent. They generally wrote each other letters, especially if the matter in question was delicate and required careful reflection.

This pattern had obviously been interrupted at some point in July 1963. Laurence read the first of the letters from Joyce with increasing trepidation. It referred to what had happened one evening. *I really cannot understand your refusal to go to the police and tell them about the rape. You owe it to yourself and not least to Keith. You always told me that people needed to be punished for what they did and how you hated the Germans because they had to be punished for killing Mum and Dad. How can you let this man go unpunished?*

The shock at reading those words winded him. He reread the passage. His mouth went dry. He could hardly breathe. His hands began to shake. Then he was back once more in the late nineties, watching the film about the *Titanic* he had taken Rosie to see. Even after the arrival of their two children there were still nights when they could go out and enjoy the latest movie blockbusters. As the ship finally began to break up, the surround system in the cinema had produced a succession of terrifying sound effects, the immediacy of which startled everybody watching. The wood creaked and splintered and snapped and the icy water that burst through the superstructure started to drag people down. The icy water that claimed its victims and swallowed them into its black hole was like the icy water that had claimed his father.

Laurence opened his mouth, expecting sounds to issue forth. None came. He was being pulled down himself, through the murky depths, ever deeper into a sea of darkness. Then came a feeling of dread that made the remains of the sandwich in his stomach begin to churn violently, sending up waves of nausea. His mother had been raped!

He sat back on his haunches and took several deep breaths. The next set of letters were reactions to further telephone conversations and a promise that Joyce would come down as soon as she could before Keith was due back for extended shore leave. Laurence attempted to piece together the broad outlines of the incident, not knowing what Roberta had written in her letters to Joyce or what had transpired during their phone calls. One thing was incontrovertible: Roberta was suffering from a sense of guilt, despite her apparent innocence in the matter, and her sense of shame, coupled with an absence of further evidence, made it impossible for her to give in to her sister's pleading to go to the police.

When exactly Keith's shore leave had been due to begin and for how long could not be deduced at this stage of the correspondence. Nor was it clear until another letter in early December that Joyce had been told about her sister's pregnancy. At that point Joyce began to confront Roberta with a series of uncomfortable questions, having concluded that she knew exactly why her sister had been unable to conceive a child with Keith. *Do you think he has any idea at all about his own infertility? If he suspects something, how are you going to react? What is he going to do if he finds out about the rape? Are you prepared for the possibility of a divorce? How will you support yourself on your own? Have you considered giving up the child for adoption?*

Laurence had no way of telling if Roberta had even talked to her sister about an abortion, but he thought it highly unlikely, given the fact that in 1963 all abortions were still illegal and the backstreet operations fraught with all kinds of danger.

He had to stop reading in order to take it all in. There were too many facts clamouring to be processed, weighed up and understood. Moreover, his eyes were starting to brim with tears. He no longer saw any point in holding them back. It was all too much for him, so soon after his mother's death. So he was the child of a rapist. Yes, the child of a rapist. The father he'd learned to worship was not his real father. That man had not even had any lead in his pencil. The whole business of one happy family presented to the photographer's lens and eternalised on his mother's sideboard was a hollow sham.

He was no longer able to separate fact from conjecture. Perhaps the rape was itself a deception, advanced as a ploy to assuage his mother's guilt. Perhaps his mother had been having a secret affair and her lover had dumped her when he knew she was pregnant. Even if she had been trapped by the man who deliberately violated her, perhaps she had failed to resist, hoping, believing even, in her desperation to have a child, that some good might come from the bad.

The questions continued to swirl around his throbbing head. How was he ever to know? There was nobody he could ask. Absolutely nobody. The unknown rapist, if there had indeed been one, had long since disappeared into the mists of time. How could he possibly find out who it was, even supposing the man were still alive, nearly forty-six years later? He was fatherless, the product of some random coupling in a dark alleyway, a park or somebody's dwelling. For the first time in his life he felt soiled, defiled, stained indelibly. No love had been involved in his conception, only a cheap physical thrill. Force had been used to bring him into this world. He wasn't the individual he had been led to believe he was. The man he had spent his whole life looking up to wasn't his real father after all.

He again became aware of the excrescences he had brushed against in the loft. The filth of the past had left its mark on him. He was suddenly overcome with a desire to scrub himself clean. Minutes later, stripped of his sullied clothing, he stood in the bathtub under the shower-head and allowed the hot water to run down his naked body. He pressed his eyes together, oblivious to all his physical imperfections and the gradual signs of ageing, the receding temples, the sagging jawline and the generous folds of flesh around his abdomen. Who was he anyway? It was a question that had repeatedly troubled him in childhood. Anybody to whom he needed to give his full name struggled to get it right first time. Constant confusion had pursued him well into adulthood over whether he was Stuart or Stewart, Lawrence or Laurence, and in what order, and the constant need to check and correct the mistakes made by others who had written down his name but who hadn't even bothered to verify the spelling. Why else did he hate having to deal with the Scott Maxwells or Maxwell Scotts, the Morgan Craigs or Craig Morgans, the Russell Howards or Howard Russells of this world? Which was the front end and which the back? How many times had he himself paused when taking down details – was it Faulks or Fawkes, Pole or Powell, Reece or Rees?

He stood motionless in the bathtub for a while, as the shower-head continued to send irregular drips and then a final cascade across his body. On the outside the scouring was complete, but on the inside the stains remained. He felt betrayed. In his early years his mother had repeatedly warned him, 'Laurence, lying is the coward's way.' Yet her whole life had been a lie.

He went into the bedroom that had once been his, looking for something warm to pull on, and found an old jumper, faded in colour and the surface roughened through pilling, with a thread of the wool exposed on one arm where he must have made contact with something sharp. Despite its imperfections it was still recognisable as the garment his mother had knitted for him during the first winter he was away from home as a student. It warmed him as he crouched down again.

There were further bundles of letters that Joyce had written in the late sixties and early seventies. She was writing far less frequently than before, normally just once every quarter; presumably when she came on her annual visits to Horndean she would have had other opportunities to spell out her concerns. One recurring theme was the way Roberta was treating her child. *I sometimes think you are not only trying to punish yourself but you are trying to punish the boy. How can you be so hard on him?* Later she became even more emphatic in her views. *You do realise that sooner or later you will have to tell him that Keith is not his father. Keeping up the pretence is simply not fair. He will want to know who is, of course, so you'd better have a good story ready. He only needs to take a very close look at the photos of Keith to realise that there's nothing of the Radio Officer in your poor wee boy. He might even have noticed already.* Once, after a visit when he couldn't have been more than seven, she had written the following: *I was beginning to feel quite sick after witnessing the way you berated Laurence. It was so unnecessary. Your whole problem is that you don't want him to have a proper childhood. You want him to grow up and become an adult as quickly as possible, so you can push the events of the past to the back of your mind, but you continue to treat him like a tiny child. For goodness sake, try to remember you are a mother and not a law-enforcement officer.* Then towards the end of her life there was a troubling new reference. *As you know, I'm now having therapy, but I can't see that it's helping much. Steer well clear of people who think they can tinker with your mind. If you've got any sense, you'll hold on to what you've got and be much kinder to Laurence. He's such a sweet boy really.*

Just before Christmas 1973, she had sent something that must have made Roberta's eyes prick as she read it. *I've been going through the obituaries on Laurence Harvey. You used to drive me mad dragging me along to all those films of his. You always made out he was such a darling matinee idol, English to the core. You clearly had the wrong end of the stick. His original name was*

*Laruschka Mischa Skikne and he was born in the Soviet Union
and had Jewish blood in him. Well actually Lithuania, but it's
all part of that awful communist bloc. He only sounded so posh
because he was brought up in South Africa. How's that for pure
British blood?* So Laurence Harvey was a bit of an impostor too.
Pretending to be somebody he wasn't. That was what his mother
had saddled him with. A name with not much of a pedigree. And
if he wasn't even Keith Stewart's child, what was the point in
continuing to take that name? Laurence Paterson, borrowed from
his mother's maiden name, would at least be more accurate.

He took up the last bundle of letters from Joyce to his mother.
The handwriting was more difficult to read, the loops attenuated
to the extent that they now looked like plain vertical strokes
on the page, with irregular spacing between letters and words
and an unstable baseline. Whereas previously Joyce had written
complete sentences in which a train of sustained thought was
properly developed across the entire letter, she was now peppering
her final epistles with brief instructions and all kinds of allusions
that were lost on Laurence. *Many a mickle makes a muckle. For
whom the bell tolls, Roberta. For thee perhaps? Remember to put
the bins out. Delays result in dangerous endings. Living well is the
best revenge. Tell Laurence lang may yer lum reek. The silence of
the mind is the true religious mind. Still falls the rain, dark as the
world of man, black as our loss. Comfort ye, my people.*

At the bottom of the pile was a brief newspaper cutting from
the early part of 1975 which again referred to the findings of a
coroner. This one pronounced that Joyce Paterson had ended
her own life while the balance of her mind was disturbed. A
suicide? Roberta's explanation to her son was that her sister had
always had a weak heart and one day it just stopped beating. In
the months after the news Laurence recalled seeing his mother
secretly wiping away her tears. He had taken this to be a simple
expression of her grief at the loss of her sister. If Roberta ever
bore any responsibility for her sister's descent into darkness,
there was no way of ever knowing. Without her side of the

correspondence and the precise content of their phone calls and conversations when he was out of the room, it was all going to be speculation anyway. Once or twice he had happened upon them in the big kitchen or in the front room and they would suddenly fall silent. At the time he assumed they had been talking about what his mother called "grown-up things".

It was already late in the afternoon. Laurence was physically tired, but more than that he was emotionally exhausted. Even if he was prepared to concede that his mother had erected a wall of protection for his benefit as much as for her own sanity, he was finding it hard to accept why there had been so much deception about the precise nature of his father's death, the circumstances of his own conception and the death of the only other close relative in his life. Unless Roberta had kept all the letters in neat bundles in a sturdy trunk because she knew that at some point after her own death Laurence would surely find them and discover the truth. Would she have wanted this to happen? Except that so many pieces of the jigsaw puzzle were still missing and there could have been no certainty that the busy entrepreneur who was her son would take the trouble to investigate the contents of a dirty old suitcase under the eaves.

It was the rape that continued to prey on his mind as he slowly drove home through the rush-hour. For all her failings as a mother and as a human being, she had been a victim too. As he put the car into the driveway, he struggled once more to hold back the tears. The day's discoveries had all happened far too quickly for him. He had been called to a final feast, and the dishes had kept coming at him until they had been too much for him. He closed the front door quietly behind him, walked unsteadily into the living-room and collapsed onto the sofa.

'I thought I heard you coming in,' Rosie said a few minutes later as she entered, and then, seeing the silent stream of despair running down his cheeks, she rushed to where he was sitting. She put a caring hand on his brow and asked, 'Laurence, whatever's the matter? I've never seen you so miserable before.' He had so rarely wept in front of her. The last time she could recall seeing him like this were the tears of joy that overcame him when attending the births of Kieron and Estelle.

'It's too terrible, I don't know if I can tell you. Where are Kieron and Estelle?'

'They're upstairs. I said I'd call them when the meal's ready. I'm surprised you came home earlier than usual.'

They were talking again like normal human beings, instead of confining their interaction to the transaction of domestic business.

'I feel like my whole life has been one gigantic lie.'

'Laurence! Whatever makes you say that?'

It all came out in fits and starts. He could no longer hold back. As she listened to his account of the terrifying details, she too could no longer hold back. She wept for her mother-in-law, she wept for the husband and the marriage that had lasted for almost eighteen years, and she wept not least for herself, releasing the shame and guilt that had wrapped itself around her in recent days, realising almost incidentally that her own release would be perfectly masked by the grief her husband was permitting her to share in. The two rapes were like Siamese twins, tying them together irrevocably. Neither of them would ever be able to escape the consequences.

Rosie brushed away her tears and held his arms. 'You're still shaking,' she said.

'There's too much to take in. It's like being hit by sledgehammers from all sides. Do you know what I keep coming back to? It's something Mary said before I went into the house. She said she and Mum had been having a conversation some time ago. Mum said...' He began to choke at the thought again.

She was watching the slow disintegration of the wall of self-confidence he had always projected to the outside world, even within his domestic surroundings. He had always wanted to appear strong. She had never supposed that his hidden core of vulnerability would be so mercilessly exposed at the very time when she was struggling to keep hers concealed.

'Rosie...' – he was finding it difficult getting the words out – 'she said mum had admitted to making a big mistake in her life. I think she might have meant me. I'm her big mistake. She never really wanted me.'

'Don't be silly,' she said after a while, when he was breathing more normally again. 'I've never ever had any doubt that you were the apple of her eye. She loved you the way she never loved anybody else, so put that thought right out of our mind.'

'But the mistake...'

'Shhh. What makes you think it was a person? It could have been a big business opportunity she got wrong. It could have been moving away from your family home to the place in Horndean. It could have been lots of things. Don't tell me you've never made any mistakes. You might not have admitted them to me, but at least admit that fact to yourself.'

But even if he was prepared to concede his fallibility, and he was on the point of doing so, there was one thing he felt he had to lock away in his heart forever. He couldn't admit to Rosie what had been simmering for days at the back of his mind, that he was the unwitting agent of his mother's death, that he was guilty as charged with cutting her life short. It was all his fault, nobody else's.

Estelle suddenly appeared at the door of the living-room. 'Mum? Dad? What's going on? What's happened?'

'It's not what you think,' Rosie said. 'We haven't been arguing.'

'But I can see you've been both crying.'

'It's been the last few days, love. We've both been keeping everything in check. We were burying your gran only yesterday and now all the emotions have caught up with us. She was your dad's mum. She was so special to him.' Then she added meaningfully, 'And it's all brought back memories of when I lost my own mum and dad. Losing your loved ones is always so painful.'

Laurence held out an arm to Estelle. 'Come here, sweetheart,' he said. 'Daddy wants you to know how much he loves you.'

She approached and sat on the edge of the sofa. 'But do you still love Mummy too?'

'Your mum is the best thing that's ever happened to me. Why wouldn't I love her?'

The dam inside Rosie was breaking again. This was the man she'd committed to, this was the father of her children, this was the husband she'd betrayed.

'Mum, why are you crying again?'

'It's OK, Estelle. There are just moments when you've got to let it all out.'

Rosie looked across to see Kieron leaning against the jamb of the door. 'Come on, son. It's time for one big group hug. Time to show our feelings.'

46

The following morning Laurence still felt as though he had been sleepwalking through a dream sequence, able to take in aspects of the landscape but unable to express a comment. He remembered Rosie saying, as they switched off the downstairs lights and prepared to walk up the stairs, 'I don't want you to be on your own tonight. Not after everything that has happened. Come back to our bed.' Their bed, she had actually used those words. The flannelette sheets and her warming presence on the other side of the bed pushed him towards the slumber he craved. But the pandemonium in his mind, the place where all his demons had gathered to celebrate their strength, would not let him rest. He felt at one stage as if his skull was about to shatter, so violent was the hammering and shouting and drumming against the interior walls. He toyed with the idea of getting up and swallowing some painkillers, but Rosie had decided years ago that the medicine chest would be kept in the utility room. So much easier that way, she said, to attend to cuts and bruises on the children when they came in from the street. More sensibly located too, as a deterrent to any ill-considered rush to find a quick fix to the problems of pain and constipation. He doubted whether his body would carry him safely down the stairs and back up again.

On the other side of the bed he detected signs of shallow sleep, and he wanted to avoid waking Rosie by making a noise, so he lay where he was, pinioned like Gulliver among the Lilliputians, while siren voices began to call, 'She loves me, she loves me not. She hates me, she hates me not' over and over again. When he heard a marked stirring, as the blackness of the night gave way to the first shafts of dawn, he stretched out a hand, felt a clammy nightdress and then the softness of her fingers. He enclosed them in his, and she did not withdraw.

47

When he walked into his office somewhat later than usual, Ilona's reaction was very direct. 'You look terrible,' she said. 'What's happened?'

He knew that if he even began to revisit the territory of the previous day, it would sap him of his remaining strength 'Oh, I'm getting on,' he replied. 'Not sleeping as well as I used to. Just one of those days. It'll pass.'

Steve had sent him a text, wanting to meet up again at lunchtime. In the afternoon he was due to show Denis around the property that had become unexpectedly vacant. He sat in front of his computer screen, staring at the flood of incoming emails and online bank statements, seeing a blur of numbers and figures. Perhaps this was a 5 or maybe an 8, a 3 could just as easily look like a 9, and a plus and a minus were reversible. Didn't two minuses always make a plus? The whole world was living on tick, so what? Energy had no finite limits, everything could keep growing and expanding. The more you had, the more you wanted, but surely that was normal? You had to keep buying stuff in order to increase demand in the economy. Without that there could be no new investment, jobs would be lost and the retail sector would begin to crumble. It all sounded so self-evident. That was the way things had always been, that was the way things would always be.

But he was becoming less convinced that this was unassailable logic. His mother had not been not the person he thought she was. *He* wasn't the person he had thought he was. Why should the certainties of the past automatically become the certainties of the present? Suddenly he was hearing again all those inspirational words of the politicians he had grown up with and who had fashioned the way he saw the world in the eighties, who had stressed the importance of wealth creation, the opportunities for home ownership and personal advancement, and the brightness of a future in which everybody could be masters of their destiny. Now those fine words, repeated incessantly by those who had the power to dictate values and ideals to ordinary people, were no longer the bright and shiny beads that everybody wanted to play with. The seemingly unshakeable structures of the economic world were toppling around him. He knew it was going to take a long while before the dust finally settled, before new edifices could emerge. Hadn't a famous economist once said that when the facts changed, he changed his mind?

Several hours later he found himself sitting opposite a very different Steve from the morose figure he had witnessed two days previously. 'I wanted to share my good news with you,' he told Laurence as they sipped their pints. 'What do you think's happened?'

'You've found yourself a new job,' Laurence ventured without much enthusiasm.

'I don't know why you're looking so down today, mate. You're normally the one who has to cheer me up. Actually, I don't have a new job. But I have something far, far better.'

'Go on then.' Laurence didn't really know what to expect. The glass might just be half-full rather than half-empty.

'Linda and I had a heart-to-heart last night. In fact, it was your Rosie who pointed me in the right direction. I proposed to her and she accepted. We've decided to look at job opportunities down under. She's always wanted to go somewhere warmer to live. And, Laurence, the great thing is that she said she loves me.'

His eyes were beaming with a new-found assertiveness. 'Now comes the big question, mate. Will you be my best man?'

'I'm really pleased for you, Steve. This is just what you need. Of course I'll be your best man. And I'll organise the best stag do there's ever been.'

Driving to Miriam's address to pick up Denis, Laurence was reliving the waves of euphoria after he had popped his own question to Rosie. He had never doubted that she was the one he wanted to tie the knot with, but until the moment of her radiant acceptance he had not been able to dispel the notion that he was being constantly compared to the previous man in her life. That relationship had lasted for over a decade, whereas he had had half a dozen girlfriends in far less time, each no more than an extended fling until both realised that the attraction was insufficient to warrant a lifetime's commitment. But there hadn't been the slightest suggestion of any hesitation on Rosie's part, and he had withstood all his mother's attempts to chip away at the certainty of his convictions. Leaving aside the more recent wobble, nothing had intervened to shake those foundations. If the house now needed some underpinning to maintain its solidity, he would be there with all the structural gear that was needed. Had Rosie reacted any differently the previous evening, he might have begun to wonder whether the cracks were symptomatic of large-scale subsidence. But she hadn't. Instead, he was inclining to the view that the cracks merely reflected the kind of earth movements all older properties were subject to over the course of time. Nothing was set in stone for ever.

Denis looked at him quizzically when he answered the doorbell. 'The last time I saw you, you seemed to be charged up with endless enthusiasm, a bit like some of my students when they finally grasped something I'd been trying to teach them,' he said. 'But today the mood's different.'

'You're pretty good at sussing people up, aren't you? I reckon in a different life you'd have made a good estate agent.'

'But in your world it's all about money. I don't think that suits my temperament.'

'I would hope it's not always about money. Trust and confidence should be part of the game too. What made you think my mood is different today?'

'It's not just one thing. It's something holistic, the whole body. As a teacher you learn to watch how a person moves, the way they speak and react. And the eyes are windows to the soul, of course.'

'OK, Denis, I was wrong about the estate agent thing. Perhaps you should have turned your attention to psychotherapy.'

Denis laughed. 'If you're in teaching, that's included in the bigger picture. You're dealing with human beings and you have to be able to motivate them. If you can't read the faces in front of you, something's wrong.' Putting on a slightly darker mien, he continued: 'The really challenging thing is that the face never stays the same. It changes. Above all, it ages. I always remember the years I was in Japan. The cherry blossom time is celebrated with an intensity I've found nowhere else. It means so much to the people there because of its transience. A week later the blossom is gone. It's a reminder of the brevity of human life. All you can do is to treasure each special moment.'

'I used to think that you could deal with sadness the way you deal with headaches. You just pop a pill and it goes away. In my case, the remedy was always putting a brave face on it. My mum used to tell me that suffering comes from being too preoccupied with the inner self and that was something I needed to avoid.'

'I understand the idea, though you should never neglect the inner self. You're obviously a dandelion.'

'Dandelion? Come again?'

'Basically, kids are genetically predisposed to being one of two types. Some are dandelions. They flourish anywhere, they take knocks as part of the rough and tumble, and simply get on with life if something goes wrong. You strike me as being one of those.'

'I see. Thanks for the analysis. And the other type?'

'Those are the orchids. They flourish only if the environment is right. They're especially sensitive and find it difficult coping with social setbacks.'

'So which one are you?'

Denis laughed again. It reminded Laurence of the spontaneous reaction he had so often got from Rosie in the early days of their marriage after saying something outrageous and unexpected or sharing with her details of his next outlandish project. 'I thought you'd probably ask that. Self-analysis isn't really my thing, but if you could create a hybrid between those two flowers, I suppose that would be me.'

'You'd have to ask my wife if there was any chance of doing that. She's the one with the green fingers.' They had pulled up outside the property in Southsea, and Laurence was glad he could again turn Denis' attention away from his philosophical musings towards more practical matters. He knew when he was out of his depth, when he had to struggle to keep up. The competitive streak with his core reminded him that a graceful retreat did not signify a defeat.

On paper it wasn't the flat that he would automatically have picked for Denis. But he had never stopped being surprised by what people said they wanted and needed and what they were prepared to settle for. The property was not exactly generous in its proportions, with one bedroom that would comfortably take a double bed and another that was a tight squeeze, but could be used as a workroom. At one end of the living-room was a kitchenette, but the crowning glory was the sea view it offered.

Denis sounded very positive. 'You know, I don't have that many possessions, so it's not as though I need a lot of space. Japanese homes are really quite tiny. In any case, people of my age often end up downsizing. The wow factor for me is how far you can see into the distance across all that water. It's like looking into infinity. Miriam's place is nothing like this.' Denis was making all the right noises; at this stage Laurence would often have wanted to press home the advantage, but he saw no reason to force the pace. 'Take your time and then let me know if it's right for you,' he said.

By the time they started the journey back, Laurence's spirits had lifted further. He was still feeling the effects of too little sleep; he was still aware of the shadow cast by the previous day's events. However, he was in his element. Taking potential clients around properties and highlighting all their positive features, picking up important signals in conversation and responding appropriately to them, having options in reserve in case things didn't quite work out as expected: this was what he was good at doing, and he knew it too.

48

After weeks of self-imposed isolation at night, Rosie was slowly adjusting to the presence of Laurence on the other side of the bed. The shock of hearing about what had happened to her mother-in-law was still reverberating through her system. She wondered whether the bitterness, the sharpness and the barely-concealed dislike that had characterised their relationship were really a form of repressed rage, a feeling of impotence that the possibility of retribution was negated by the circumstances of the time. She knew in her heart that her mother-in-law's generation could never count on being believed, least of all in a court of law. Now she was ready to identify not only with the one victim that had been raped but with the other victim, the one who had been deceived. Roberta Stewart had been hard and demanding on the human consequence of that rape, but she had chosen to conceal the pain of that encounter from her own son and suffer in silence. The pain was referred; it simply found another outlet.

Rosie sensed from the first moment Laurence began to tell her about the content of the letters that without her emotional support he would break. For her, seeing a grown man cry was not in itself upsetting; as far as she was concerned, adherence to the traditional stiff upper lip resulted in the true state of one's feelings being concealed rather than shared. Northern grit was fine in the face of adversity, but it had its limits. Here Laurence now was, a diminished figure in her eyes, having to cope with emotional baggage from his past far weightier than he could ever have imagined, and she had to be strong for both of them. The fact that she too had been raped – and she increasingly made herself think that there had been no consent on her part – meant it was much easier for her to understand the deception her mother-in-law had maintained. Sometimes, she thought, you had to pursue what was morally indefensible simply in order to forestall a greater disaster. There were lessons here for her too.

Yet she knew, even without thinking about it, that keeping everything together was always going to involve a colossal strain. She was sleeping fitfully, sometimes waking to find herself in a cold sweat, the effects exacerbated by the warmth coming across the divide from Laurence's body. The symptoms of the past few months were part of a pattern. There was no point pretending she had somehow dodged the bullet; everything was pointing to the end of her fertility. Dr Famotibe was sanguine that the HRT course she had prescribed would help to regulate the changing biochemical flows in her body, but the psychological effects were already gnawing at her self-confidence. Laurence's received identity had been called into question and repairing that damage was going to be a long-term operation with no quick fixes, but she too was no longer the person she thought she was. What had previously felt whole and complete had lost shape and definition. Her biological function was being disabled; she was but half a woman. Everything that now followed on from this would place her on a downward trajectory. The greying hair, the wrinkles, the flabbiness about her midriff would all increase. Her levels of vitality would decline, her powers of recall would wane. Even more disconcerting was the knowledge that the attention paid to her by an attractive man was not a confirmation of her desirability as a woman and a partner, but merely her availability for a sordid dalliance. In the days after that sexual encounter she had waited, hoped even, for some kind of communication from John. Had she got back safely? Was she OK? Did she want to meet up again? That was one scenario. Or, in another scenario, in which he acknowledged misreading the signals, perhaps they'd both been a little tipsy and he'd assumed that was what she'd wanted, but if he'd gone too far then he apologised for his brashness. Instead, she'd been thrust into a state of limbo, her feelings in turmoil, all the certainties in her life under attack, her need for emotional stability stronger than ever, only to find within days that there was somebody very close to her who was weaker still and more exposed than she herself.

As if to underline his impotence, Laurence continued to let off steam about the incompetence of the local police, railing at their inability to find the mastermind responsible for the blackmailing of Kieron as well as their lack of progress in identifying the perpetrators of the Lindon Road burglary. With the flimsiest of evidence at her disposal, she failed to see why any law enforcement officers would pay much heed to an official complaint she might want to make about John Bibby. Who was to say how he might react if she decided to take such a step? A local bank manager, a pillar of society, he would probably sue for defamation of character. She knew her options were therefore severely limited. On the other hand, if she felt strong enough to support Laurence through his current crisis, she would be a fool to do absolutely nothing on the grounds that the odds were stacked against her. She thought about going to his bank and confronting him, even in the presence of customers. But most probably he inhabited a back office somewhere, shielded from the tiresome public, protected by someone who answered the phone, kept his diary and organised his meetings. How would she get past such a gatekeeper? She considered the possibility of adopting an alias and making an appointment, but then there would have to be a very pressing reason why she would need to be seen by the top man in the branch rather than one of his minions. Off-hand she couldn't think of one. What had she once heard Dulcie saying to Lucie in the days of her early teenage innocence? Revenge is a dish best served cold. She would find a way. Somehow.

It was the last week of January, and the piercing cold that made Rosie wrap up warm was giving way to milder air from the Atlantic with rain-bearing parcels of cloud that leapt off the conveyor belt at regular intervals. The first snowdrops in her garden were already nodding their ivory heads, the first buds on the primroses pushing out from the coronal clusters of leaves. What for so long had seemed utterly dead was showing the first signs of resuscitation.

At Florabellum there was plenty to do. She and Lorna had decided to broaden their range of greetings cards, and the first boxes were waiting to be unpacked and the contents placed into the upright holders. After that she would have the weekly order for table decorations at the Callas to see to.

'Spring can't come soon enough,' Rosie said, as she rearranged some of the stands. 'I've had too much on my plate these past few weeks and no time to enjoy any of the food.'

'Then I almost hesitate to mention something that Pete and I have been mulling over since New Year,' Lorna said, folding the cardboard into neat piles.

'Oh, what's that?'

'You're lucky to have somebody like Laurence who's such a rock in your life. Pete's always been a little chaotic, coming up with these bird-brain schemes of his.'

You'd be surprised if you knew the full truth, Rosie thought. Perhaps all husbands tended towards the manic, and it was left to the wives to bring order and stability to the world. Except that such an assumption was wide of the mark in her case. She had allowed herself to be thrown out of kilter, slipping down a rock-face in search of a secure hold, when she could have chosen to keep both feet planted firmly on the ground below.

'So, what's the latest one?'

'He's always had this hankering for a rural life. Not just the country cottage with roses round the door, but the complete way of life. I used to let him dream on, thinking it was all part of a midlife crisis. But he's really serious about it. A smallholding or a nursery, perhaps even with a garden centre attached, that's what he has in mind.'

'I'd have thought that in the present economic climate it would be madness to take on a new project. Though that hasn't stopped Lee and Matthew pouring their heart and soul into the Callas.'

'Yes, but making shedloads of money isn't Pete's thing. I've always earned more than he has. He just thinks that self-sufficiency or as close to it as we can get would make life worth living again.'

'Are you saying that you haven't been happy here?'

'No, I'm not saying that. I can cope with the routine. The point is he's so frustrated. I think that if you're basically happy in your relationship, there are compromises you just have to make. I'm willing to do that; I'm certainly not looking for a new fella.'

'Does this mean what I think it means? That you'd be giving up Florabellum?'

'That's a hole in one, Rosie. I really wanted to sound you out, to see if you would be interested in buying me out. You'd be in sole charge of the business.' Noting the slight look of apprehension in Rosie's face, she added: 'Don't worry, I'm not planning to leave a month from now. We have to find the place of his dreams first and that'll take some time. It would help of course if I knew that you were interested. Have a think and then tell me if you are.'

The place of his dreams, she thought, not the place of our dreams. She'd never had Lorna down as somebody who would put her husband's interests first, and she hadn't even referred to their own children. Was Lucie really so different from Lorna? The scales had long since fallen from her eyes and yet she was still prepared to let Ian be, to tolerate his excesses and to accept that he remained the most important man in her life. There's nowt so queer as folk, went the little voice in her head. Except for me and thee – and even thee's a little queer.

When she got to the Callas, Lee and Matthew were both sitting at their laptops, their arms on the reception counter propping up their chins. 'It's that time of the week again,' Lee said, motioning her to sit down. We're poring over the numbers and you've come with the flowers. What a conjunction of opposites!' They both smiled at her, the kind of smile she instinctively judged to be sincere. Here there was no deeper sexual malevolence masquerading as gentlemanly charm, the kind of charm that would undoubtedly unsettle her if she encountered it again.

'We've been so lucky with our business partners,' Lee went on. 'You especially of course, with all your good ideas. But our suppliers too and then there's John. If he hadn't been prepared to take a risk with us, who knows where we would have found the missing cash?'

At the sound of his name, she froze. Taking a risk... there was something more than a little alarming in the fact that this bank manager in particular was not averse to taking risks in both his professional and private life. Perhaps this was what everybody in finance and high finance did. They took risks with people's lives, they lounged at some gigantic roulette table playing the game that everybody else was playing, upping the stakes whenever a prize beckoned. Sometimes they won and sometimes they lost. She was not going to stand idly by on the sidelines and let one such representative walk off unhindered with all his winnings.

It was Matthew's turn to speak. 'We're really glad you're here, because there's something we'd like to discuss with you.' As so often, when the two of them were together, he provided the prelude and Lee the rest of the opera. Their roles were pretty much defined. Matthew ruled in the kitchen and Lee looked after the business side.

'But here's the thing,' Lee said. 'I'm perfectly happy to do all the ordering and maintain the books, but I'm not a natural greeter. We want somebody with a lovely smile and a big personality who can bring the punters in and make them feel special. In other words, we want a manager for front-of-house. It's mostly evening work, as you know. And we, well, we were wondering whether you might be interested in that position. We know you're only part-time at Florabellum, so we thought you might at least be prepared to consider it.'

Two new doors had opened for her within the space of a few hours. Most of her life had been spent in floristry; now the prospect of running her own business outright had been offered to her on a platter. Yet if it was new vistas and new challenges she really craved, here was a chance to show the world that she had more than one string to her bow.

'Well, I'm really flattered that you should think of me,' she heard herself say. But she knew without a second thought that there was no contest between the two options appearing on the horizon. The one door took her to the sunny uplands on which she would be monarch of all she surveyed; the other opened onto a grand pier around which sharks circled. 'I'll think about it and let you know.' New adventures no longer carried with them the automatic promise of new happiness. That was one disagreeable insight she had recently gained.

49

Candlemas 2009 fell on a Monday. It was the start of a new week and it was Rosie's forty-sixth birthday. As a child she spent the days between Christmas and the second of February anticipating the next happy stage in her life, eager to catch up with the experience of the world her two elder sisters had over her while holding on to the imagined security she derived from reading her romantic fiction. It was enough to believe in the fundamental goodness of human beings and then everything would turn out right in the end. The few scoundrels there were would always be found out and punished for the suffering they inflicted on others.

The intervening years had been a period of painful adjustment. Her parents, who had worked so hard to make a success of their butchery and to be upstanding members of the community, had not been rewarded with a long and serene retirement. For all the family likeness and directness they shared, her two sisters saw the world in quite different ways; neither could identify with the ambitions of their kid sister, or would want to. Adam had not turned out to be her knight in shining armour and Laurence, despite his many admirable qualities, had repeatedly chosen the path of self-advancement over the need to be first and foremost a husband and father. As the latest milestone approached, she realised that she too had fallen short of the goals she had set herself. For all the striving after perfection in her own life as well as in the lives of others, her mother-in-law had never struck her as being utterly fulfilled. Wherever Rosie looked, she found individuals who usually set out with the best of intentions but were then quickly strapped to the rack of life, twisting and turning the moment a more powerful force was upon them. Not even an iron determination could always guarantee the ultimate triumph. Fighting against the impossible in search of the immeasurable was in itself a laudable idea – it had served the heroes of her early story-books so well – but the toll on energy reserves, the frustration at being constantly thwarted and the humiliation of having to accept defeat had never been regarded as a model for universal replication. Sometimes it was more prudent to bow to the inevitable and only to take up cudgels when vital interests were threatened.

That morning, as she entered the forty-seventh year of her existence, she had lain on the edge of consciousness, fretting once again that she been denied the restorative powers of unbroken sleep. Long after the witching hour she had heard those familiar voices attempting to make sense of her life and plot its future direction. There was nothing, they murmured, to be gained from maintaining a steely detachment towards Laurence in the interests of her own self-preservation. The shock he had experienced was not of his own making. It had visibly aged him in a matter of days. The increased worry lines on his face were giving it a fragile, haunted quality which appealed to her compassionate instincts. The brash optimism in his speech had been tempered, the infectious self-confidence he projected to the world diminished. The old Laurence was no longer what she saw when she looked at him. Instead there was a childlike vulnerability in his eyes which sought reassurance and acceptance from her. She felt his pain, just as he had been made to feel his mother's pain.

In past days she had also toyed with, and then rejected, the idea of having another long heart-to-heart conversation with Lucie on the phone. There was little point; she alone would have to set the priorities in her own life and, where necessary, seek out those interior spaces where she could be the person she wanted to be and not the person others might want her to be. Rejecting the role she had previously played as a wife and mother, and not least as a human being, would ultimately be an admission of failure and an abrogation of responsibility. This much she knew: what she still had within her, she was prepared to give to those who depended on her. Nothing would ever be quite the same again, but everything was now negotiable. The woven figure was a thing of the past; it was the pattern of her existence which had come to define her, just as it defined Laurence and those around her. But the future was already waiting for fresh skeins of wool to be taken up and knitted into place. And then the process would begin all over again, as it had so often done before.

She had waited for the first rays of confident early sunlight to begin teasing at the curtains before she fully opened her eyes. Her nightdress again felt slightly clammy, but the head was mercifully clear. She had a husband, a son and a daughter; she had a job she loved doing; she had friends who valued and supported her. They too were part of her own identity, what made her the person she was. As the gentle snores on the other side of the bed subsided and she felt the stirrings of the familiar large frame, she stretched out a hand and met a reciprocal limb stretching out to her.

'Happy birthday Rosie, my love,' he whispered across the divide.

At the end of the breakfast they all shared, Laurence gave her an envelope. 'Go on, open it,' he said. Inside she found two tickets for a Glyndebourne performance later that summer. 'I know nothing about opera,' he continued, 'but I know you've poured your heart and soul into helping to make this Callas place a success. If opera has inspired your passion, there must be something good about it.' Once more he had surprised her with his knack of coming up with totally unexpected and yet appropriate presents.

Towards the end of the afternoon, after finishing the binding of a bouquet for a middle-aged woman whose daughter had just presented her with her first grandchild, she knew what she had to do next. She set off in the direction of Hayling Island, towards the house where she had once been so royally entertained. She knew its principal occupant would return to its security at the end of his working day. And when he did, she would shatter that security and confront him with the full iniquity of his wrongdoing. She would speak to him in the name of all those whose voices had been left unheard amongst the clamorous denials of responsibility. And having done so, and restored one small element of stability in her life, she would wrap up the secret of that encounter and all that had preceded it and lock it away in the deepest part of her being, just as her mother-in-law had once done.